H.M.S. UNSEEN

Also by Patrick Robinson

Classic Lines
Decade of Champions
The Golden Post
Born to Win
True Blue
One Hundred Days
Horsetrader
Nimitz Class
Kilo Class

H.M.S. UNSEEN

Patrick Robinson

C

CENTURY · LONDON

Published by Century in 1999

3 5 7 9 10 8 6 4 2

First published in the United Kingdom in 1999 by Century
Random House UK Limited
20 Vauxhall Bridge Road, London SW1V 2SA

Random House Australia (Pty) Limited
20 Alfred Street, Milsons Point, Sydney,
New South Wales 2061, Australia

Random House New Zealand Limited
18 Poland Road, Glenfield
Auckland 10, New Zealand

Random House South Africa (Pty) Limited
Endulini, 5a Jubilee Road, Parktown 2193, South Africa

Random House UK Limited Reg. No. 954009

A CIP catalogue record for this book
is available from the British Library

Maps by Justin Spain

Papers used by Random House UK Limited
are natural, recyclable products made from wood grown in
sustainable forests. The manufacturing processes conform to
the environmental regulations of the country of origin

ISBN 0 7126 7879 4 Hardback
ISBN 0 7126 7928 6 Paperback

Phototypeset in Bembo by Intype London Ltd
Printed and bound in Great Britain by
Mackays of Chatham, plc, Chatham, Kent

This book is respectfully dedicated to the military Intelligence services of both the United States and Great Britain, the men who watch the oceans and the skies, and whose diligence and brilliance are often unheralded.

ACKNOWLEDGEMENTS

For the third time, Admiral Sir John Woodward was my principal technical advisor in the construction of a novel. HMS *Unseen*, a stealthy Royal Navy submarine now being leased to an overseas government, was chosen for the title as it represents the central area of the book.

The Admiral was obliged to use all of his considerable ingenuity to convert it into precisely the kind of boat we required for the plot. He was also obliged to 'invent' a missile system which would (a) stand some chance of working, and (b) not take us too far into the realms of the impossible.

Loyally, my supersonic flight advisor said it would never work, could not achieve its objective. The Admiral disagreed . . . 'maybe not today . . . but in six years?'

Their good-natured disagreement, conducted over several high-tech weeks, has, I hope, brought *HMS Unseen* (the novel) home with suitable, grim reality, and I thank them both.

Readers may note a stark similarity between an event in this book and a later actual happening on the world stage. It was recounted in the completed manuscript of *HMS Unseen* several months before it actually happened, and for this I am again grateful to Admiral Woodward.

My thanks too, to my two Scottish advisors (rural, geographic and social), Penelope Enthoven and Olivia Oaks. For insights and religious advice concerning the Muslim faith, I am indebted to the kindly and patient Syed Nawshadamir (Ronnie), originally from Dhaka, Bangladesh, and now of Dublin, Ireland.

Patrick Robinson

PROLOGUE

January 17, 2006.

IT WAS A morning of savage cold. The raw, ravenous January
wind hurled snow at the driver's side of the car as the vehicle
crunched along a freezing man-made ravine between drifts
ploughed a dozen feet high. It had been snowing here in Newfoundland now for over three months. But Bart Hamm did not
care. He chuckled at the banter of the local radio station's DJ as
he pressed the car on through the howling polar blizzard of his
homeland, heading resolutely for the big trans-Atlantic air base
outside the eastern town of Gander.

Bart had been working there for ten years now and he was
used to the job's routines and regimentation. Unlike most of the
working people of the island's coasts, he never had to worry about
the cold. All through the autumn and winter the weather in
Newfoundland is unbearable, except to a polar bear or possibly
an Eskimo. But Bart was the first male member of his family in
five generations not to have gone to sea, his attitude to life being
guided by one solitary thought: *Whatever the disadvantages may be
to this job, whatever the freedoms I have sacrificed, it's a helluva lot better
than being out in a fishing boat.*

The Hamms were from the tiny port of St Anthony, way up
on the northern peninsula. Down the years since the middle of
the 19th century they had treasured their independence, earning
a harsh living from the dark, sullen waters that surge around the
Labrador coast and the Western Atlantic. In the past century
the Hamms had been saltbankers, sailing the big schooners out
to the Grand Banks for cod; they had fished for turbot from the
draggers, they had trapped deep-water lobsters, they had hunted
seals out on the ice at the end of winter. A lot of teak-hard, rock-
steady men named Hamm had drowned in pursuit of this most
dangerous of industries – three in one day back in the early 1980s

I

when a fishing boat out of St Anthony had iced up and capsized in a gale east of Grey Islands. Bart's father had been one of the men lost in that incident, and Bart himself, his only son, had never quite recovered from the ordeal of waiting helplessly with his mother and sister for six hours in the snow and a biting nor'easter on the little town jetty. Every 30 minutes, they had walked up to the harbormaster's shed, and Bart had never forgotten the old man repeating over and over, into the radio, 'This is St Anthony . . . come in *Seabird II* . . . come in *Seabird II* . . . *Please* come in *Seabird II*.' But there had always been just silence in reply.

That had been 23 years ago, when Bart had been 13; it was the day he knew that, whatever else, he was never going to become a fisherman.

Bart was a typical member of the Hamm family: thoughtful, quiet, accepting and as strong as a stud-bull. He was a good mathematician, and had won a scholarship to the Memorial University of Newfoundland in St John's, where he had earned two degrees, one in mathematics and the other in physics. He possessed the perfect temperament for an air-traffic control officer, and had settled into a well paid place in one of the warmest, most protected modern buildings in the entire country. Stormswept ATC Gander is where they check in every incoming trans-Atlantic flight to Canada and the northern United States, the big passenger jets heading back into the civilized world from under the huge freezing sky which umbrellas the desolate North Atlantic waters at the 30° line of longitude. Bart loved the job, and not just because of the warmth. He had excellent powers of concentration, and his rise to supervisor would not be long in coming.

Today, driving through the snow at half past six in the morning, headlights cutting through the endless winter darkness, Bart was starting a seven-hour shift with an hour's break midway. He would begin at the busiest part of the morning – any time after seven you were talking to a different airliner every three minutes, and you had to stay alert, on top of your game, every moment of your shift. The Gander Station was a key ingredient in Atlantic air-traffic safety, and the controllers there were inevitably the first to know of any problem.

Today Bart's shift began at 0700. And he began to talk into his headset almost immediately he arrived at his station, connected on the HF radio to the great armada of passenger jets trundling westward, identifying themselves in their airline's code and then reporting their height, speed and position. At 0717 he was talking to the co-pilot of a Lufthansa Boeing 747, out on 40°W, handing him a weather check and confirming the position of an offshore blizzard to the south, off the coast of Maine.

Two minutes later he picked up a new call and his heart, as always, skipped a beat. This was Concorde, British Airways' supersonic star of the North Atlantic, streaking across the sky at 1330 mph. Bart heard a calm British voice saying, 'Good morning, Gander. Speedbird Concorde zero-zero-one. Flight level five four-zero to New York. Mach–2. Three-zero-west, five-zero-north at 1219 GMT. ETA 40 West 1241 GMT. Over.'

Bart replied carefully. 'Roger that, Speedbird zero-zero-one. We'll be waiting 1241. Over.'

The information was entered on his screen, and at 0738 Bart was waiting. Concorde was usually a couple of minutes early calling in because of the high speed at which she crossed the lines of longitude. To cover the 450 miles between 30°W and 40°W, she required only 22 minutes.

At 0740 he was still waiting, but nothing was coming through from the cockpit of the packed British supersonic craft as she raced through the skies out on the very edge of space.

Bart was already, by this time, feeling distinctly uneasy. He watched the digital clock in front of him go to 0741, and he knew that Concorde must be well past 40°W. But where the hell was she? At 0743 and 40 seconds he opened his High Frequency line and went to SELCAL (selective calling), causing two warning tones to sound in Concorde's cockpit to alert the pilots to the signals. He began transmitting on the private voice channel. But there was no reply.

Seconds later he transmitted a radio signal designed to light up two amber bulbs right in the pilot's line of vision and followed this up with: 'Speedbird zero-zero-one, this is Gander. How do you read? Speedbird zero-zero-one, this is Gander. How do you read?'

By now his heart was pounding. He felt as if he were driving the supersonic jet himself, and he willed the voice of the British pilot to come crackling onto the headset. But there was nothing.

'Speedbird zero-zero-one, this is Gander. How do you read?' Frightened now, Bart raised his voice and departed from the procedural wording. 'Speedbird zero-zero-one, please come in. *Please* come in.'

He checked his own electronic connections, checked every step he was taking. But he could not remove the lump in his throat, and, unaccountably, a new image stood before his mind's eye — the image that still wakened him on stormy nights, the image of himself on that terrible morning in St Anthony when he had stood in the snow and then in the radio shed, clutching the hand of his mother and praying for news of his lost father, the skipper of the missing fishing boat *Seabird II*.

He tried one more time, calling through to the cockpit of the Concorde. His hand was shaking as he finally pressed the switch to summon his supervisor. At 0745 Concorde should have been more than 100 miles beyond 40°W; continued radio silence could only be the harbinger of disaster. Because this aircraft was nothing short of a flying hi-tech masterpiece in which electronic backup was layered threefold.

At that precise time, Air-Traffic Control Gander sounded the alarm that a major passenger airliner was almost certainly down in the North Atlantic. They alerted British Airways and the Canadian and US navies, and sounded the alarm on the international search and rescue wavebands.

The naval drills were routine and precise. Commanding officers were ordered to divert ships into the area where Concorde must have hit the ocean. While all this was happening, the haunted face of Bart Hamm was still staring into his screen as he listened to his headset. His urgent, despairing voice continued broadcasting, unanswered, on the great plane's private frequency: 'Speedbird zero-zero-one, this is Gander. Gander Oceanic Control. Please come in, Speedbird. *Please* answer. Speedbird zero-zero-one.'

CHAPTER ONE

May 26, 2004.

THE LIGHT WAS fading now along Haifa Street, and it was almost impossible to spot any westerners in this seething, poor section of Baghdad. Men in *galabiyyas*, long loose shirts, occupied much of the dirty sidewalks, sitting cross-legged, smoking waterpipes, selling small items of jewelry and copper. On one side of the main thoroughfare, dark narrow streets ran off toward the slow-flowing Tigris river. Tiny car workshops were somehow crammed along here between the cramped, decaying houses. The stifling smell of oil and axle grease mingled with the dark aromas of thick, black sweet coffee, incense, charcoal fires, cinnamon, sandalwood and baking bread.

He should have stood out a mile, wearing a smoothly cut, gray Western suit as he hurried out from the inner canyon of a green-painted garage. The club tie should have given him away, and certainly the highly polished shoes. But he turned around as he walked out and embraced the elderly, oil-coated mechanic with warmth and affection, staring hard into the man's eyes – an unmistakable Arab gesture, the gesture of a Bedouin.

No doubt, the man was an Arab, and he caused few heads to turn as he headed back west toward Haifa Street, cramming a length of electrical wire into his pocket as he went. He seemed at home here in this crowded, sprawling market, striding past the fruit and vegetable stalls and nodding occasionally at a purveyor of spices or a rug-seller. He held his head high, and the dark trimmed beard gave him the facial look of an ancient caliph. His name was obscure, foreign-sounding to an Arab. The people called him Eilat. But, in the circles that knew his trade he was more formally referred to as Eilat One.

He made just one more stop, at a dingy hardware store 40 yards before the left turn onto the Ahrar Bridge. When he emerged ten minutes later he was carrying a white box with a picture of a lightbulb on the outside and a roll of wide gray heavy-duty, plastic tape, the regular kind that holds United Parcel together all over the world.

Eilat kept walking fast, sometimes straying off the sidewalk to avoid stragglers. He was thickset in build, no more than 5 feet 10 inches tall. He crossed the bridge into the Rusafah side of Baghdad and made his way up Rashid Street. In his left jacket pocket there was a small leather box containing Iraq's national Medal of Honor, which had been presented to him personally that morning by the somewhat erratic president of the country. The coveted medal counted, he feared, for little.

There had been something in the manner of the President which he had found disturbing. They did not know each other well, but even so the uneasy distance between them had been noticeable. The President was known for the almost ecstatic greetings he gave to those who had served him faithfully, but there had been no such display of emotion that morning. Eilat One had been greeted as a stranger and he had left as a stranger, escorted in by two guards and escorted out again by the same men. The President had seemed to avoid eye contact.

And now the 44-year-old intelligence agent experienced the same chill that men of his calling have variously felt over the years in most countries in the world, the icy realization that, no matter what their achievements, the past had gone and time had rolled forward. The spy was being sent back out into the cold. Or, put another way, the spy had gone beyond his usefulness to his master. In the case of Eilat One, he might simply have become too important. And there was only one solution for that.

Eilat believed they were going to kill him. He further believed they were going to kill him tonight. He guessed there was already a surveillance team watching his little house, set in a narrow alley up toward Al–Jamouri Street. He would be wary, and he would be calmly self-controlled. There could be only one possible outcome of any assassination attempt on his life.

Still walking swiftly, he reached the huge wide-open expanse of Rusata Square. The streetlights were on now, but this square needed no extra illumination. A 50-foot-high portrait of the President was floodlit by more voltage than all the city streetlights put together. Eilat swung right, casting his eyes away from the searing dazzle of his leader, and pressed on eastward toward the great adjoining Amin Square with its mosques and cheap hotels.

Now he began to walk more slowly, tucking his white box under his arm, and staying to the right, hard against the buildings. The traffic was heavy, but he had no need to leave the sidewalk, Almost subconsciously he slipped into the soft stride of the Bedouin, moving lightly, feeling at the small of his back the handle of the long stiletto-bladed tribal knife that was his constant companion in times of personal threat.

He followed the late shoppers into Al–Jamouri Street and slowed almost to a stop as he reached an alleyway beside a small hotel. Then he quickened again and walked straight past the narrow walkway, with its solitary dim streetlight about halfway along. He gave a passing glance into the alley and saw that it was empty except for two cars parked at the far end. They were empty too, unless the passengers were curled up on the floor. Eilat had excellent eyesight, and was good at remembering pictures in his mind.

And now he stopped completely. He stood apparently distracted outside the hotel, looking at his watch, checking the passers-by, watching for someone who hesitated, someone who might slow down and stop, just as he had done. Twenty seconds later he moved into the alley and walked slowly toward a narrow white door that opened through a high stone wall into a courtyard that housed the Baghdad headquarters of Eilat One.

He heard with satisfaction the rusty grind and squeak of the hinges on the outside gate. He walked past an old bicycle and opened the door to his dark, cool house noiselessly. 'I wonder if they'll come as if in friendship,' he said to himself. 'Or will they just come busting in with a Kalashnikov and blow the place apart?'

He turned on the light-switch in the wide downstairs hall and checked the setting on the low laser beam he had installed to inform him if anyone had entered during his absence. There had been nobody. The white light on the wall panel, which flickered red if anyone had opened a window, was steady.

On reflection, he thought, *they'll probably try to take me out in the small hours of the morning. Stealth will be their method, and I suspect they'll use knives. Messy, but silent. At least, that's what I'd do if I were an assassin. I can't see them risking gunfire, and I can't imagine them confronting me, even in friendship. Not with my reputation.*

It was after 8pm now. Eilat went to work with two screwdrivers, a large one for fastening a bracket into the wall and a small one, for electrical connections. 'The key to murder in the dead of night,' he muttered, 'is vision. Night vision.'

When his tasks were completed he placed a firm wooden chair behind the door, turned out every light and drew the shades across the windows. He settled down to wait in the pitch black. Eyes open wide, he strained to make out shapes in the darkness; it was a full 20 minutes before he could distinguish the curved outline of the water pitcher on the table at the end of the hall.

Midnight came and went. Still Eilat waited calmly. He hoped there would not be more than three of them but, if there were . . . well, so be it.

At 1am he stood up, walked to the pitcher and poured himself a drink, splashing the water into a stone cup. No spillage. Then he walked back to his chair behind the door without crashing into it. His night-sight was perfect now, a circumstance which he would use to best advantage. The last thing he wanted was 'equal terms.'

They came for him at 19 minutes after 2am. Eilat heard the gate squeak and the doorknob turn, and was on his feet. The first man, dressed in dark combat gear with desert boots, entered silently. A second man followed the first, sensed rather than observed. Eilat remained by the door with his eyes clenched shut, his hands covering his face, protecting his night vision from the glow of the city outside.

Suddenly, very suddenly, without opening his eyes, he moved. Raising his right foot he booted the door shut with shuddering impact. And then he turned toward the wall again, his eyes still clenched tight.

The two visitors turned automatically to the slammed door. The big theatrical lightbulb set above it came on with blinding brightness and caught them bang in its ferocious glare. For a split second the men stood transfixed like rabbits in a spotlight. Their hands flew to their faces, but it was too late. The bulb was on for only two seconds but it destroyed their night vision completely at a vital moment for them both. And Eilat still had his.

He moved quickly behind the unseeing first man and crashed

a smooth, heavy glass paperweight into the critical nerve-center behind the intruder's right ear. He slammed the second assassin with a similar blackout blow, then turned and softly opened the door. 'I suppose they have a lookout,' he murmured to himself. 'I may have to kill him as well.'

He walked swiftly across the yard and, ignoring the gate, climbed to the top of the wall with the assistance of an old wooden bench. For two minutes he scoured the alley with his gaze, watching for a movement, any movement, a person, any person. But there was nothing.

Finally he stepped down and walked back into the house. Once he was in the main room he switched on a small desk-light and collected his roll of sticky plastic masking tape. Slowly and with steady efficiency he bound together the wrists and ankles of the unconscious intruders using layers of tape. Then he placed one wide piece right across each of their mouths and arranged the two inert bodies to his satisfaction, dragging them down the middle of the hall and resting the head and shoulders of the second across the first man's chest. Immediately after that he went into the kitchen and poured himself a cup of the coffee which had been percolating for the past several hours. Exactly eleven minutes had elapsed since Eilat had floored his assailants. He returned to the hall, holding his stiletto-bladed knife, and positioned himself right behind the head of the uppermost man, who was just regaining consciousness.

Leaning over, Eilat made a small incision on the left-hand side of the assassin's throat. Then, with a surgical twist of the knife, he severed the jugular vein, the third largest artery in the human body. He stepped back quickly to avoid the surges of blood. After a moment he walked back to the kitchen and finished his coffee.

Grunts from the prostrate man on the floor drew him back to the hall a few minutes later. The assassin's eyes were wide with terror as his colleague bled messily to death all over him. Almost a half-gallon of blood now saturated the two tangled bodies and still more was pumping out of the dying man's neck wound.

'*Salam aleikom* – and perhaps sooner than you think,' said Eilat. 'I expect you've noticed I just cut your assistant's jugular. In a few moments I shall have absolutely no hesitation in doing precisely the same to you. That would give you about eight minutes to live. It takes that long, you know, for six pints of blood to unload. He's just about gone now. Were I you I should wish him well in the arms of Allah.'

Eilat walked away, seemingly indifferent to the frenzied head-shaking, two-footed kicking and muffled screams of the man who still lived. When he returned he was once more carrying the knife.

Again he leaned over, careful to avoid getting blood on his suit, and placed the sharp tip of the weapon firmly against the assassin's throat. When he spoke now it was with a hard edge to his voice. 'If you want to live you will tell me precisely who sent you, precisely who issued your orders. You will speak softly when I remove the tape from your mouth. If I suspect a lie, you'll be on your way to join your colleague. If you speak too loudly, the result will be the same. It takes about eight minutes, as I told you.'

With his left hand he slowly ripped the tape from the man's lips. With his right he pressed the knife harder into the assassin's throat, though still not making a cut, and said: 'Speak softly and truthfully.'

'The President, sir. He ordered it himself,' the man blurted. Trembling uncontrollably, he poured out a mixture of facts and implorations. 'Please don't kill me – I have a wife, children. Please . . . The President, he told my boss what we were to do. I was told to be in attendance in the President's office today so I'd know who you were. My boss was there too.' Eilat nodded. He had already recognized the dying man as one of the guards who had escorted him into the President's presence. 'He said you were to die after midnight . . . quietly. Please, sir, don't kill me. I had no choice . . .'

Eilat removed the knife and stuck a new piece of tape hard across the man's mouth. Then he walked back into the main room and took from a drawer three passports and some travel agency documents. He slipped the paperweight into his pocket; he would keep it as a souvenir of tonight's encounter. Then he straightened his tie, buttoned his jacket and moved back into the hall, putting the passports and documents on the table by the water pitcher in plain view of the bloodsoaked assassin.

He went into the bathroom, collected his shaving gear, tooth-paste and soap, and re-emerged holding a small, smart-looking leather case. He turned out all of the lights and sat quietly in the darkness for fifteen minutes while the irises of his eyes slowly grew larger, recovering his night vision. Eventually he stood up and said casually, 'Well, I'm going now. And I won't be back for a while. I have rather a long journey ahead of me. I expect they'll send someone for you in a few hours. By the way, you don't have a lookout posted in the alley, do you? Don't lie to me, because if I have to kill him I'll come back here immediately and kill you as well.'

He felt rather than saw the man shake his head feverishly. 'Very well, old chap,' said Eilat. 'I expect you won't want to see me again. And nor will you, unless of course you've lied to me.'

The petrified palace guard nodded firmly. Eilat left him and stepped out into the courtyard, where he pulled a battered old bicycle away from the wall where it had stood in the shadows. Swiftly he took off his suit, shirt, tie and shoes. From a cloth bag behind the bicycle he produced old, soiled Arab robes, a turban and thonged leather shoes, and put them on. He stuffed his Western clothes into the sack in their place and slung it over his shoulder. Then, adopting the stooped posture of an elderly man, he pushed the bike out through the gate and made his way, limping painfully, away from Al-Jamouri Street toward the alley's far end.

For over a year now he'd rented a disgustingly dirty little garret on the top floor of a small block of apartments less than 50 yards from his house on the same tiny street. It took him only moments to get there, leave the bicycle in the downstairs hall and climb the three flights of stairs. Once inside his room he shaved his beard, leaving just a thick black mustache. As he did so he prepared his mind for the new persona he was going to adopt, that of a street pedlar plying his wares among Rashid's copper and gold bazaars. He would lead this new life for at least the next month, during which time the President's security men would place an iron grip on every airport, seaport, bus and rail terminal in the country, while they tried to run down Iraq's most wanted intelligence officer. The one with three passports.

'If they searched this land for a thousand years,' mused Eilat as he cleaned his razor, 'I don't suppose they'd ever, ever look for me along the street from which I vanished – my last known position.'

★

A month had gone by. For the past four days Baghdad had simmered in flaming June temperatures of around 110 degrees. The nights had brought no real respite, not even a cooling breeze off the eastern edges of the Syrian Desert. There had been terrible dust storms out in the central plains all week, the winds were hot, and Baghdad's four million people were wilting under the hammer of the sun.

Nonetheless, Eilat had to go.

He waited until 10pm on the night of June 26 and then gathered up his heavy cloth sack and cleared his room. He collected his bicycle from its usual place in the downstairs hall. The heat hit him like a blast from a furnace as he shambled out into the dark alley. As he had remarked to the man whose life he had so scrupulously spared a month before, he was leaving and might not be back for some time.

Eilat was fit but he was currently, by deliberate design, overweight: during the past month he had gained 14 pounds by following a careful diet of chicken, lamb, rice and pita bread at least twice a day. By the time he reached Al–Jamouri Street he was already sweating heavily. Once on the wide thoroughfare he mounted the old bike and set off slowly in a southeasterly direction, heading for the great bend where the Tigris swings suddenly west around the university before turning east again in a nine-mile loop out on the southern edge of the city. He pedaled gently, making for the long sweep of the Dora Expressway at the point where it crosses the river. The city was darker and quieter down here along Sadoun Street, and there were few people walking in Fateh Square. Eilat kept going until he could make out the huge yawning overpass of the expressway near where it becomes a truly spectacular bridge.

Here he dismounted and turned off the public roads, pushing the bike through the dark until he came into the deeper shadow of the bridge. He dumped the bike under a clump of bushes and began to move on foot along the banks of the Tigris. This was the great river of his boyhood, and he was aware this might be his last walk beside its quietly flowing brown waters.

It would be a long journey downstream, all 225 miles of it. He had the route laid out in detail, but without a single name penciled in, on a hand-drawn map he carried in the pocket of his robe. It was a critical drawing to him, but he had done it so

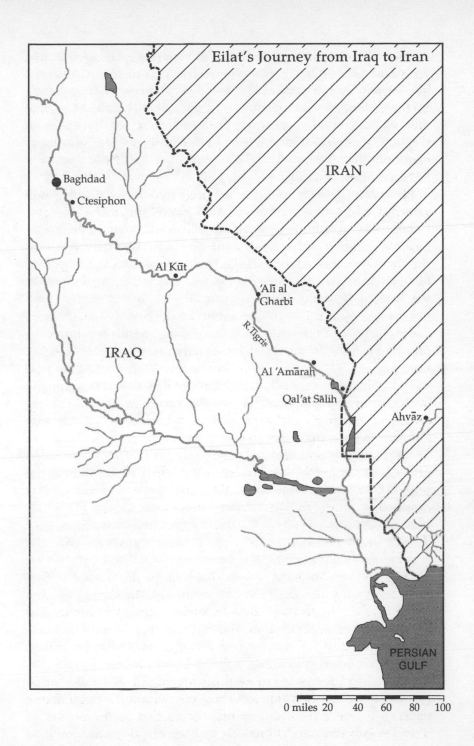

Eilat's Journey from Iraq to Iran

IRAN

Baghdad
Ctesiphon

Al Kūt

'Alī al
Gharbī

R. Tigris

IRAQ

Al 'Amārah
Qal'at Sālih

Ahvāz

PERSIAN
GULF

0 miles 20   40   60   80   100

13

it would be complete gibberish to anyone else. He also carried with him a tiny military compass he had owned for many years. He intended to proceed at the speed of Napoleon's army on its way to Moscow – four miles a hour, despite full packs and muskets. If he could find shade, he would sleep by day and walk through the night, which was at least a little cooler – albeit not much. As he proceeded south toward the marsh the humidity would become stifling, and he guessed he would lose weight progressively. If there was no shade to be had by day he would keep walking beneath the glare of the desert sun.

Eilat was a Bedouin by birth, and he possessed the proud Bedouin belief that his kind alone could survive in the pitiless summer climate of his homeland, that he could go without food for days if he had to, and that he was not intimidated by even the worst dust storm. Water he carried with him, but he would not require as much of that as another man would.

He wished, not for the first time, that he still had access to one of his father's camels. If he closed his eyes he could easily imagine the tireless, swaying rhythm of the stride, the endless beat of the wide hooves on the desert floor. But that was all in the far-lost youth he had spent out on the rim of the central plains, a long way north up the river, when life had been simple and he had been a true son of Iraq.

Iraq – the country which had used him for years, often under circumstances of unthinkable danger, and which had now betrayed him in the most brutal possible way. Eilat inwardly seethed at the injustice of the treatment handed out to him by the President. He had seen the coldness in the man's eyes when he had presented the Medal of Honor, and he still failed to understand why he should have been singled out for summary execution after all that he had done in the cause of his nation's greatness. In the past they had paid him, and paid him well. He still had close to a million dollars on deposit in four banks around the world, and he had some cash with him too, dinars and rials. But the thought kept returning: the President had not just rejected him but had wished him dead. And now, in the space of just one month, he, Eilat One, had redirected all of the hatred in his soul, the hatred that had sustained him through the loneliest years, toward a new enemy.

In the Arabian mind, the great flagstaff of pride stands tall. In the Bedouin mind it is unbending. The biblical concept of revenge is universal in Iraq, accepted by all. Time is no barrier — there is no time. In a land which has survived for six millennia, a single year is only a heartbeat, a decade just an interval. Eilat would have his revenge. Of that he was certain. He had spent his life in the service of his country, never marrying, never loving — except once. And the realization of the years wasted, squandered on an unfaithful master, burned into his mind as he walked steadily along the eastern bank of the dark Tigris.

By midnight the moon was bright, and it lit his way. Out to his left he could see car headlights in the distance, on the main road which connects Baghdad to the southern port of Basra. If he were to cross the sparse sandy flatlands between the river and the highway he could probably pick up a ride or even a bus, and at the very least the flat terrain of the road and its hard shoulder would be easier to walk upon. But Eilat was a wanted man, on the run in his own country, and he did not wish to be seen up close — not by anyone. He assumed the army and the police would have descriptions of him and that he would by now be branded a murderer and an enemy of the state. Which was, he had decided, a bit depressing . . . but considerably better than being dead.

He smiled when he imagined how long and determinedly they must have searched for a smartly dressed, bearded businessman, in Western clothes, and heading abroad. The chances of anyone connecting such a man with this scruffy country Arab, walking south with his pedlar's sack and the stooped gait of an old man, were, he knew, remote. But Eilat was not into 'remote'; he operated only on cold-blooded near-certainty. If no one saw him, he could not be recognized. And so he continued through the hot night, moving over the sands as swiftly as he could, if not so fast as Napoleon's army.

The sun came throbbing up into the eastern sky shortly before 6am. In the distance Eilat could see the ancient remains of the Parthian city of Ctesiphon, which lies on the banks of the river 20 miles south of Baghdad. He could just make out in the dawn light the great vaulted arch, built in the second century BC, which still dominates the ruins. Eilat still had 45 minutes more to walk. He took his first drink of the new day, swallowing almost a pint of water; if need be he could refill his two leather flasks some-where in the old city.

By 8am the sun was high and the temperature was on its way to 110 degrees. He had found the city's only café deserted of customers, and now he sat alone in a corner facing the wall, devouring a large breakfast of eggs, toast and chicken with rice. He drank orange juice and coffee, and paid the staff to fill his water-holders. The price was minimal compared to what he would have paid in Baghdad.

The next stretch of the river, winding 100 miles down to Al Kūt, was not a walk which held any appeal to Eilat. The flat landscape, hammered brown by the sun, was practically bereft of life, human, animal or plant. He knew that close to the water he would occasionally pass scattered date-palms tended by kind and generous rural families who would perhaps offer him a drink, and they would want to talk. But he would have nothing to say to them. The President had made him an outcast in his own land, and he already felt foreign, as if he must hide all of his inner thoughts even from simple country people, people for whom he had once been prepared to die.

Perhaps that had been inevitable anyway, because he had spent so many years away the men in power felt he could never be completely trusted. He could understand that thought process – just. But the blind injustice of it represented to Eilat a violation of his honor. And *that* was what he found himself unable to live with.

He left the café before 10am and wandered out to the ruined outskirts of Ctesiphon, avoiding people, searching for a quiet, sheltered north-facing place to sleep until the late afternoon, when he would eat and drink again before setting off on his second night's trek. He found a small, low dusty building – just three stone sides and a roof – which faced back up the river, the way he had come. It was hot inside, but the shade was deep. Eilat was exhausted, and breakfast had made him sleepy. But first he turned toward the back wall, on a bearing of two-zero-five, a line down which, more than 800 miles distant, lay the holy Muslim city of Mecca. He knelt in the dust and humbled himself, seeking the forgiveness of his God.

Eilat slept for eight hours undisturbed, his head on his soft water bags, his right hand on the handle of the desert knife beneath his robe. By 8pm he was under way again, striding forward along the river, wishing it ran a straighter course, hoping not to meet anyone, cursing the ground upon which the President of Iraq walked.

Eilat once more wondered what the future held for him. He had a plan, but it might not work. For the first time in his entire life he faced the world alone – entirely alone. The cord which had joined him for so long to Iraq was severed, and it could never be repaired.

He walked generally southeast with the river for almost four days, alone and, so far as he knew, unobserved. He spoke to no one, and eked out his water and his pita bread. The sun was pitiless during the day, and shade was so sparse that his planned schedule went awry almost immediately; he just slept when he could and walked the rest of the time, making on average 25 miles a day without incident except that he lost some ten pounds body-weight.

On the first day of July, late in the afternoon, six miles north of the riverside town of Al Kūt, he spotted, about 200 yards ahead of him, his first potential problem. There on the edge of a small grove of date-palms was a camouflaged Iraqi army jeep He could see no sign of local farmers, there was no house, and the area seemed completely desolate aside from two uniformed soldiers leaning against the vehicle. It was too late to stop or turn off the path. They must have seen him and, despite the comforting protection of his Arab robe, complete now with the customary red-checkered head-dress, Eilat knew they might very well ask to see his identification documents.

Walking with the aid of a long stick he had cut, he slowed slightly as he made his approach, limping, stooping forward. He did not avert his gaze as he continued straight toward the jeep and the soldiers, each of whom carried a short-barreled machine-gun, probably old-design Russian.

He was almost level when the senior man spoke, brusquely, with authority. 'Hey, old man. Iraqi?'

Eilat nodded and kept going, moving past them, exaggerating the limp. He thought for a split second that they would ignore him, but then the soldier spoke again. 'WAIT!'

Eilat was not surprised. He was moving into a particularly sensitive area of the country. Al Kūt is the town where the Tigris splits, and here a great drainage program had been instituted to dry out the marshes and destroy the wild wetland homes of the ancient and potentially troublesome Marsh Arabs. Eilat knew the place was crawling with soldiers: it was still regarded as somewhat out of control – drier, but out of control.

He obeyed the command of the Iraqi officer, turning slowly and saying softly the traditional greeting of the desert: '*Salam aleikom.*' Peace be upon you.

The officer was a man of about 35, tall and thin with a hooked beak of a nose, hooded dark eyes, and a full mouth. He did not smile. 'Documents?'

'I have none, sir,' replied Eilat. 'I'm just a poor traveler.'

'Traveling to where?'

'I'm looking for my son, sir. I heard from him last in An-Nasiriya three years ago. I have no money except for a few dinars, enough for some bread in Kūt.'

'And then you plan to walk right down the Shatt al Gharraf? One hundred twenty miles?'

'Yes, sir.'

'With a loaf of bread, on your own, and no documents?'

'Yes, sir.'

'Where do you live?'

'In Baghdad, sir. In the south of the city.'

'A city Arab with no documents?' The officer's tone was questioning. 'And what do you carry in that bag?'

'Just water, sir.'

'Show me,' said the officer, uttering the two words which would end his life.

Eilat turned away slowly, but he came back as fast as a striking cobra, jamming the end of his stick with colossal force into the small space between the officer's eyes, just above the bridge of his nose. All three men heard the bone of the forehead splinter, but it was the last sound the Iraqi officer ever knew. Eilat slammed the butt of his right hand upward into the great beaked nose, ramming the jagged bone into the man's brain.

The younger soldier just stood there, his mouth open in total amazement, as this elderly crippled traveler killed his commanding officer in two seconds flat. He held his hands open wide, trying to speak – perhaps to surrender. But it was too late for that. Eilat was on him, thrusting his knife between the ribs and straight into the young man's heart. The soldier was dead before he hit the sand.

Eilat kicked and rolled the two bodies under the jeep, located the toolbox and shoved that under there alongside them. Then he cut and sliced three long strips of material from the front seat and tied them together to make a jury-rigged strip, about six feet long, which he shoved into the petrol tank. Once he was sure the material was saturated with petrol he pulled most of it out and laid it on the sand. He lit the end furthest from the tank and hurled himself flat about 20 feet away as the jeep blew up in a blast of flame and black smoke. After a few moments he picked up his bag and stick and fled the blazing wreck, racing along the river for more than two miles before he finally slowed, resuming his careful, stooping old man's gait. He hoped the burned-out jeep and corpses would not be discovered for a few hours, but he did not bank on it.

'Anyway, who would suspect me?' he muttered. 'It'll take them a few days to run an autopsy on the soldiers – a few days before they find out their men were taken out by a professional.' He thanked God for the training of the military in which he had served, especially for the courses he had attended in unarmed combat – and armed combat, for that matter. He had finished first in both disciplines, as he had in every course he had ever taken.

He reached Al Kūt by nightfall, limping into the city. Food was easy to find – he purchased grilled lamb and rice with extra pita bread from a street trader – and he was able to refill his water bottles from a hose at a gas station. He slept on a bench in a dark corner of the bus depot. So far as he knew, only the curbside cook had seen his newly bearded face, and even then he had kept his head well down, mumbling his order and offering no conversation.

Eilat left before dawn, following the river as it swung east away from the city toward the Iranian border. His little map marked the spot 80 miles further on at the oasis settlement of 'Alī al Gharbī where the wide stream would turn southward again, toward the Gulf – and the marshes.

For four more days and nights he walked and slept intermittently, both under the raging desert sun and through the unbearably hot and clammy nights. He saw few travelers, spoke to no one, and ate and drank only what he carried with him. His ration was three pieces of bread and four pints of water every 24 hours. Twice each day he would move down to the river and immerse himself in the water; then he would walk on, in a robe that was at first cool and heavy but which dried out all too quickly.

He arrived exhausted and dehydrated in 'Alī al Gharbī just before midnight on July 5. He located a water pump in the middle of the town and stood drinking alone in the dark for almost ten minutes. He filled his water bags again and found an abandoned market stall on the sand, where he slept until dawn. He was two days away from Al 'Amārah, which was a much bigger town, but there was nothing along the route: before he left Gharbī he would have to replenish his food supply, and he hoped there was a café which opened early.

His luck, which had held for a long time, ran out here. Nothing opened until 9am, and so he was obliged to wait around for three hours. He finally ate breakfast, drank copious amounts of fruit juice, and found another shop where he could buy bread for the journey. He was wary of taking even prepacked meat because of the heat, but he risked a few tomatoes and some tired green local lettuce leaves. In a second shop he noticed a newspaper which carried a front-page photograph of a burned-out army jeep under the headline 'IRAQI SOLDIERS DIE REPAIRING ARMY VEHICLE.'

It took him another three and half days to reach his turning-point, at Qal'at Sālih, deep in the eastern marshes, only 30 miles from the Iranian border. It was easily the most hellish part of the journey. The unforgiving sun beat down from morning to night, and the days grew hotter as he went south while the humidity became worse. He was now 16 pounds below his regular weight, and the insects which hovered above the still waters were vicious. Eilat used his repellent spray sparingly, and only when the mosquitoes were at their worst. He stuck to the river.

He knew that out to his east were the surviving ancient lands of the Madan, the Marsh Arabs. Away to the right, on the west side of the river, Saddam Hussein had drained hundreds of square miles of the marshes right down to the confluence of the Tigris and the Euphrates. For hundreds of years those wetlands had provided a haven for escaped slaves as well as Bedouin and those who had offended against the state. The area was accessible only by small boats, and no army, however determined, had ever operated successfully in this treacherous swampland. Saddam had a solution to that. He diverted the rivers and built a couple of gigantic canals to cut off the water supply to the entire Al 'Amārah Marsh. The result today is an arid, silted-up land whose entire ecosystem has been destroyed. A huge range of wading birds, storks, pelicans and eagles lost their homes, not to mention another vast array of fishes, small mammals . . . and people. The Marsh Arabs, whose families had lived there for thousands of years, were forced to leave in the 1980s as the Iraqi Army drove through the dried-up swamps, laying down great causeways for armored vehicles to move more easily eastward, toward Iran, Iraq's smoldering enemy across the border.

Eilat did not approve of the drying-out program, but right now he was much more concerned about his own side of the river, where the great surviving marsh stretches for 50 miles to the border and on into Iran, approaching the foothills of the Zagros Mountains.

He rested for a whole day at Qal'at Sālih, regaining his strength after his 16-day march from Baghdad. He ate chicken, lamb and rice, fruit and vegetables. He risked no other human contact except for the two elderly street traders who served him. Then, in the late afternoon of July 12, he started his journey again, turning away from the Tigris for the first time through the marshes to the border. His little map marked the causeways he could follow, but there were no road signs and his only navigational guides were the most rudimentary: the Pole Star showed him due north and, so long as the sun rose directly ahead, he was on an eastward bearing.

Eilat intended to walk until dawn, until he could see the watery landscape. That meant 11 hours' travel, including three stops, and he expected to cover close to 25 miles in the long humid night. He would have to take care not to walk over the edge of the path into the swamp. He knew that the moon, now 16 days after full, would be no help at all, but luckily he was a man with excellent night vision.

Unsurprisingly, he met no one throughout his hours of walking. The waters were low at this time of the year, and many of the nomadic buffalo herders had moved to the rivers. Occasionally Eilat spotted the dim lights of a small cluster of *sarifas* – houses set on poles above the water – with their ornate latticework entrances. Outside in the shadows, moored in the high reeds, floated a scattering of the long slender poling canoes – the *mashufs* – that are just about the only boats which can operate efficiently in these long lagoons and shallow lakes: not many boat-designs remain virtually unchanged for 6000 years.

When the sun rose – dead ahead, thankfully for Eilat – he was seven miles short of the Iranian border. The causeway he now walked on was wide and firm. It was along here in September 1980 that the great armored divisions of Saddam's army mounted their opening attack on their Persian neighbors, roaring through to the old capital of the border province of Khuzestān – the city of Ahvāz, to which Eilat, too, was now headed.

However, between him and the border lay a patrolled frontier, and he had no wish to further cross swords with the government forces of Iraq – nor those of Iran, for that matter. Although he had an Iranian passport with him, he elected to lie low all day and then make his crossing by night, heading for the tiny border town of Bostan. He kept his distance for the remaining daylight hours and waited until 11pm before finally making his move. Two hours and forty-five minutes later, in the small hours of July 14, he slipped into the Islamic Republic of Iran, crossing illegally the unseen line which divided two of the world's most implacable enemies.

He was still in the marsh, but soon the land would rise and become drier. Ahvāz was 60 miles distant, with two towns along the way, Bostan and Sūsangerd, where he could eat and find water, but he wouldn't pause in either of them long. He had arranged to pick up a letter in Ahvāz, and there he could also purchase Iranian clothing, find a decent meal and in due course board a train for the long journey to Isfahan, almost 500 miles away across the great range of the Zagros.

Eight o'clock on the evening of July 17, and Eilat could see clearly the bright lights of the sprawling industrial city of Ahvāz, three miles away and directly to his south. All along the north side of the city there are huge oil refineries, burning off excess gases 24 hours a day. These towering beacons light up the city permanently: it never gets really dark in Ahvāz.

Half a mile from the city's boundary Eilat changed back into his Western clothes. He dumped his Arab garments and his bag and strolled up to the main square, Meidun-e Shohada. From there he located the Hotel Bozorg-e Fajr, checked into the best room he could find ($75 a night), immersed himself in a hot bath and made a single phone call. Then he persuaded a rather sullen room-service waiter to bring him sandwiches and coffee while he awaited the arrival of the *talabeh*, the young theological student who would take him to the meeting place he had set up on the phone.

Another 45 minutes went by, and it was close to 11pm before Eilat and his guide, a bespectacled 24-year-old Iranian named Emami, left the hotel. They turned immediately west, walking quickly through the shadowy but still busy streets.

Ahvāz is a late city, probably because of the endless twilight afforded by the flaming oil beacons, and many shops and restaurants stay open until after midnight. But here, less than a mile from the main square, it was very gloomy. The streets were like those of most industrial towns, poor and dirty, and they were made even more melancholy by the closeness of the factories and refineries in which most of the male population worked. The heat was oppressive and the smell of oil saturated the atmosphere.

The two men turned into a small deserted square surrounded on three sides by high dark walls. The young *talabeh* led the way to a tall wooden gateway, tapped softly – once, twice – and then said quietly, 'Eilat,' before tapping twice more.

The gate was opened by a guard, who led them across a courtyard and into a small house situated at the rear of an unprepossessing city mosque. Inside stood a tall, elderly cleric dressed in the long dark robe of his calling and wearing a white turban. Eilat had known that, as an Iraqi Sunni Muslim, he would have some adjustments to make. Standing before the Iranian Shi'ite, he raised his left hand to his forehead and then lowered it in the traditional greeting of Islam: '*Salam aleikom.*'

The cleric wasted little time. He nodded his head and said, 'Your suggestions have aroused curiosity in certain places. The *hojjat-el-Islam* will see you in Isfahan. I will give you a letter of introduction, with a phone number. You should call it, and a student will take you to him. You must explain everything to him. But it is better that you leave now. The train departs at 8am, and before that you must sleep. Allah go with you.'

23

Eilat bowed again and took the letter which was handed to him. After offering his thanks he followed his student guide back across the courtyard and through the gate to the square. Fifteen minutes later he was in the hotel and by midnight he was in bed. Before he slept he assessed his progress. 'Out of Iraq. Good. Into Iran. Satisfactory so far. But will they listen, or will they just kill me first? It's beginning to look as if they might listen . . .'

The following morning, after a deep six-hour sleep, he rose early, badgered the hotel staff for tea, bathed, shaved and wished to hell he had a clean shirt. But that would have to wait. He got someone to call a cab to take him to the railway station, and there he bought himself a first-class ticket to Isfahan, paying in cash. The journey would take 12 hours, including a stop at Qom.

Iranian trains are fast, and the comfortable compartments of the first-class section are each designed for only four passengers. Seats in here can be converted into beds at night, and the guard comes around often, taking orders for meals and tea. The compartment Eilat found himself in was otherwise empty, and the train was only ten minutes late, as it pulled out of Ahvāz bound northward 70 miles across the southwestern desert to the town of Dezfūl. From here it climbed into the high peaks of the Zagros, steaming through rough and often spectacular country to arrive at 2pm at the mountain town of Arāk, a religious center in which the young Ayatollah Khomeini had begun his theological studies in 1920.

Arāk was almost the halfway point. From here it was a fast downhill run of almost 100 miles to the sacred Shi'ite city of Qom, home of the gold-domed Astane, the shrine built over 400 years ago in honor of the Imam Reza's sister Fateme, who died in 816. Non-Muslims are banned from entering the holy shrine and even from the hotels around it, and photography in any form is absolutely forbidden. Ayatollah Khomeini studied here for 15 years under the legendary Muslim theologian Shayk Abdul-Karim Ha'eri.

The train waited in Qom for only a few minutes. Four hours later Eilat arrived in Isfahan, checked into the great ornate Hotel Abbassi, and made his phone call. He agreed to meet the student at 11am and that together they would find the *hojjat*.

Early the following morning Eilat purchased a soft leather traveling bag and some expensive robes in the Iranian style. He also bought a turban and new underwear, socks and shirts, and laid siege to a city pharmacy, acquiring aftershave, toothpaste and toothbrush, shaving foam, eau de Cologne, and luxurious bath oil. On reflection, he decided, he was glad to be shot of the life of a traveling Bedouin pedlar.

When he met the *talabeh* at the appointed time in the hotel foyer he was wearing his new robes and feeling clean and comfortable for the first time since the night he had dealt with the Iraqi Government's assassins, more than seven weeks ago.

The new student was a slim youth of just 21 from Tehrān, taller than Eilat, and he walked along reading an open book, saying nothing whatsoever. Eilat saw no reason to disturb these theological ponderings, and followed just behind, taking in the sights of a place he had known only in Muslim folklore.

Isfahan was once the most glorious city in the Middle East, and it still contains the greatest concentration of Islamic architecture in Iran. Beautiful, translucent blue tiles decorate many of the buildings. Like most tourists, Eilat had never seen anything to match the ancient splendors of this place. He and his guide walked along winding streets to Imam Khomeini Square, a majestic shop-lined area some 20 acres in extent right in the middle of the town; it is the second most dramatic urban square in the world, after Beijing's Tiananmen Square. They crossed its entire length, and Eilat began to think he had walked far enough by now. He asked how much farther it was to the meeting place.

'One more mile, sir,' replied the *talabeh*. Eilat silently considered it would have been churlish to protest since he had just walked over three hundred miles without a word of complaint.

They kept heading north for another fifteen minutes, finally turning into the precincts of the Great Mosque of Isfahan, the Masjed—e Jame, a truly momentous building whose twin minarets towered over its pale-blue-tiled exterior. This most glorious of mosques is unique for many reasons, particularly its soaring eleventh century north dome; still regarded as a geometric miracle, this was designed using structural theories developed at that time in Isfahan by the eminent local mathematician and poet Omar Khayyam.

Eilat and his guide entered from the east and walked across the great courtyard into the large covered area in the southeastern quadrant. It was cool in here and some parts were in deep shade, almost darkness. Standing beside one of the ornate stucco pillars, his face completely hidden, was the *hojjat* whom Eilat had come to meet.

Not moving from the shadows, the man offered a formal greeting. Eilat stepped forward to enfold the eminent cleric's outstretched hand in both of his, in the ancient Muslim way. The *talabeh* was dismissed somewhat curtly, and the learned man moved swiftly to business.

'It's quiet in here, and private,' he said. 'We will speak in Arabic. If that's agreeable?'

'Perfectly,' replied Eilat. 'How would you like me to begin?'

By now he could see the face of the *hojjat*. It was the face of a masterful man. Even partly covered by the white turban, the high, intelligent forehead was obvious. The mouth was thin and even, the dark eyes steady but alive. The cleric might have been 70 years of age, but there was a youthfulness in his manner – and an edge of wariness. Eilat would not have been surprised to discover the *hojjat* carried a revolver, as he himself carried his desert knife.

The holy man walked slowly between the great supports in the vaulted area, and the Iraqi fell into step with him. 'Perhaps,' began the cleric, 'you should begin by telling me why I, or any of my colleagues, should trust you.'

Eilat smiled and then said slowly, 'In my line of country, there must always be some risk. I'm here to offer you my services for an extended period of time. I expect to be highly paid, because I have a unique service to offer. But you may feel I oughtn't to be paid until my tasks for you are complete.'

'That wasn't quite what I meant,' replied the *hojjat*. 'I was asking, *why?* Why should we listen to you? Who are you? How can we know you aren't working for a foreign government? How can we know you're not an enemy of Iran? What proof have you that we should confide in you in any way at all?'

'Sir, I will tell you as much as I can without placing myself in more danger than I already am.'

'Very well. Please do.'

'I've spent almost all of my working career operating on behalf of my government under deep cover in other countries. I have taken some very large risks, and I have occasionally struck a savage blow against the West on behalf of the nation of Islam.'

'Are you a terrorist?'

'No, sir. I have always been connected with the military.'

'Are you Syrian, or perhaps Libyan?'

This was the difficult moment. 'No, sir. I'm an Iraqi.'

'And do you intend to return to Iraq should your mission for us be completed?'

Eilat elected to use a term of high respect as he replied, 'No, *mullah*. I will never return to Iraq. I would not be permitted to do that, except so that they could kill me. And, anyway, I have come to hate Iraq. I would rather be dead than ever set foot in the place.'

'So would I,' commented the *hojjat*. 'And what has happened to make you so bitter? What have they done to this loyal servant of Saddam's regime who stands here with me today?'

'They presented me with a medal, sir, for my long, untiring efforts on their behalf. And that same night the President sent two of his palace guards to assassinate me.'

'I see they were not successful.'

'No, sir, they were not. But it was close. I had to kill one of them in order to escape.'

'Are you publicly hunted?'

'I do not believe so, sir. They would never admit openly to anything like this. But I imagine you have sources in Baghdad, and I expect someone will confirm to you that Eilat One is missing, and wanted, and is believed to have left the country.'

'Do you have a valid passport you can show me?'

'I do. It's Iraqi and old. For obvious reasons I have placed tape over my real name, which I do not wish you to know yet. But the photograph and all the other details are accurate.'

'Very well. Might I ask you also whether you seek to enforce terrorist action against America and the West for fundamentalist reasons? Or is it that, because you intend to carry out your attacks in such a way, the blame will surely be leveled at Iraq?'

Eilat was momentarily shaken by the directness of the question, and indeed by the acute observation of his interrogator. But he knew that to hesitate would be fatal. He replied instantly: 'Both.'

The cleric walked slowly onward, keeping silent for more than a minute. Then he asked, 'Have you ever attacked a target in the West in, shall we say, a high-profile way?'

'Yes, sir.'

'Do they search for you? Are you a man wanted not just in Iraq but by nations all over the world?'

'I cannot say, sir. No one ever mentioned that I was wanted by the Americans. But I shouldn't be terribly surprised if I were – although I've no idea whether they have any clue as to my identity.'

'I share that ignorance with them, of course.'

'Yes.'

'Well, Eilat, I must tell you that I shall recommend that our source in Baghdad substantiate this story about your . . . er . . . demise in your home country. Could you give me a time and date when it happened?'

'I could. In the early hours of May 27, around 0215.'

'How did the man die? What did you use?'

'A knife, sir. To the throat.'

'Quieter, hmm?'

'Exactly so, sir.'

'Any other details?'

'Yes. After a long manhunt, they were unsuccessful in finding me.'

'Very clever, Eilat.'

'Just professional.'

'Would you have any interest in telling me precisely what you intend to perpetrate against the Great Satan?'

'I should prefer not to unless I were in the presence of the man making the decision and of the military commander with whom I would have to work.'

'I understand. But do you propose the targets be military ones?'

'Not necessarily.'

'Reverting to the question of fundamentalism, would you say your religious beliefs are your prime reason for wishing to carry out such operations?'

'No. That was the case when I was an idealist, serving my country abroad. But no longer. I have simply come to the realization that I know no other trade – it's all I have to sell. And every man has to earn a living. I believe my talent is valuable, and I see your country as a place which might use me in a way which would put Iraq into the worst possible light on the world stage – especially in the Pentagon, which would be likely to move against them.'

'I agree with you. The idea has considerable appeal to me personally, and I suspect it will have for several others as well.'

'Yes, sir. Might I ask who will make the final decision?'

'Oh, the Imam himself. In association with one or two senior military commanders.'

'The fewer people who know the precise nature of the missions the better.'

'Correct, Eilat. That is correct.'

They walked once more in silence for a few minutes, pacing through the great stone vault in the southeastern corner of the mosque. Then the *hojjat* spoke again. 'Is there any further evidence you can make available to us to show that you are who you say you are?'

'Sir, I have written my address – the address where I killed the assassin – on this piece of paper. I'm sure you could send someone in to make inquiries. Even if the place has been cleaned and set in order, you should still be able to detect bloodstains on the floor in the main hall, and certainly you ought to find holes in the wood above the door where I fixed a bracket into the wall. I expect my possessions have been removed.'

'Thank you, and yes, we will conduct those checks in Baghdad immediately. If you are lying, we will of course not contact you again. But, if the checks confirm your story, as I suspect they will, we'll be in communication very quickly because obviously you could prove extremely useful to us. Whether or not you're able to conduct the military operations you plan will be for others to decide.'

The two men shook hands as before, and Eilat walked back outside to where the student waited to escort him back to the hotel. The *hojjat*'s final instructions were succinct: 'Remain in place for the next few days until we contact you again.'

At $80 a night in the Hotel Abbassi, I trust they'll be quick, he thought, as he and the *talabeh* strolled back through the vast expanse of Imam Khomeini Square.

The next three days passed slowly. Eilat spent his time sleeping and regaining the weight he had lost. Finally, on the morning of July 23, the phone call came. It was from the young student guide. 'Please catch the noon train to Tehrān. A room is booked for you at the Hotel Bolvar under the name "Mr Eilat." You will be contacted there this evening.' He said nothing more but simply replaced the phone.

The train ran into Tehrān on time, shortly before 4pm. Eilat wore his Iranian robes and turban and carried his leather bag. He settled down in the modest room on the third floor of the Hotel Bolvar, to await his call. It came at six minutes past five. A new *talabeh* announced that he was in the lobby and would Mr Eilat come down at once. There were important people awaiting him.

Outside the hotel an orange taxi was parked with its meter running. The vehicle wended its way north through the city's heavy evening traffic – straight up the Vali-ye Asr, the world's longest urban road, lined with shops beside the Tehrān railway station at the shabby southern end and leading all the way to the former Shah's summer palace up in the select, rarified hills of Shemiran, a distance of 16 miles. Their taxi did not go the whole way, instead veering off to the right at Keshavarz Boulevard, past the Iraqi Embassy, and ducking into the Kheyabon area. From there it traveled less than 200 yards before stopping opposite an elegant city mosque. The *talabeh* paid the fare and they walked 50 yards down a narrow street beside the building to a white gate with a doorbell at the side. Their ring was answered immediately, and Eilat was escorted into a shaded, completely walled courtyard containing a slender date-palm and the great awning of a tamarisk tree. The waters of a stone fountain splashed quietly in the center; beyond, directly opposite the west entrance to the mosque, stood a tall house the color of sandstone. Eilat was led through the door to this house into a large stone-floored hall similar in design to that of his former residence in Baghdad but about three times larger. Seated on a heavy wooden chair, attended by two disciples, was an *ayatollah* wearing a black robe, and a black turban which contrasted with his white beard. Next to him was the *hojjat* who had first interviewed Eilat in the Great Mosque of Isfahan.

Both men rose as the Iraqi entered, and one of the disciples poured him water from a large dark green ceramic jug which Eilat estimated would hold about one and a half gallons. The *hojjat* made the introductions, and the *ayatollah* offered his hand to the visitor.

'You certainly caused a commotion in Baghdad,' said the *hojjat*. 'We had your story checked by two sources, and one of them knew all about it without having to make even a single inquiry.

Our other man was actually in Syria at the time, but he telephoned back within five hours. He told us the Iraqi security forces are still watching all airports and seaports, and they even have men on buses and trains, searching for the intelligence officer who fled with all his secrets after murdering a palace guard.'

'I suppose no one mentioned the fact that two armed men entered my house at two in the morning and, on the admission of one of them, with intent to assassinate me? On direct orders from the President?'

'Yes, as a matter of fact. Our first man knew everything. Apparently there are many people who are angry at the Iraqi Government's propensity to have people quietly executed, and quite a lot of them thought the President deserved to be thwarted. Eilat One is a name on every insider's lips. But nothing of that kind has been officially announced.'

'No. I thought probably not.'

'I would like to ask you two things. First, how did you make one of the assassins tell you what he was there for? Second, how did you get away?'

'To answer the first question: routine persuasion. As for the second, I walked.'

Both the *hojjat* and the *ayatollah* smiled. 'You mean you killed one of them,' said the *hojjat*, 'and threatened the other with a similar fate?'

'Yes. The use of lethal force seemed reasonable, since both of them had been intending to kill me, and for all I knew there were others outside with a similar brief.'

'And about this walk. How long did it take?'

'About 22 days from Baghdad to the train station in Ahvāz. I suppose I averaged around 15 miles a day. It was fiercely hot and I walked at night when I could. Parts of the journey were very slow. I stuck to the river, and in places there was no hard surface so sometimes it took almost an hour to cover a mile. Other parts were much better.'

'Well, Eilat, you are a man of considerable resources. Before we ask you to outline your plans there is one further question I would like answered.'

'By all means.'

'Did the President have any reason whatsoever to distrust you?'

'No. He did not. Except for the fact that I had been unavoidably away for a very long time. He may have felt that I had become distant, and could never really be further trusted. But I gave him no cause for suspicion and I acted only on behalf of Iraq. For my entire working life.'

'I see,' replied the *hojjat*. 'But it has been very hard to discover anything about your career. No one appears to know exactly what you have been doing, or even where.'

'For that I should perhaps be congratulated, sir,' replied Eilat. 'Secrecy is, after all, the difference between life and death in my trade.'

'That and your sharp knife,' interposed the *ayatollah*. 'By the way, do you have it with you?'

Eilat smiled. He was not afraid of the holy men with whom he conversed. 'Yes, sir. I do.'

'Perhaps you would do me the honor of placing it on the table until you leave. We, of course, are not armed.'

Eilat recognized a test of trust when he heard one, and he walked across the room, drew his knife from inside his robe and placed it next to the water jug. One of the disciples chuckled, archly, at the size of it. 'You are Crocodile Dundee,' he said, betraying the terrible truth that he had been watching Western videos. 'In disguise,' he added.

The *ayatollah* looked puzzled but after a moment ignored the young man's remark and spoke only to his visitor, offering simply, 'Thank you, my son.' It was, Eilat knew, an expression of trust, and for that he was grateful. He also knew that he would need to tell these men more about his life than he had ever told anyone. They were plainly going to check him out ruthlessly, and if he wanted to earn their confidence he would have to level with them. Otherwise the entire exercise would become futile. There were risks attached to telling the truth, but he could face death as a spy should he attempt to conceal his background from the Iranian *ayatollah*.

'And now, Eilat,' the religious leader continued, 'the *hojjat* and I would like to hear your plans.'

'Sir, may I begin by suggesting that we are dealing with two acts of revenge here? Mine and yours. Mine we know about. By yours I refer to the occasion, almost two years ago, when all three of your Russian Kilo-Class submarines were mysteriously destroyed in Bandar Abbas. I know from the newspapers that the

Iranian Navy officially put the entire episode down to accident, but I'm sure we all know it was anything *but* an accident. And, when you think about it, no other nation except the Satan could possibly have done it. The Americans had the motive, the power, the finance and the know-how.'

'And what was that motive?' asked the *hojjat*.

'I don't really know, sir. But I would guess they secretly blamed Iran for the destruction of that aircraft carrier of theirs in the Gulf a few weeks previously. They publicly announced that that was another . . . accident. But I don't think they believed it – though I do think you were innocent of it.'

The *ayatollah* nodded. 'Please go on.'

'I am therefore proposing that we hit back three times – one blow against America for each of the lost submarines.'

'But why do you think they will not blame us again? And perhaps launch an air strike against Bandar Abbas and wipe out the rest of our ships?'

'Because, sir, we will arrange our actions to coincide with irrevocable evidence that it must have been Iraq.'

'Such as . . . ?'

'We will hit them on a selection of the following dates: January 17, the day the US Army launched its opening attack on Iraq in the Gulf War April 6, the day Iraq was forced to accept the terms of surrender as laid down by the Americans' puppets in the United Nations. And July 16, the anniversary of the day Saddam Hussein became President of the Republic of Iraq.'

'I see . . . Yes, I suppose such coincidences of dates would be irresistibly persuasive for an American intelligence officer.'

'And of course there is one other method we could employ, sir. Once I'm clear, and back in Iran – where I hope I'll be welcome – we can leak some judicious details to the CIA field officers in Baghdad, details which could have been known only to the mission commander, a serving Iraqi intelligence officer who has now gone into hiding . . .'

'Yes . . . You have given this considerable thought, have you not?'

'I have, sir. And I am of course assuming that I am speaking to one of the Imam's closest advisors.'

'Two of them, Eilat,' replied the *ayatollah*, 'on matters such as these. But so much for your overall strategy. Are you yet prepared to divulge how you are going to put it into practice?'

'Not quite yet, sir – not until we have an agreement in principle. Save to mention that I shall require quite substantial refitting work to be carried out at one of your military bases, and that I anticipate using a surface-to-air missile, possibly a regular Russian SAM. My advice is that you order four such systems, claiming that you are improving the anti-aircraft defense on your surface ships. You will have to pay about three hundred million dollars, but I think it might prove a bit of a bargain. The system I have in mind has a vast array of radar, and I will merely require certain parts of one of them.'

'Will you take charge of this work personally, or will you leave it to our people?'

'I shall take charge myself, sir. I do not know of anyone else in the Middle East who would be qualified. Which brings us to a minor point: I shall have to be seconded into your armed forces, with appropriate rank.'

'Yes, you will. But I do not anticipate that being more than a formality. However, there is one aspect I should clear up. You have mentioned the cost of the missile system, but have you any idea of how much your further expenses will come to?'

'Not really, except for the value of time and people. I am talking about major hardware costs, but they might not be as great as you think. And then, of course, there is the question of my own fee.'

'And what might you assess that to be, Eilat?'

'I think three million American dollars would be fair. I shall ask you to put a quarter of a million in my Swiss account when we start, followed by three-quarters of a million when the initial stage of the mission is accomplished. Then I shall require five hundred thousand dollars when we set off and a final one and a half million when, and only when, the three objectives have been achieved. That way, should we fail, I will have been working for half-pay. But I do not anticipate this.'

'And what, Eilat, if you should be caught? What if my country is held up to ridicule in front of the entire world as a bunch of lawless international gangsters?'

'Sir, we will not be caught. *Cannot* be caught. But, if by a million-to-one chance we were, suffice it to say that death would be preferable to me. I have no fear of death. Suitable arrangements to that end would already be in place.'

'Eilat,' replied the *hojjat*, 'you come to us with a vague and expensive scheme. I can take it no further without a much clearer plan from you, and I shall of course also have to consult with the Imam and the military. Nevertheless, you may assume we agree in principle to explore this project with you, and that you will remain here as our secret, honored guest for as long as that may take.'

'Thank you. I am grateful, and may Allah always go with you. Just one thing, sir, before I leave. I hesitate to ask this, but I have been alone for a very long time. I wonder if we might pray together . . . ?'

'Of course, my son. You have been very badly used. Let's walk together across the courtyard. Ayatollah, will you join us?'

'No, I have some writing to finish. I will pray in an hour.'

The *hojjat* and the Iraqi left the house and entered the courtyard together. They walked slowly past the fountain to the door of the mosque, where they removed their shoes. It was there that the learned man turned around to ask his final question. 'Eilat, I wonder if you are yet ready, as we prepare for prayer, perhaps to tell me your real name?'

'Yes. You have been very kind to me, and I think I am ready now. My name is Benjamin. I'm Commander Benjamin Adnam.'

CHAPTER TWO

September 12, 2004.

THEY WERE 9000 feet above the desert floor now, flying low in the thicker air. The big Iranian Navy transport aircraft, a C130 Hercules transporter, was making 240 knots through crystalline skies. Down below, along the northern edges of the Dasht-e-Lut – the Great Sandy Desert – the temperatures hovered around 114 degrees. The Air Force colonel at the controls of the Hercules made his course adjustment to the south as they inched their way over the old city of Yazd, which has been trading silk and textiles in the middle of Iran's vast broiling wilderness for 1000 years.

'Can you you imagine living in a place like that, Commander?' muttered Rear-Admiral Mohammed Badr, the Iranian Navy's most senior submarine expert, as he stared down at the desert city, all alone in the midst of thousands of square miles of sand.

'Only in the line of duty, sir,' replied Benjamin Adnam, elegant in his new Iranian uniform with the three gold stripes on the sleeve.

The Iranian admiral smiled. 'Where's your family from, Ben?'

'Oh, we've lived in Tikrīt for generations.'

'Where exactly is that?' asked Badr. 'Close to Baghdad?'

'Well, it's on the Tigris, like Baghdad, but about 110 miles upstream, on the edge of the central plains. If you start heading west from Tikrīt you encounter precisely nothing for 150 miles, all the way to the Syrian border.'

'Sounds like Yazd.'

'Not that bad, sir. To the south of Tikrīt, heading for Baghdad, it can be quite busy. We're only 34 miles from Sāmarrā. And you presumably know that Tikrīt was Saddam Hussein's home town. When he rose to power it gave the town a new life and a new prosperity. Half his cabinet came from there. My father says the old rural feel of the place vanished once it became known as a cradle of government power.'

'Did you spend much time there as a boy?'

'No, not really. I went away to school in England, and when I returned I was drafted into the navy – the Israeli Navy, actually.'

'The *Israeli* Navy?' exclaimed Admiral Badr. 'How did you manage that?'

'Oh, there was a group of us. The chosen Iraqi youth. Fanatical fundamentalists – which I was, then. When everyone thought I was 16 – in fact I was 18 – we were all placed with families abroad, operating under deep cover in different countries. I was sent to Israel and ordered to join the navy. Everything was arranged for me. I was spying for Iraq for years.'

'You were a submariner, weren't you, Ben?'

'Yes, for several years I was. Trained in the Royal Navy in Scotland after Israel bought a diesel–electric boat from the Brits.'

'Think they'd train a few of our men if we bought a submarine from them?' Badr was smiling.

'Probably not. You guys are generally regarded by the world community as dangerous outlaws.'

'And soon we show them *how* dangerous, eh, Ben?'

'Yes. Except they'll think it's Iraq.'

Both men laughed. They were the only passengers in the big, noisy military aircraft as it thundered on toward Bandar Abbas, but such was the deadly nature of their business that they still spoke in the guarded tones of strangers, even though they had worked closely together in Tehrān for the past three weeks and more. The two officers were already kindred spirits, mainly because of Ben Adnam's certainty that it had been the Americans who had destroyed the three Iranian submarines.

Rear-Admiral Badr had been the project manager for the entire Kilo-Class program in 2002. He had been at his home in the Bandar Abbas dockyard when the American hit squad had struck, smashing all three of the Russian-built submarines to the bottom of the harbor. For Badr it had represented ten years of work in ruins. He was fortunate not to have been dismissed from the navy, but the *ayatollahs* liked the big, bespectacled submariner from the south coast port of Būshehr, and he was held in great respect by his fellow admirals. No one in Iran knew more about submarines than Mohammed Badr. At least, not before Commander Adnam arrived.

In the months after the attack the admiral had, like almost everyone else in the Iranian Navy, concluded that the American President had blamed the *ayatollahs* for the loss of the *Thomas Jefferson* and acted accordingly. But the Americans were wrong. Iran was innocent, and the gnawing desire for revenge against the Satan seemed only to grow with each passing month. Especially in the mind of the man most affected by the loss, Rear-Admiral Mohammed Badr himself. For him the sudden appearance of Benjamin Adnam now represented a beacon of light in the murky waters of naval sabotage, that no-man's-land of world politics where no one admits anything – neither the criminal, for obvious reasons, nor the victim, for fear of humiliation. In this former Iraqi intelligence officer Badr could see a man with a plan – a plan of such monumental dimensions it would be a miracle if it worked. But the ex-Israeli submarine commander seemed coldly sure of his own abilities, and Iran had the money and the will to make it happen.

The admiral smiled again. It was a smile of good nature, of contentment with his new colleague, and of anticipation of the future.

'You know, Ben,' he said, 'I really admired your planning for these missions. But one thing puzzled me. Why did you turn down their offer of becoming a rear-admiral?'

'I suppose I'm a purist about some things. Remember, I *earned* my rank in the Israeli Navy. I was Commander Benjamin Adnam, and I was CO of a submarine. I'm very proud of that. And I'm proud of my rank. It does me honor, and so I don't want to be a fraud admiral. I am *Commander* Adnam. I expect you heard me tell them I'll accept the rank of rear-admiral when the project is successfully completed. Because then I will have earned it.'

'Very admirable,' replied Admiral Badr. 'And now I have another question. I heard you say twice in that last meeting that the West believes you are dead. How can they? They don't even know you. Who told them you were dead?'

'The Mossad, I expect. There was a pretty serious hunt for me after I absconded from the Israeli Navy. But they thought they found me.'

'Can you explain that, Commander?'

'Well, I suppose I can, now. OK. This is what I did. I'd known for months this professional forger, you see, an Egyptian who specialized in passports and official documents – lived in Cairo. He did the most exquisite work, and I'd often used him before. The strange thing was that he looked very like me – same height and build, same complexion – and he even walked like me, the big difference being that he had a very slight limp; he always walked using a black cane with a silver top.

'And so, not to put too fine a point on it, I set him up. Phoned him and asked him to meet me privately one night in a secluded place up in the precincts of the citadel, on the southeast side of the city. There, I told him, I'd hand him a small attaché case made of soft leather in which would be several documents I wanted him to copy for me. I'd also hand over to him three hundred US dollars as a down payment.

'I made the appointment for half past seven in the evening because I knew he'd then walk straight down the hill to the mosque he attended every night at eight o'clock. Then I called the Mossad in Tel Aviv and spoke to a duty officer. Told them I was a sympathetic member of the *sayanim* and that I had valuable information that'd cost them $100,000 if it proved to be accurate. I gave them the number of a Swiss bank account, and I told them I had many contacts and might be able to inform them of other important matters. Right now, however, my information was this: the missing Israeli Navy officer Commander Benjamin Adnam was to be kidnaped and interrogated this evening by an Iraqi hit squad. The Mossad had one chance to take him out themselves – on the dark and lonely lower part of the hill that leads down to the Mosque of Sultan Mu'ayyad Sheikh.

'Obviously I told them the man would be wearing Arab dress and walking with a slight limp, using a black cane with a silver top. Their operatives should be dressed in Western suits and approach under the guise of the Egyptian Secret Police, asking to see his papers. I was working on the theory that a criminal like my forger friend would carry no papers of his own – that would leave only the attaché case. After that it was up to them, because in that case was every one of my most valuable documents – you know: navy record, passport, driver's license, birth certificate . . . not to mention my cigarette case and my precious Israeli submariner's badge.

'After my own transaction was complete, I slipped away and followed the forger from a distance. I watched two men approach him and examine the contents of his briefcase. Then I watched one of them kill him instantly from behind with a single shot from a silenced pistol. I watched them leave, taking the briefcase with them.

'I'd made sure there was ample evidence for the Mossad, and there was no doubt in their minds about who the dead man was. Someone found the body a few hours later, and the Egyptian police took over – but of course *they* knew nothing because there were no documents left on the corpse. Two weeks later the Israelis sent one hundred thousand dollars to my account in Geneva, just as I'd asked.'

Rear-Admiral Badr burst out laughing at the sheer brass neck of the scheme. 'Ben, I guess a lot of people in Tel Aviv think you are dead.'

'Yes sir. And they will have undoubtedly informed the Americans.'

'But what precisely had you done to make the Great Satan so interested in you?'

'I don't think I can reveal that. Except to say that I know your country had nothing to do with the elimination of that American aircraft carrier.'

'My God, Ben . . . was that *you*?'

The Iraqi just smiled. 'Admiral, let's look to the future . . .'

Badr remained thoughtful. 'Is your vision of the future the same as ours, Commander?'

'I believe so, sir – assuming you're referring to a general belief that one day the nation of Islam must dominate the earth, to the everlasting glory of Allah.'

'That is our dream, Ben. That is our dream. And there are many of us in the military here in Iran who believe the only way to achieve this aim is to cause chaos in the West.'

'You mean, sir, that if we frighten them often enough they may begin to fall apart?'

'I believe they will, Ben. Because, unlike us, they're a godless society. They have no central rallying point except money. In fact they have nothing except money. Their god is material possessions. They have no ideals.

'Great wars of the past have often been won behind a religious banner. But in this millennium Allah alone can inspire brilliance and courage . . . because Allah is great and all-powerful. Allah makes *us* great, and when we attack we attack behind his power, for a common cause. In the end, nothing can withstand us. Certainly not the infidels of the United States.

'We must strike hammer blows against them, over and over, until their will dissolves – as it must, because they have no god. They are just overfed disciples of a lesser god – the god of money, and country clubs, and huge cars, and beautiful houses. But in the end they are nothing because they believe in nothing and have no true god. The Koran does not guide them. Nothing holy lights their way.

'They are the rampant heathens of the twenty-first century, sucking the world's resources dry. Taking, grabbing, using, claiming the rights of other countries, treating our own Gulf of Iran as if it were theirs. But one day we will rise up and take back what is ours, what has been ours for thousands of years. And when that day comes the power of the United States will be returned, finally, to the Nation of Islam.'

The two men sat in silence after that. To each of them the words possessed profound meaning. Not everyone in Iran agreed with such thoughts, nor with Admiral Badr's preferred course of action. But there were senior military figures who did share his views, very firmly. Which was why he had been singled out to work with the newly arrived Benjamin Adnam, the world's most wanted terrorist.

In due course the big Hercules began descending toward Bandar Abbas Airport, slipping down through the hot clear skies. Ben could see from his window the submarine docks in the distance. There would be much activity there this week, what with the arrival from St Petersburg of the first replacement Kilo, Russia's special export model, the 877 EKM. This submarine was to be named the *Yunes-4* for the prophet Jonah, who was swallowed by a whale but saved by God.

Ben could imagine the 235-foot 3000-tonner from the Baltic quietly berthed in the submarine pens, and as he did so he envisaged himself in the control room, as once he had been in a similar vessel. Admiral Badr, too, wore a faraway look, remembering as he so often did the black night of August 2, 2002, around the midnight hour . . . and the scene of absolute devastation which had greeted him at the Iranian submarine base. The confusion. The fear. The desperate unavailing attempts to save the men on board the two hulls which had been sunk alongside the jetties.

Today would offer Badr his first sight of an operational Kilo in the harbor of Bandar Abbas since that terrible night. And the prospect gave him heart, for he assumed that, under the guidance of the quite brilliant Iraqi officer with whom he now shared a common goal, they would harness the new Kilo to attack the hated, imperious enemy from the Western hemisphere.

A naval staff car greeted them when they disembarked, and they were driven immediately to the base. Ben transferred his few possessions to the house which had been provided for him, next door to the rear-admiral's residence. Twenty minutes later they were in the Special Ops room, which took up the entire top floor of a small executive block. Each man had a private office, complete with secure phone lines. A wider conference room between these offices contained drawers full of naval charts and architectural plans, shelves of reference books, a fax machine, a copying machine, and three computers, one containing all of the world's naval charts and another a myriad of marine-engineering and design data. Ben guessed most of his work would be done on the third computer.

There was no sign of staff or assistance in any form, although four armed Iranian Navy guards stood duty in the upstairs corridor, beyond the big locked wooden doors. Ben approved of that arrangement, and checked the guards would be on duty 24 hours a day. Every day. He also requested that the two-man guard on the main entrance be trebled.

'You like security, hah?' said Badr.

'Admiral, the repercussions should a foreign agent breach our defenses and ascertain our plans would represent your very worst nightmare. If they happened to work for the CIA, I think you could assume a full-blooded American air strike on this port from one of their carriers within 48 hours. We, you and I, probably would never know what hit us. But, should we survive, we would be rightly blamed. And executed. I don't care how many guards you deploy – 40, 60, 100 or more – the consequences of not having enough of them are utterly unthinkable.'

'You're right, Ben. You're usually right, hah?'

42

'Mostly. Which is, essentially, why I'm still breathing.'

The rear-admiral nodded gravely. Then he hit his bleeper to summon his regular chauffeur to take them for a tour of the dockyard to inspect the work in progress, in readiness for the Three Strikes against Satan.

The two officers wore the new summer uniform of white shorts, socks and shoes plus dark blue short-sleeved shirts with epaulettes and the insignia of rank. They each carried a two-foot-long officer's baton. All of which set them apart as they stood on the dusty edge of the massive construction site that was being dug out of the shoreline on the southeastern corner of the harbor, directly opposite the regular submarine docks, facing inland, with the road and the open waters of the Gulf behind them.

A fleet of 40 trucks was moving sand from a hole almost 300 feet long, 150 feet wide and 120 feet deep. It was separated from the harbor waters by a 50-foot 'beach.' As the trucks hauled away the mountains of sand, more like them were grinding their way up to empty tons and tons of hard-core and rubble into the floor of the hole. It was going to be a mighty foundation.

'Just as you instructed, Ben,' said Badr. 'One reinforced-concrete submarine drydock. Walls 30 feet thick to withstand the impact of a 10,000-pound bomb. The boat will just float in and we'll pump out the water and get to work.'

'Very impressive,' said Adnam. 'Did you decide yet where to build the model room?'

'Right here, Ben. We build it 300 feet long of scaffold and wood. Right now we're just waiting for them to pour the concrete foundation for both buildings. Maybe a week, then we'll have it erected inside twenty-one days. You have preliminary plans ready for the model?'

'Almost. By the way, how is your man at the Vickers shipyard in England? I need his details now.'

'I don't know off the top of my head whether we have them here quite yet, but I'd be surprised if we were not very much on the case. We have men in all of the big submarine bases in Europe. The one we've positioned at the greatest submarine-builders in the world will be very efficient indeed. Let me check later.'

Barrow-in-Furness, England, September 17.
The afternoon was drawing to a close in the brightly lit drawing-

office block out on the edge of the sprawling yards of Vickers Shipbuilding and Engineering. Most people here left sharp at five o'clock these days. Vickers, whose engineers had built the spectacular Trident submarines, was undergoing something of a morale problem. People did not work late any more. There was hardly any point. All successive governments ever wanted to do, it seemed, was to cut programs, scrap submarines and generally run down one of the finest engineering firms in the world – some think *the* finest.

Up in the drawing office, desk lights were going out. Young draftsmen were preparing to leave. The big computers which contained the database for all the submarines built here were switched off. In the outer offices, where the senior engineering draftsmen worked, only one light was still burning.

John Patel, a tall, sallow-faced man aged 38 years old, with two outstanding degrees from the University of London, was working quietly on. His field lay on the leading edge of new submarine design – indeed, he was widely regarded as the most important man in the department. He was a brilliant engineer with an equally brilliant career ahead of him, either here or possibly in the United States, where such men are valued far more highly than they are in the United Kingdom. For the moment, however, he belonged to Vickers, and that was greatly to the company's advantage.

Except for one unknown factor. John Patel was not what he seemed – a youngish married man of Pakistani parentage living in the village of Leece, on the outskirts of Barrow. He was an Iranian who had been skilfully inserted into England during the 1970s with his father. At the time John had been still been a schoolboy. Both father and son had beaten the immigration system by using Pakistani passports. They had now lived in Britain for 27 years, the father – an ex-Iranian Navy officer – working undercover for first the regime of the late Shah and subsequently for the burgeoning navy of the Ayatollah Khomeini and his successors.

The young John Patel had succeeded beyond anyone's wildest dreams, after graduation obtaining a job deep inside the Vickers corporation. Taught by his father from an early age, he was one of the shrewdest and most valuable field operators in Tehrān's worldwide spy network, because his speciality lay in the one area in which Iran nurtured overwhelming ambition – the formation of a strike submarine fleet which could blockade the Gulf of Iran, the country's own historic waters.

When John Patel finally returned to his homeland he would do so as a rich man. Both sets of employers had paid him well for the past six years, during which time he had systematically raided the Vickers computerized database, copying for his government countless high-tech secret documents involving submarines and their systems. Tonight he would do so again. Within the next 15 minutes he would be the only man left on the floor, as often happened.

The room which housed the database was in darkness and securely locked. No one had access except between the hours of nine and five when the office was staffed. Six years previously it had taken John Patel approximately 15 seconds to take an impression of the key in a piece of window putty from which he had had a duplicate made. Today, such was his eminence in the department that no one would have given it a thought had he been observed working at the computer after hours.

He waited until the cleaning staff had completed their tasks before he made his move, at 6.30pm. Then, carrying his own powerful Toshiba laptop computer, he walked softly through the darkened main floor and quietly opened the door to the database room, closing it softly behind him. He turned on the light above the console and heard the hum of the big corporate computer as it came slickly to life. He promptly tapped into the database for the section which dealt with the now-extinct Upholder Class diesel–electric submarine – a program killed off by the government in the 1990s, to the fury of the Royal Navy.

Only four of the subs had been built, at Vickers's Cammell Laird yard in Birkenhead, fifty miles to the south of Barrow. But they were excellent ships, highly efficient, as good as if not probably better than the Russian Kilo-Class, and they were the only diesel–electric submarines the Royal Navy had built since the 'O'-Class back in the 1960s. They were called *Upholder*, *Unicorn*, *Ursula* and *Unseen*. The government planned to sell all four of these stealthy 2500-tonners to foreign governments, a course of action most British admirals considered to be somewhat shortsighted.

John Patel hooked up his Toshiba on the laplink system and hit the 'copy' and 'start' keys. The operation would take about

45

four hours, but he would not have to monitor it. The Toshiba, with 4.3 gigabytes on its hard disk, would silently absorb every last sentence and diagram of the thousands and thousands of details contained in the computerized library which represented the Upholder-Class submarine. Every working part – every system, the propulsion, the weapons, the generators, the location of the switches, the valves, the torpedo tubes, the air purifiers – the entire blueprint of these miraculous underwater warships would be copied. The data would take up almost the full capacity of the hard disk. It was the biggest request John Patel had ever received, and he wondered what on earth the Iranian Navy could want with such a mammoth quantity of data. And the note, delivered personally by his father, had contained an air of urgency, emphasized by the rare specification of the amount of money he would receive for this service – $50,000, payable to his usual numbered account in Geneva.

John thanked Allah for the general weakness of Vickers's security. He planned to spend the night in the building rather than risk being searched, as he might well be if he left via the main gate at around 11pm; the chances of his being discovered if he spent the night hidden somewhere in the building were almost nonexistent. The sole security guard on duty in the drawing-office building, Reg, was normally asleep or watching television: he usually took a walk at around 10.30pm, right after the evening news on ITV, but it was not a long walk. Reg liked to be back in his little office for the late movie at 10.45pm.

At 9pm John checked the computers. They were still running flawlessly, the little Toshiba sucking off the priceless information from the database. He turned out all of the lights, locked the door, and then slipped across the main floor into his own office, where he also switched out all the lights. He sat behind his desk, looking out through the door to the unlighted corridor along which he expected to see Reg advance in 90 minutes' time.

It was a boring wait, but at 10.35pm the lights went on in the outer corridor. John Patel softly closed his office door and positioned himself directly behind it. He could hear the security man opening and shutting doors swiftly, each time sounding a little closer. When he reached John's office he opened the door and stepped inside, but did not bother to turn on the lights and certainly did not look behind the door. He was gone inside ten seconds, and John heard him check the next office immediately afterwards.

Reg skipped the computer room altogether, but even had he entered he would not have tampered with a running program. His brief was to locate intruders, nothing else. And anyway the late movie tonight was a repeat of an old 1997 comedy called *The Full Monty*, which he thought was the funniest film he had ever seen.

John re-entered the computer room at 11pm, disconnected his laptop and turned off the main system. Then he retreated to his pitch-dark office, locked the Toshiba into his briefcase and spread out on the floor behind his desk, guessing correctly that Reg was done for the night.

At 8.15 the following morning John Patel opened his office door, switched on his desk light and began work. No one else would appear before 9am. No one ever did at Vickers, not these days.

Tonight he would leave on time with all the others, and he looked forward to that. This evening he and Lisa were driving over to his father's Indian restaurant in Bradford, 80 miles away across the high Pennines. That was always fun. But, while he and his wife drove home, Ranji Patel would journey 175 miles southward through the night down the M1 motorway to London, taking the Toshiba laptop to the Iranian Embassy at 27, Prince's Gate, Kensington, for special delivery to the Naval Attaché. Old friends would be waiting up for him in the small hours. And the little computer would be in the Iranian diplomatic bag on board Syrian Arab Airways' morning flight from Heathrow to Tehrān.

November 2, Bandar Abbas.
In the past two months there had been immense progress on two fronts. Commander Adnam had mastered the rudiments of the Farsi language, using every modern computerized technique. And the Iranian contractors had completed the foundation for the concrete drydock. They also had in place the 30-foot-thick wall, towering 60 feet high, on its left-hand side, facing the harbor. The wall on the other side was nearing completion, and the great steel girders of the roof were in place. Against the long left-side wall the 300-foot model room was already under cover, and teams of carpenters were hammering home the side walls.

47

Beneath the roof, concealed by sheets of tarpaulin, a huge full-scale cylindrical model of a diesel–electric submarine was being created out of wood and gray plastic. Commander Ben Adnam spent several hours each day in there with Iran's senior naval architects and submarine experts. The boat could almost have been a Russian Kilo except that it was not quite so big and contained many significant differences of detail, particularly of internal layout. To the expert eye, it was several degrees more sophisticated.

Commander Adnam had been careful to reveal to no one other than Rear-Admiral Badr the precise type and class of submarine they would use on the mission. He had slightly irritated the Iranian Navy hierarchy by brushing aside their questions concerning when, how and where the Special Ops submarine was coming from. To every question the Commander's answer was the same: 'I am not yet ready to reveal the whereabouts of the submarine we will use. But you may trust me implicitly – the entire plan depends on it. At the correct time I will inform you how I propose to acquire it.'

'But Ben,' they protested, 'we must know. Do you intend to rent one, borrow one, or even buy one? If so, from whom? We need to be told the costs and who the provider might be. There may be great political ramifications.'

'Not yet,' Adnam would reply curtly. 'When the time comes I will of course present you with a detailed plan and report. At that point you will be free to accept or decline, as you wish. Bear in mind that I do not anticipate your declining, because that would cost me $2,750,000; this I consider to be a sensitive area.'

Out beyond the model room, work continued under the wilting rays of the sun by day and under lights at night. Security was phenomenal: It was impossible to reach the buildings without crossing a cordon of armed guards, placed two hundred yards from the new dock. Miles of barbed wire protected all approaches to the site. Every worker wore a plastic identification badge. Every man employed on the site was photographed and fingerprinted, checked and searched, both incoming and outgoing. A simple sign on the main gate along the road to the base read:

AUTHORIZED PERSONNEL ONLY
INTRUDERS WILL BE SHOT ON SIGHT

Three drivers who had arrived without their badges had been incarcerated in the Navy's jail for a week as suspected spies. Special-patrol craft criss-crossed the waters of the inner harbor with unprecedented frequency. A frigate remained on permanent patrol outside the harbor entrance, ready to intercept and if necessary sink any unauthorized visitor.

By the year 2004 the Iranian Navy was 40,000 strong, comprising 20,000 regular personnel plus a further 20,000 members of the Islamic Revolutionary Guards Corps (IRGC), special forces loosely modeled on the US Navy SEALs, or the British SAS. These forces managed some heavy practice during the 1980–88 war with Iraq, but have never achieved the sophistication of their American or British counterparts. Nonetheless, the young Iranian naval commandos were tough, fit and quite incredibly brave, believing as they did that in the end they were fighting for Allah, and that he would protect them and lead them to glory.

From the ranks of these commandos Adnam would hand-pick two hitmen for his mission. Another eighteen crew-members would be recruited directly from the submarine service – men who had been essentially without ships since the American attack two years previously. He expended long hours in consultation with the commanding officers of the IRGC, poring over the records and finally selecting five outstanding veterans for interview, of whom he would reject three. He spent, of course, even longer with the submarine commanders looking for the individuals who would one day man the watches on the long submarine journey.

When he was not involved in selection, Ben passed many hours alone in the Black Ops inner office, studying the superb data which had been brought on the little Toshiba computer from Barrow-in-Furness. Then he would consult his designers and go to the model room to help build and perfect another aspect of the phantom submarine he had masterminded.

By early December the model was almost complete, and Commander Adnam had selected his personnel. In company with Admiral Badr he made his way out to the building site to meet the busload of 20 young men with whom he would soon go on a mission of justice for their country.

Both officers stood and watched as the select few disembarked and formed two lines of ten. The admiral and the commander

49

walked carefully along the lines, addressing every man by name and rank, talking for perhaps two minutes with each of them. They then ordered everyone into the air-conditioned conference room set beyond the stern end of the 200-foot model. Here it was that the world's most notorious terrorist outlined their duties for them. Most of the men had some Arabic, but Ben spoke mainly in Farsi, using phrases he had learned especially for this talk. 'Most of you,' he began, 'are already familiar with the workings of a Kilo-Class submarine, and you will understand that I have deliberately selected officers who have worked in specialist areas – I mean, of course, people who have been in charge of propulsion, electronics, generators, sonar, hydrology, communications, navigation and hydraulic systems.

'The submarine I shall acquire for our mission will be one with which you are not familiar, and in anticipation of that we have constructed here this full-scale model. In the coming three weeks I want all of you to familiarize yourselves with its workings – every switch, valve and keyboard. And when I say "familiarize" I mean that I would expect you to go on board the real submarine in the pitch dark, find your area of operation and work your systems without error, possibly still in complete darkness.

'This is to be a time of extensive study, note-taking and memorizing. Pure concentration. I have selected each one of you because I know you have the precise characteristics this mission demands. Even so, it is likely that during the course of the next four weeks some of you will not measure up, and we may have to replace you. That, however, will be up to you.

'This mission will not be without its dangers, but I am confident in our skills and in the abilities of each one of you. And now, perhaps, we should go and make a tour of the model . . .'

January 6, 2005. Office of the National Security Advisor, the White House.
The National Security Advisor, Admiral Arnold Morgan, was in deep conference, studying satellite photographs with Admiral George Morris, Director of the National Security Agency, Fort Meade, Maryland.

'What the hell's that, goddammit?'
'Er, a building, sir. A large building.'
'I can see that, for Christ's sake. What kind of a building is it?

Looks like a fucking indoor football stadium. What the hell's it doing in a naval dockyard? Eh?' Then, warming to his theme, as he was always prone to do, Morgan added, 'Fucking Arabs taking up football? Nah, bullshit – they ain't big enough, betcha you couldn't find a halfway decent lineman in the whole Middle East. Come on, George, what kind of a building is it?'

'Sir, at a guess I'd say it was a concrete drydock for a submarine. But there's another big building on its left-hand side that seems to have a steel roof, judging by the sun glinting off it. God knows what's inside it – there are massive doors at the seaward end and a thick concrete wall at the landward end.'

'Hmm. Let me ask you this: if it's gonna be a drydock, how come it's not connected to the water? Look – you can see the land runs right across the entrance.'

'Yes, sir. I do see that. But these buildings are pretty compli-cated. I'd guess they're fitting all the flooding systems right here where this excavation is . . . I'd say they'd remove that strip of land along the shore at the conclusion of the building project. That way the submarine could just float in and settle, and then all they'd have to do is pump the water out.'

'Correct.'

The two men had worked together for years. Lifelong naval officers, they were as different in character as it was possible to be. Morgan was tough, hard-looking, irascible, brilliant, rude and curiously admired by many, many people. Morris, an ex-Carrier Battle Group Commander, was soft-spoken, lugubrious in delivery and appearance, and thoughtful in the extreme. He had succeeded Morgan as Director at Fort Meade when Morgan had been promoted to National Security Advisor; his biggest problem was that Morgan now frequently believed he was doing both jobs. But this concentrated attention, which the President's chief advisor leveled on the ultra-secret Fort Meade operation gave the place a greater importance than it had enjoyed for many years.

'I wonder why the hell they've built a big secure drydock,' pondered Arnold Morgan out loud.

'Possibly, old buddy, because they don't want us taking out their new Russian Kilo. They're . . . er . . . a bit short of sub-marines these days. But you wouldn't have thought all this activity necessary for just the one boat, would you?'

'Not unless those stupid fucking Russians have agreed to sell 'em an entire new fleet of Kilos,' Morgan rasped. 'And, if they have,' he added, 'we'll remove them. Even Rankov understands that. When we saw the first new one in BA last week I made it clear to him on the phone that the USA would not stand still while the Iranians held up half the industrial world to ransom because of some mad fucking Muslim belief that they own the Persian Gulf.'

'Absolutely, sir.'

'Anyway, George, I guess that new building is big enough and serious enough for us to take an interest. Thanks for bringing the photographs in. I think we better get a couple of guys in there to take a look, since the satellite can't do it for us. You better get back. I'll talk to Langley.'

Five hours later the CIA's Middle East Chief, Jeff Austin, was on the secure line from the White House imparting the news that the agency was well aware of the new building, but at a loss to find out what precisely was going on. 'Admiral,' he said, 'everyone in the area is aware of the construction. Apparently they dug out a foundation half the size of the Grand Canyon and then dumped the sand back in the desert . . . caused a daily dust storm. Our best guess is a drydock, possibly for submarines. I believe they lost their little fleet . . . er . . . coupla years back in some kind of an accident.'

'Oh, yes, that's right. I remember reading something about that.'

'Well, sir, I'm not sure how strongly you feel about it, and the security at the Bandar Abbas base is very hot right now, but I could try and get a couple of guys in there to take a look. Trouble is, they'd have to swim in, and even if they reached the building I'm not sure they could get close enough. And if they did they wouldn't really know what they were looking at.'

'Uh-huh. I see that. Do we have anyone inside the base?'

'One man, an Iranian. White-collar guy in the procurement office. Middle level. Useful, too. We find out most of the ships they're buying before the order gets placed.'

'Didn't find out about the new Kilo, did he?'

'No, sir, he did not.'

'Could he get one of our top guys into the base?'

'Possibly, sir. Leave it with me. I'll get back to you in the morning. It's the middle of the night in Iran.'

'OK, Jeff. Make it early. I don't like submarine activity among the towelheads, right?'

'No, sir.'

At 0830 the following morning Jeff Austin reported back. 'They're working on it, sir. There is, it seems, the possibility of a VIP pass to the base. Our man in there has used it before. He thinks the pass might just get him through the gate out near the building, but he's not sure. They'll be back to me in a couple of days.'

'Fine. Keep at it. I'm concerned about the Iranians.'

'Yes, sir.'

Midday, January 14, 2005. Special Ops Room, Bandar Abbas Naval Base.

'Did you see this report, Admiral? The one just in.'

'Not yet, Ben. What's it say?'

'It's brief. From the security chief out on the main gate to the new dock. "In accordance with your instructions, I am reporting on two men we turned away at 1052 this morning for having incorrect identification passes. One of them was an office executive, Abbas Velayati, who has some clearance but not enough to enter the site. The other was a VIP guest with a correct pass, but again without clearance to the site. He said he was from the Ukraine. I believe both men may be found via the procurement office, according to Velayati's identification pass." '

'We must place them under immediate arrest,' snapped Rear-Admiral Badr. 'Neither of them could have any reason for going out there, except to snoop around. We should interrogate them both. Harshly.'

'I would be inclined to do none of that,' responded Commander Adnam. 'In fact, I'd prefer to do the exact opposite. I think we should apologize for treating a guest here in such a brusque manner, and then issue the correct documents for them to go out and visit the new dock, and even the model room. Perhaps at 1800 when the day shift is packing up. Then we could shoot them both. It would save a lot of time, and we'd be confident our secrets were safe.'

'My God, Ben! You mean I should instruct one of the guards to execute them?'

'Absolutely not. Say nothing to anyone. I intend to deal with them myself . . . in my new capacity as tour guide. I believe they're pouring the concrete foundation in the morning out by the new pumping station. Most convenient, don't you think?'

January 19. Office of the National Security Advisor, the White House.
'Bad news, I'm afraid, Admiral,' said Jeff Austin even before he had pulled up a chair to Admiral Morgan's desk.

'Lay it on me.'

'We've had a disaster in Bandar Abbas. Lost two men, one of them our only insider in the naval base. The other's Tom Partridge, a senior field officer. Comes from Connecticut, speaks Russian and Iranian. The two of them disappeared five days ago.'

'Where?'

'Out at the base. Our man in Abbas got Tom in on some kind of a VIP pass, and neither of them have been seen since. The Iranian's wife has kicked up a huge fuss, but the military police say they have no knowledge of anything. They say both men left the base at the regular time. The civil police say it's nothing to do with them. My guess is they were both caught and shot.'

'Jesus Christ, Jeff. That's bad. Did it get into the papers out there?'

'Not a word. Ever since that building got started, the security's been castiron. We got a man works for the local newspaper and he knows absolutely nothing. Nor is he planning to investigate. We only found out when both men missed their check calls two days after they went to the base.'

'Hmm. We better sit on this for a few days. See if anything pops up. One thing we do know – they're pretty darned touchy down there, whatever the hell it is they're up to.'

January 20. Special Ops Room, Bandar Abbas Naval Base.
'OK, Ben, we got a communication back from Moscow. They've agreed to sell us the systems – four of the new SA-N-6 Grumble Rifs. The one you suggested in the first place. It took 'em long enough, and it's not cheap – three hundred million US dollars, including fifty SAMs.'

'All those Russian missiles are pretty reliable – maybe a 95 percent chance of a successful launch and flight. Kill probability depends on target maneuvers and countermeasures. But this one is very fast, hits Mach 2.5 almost immediately. It's good to altitude 90,000 feet. Carries a 90-kilogram warhead. The export version may need minor modification.'

'Are the Russians using 'em themselves?'

'Yes. I think they're replacing a lot of the old SA-N-3s with them. I read somewhere they've been testing the system on one of those old Kara-Class cruisers – the *Azov*, I think: she's in the Black Sea. What do they say about delivery? You know what they're like.'

'I think we can look forward to something in the next month, Ben. This system is fairly new, it's in production, and we're very good customers. All four of the Grumble Rifs are coming on a freighter direct from the Black Sea and through the Suez Canal. According to this, the freighter will clear Sevastopol in four weeks, pending the arrival of our money.'

'The Russians do not, of course, have the slightest idea why we are buying Grumble-type surface-to-air missiles?'

'No, they do not. We told them we live in constant fear of an air strike against us by the United States. We require the missiles strictly for anti-aircraft defensive purposes to protect our Navy base here in Bandar Abbas. These things could just as easily be used to take out incoming American fighter bombers. The Russians had no reason to question us further. Besides, I think they'll just take the money from anyone these days.' Badr looked at his watch. 'Ben, we have to go. The flight's taking off in a half hour.'

'Since we're the only passengers, I expect they'll wait for us,' said Adnam with a smile. But he stood up, quickly tidied his desk, checked out with security downstairs, and soon joined Admiral Badr on the upstairs landing.

1700, January 20. The home of the ayatollah *in the Kheyabon area of Tehrān.*

One of the disciples opened the side door to the courtyard for the two naval officers. He touched his left hand to his forehead and brought it down in an elegant arc. 'Admiral,' he said, nodding his head with respect. To Ben he added, 'Good afternoon, Mr Dundee,' barely suppressing his overwhelming joy at the keenness of his wit. Commander Adnam smiled, turned to the admiral and said, 'Sir, in the Royal Navy that would be described as an in-joke.'

They walked past the fountain and into the cool stone-floored room in which the *ayatollah* sat, accompanied by the *hojjat-el-islam* and a robed Iranian politician from the Ministry of Defense. Greetings were exchanged with grace and eloquence, as is the custom among the educated classes of Iran. But there was an edge to this gathering, and both Ben and Badr sensed it immediately.

The *ayatollah* was anxious to begin, but he did not rush to address the most pressing aspect of the discussion. Instead he started carefully, summarizing the progress report he had received from the top-secret project down on the south coast. He confirmed that he understood the team had been selected from among the best men in the Navy. The drydock was just about complete, and would be flooded down inside ten days. The new missile system would leave the Black Sea on a freighter within a matter of days. Everything was slightly ahead of schedule, and there had been no serious outside inquiries as to the nature of the operation – the only sign of any outside interest at all had been the two CIA spies who had tried and failed to investigate the building site.

For all of this he congratulated his admiral and his new commander. But then his face took on a look of concern, and he spoke very quietly. 'Commander Adnam,' he said, 'before I approved this project you told me you intended to fit this missile system to a submarine. You even undertook to provide one. As you know, I authorized the expenditure because the dock would always be useful for our new Kilo, and the SAM system will serve as strong air defense for the base. However, before I assign further funding I need to know a great deal more detail about how you intend to proceed from here.

'For instance, to which vessel do you intend to attach this extremely expensive Russian missile system? I think the time has come for us to know that.'

'Sir, it will be engineered onto a submarine, right behind the fin for vertical launching.'

'I see. Is this liable to be a difficult operation? I mean, fixing a surface-to-air missile system onto the deck of a submarine.'

'I don't believe so, sir. It's just that it's never been done before. You see, it's not the same as the big intercontinental ballistic missiles, with their extremely complex systems. We're operating with a much smaller, simpler beast, a wickedly accurate guided missile which travels at two-and-a-half times the speed of sound – but for only about 40 miles.'

'Well, why do you think no one has ever before wanted to fire such a weapon from a submarine?'

'Oh, I think it's been talked about often, but there was never a very strong reason for doing it. They fit better on surface ships. Nonetheless, I've always considered it the most formidable possibility. A missile fired, as it were, from nowhere.'

'Commander, do you envision using our only suitable submarine, the new Kilo from Russia?'

'No, sir. The Americans will be watching that too vigilantly. I'm afraid we'll have to be a great deal more subtle than that.'

'You mean we must acquire another submarine, one which the Americans know nothing about?'

'Yes, sir.'

'Then my colleagues and I believe that now is the time for you to explain precisely how you propose to obtain it. Are you suggesting the British, of all people, will sell us one? Or are you asking us to rent one, an old one from some moribund navy around the Gulf or North Africa? You have never told us, you know. And so far as I can see the entire project depends on the acquisition of the right submarine, and the skill of our engineers.'

'Yes, sir. It does.'

'Well, Commander? Will you tell us your plan at last? Then we can proceed to release the funds to go ahead. It may take a little time – you realize the new Kilo now costs even more: three hundred and fifty million dollars?'

'Sir, had I intended to involve you in high expenditure for a submarine, I would have advised you accordingly many months ago. But I do not intend to incur such expense.'

'Then you are proposing we contact the British and make some attempt to lease one for a year, or something like that?'

'No, sir. I was not planning to do that either. I think that would be impossible.'

At this point Admiral Badr stepped in, sensing the meeting was approaching an uncomfortable level of frustration. 'Ben,' he interjected, 'you've drawn me to the inescapable conclusion that you intend to use the plastic model submarine we have in the shed!'

Adnam shook his head and said gently, 'Not quite. Actually, I intend to steal one.'

CHAPTER THREE

March 23, 2005.
'230200MAR05. 31.00N 13.45W. Course 060. Speed 12.'

Commander Adnam carefully wrote down the date, time, position, course and speed in the manner of a lifelong naval officer. He made the note only in his own diary, for he was a guest on board this ship, *Santa Cecilia*, but the old disciplined habits of the navy – the endless recording, the accuracy of even the smallest detail – never fade from the mind of a senior sailor. And for good measure he added, 'Weather gusty, *Santa Cecilia* rolling forward in a long swell.'

They had been out for 47 days now and had run nonstop for 13,500 miles, all the way from the Arabian Gulf down the coast of East Africa, around the Cape of Good Hope and up the endless coast of West Africa. They were now ploughing north, 200 miles off the shore of Morocco, where the Atlas Mountains sweep down to the ocean south of Marrakesh.

The quarters were not comfortable: just a converted freight hold in this aging Panamanian-registered coaster of 1800 tons. There was not much room for 21 fit men to sleep, but the Iranian Navy had done its best: bunks and hammocks had been rigged, there was plenty of water, the decks were roomy even if they were sweltering hot, and the food was excellent. The rolling motion of the half-empty ship had caused some seasickness among the submariners, and the throb of the big diesel engines filled the hold 24 hours a day. When they'd been crossing the equator it had been simultaneously too noisy below and too hot on deck, but the iron discipline of Ben's men had held. No one had complained.

The second of the two holds was full of fuel, so that the freighter would not need to put ashore. That had been Ben's idea, stated forcefully during a day-long argument when all the other planners had wanted the ship to turn northwest through the Red Sea and steam straight across the Mediterranean, thus cutting the overall distance by almost one half. But the Commander had been immovable. 'One visit by Egyptian Customs at the Canal,' he had said slowly. 'Just one visit. And they find a freighter with a full crew plus 21 other guys below and a hold full of fuel. It's just too unusual. All right, I know we could be tourists, fishermen, a crew going to pick up another ship . . . But in my line of country you learn never to take that kind of a chance. And you certainly do not leave half a dozen Customs officers wondering who the hell you really were. Gentlemen, I'm sorry but we go offshore and make the voyage around the Cape. In private. No Customs. No intrusions.'

And now, on this dark windy night out in the Atlantic, Ben Adnam was leaning on the starboard rail, gazing to the east, watching for lights. In his mind he had been calculating precisely when they would arrive at a selected spot in the middle of the English Channel, and now he jotted it down. He headed back to the ship's radio room, which was currently empty.

Once there he tuned to medium frequency, encrypted, and began transmitting his call-sign, speaking clearly: '*Calling Alpha X-Ray Lima Three. This is November Quebec Two Uniform. Radio check. Over.*'

The radio crackled a bit but otherwise remained silent. Ben transmitted again: '*Calling Alpha X-Ray Lima Three. This is November Quebec Two Uniform. Radio check. Over.*'

Then suddenly, after a delay of only a few seconds, there came a reply: '*Roger. This is Alpha X-Ray Lima Three. Over.*'

Ben spoke again. '*Two-eight-two-two-zero-zero Mike Alpha Romeo zero-five. Four-nine-five-zero November. Zero-four-two-zero Whisky. Over.*' He repeated the message slowly and carefully.

The transmitter crackled again. '*Roger that. Out.*'

It was 0220 now, and the Commander returned to the hold to sleep the rest of the night. The rendezvous was fixed.

241100MAR05.

By any standards she was a beautiful boat, a traditional white cruising yacht which looked as if she might have once belonged to the Great Gatsby or at least to his French equivalent. Moored alongside, in the port of St Malo on the picturesque northern coast of Brittany, the bright teak door to her magnificent wheel-house glinting in a pale wintery sun, the *Hédoniste* was a splendid sight. Eighty feet long, she had two staterooms, an exquisite covered quarterdeck with an outside bar, a canopied helm above the wheelhouse, and luxurious sleeping quarters for ten. Her big twin screws were powered by two diesels. She could cruise through a good sea at 20 knots. Her call-sign was Alpha X-Ray Lima Three.

On board the *Hédoniste* were the three men who had chartered her for the week at a cost of $20,000 – off-season rates. Perfectly dressed in designer yachting kit and carrying expensive leather luggage, they had arrived in St Malo in a chauffeur-driven Mercedes limousine. They had brought with them, in another car, their captain, an engineer and a chef-butler.

The French hire agent had taken a cursory glance at their Turkish passports. All three addresses were either on or close to Paris's Avenue Foch and so the agent had rapturously handed over control of the boat to Arfad Ertegan, whose current French Master's certificate fully entitled him to command the *Hédoniste*. 'You will be very happy, gentlemen,' the agent had said, pocketing the banker's check for $20,000 cash, 15 percent of which was now his. 'See you in a week.'

The six young Iranian naval officers who were posing as three Turkish millionaires and their staff had never known such a wonderful time. This was a very beautiful boat, built in England by Camper & Nicholson; they all appreciated that. And now they were ready to set off on the voyage across the Bay of St Malo to make an overnight stop at St Peter Port in the Channel Island of Guernsey before pressing on to the meeting point. Essentially they were going to have four days off. The only dark cloud on their horizon was that the sixth of their number, Abdul Raviz, the 'chef', was in fact the gunnery and missile officer of Iran's *Hudong*-Class fast-attack craft P313-4, out of Bandar Abbas. He had never actually been in a galley before. Neither had the other five. Though the *Hédoniste* was laden to the gunwales with the finest French delicacies, the combined culinary talent of those aboard would have had serious difficulty producing a piece of buttered toast.

They resolved to make a fast run to St Peter Port and dine in the hotel there. They carried with them a leather pouch full of

French francs. The world, they knew, could be their oyster, if they could just work out how to shuck it.

282120MAR05. 49.50N 4.20W. Course 020. Speed seven.
The *Santa Cecilia* was making a racetrack pattern on this dark cloudy night. The moon was completely hidden, and the westerly wind gusted occasionally over the short sea. Commander Adnam could see no ships anywhere along the horizon. All he could hear were the engines and the hiss of the spray slashing back off the steel bow as the old freighter shouldered her way forward.

He had been on deck for half an hour now, staring out to the southeast, watching for the running lights, listening for the deep throb of the twin diesels of the French-based luxury yacht. Twice he had thought he heard something, but the sound had come from too far east. He knew the bearing for her approach, and he stared through binoculars into the darkness of the English Channel straight down bearing one-three-five. But there was nothing out there, so far. Below, in the sleeping hold, his men were ready, each of them in a black wetsuit and all variously armed, the two hitmen from the Islamic Revolutionary Guards Corps rather better than the rest.

At 2145 he picked up the running lights of the *Hédoniste*, her white hull visible half a mile away. She was bang on time, making good headway through this bumpy sea. Ben ordered the captain to reduce speed to two knots, and huge fenders were hung off the starboard side as the 'Turkish millionaires' maneuvered alongside.

The sea was rough enough to be a nuisance during the transfer, the 80-foot yacht rhythmically rising and falling through six feet. The men from the *Santa Cecilia* used a climbing net and two rope-ladders to cross to the yacht, but even so it was a dangerous maneuver in the dark. Ben noticed how the two commandos from the IRGC waited for their moment and jumped straight onto the *Hédoniste*'s foredeck; the other 19, himself included, took it more steadily. Ten minutes later, Captain Ertegan revved the *Hédoniste*'s starboard engine and reversed the craft away from the Panamanian freighter, which would now head southwest.

Ertegan set a course of zero-two-zero, and the overloaded cruising yacht swung north, making her way toward the great 133-foot-high lighthouse standing guard over the legendary sailors' graveyard of the Eddystone Rocks, 25 miles away. Ben calculated that, if they maintained eight knots, the lighthouse's white warning beacon should be a couple of miles off their port beam by 0045. But they would see its signal – two bright flashes every ten seconds – long before that.

Meanwhile the men were making their own introductions, though most of them had been acquainted before back at Bandar Abbas. Ben Adnam went briefly through the plan with the 'Turkish playboys', and everyone could feel the atmosphere tightening as the team began to run last-minute equipment checks, paying particular attention to their breathing apparatus.

By midnight the Eddystone Lighthouse, less than three miles away off the port bow, was looking close. 'Hold course zero-two-zero,' ordered Ben. 'Make your speed ten knots. Remember, we're just a luxury yacht running in late from the Channel Islands. Keep the decks clear for the moment. We've plenty of water and we're well clear of the rocks.'

By 0100 the towering light, which has warned sailors of the dangers since 1698, was slipping behind them, brightening the black water off their portside quarter. The sharp white flashing light was certainly more efficient than the 60 great tallow candles of the 18th century, but Ben would have been glad of pitch black right now, as the *Hédoniste* drove forward toward the coastline of southwest England. He had chosen a pleasure craft such as this because it was unlikely to attract the attention of the notoriously vigilant British Coastguard, who might certainly stop something like an old foreign freighter making its way to port in the small hours of the morning but would probably leave a leisure yacht alone.

There were still about nine miles to run. The sea was almost deserted along the inner, east-going traffic lane. The men were starting to blacken their faces with special oil and little was being said as they prepared for their mission. No one was in any doubt as to what was expected of them.

At 0155 Ben spotted the line of red lights on the radio masts high up on Rame Head. He estimated they were four miles away, right off the port bow, one of them flashing a warning to aircraft. The light on the western end of the breakwater was dead ahead.

Ben Adnam and his navigation officer, Lt-Commander Arash Rajavi, aged 31, were alone under the canopy of the exposed upper bridge while Captain Ertegan steered from the warm wheelhouse below. Both men were protected from the chill March night by their wetsuits; on their heads they wore dark balaclavas which they would keep on under the tight-fitting black rubber hoods they would need for the mission.

Suddenly Rajavi said in his naturally soft voice, 'Sir, can I ask you a question?'

'Fire away,' replied Ben.

'How do you actually know the submarine is there?'

'I know,' said Ben.

'But how?'

'Well, first I read last August that the Brazilians were negotiating to buy one of the Royal Navy's Upholder-Class submarines, HMS *Unseen*, and they hoped to take delivery in the submarine base in Rio de Janeiro around May 15 this year. I calculated 28 days at nine knots for the 5500-mile journey, so they probably intended to clear Plymouth Sound around April 18.

'I knew there would be a six-week work-up period for the Brazilian crew right out here in the Channel, beginning about March 7. That would mean the submarine would arrive in the Devonport Naval Dockyard for maintenance three weeks before that. On February 1, just before we left, I asked one of our agents in England to check when HMS *Unseen* was scheduled to leave the base at Barrow-in-Furness. That part was easy. They were having a little ceremony to say goodbye to her on February 14. So I knew everything was bang on schedule. She has been sighted since then, working down here.

'So, Arash, you'll find that *Unseen* will be right out there where I say she'll be. Moored on the big Admiralty buoy a quarter of a mile inside the breakwater. That buoy is huge – they say it could hold an aircraft carrier in a full gale. And that's where she'll be, three weeks into her work-up, with about 40 Brazilians on board. I know. I've moored on that buoy in a submarine while I was training here. That's where all the Royal Navy work-up submarines tend to spend their weekday nights if they're not out at sea.'

'Sir, you are a very smart man.'

'Still breathing,' said the Commander absently.

By 0220 the sea was calmer in the lee of Rame Head and Ben ordered an increase in speed to 12 knots. The *Hédoniste* looked like a typical big motor yacht with nothing to hide, charging in from the Channel Islands, running late and anxious to make Oliver's Battery – the big marina northeast of Drake's Island, deep in Plymouth Sound. Innocence, thy name is Benjamin, and to underline it he personally called the marina on Channel M to check the allocated berth and give an ETA.

The sky was brighter now, the streetlights of Plymouth casting a glow in the sky to the north. Through his binoculars Ben could make out the old breakwater which guards the sound – right out in the middle, more than three-quarters of a mile long, a low manmade construction of concrete and rocks with a lighthouse on each end. Ben could see the western of these lights flashing and, as they drew ever closer, he picked up the little intercom, and snapped: 'Stand by!'

No reply was needed.

Soon they were right opposite the light. 'Four hundred yards,' said Ben. 'Lead swimmers prepare to go. Reduce speed to eight knots for the next half-mile.'

He lifted his night-vision binoculars again. Now he could make out the dark hulk of the submarine out on the buoy, a quarter-mile off the starboard beam.

'This is it,' he said. 'Lead swimmers . . . *go.*'

He heard a soft splash as the flippers of the two Islamic Revolutionary Guards hit the dark waters of Plymouth Sound together.

'OK, everyone, let's the rest of us go. Six at a time over the port side. I'll come last. Then we regroup and swim in together 50 yards behind Lieutenant-Commander Ali and his man.'

Ben pulled down his facemask, fixed his breathing gear, and dropped over the side of the *Hédoniste.* He checked with all three group leaders that everyone was safe, then gave the order to swim forward, using flippers just below the surface. The 19-strong Iranian hit squad began to kick slowly through the water toward HMS *Unseen.*

Out in front, Ali Pakravan heard the motor yacht head on up the sound, lights still on full, the noise growing fainter. He kept swimming: kicking and gliding, no splashing, no arm movement, just the legs, as he had been trained. His colleague, Seaman Kamran Azhari, swam just behind him, a rifle with nightsights clipped to his back.

After seven minutes Pakravan came to the surface and tried to see the submarine. It took a few moments for him to focus and then he could indeed see her, about 100 yards ahead. With a few more kicks he would be able to see on the fin the white identification S4, the individual mark of the jet-black 230-foot torpedo- and mine-laying patrol submarine that was now officially a part of the Brazilian Navy.

He and Azhari made their way slowly to the steep, slippery slope of the bow, moving under cover of its curve, and in the water they prepared their special electromagnetic clamps. Azhari placed the first two a foot out of the water, then hauled himself up and softly placed two further clamps three-and-a-half feet higher up *Unseen*'s bow. He unclipped the rifle from his back as Pakravan began to work his way up beside him, moving his four magnetic clamps one at a time to give himself purchase. Azhari gave him the rifle and it took Pakravan two more minutes to reach a point where he could safely lie on the downward curve of the bow. High above him he could see the fin, on top of which, he knew, was the night guard; according to Commander Adnam, he should just see the man's head and shoulders above the rail of the bridge. And he would see them very clearly through the night-vision telescopic sight on the rifle.

Pakravan moved one of the clamps and took up his sniper's position on the casing. Adnam had been right. He could see the sentry up there, but the man was standing sideways, hunched against the light rain that was beginning to fall; he made a very difficult target.

Pakravan, the best marksman in the Iranian Navy, was uncertain whether to wait or fire. After a few moments he decided that time was a luxury he did not have, and lined up the cross-hairs of the rifle sight against the guard's left temple.

He steadied himself, held his breath, and then from a range of 110 feet shot Seaman Carlos Perez dead.

The snub-nosed bullet blew away the entire right-hand side of the Brazilian's head as it made its exit. There was no sound save for the familiar soft pop made by a big rifle fitted with a silencer.

The Iranian lieutenant-commander stood up on the casing to signal to the rest of the swimmers that it was safe to work their way around to the port side of the submarine. Handing the rifle back to Azhari, he moved along the casing and unclipped the rope ladder he had carried with him. He made it secure, then slid it silently down the hull and into the water. Almost immediately he saw the black-hooded figure of Commander Adnam coming through the water, and Pakravan called out softly in the night, 'Here, sir. Right here.'

Ben was still using his breathing gear as he came up the ladder. Right behind him followed two other submariners, both of whom had previously served in the old Iranian Kilos. They moved swiftly to the door at the base of the fin and unclipped it gently. Ben opened it and led the way inside the fin to the top of the conning tower. They were still undetected. He pulled from his pocket a sealed chlorine grenade and, after a few seconds spent preparing it, threw it straight down the tower hatchway. He waited for what seemed an age after a soft fizzing noise indicated that the grenade had gone off, then climbed down after it followed by his two henchmen, all three of them still wearing their full breathing gear.

In the control room at the bottom of the tower they separated, one man heading for'ard and one aft, both rolling more grenades ahead of them. Ben stayed right where he was, acting as communications number to the men above as they gathered silently on the casing under the supervision of Lt-Commander Pakravan.

Of the 38 Brazilians aboard, none survived the first two minutes. Those asleep never awoke. Those awake gasped, choked and quickly died. The massive level of concentrated chlorine was sudden, silent and deadly in the confined space. It took less than ten minutes for the intruders to ensure that no one remained alive.

With the possibility of survivors now extinguished, Ben Adnam himself started the submarine's engines, running them steadily with the ventilation and battery fans working flat out to clear the hull of the poisonous gas. The Iranians tested the atmosphere constantly until almost 0400, when Commander Adnam declared the ship clean and told the cold men out on the casing that they could now come safely below. There was some nervousness among the newcomers, who did not have full breathing gear but instead wore only small chlorine-proof gasmasks. They went about the depressing business of dragging the bodies to the torpedo room, where they would be stored: each one zipped tightly into a waterproof body-bag. They would be disposed of at the first fueling stop out in the cold Atlantic off Gibraltar –

there could of course be no question of dumping them out into Plymouth Sound.

By now Commander Adnam had located the ship's weekly Practice Program and daily signal log. These two items had told him what to expect – even down to the names of the four British training staff. The dreaded Sea Riders were due to come back on board at 0755 that morning. The same team as all the rest of the week. He noted that the Brazilians were a little behind where they should have been at this stage of the proceedings. The previous day the crew had been practicing routine snorkeling drills: starting, running and stopping the diesels while submerged.

'Should have finished that last week,' he murmured as he turned the pages, trying to find out what they were scheduled to do today. 'Good job old MacLean's not training them – he'd have made them walk the plank by now.'

As he had guessed, *Unseen* was due to sail at 0800. This was listed alongside Exercise Area, Stop Time, and Type of Exercise. Today's activities were simply listed as INDEX – Independent Exercises. But there were some scribbled notes in the margin which told him they had been scheduled to practice emergency maneuvers – matters such as the avoidance of oncoming shipping; plane breakdowns, steering failure, failure of the systems governing seawater, electrics, hydraulics, mechanics . . . Break-down Drills. Fire Drills. Flooding Drills. Etcetera, etcetera. But there was also the most blinding bit of luck: the submarine was to stay out overnight practicing some much-needed special drills, in particular night snorkeling.

Ben read the Orders slowly and carefully, then located the previous day's Next-of-Kin signal, the one every submarine captain sends to his shore-based headquarters immediately before departure detailing all changes to the crew-list in the NOK book that was held ashore – the final update, ensuring accurate names and addresses of the next-of-kin of every man aboard just in case the submarine should disappear.

At 0500 he called a short briefing meeting for his officers, leaving the rest of the team to continue to familiarize themselves with their specialist areas of the ship. Of course, everything was more real than it had been in the Bandar Abbas model where they had practiced so intensely for many weeks. But, with very few exceptions, every switch, valve and keyboard was exactly where it had been in the model. The precious data from the big computer in Barrow-in-Furness had taken care of that.

'Gentlemen,' Adnam said. 'I'm sorry for the delay but I've been trying to read myself in on procedures. Our sailing time is, as planned, 0800, three hours from now. I have the Next-of-Kin update, and the Squadron Standing Orders. At about 0755 we are expecting four Royal Navy Sea Riders to arrive from the dockyard to supervise the day's exercises. We will take care of them as planned. Allow them to arrive safely and go below. Lieutenant-Commander Pakravan, well done tonight: you and Seaman Azhari did an outstanding and difficult job. I know I can leave it to you to silence the Sea Riders as soon as they come below.

'The only major change to our plan is that I intend to send *Unseen*'s diving signal to cover tomorrow's program as well as today's, because she is, by fortunate chance, not due back until tomorrow evening. That said, we must of course send in a check report every 12 hours — the ship is still in Safety Work-Up. I intend to comply with all of the external procedures when we depart, and it is vital that we make no errors in these. I also intend to *walk* out of Plymouth Sound with this ship, not run. When we leave here I do not want one shred of suspicion left behind us. That way we have many hours to get free. And, once we're free, they'll never find us.'

Lt-Commander Arash Rajavi listened carefully — as did all the other Iranians — to the intensive two-hour training program they all faced. And he tried to stay calm. But it was hard to cast from his mind the overwhelming magnitude of their crime. Here they were, sitting bang in the middle of the historic harbor of Sir Francis Drake, the very cradle of the Royal Navy, having stolen one of their submarines and killed its crew. Three hours from now Commander Adnam was planning summarily to murder two British officers and probably a couple of petty officers. 'My God!' he thought. 'If we're caught they'll execute every last one of us.'

But he fought back his fear, fought down his natural instinct to escape from here at all costs, and listened to the cool, measured words of his leader. Not for the first time, Lt-Commander Rajavi decided that Benjamin Adnam was without doubt the most cold-blooded man he had ever met.

Two hours later, neatly dressed in Brazilian Navy uniform, four

69

hands, in company with a young officer waited on the casing for the arrival of the Sea Riders. At 0750 they spotted the harbor launch speeding down the well marked channel west of Drake's Island toward HMS *Unseen*; with the Britons visible through the launch's cabin windows. Two more officers and a lookout, again in Brazilian uniform, were on the bridge.

Within five minutes the launch was alongside, and the young officer on the casing saluted, wishing the Royal Navy men 'Good Morning' in an Iranian accent which Adnam hoped would be taken for a Brazilian one.

The launch headed back to the dockyard, and one by one the four Royal Navy men came up on board, making for the open hatch on top of the casing. There was an eight-foot steel ladder inside, and the leader, Chief Petty Officer Tom Sowerby, made his way expertly downward, taking his final steps in this life. As his right foot hit the ground three of the Iranians grabbed him. A hand was clamped tight over his mouth to stop him crying out as Pakravan's knife pierced his heart. Lt-Commander Bill Colley, next on the ladder, never realized what was happening below until it happened to him as well.

Eight minutes later, all four of the Royal Navy men had joined the pile of zipped-up bodies in the torpedo room. It was 0759, and Commander Adnam was preparing to leave British waters.

At 0800 sharp, he ordered that the Brazilian ensign be hoisted on top of the fin. The diesel generators were still running sweetly as they slipped the buoy, and Ben gave the commands 'Half astern' then 'Half-ahead' as he turned HMS *Unseen* away from Plymouth, making coolly for the western end of the breakwater and freedom. No one in all the great sprawling Royal Navy base had the remotest idea that anything was other than normal.

The men accompanying Lt-Commander Rajavi on the bridge were surprised at the sight of Rame Head as they ran fair down the channel, keeping the big red buoys to starboard. The headland looked even higher by day: the steep-sided, solid, treeless rock with its small chapel on top is visible almost 20 miles out at sea. Ben Adnam's engineering officer had the big electric motor running steadily, with the diesels working to provide the power.

Below in the control center, Adnam studied the operations area where *Unseen* was scheduled to work today and headed her for the northeast corner of the 'square', a couple of miles west of

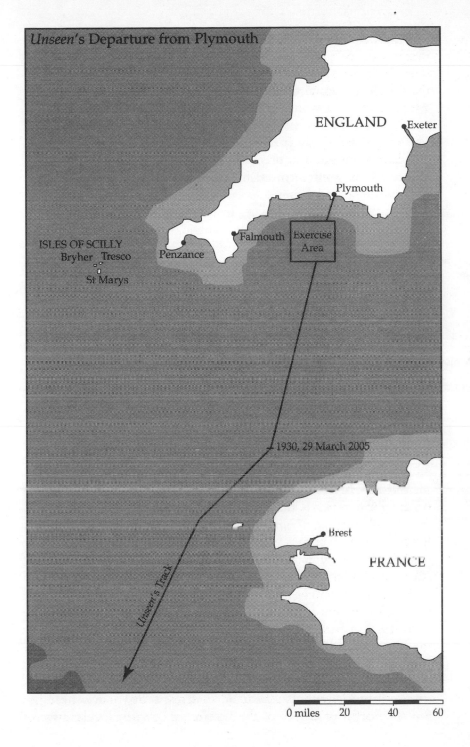

Unseen's Departure from Plymouth

ENGLAND

Exeter

Plymouth

Falmouth

Exercise
Area

ISLES OF SCILLY
Bryher Tresco

Penzance

St Marys

1930, 29 March 2005

Brest

FRANCE

Unseen's Track

0 miles   20   40   60

the Eddystone Lighthouse. There was almost 200 feet of water under the keel now, and, with all signals having been correctly sent to home base, he ordered the submarine dived. The great black hull slid down beneath the cold gray waves, leaving behind a mystery which would rival that of the *Mary Celeste* and which would last for many, many months.

Right now, Commander Adnam was in a perfect situation. The sub was located in precisely the area she was supposed to be; moreover, he wanted to test his team in some underway drills in exactly the same manner the Sea Riders would have been testing the Brazilians. In the following few hours he worked the Iranians through the electrical and mechanical systems, the sonar, the radar, the ESM, the communications, the trimming and ballasting, the hydraulics and air systems, even the domestic water and sewage systems. He checked the periscopes and low-light aids, sometimes running easily at nine knots, occasionally stopping in the water to give his officer of the watch experience at trimming this new and strange submarine. More than half the time was spent snorkeling, making certain the ship's battery was well topped up. Sometimes the commander offered quiet advice to the younger men, sometimes he pushed them harder. But there was never an edge to his voice. He was always conscious that a tired crew may make mistakes, but not so many as a tired and frightened crew.

Three times he took his vessel deep, insisting his men grew accustomed to the diving angles. Twice during the midafternoon, when they were at the southern end of his ops area, he ran her on the surface – which Lt-Commander Rajavi regarded as one of the most reckless decisions he had ever witnessed. What if anyone should see them? At one point late in the afternoon, Rajavi actually ventured to ask if the commander considered it possible there might be a hunt on for them. 'Would you not feel safer, sir, at periscope depth?'

'There's no danger,' replied the commander. 'If there was, I wouldn't be on the surface.'

At 1930, a half-hour early, Adnam sent in his check report to the operating authority, the Captain, Second Submarine Squadron (Captain SM2), in Devonport. He was 90 miles from his diving position; and now he turned the ship toward the southwest, running throughout the night on course two-two-five, heading for the northwestern coast of Brittany, snorkeling constantly to keep the battery well charged. *Unseen* went deep only twice during the small hours, once when they detected a threatening sweep of British military radar, once when a large merchant ship passed close by.

At 0700 the following morning Commander Adnam sent in his second – and last – check report. He was, of course, by now well beyond his ops area, but it was naturally assumed at the other end that the signal was being sent from *Unseen*'s designated place in the ocean. By 1800 this evening, when his diving signal was due to expire, he would be 180 miles away from *Unseen*'s specified area of activity. But by then he would be running deep down the Atlantic, 120 miles west of the big French Naval Base at Brest. Ben Adnam would take no chances here.

301725MAR05. Second Submarine Squadron Operations Center.
Lt-Commander Roger Martin, the Staff Officer, Operations, had just about had it for the day, coping as he did with the frenetic mass of tiny problems that made up this unenviable job. Aside from dealing with the endless stream of orders coming across his desk he had been coordinating all the plans for exercises among the boats in the squadron. Not just the work-up boats: Martin was also handling the exercises for all of the squadron boats based in the vast Devonport dockyard.

He took a deep swig of tea, checked his watch and prepared to hand over for the night to the Duty Staff Officer, Lt-Commander Doug Roper. He checked his list over again, as he always did when there were boats at sea, insuring that every anticipated check report and surfacing signal was recorded on the state board, complete with times when ships were due to make contact.

By now he could see the fair-haired, athletic Roper striding along the corridor toward him, and Martin greeted him cheerfully. 'Hello, Doug. We're more or less in order here – except for *Unseen*. She's not actually late, but her diving signal expires at 1800 and she's been well ahead of time with her other communications for the past couple of days. I was just beginning to wonder . . . Still, Bill Colley was her senior Sea Rider and he mentioned he might give the Brazilians an extra hard time out there. He reckons they're slipping behind with their program. Perhaps he's keeping them at it until the last minute.'

73

'Probably,' responded Roper. 'Still, one always worries when they cut it fine. I'll keep a close eye on the situation.'

'OK, old pal. I'll be off now. Have a good night.'

Doug Roper was a very ambitious officer. Aged only 31, he was not yet married. Money from his family timber business in Kent had enabled him to buy a flash, low-slung white sports car. In a predominantly middle-class operation like the Royal Navy this might have caused some envy, but this particular lieutenant-commander was universally popular and worked extremely hard; he also had a keen and profoundly watchful mind.

Roper studied the sheets he had been handed and checked his watch: 1740. He looked for *Unseen*'s surfacing signal. Nothing. And for no accountable reason alarm bells began to go off in his head. Time was running out. If *Unseen* continued to live up to her name for much longer he was going to become the busiest man in Plymouth.

He realized that Lt-Commander Colley might just have forgotten to send the surfacing signal, but he knew when she was supposed to be on the surface and by now she should actually be so, close to Plymouth. *Maybe, thought Roper, she's had a total communications breakdown, and is right now running through the harbor, trying to contact anyone in sight to pass her signal by light, VHF or word-of-mouth.* But somehow he doubted that.

At 1800 on the dot he hit the phone to the Captain, Second Submarine Squadron, to report the overdue surfacing signal according to standard Submarine Safety Instructions (Allied Tactical Publication ATP 10). Roper knew that already a disaster must be considered a possibility.

The captain instantly put into operation Comcheck, a procedure which effectively meant, 'Hey, *Unseen*, haven't you forgotten something?' but in fact alerted all Royal Navy ships in the area that a communication was urgently required with the sub. The signal from the Second Submarine Squadron was regarded as sufficiently important for a copy to be relayed to the Flag Officer, Submarines, in Northwood, over 200 miles away in West London.

Thirty minutes later nothing had been heard and it had grown to be almost impossible to believe that the submarine had not by now found some way to communicate her safety. By 1835, Captain Charles Moss was in the Staff Office, as was Lt-Commander Roger Martin. The mood was somber. The Royal

Navy had not lost a submarine since the diesel–electric A-Class boat *Affray* had gone down in the Channel in April 1951. Everyone knew it had taken months to find her.

At 1900 they went to the next phase, SUBLOOK, because each of the four officers in the room knew that if *Unseen* was on the surface someone should have reported in. If she was dived and anyone had survived they'd have released the expendable communications buoys or even the main indicator buoys, situated one for'ard, one aft. If anyone had got out, their locator beacons should have been picked up. But not a word had been heard, and the sub was now fully an hour overdue. The worst was feared.

It always is before they issue SUBLOOK, because this is a very big word in the Royal Navy. It comes in capital letters, to indicate that it is a serious message which will alert other nations, not to mention Rescue Coordination Centers all around the English Channel. It also alerts the Royal Navy Casualty Organization and the Public Relations network. 'We are very much afraid we have lost a submarine. NO SHIT.'

The word whipped around the base that *Unseen* was missing. Four available guided-missile frigates moored alongside in Devonport were ordered out to the exercise area. Royal Navy warships were signaled to stop whatever it was they were doing and start looking and listening. The senior officer out there, Captain Mike Fuller of the 4000-ton Type-42 destroyer *Exeter*, was ordered to coordinate a methodical search of the area. Two maritime patrol aircraft, big Royal Navy Nimrods, were diverted to search the waters south of Plymouth Sound under Captain Fuller's control.

By now the weather was deteriorating. With the fading light of this early spring evening, the breeze was backing southwest, and a gale-force wind was gusting off the Atlantic and straight up the English Channel. The sea was rougher than it had been for a week and Fuller, on the bridge of *Exeter*, was extremely concerned: if sea conditions worsened much more the search would become impossible.

Back in the Staff Office, Lt-Commander Doug Roper, as Duty Officer, was dealing with the minute-by-minute reports that were coming in. He could see the looks of real concern on the faces of Roger Martin and Charles Moss, and could hear the captain saying, 'Time is of the absolute essence. The quicker we find *Unseen* the better our chances of getting any survivors off her.'

All four men knew that a major accident now seemed certain, but hoped that Bill Colley and his men might still be alive on board on the bottom somewhere, their air supply strictly limited and possibly with some men injured, waiting to effect their escape when the searchers finally arrived. All submariners realize there's no point just getting out and floating up into a raging, empty sea where death is virtually inevitable. The trick is to stay aboard as long as possible and then, hopefully, float up into the arms of your rescuers, who will haul you out, administer first aid and get you to the ship's hospital, where they can at least treat hypothermia and possibly also the bends and CO_2 poisoning.

By 2130 two of the frigates were working with active sonars to check out known wrecks and bottom-contacts to see if a new one had appeared. Captain Moss had ordered two minehunters into the area because their sonars are particularly well suited for wreck-searches. In the next 20 minutes the minehunters would begin scanning the bottom of the English Channel, trying to sift out a new wreck from the thousands of others which had been there since at least World War II. In Captain Fuller's destroyer, and in the four frigates, the navigation officers pored over charts which detailed almost all of the wrecks on the floor of the Channel. Commander Rob Willmot, in the 4200-ton Duke-Class Type-23 *Portland*, thought they had something out on the western edge of the 'square.' It was not marked as a known wreck, and but for the sea conditions he would have been ready to send down a pair of divers and a television camera to have a closer look.

However, despite an evening full of false hopes and false alarms, no one had anything firm. At midnight Captain Moss issued the fateful SUBMISS Signal, six hours after *Unseen*'s diving signal had expired. There was now in place a full-scale internationally coordinated search which would continue until the submarine was found. In the hard-edged mind of the Royal Navy, submarines do not just disappear – they may go missing, because they have sunk or blown up or even *been* blown up, but the submarine or its wreckage must be *somewhere*.

The critical issue was, had *Unseen* left her area of operations? Why on earth would she do that? Bad navigation? Incorrect tidal calculations? Sheer carelessness? None of these was very likely. But the specter of the *Affray* still haunted the Royal Navy submarine operators, because that 1800-tonner, out of Portsmouth on a training exercise and full of men just in from the surface navy, was finally found on the bottom a long way outside her allocated area – right down by the Hurd Deep, off the Channel Island of Alderney, weeks after any hope of survivors had disappeared.

Shortly after midnight the next-of-kin of the four British Sea Riders were informed. A communication was drafted to the Brazilian Navy Headquarters in Rio de Janeiro detailing the Brazilians on board. The press were informed very quickly, because that way they could be controlled a little more; the alternative was that they picked something up on the naval networks and started off by asking, 'Are You Trying To Keep This A Secret?' Even so, everyone knew the journalists would do their worst, dragging up old stories about every Royal Navy submarine that had ever been lost, starting with *Affray* and then going back a year to January 1950, when *Truculent* collided with a merchant ship and sunk in the Thames Estuary, then further back, to June 1, 1939, when *Thetis* went down off Birkenhead. It had all happened over half a century ago, but still it would be sufficient for the media to conclude that submarines were not much better than iron coffins. At least that's how the news would be presented by the time the headline writers had gone to work: 'SHOULD OUR BRAVEST YOUNG MEN BE SUBJECTED TO THIS CARELESSNESS?'

At 1945 EDT the information reached the office of the Director of National Security in Fort Meade, Maryland, and Admiral George Morris became very thoughtful. He read the brief details over again and looked at a chart on one of the computer screens, tapping a button which alternately drew it in closer and took in a much larger area. 'Out of Plymouth, eh? Long time since the Brits lost a submarine. Wonder what happened?'

Ten minutes later he had reached Admiral Morgan, still in his office at the White House and interested, as ever, in *anything* to do with submarines. 'How long's she been missing, George?'

'Seven or eight hours since her surfacing signal was due.'

'I don't mean *that*. How long since they heard from her?'

'They got a check report in at 0700 their time. 'Bout 12 hours before her diving signal expired.'

'Hmm. Where was she?'

'Twenty miles off Plymouth Sound.'

'They gotta lot of ships out there searching?'

'Guess so. They've had sonars working the bottom of the ocean for several hours, but no one's found anything.'

'Ocean?' replied the old blue-water submariner. 'That's not a goddamned ocean – it's some kind of a fucking mudflat. The English Channel's only about 20 feet deep. I bet the fucking periscope's sticking out of the water! Incompetent Brits . . . couldn't find an elephant in a chicken coop.'

George Morris laughed politely. 'Anyway, they've found literally nothing. No buoys, no signals, no wreckage, no oil slick, no survivors. Damn' thing just vanished off the face of the ocean. Sorry, Arnold – off the face of the mudflat.'

Admiral Morgan chuckled. 'They asked us for help yet?'

'No. At least no one's told me. But SUBLANT will know.'

'OK, George. Keep me posted on it, will you? And, if the Brits do get in touch, would you have their Flag Officer give me a call. He's an old friend, just got promoted – Admiral Sir Richard Birley. 'Course, when I knew him he was just plain Commander Dick Birley, trying to drive a Polaris boat. We shared a few laughs in London . . . too long ago. See ya, George.'

Arnold Morgan was now late. It was after eight o'clock, which was the time he was due at a small French restaurant in Georgetown for an assignment to which he urgently looked forward. It was only dinner with his secretary, which might seem almost mundane for a 60-year-old, twice-divorced Admiral. Except that this secretary, the 36-year-old divorcee Kathy O'Brien, was possibly the best-looking woman in the entire White House. A long-legged redhead from Chevy Chase, she had worked for the tyrannical Texan since first he had entered the building and almost fired his new chauffeur on day one.

For a month she had gazed with awe at his command of the workings of the world's navies, his knowledge of international events and of the intentions of various countries, his total distrust of foreigners. For another six months she had watched him ride roughshod over men in the highest offices, contemptuous of stupidity, withering in his judgments, and cynical in his appraisal of diplomats, especially foreign ones.

The President himself, a right-wing Republican from Oklahoma, trusted Arnold Morgan implicitly – he actually *loved* Arnold Morgan. So, fortuitously, did the beautiful Mrs Kathy O'Brien. And the friendship had grown, albeit hesitantly at first.

For it was beyond the comprehension of Arnold Morgan, who had no illusions about his craggy lack of good looks, how any woman could be attracted to him, far less this goddess who worked as his secretary.

His failed marriages and the endless criticisms of his wives, both of whom had summarily left him, had created a man who believed that all women were a mystery and that, whatever it was they wanted or liked, it most definitely was not him. As such, he chose to 'get along without 'em.' It had been so long since any woman had shown the slightest interest in him that he almost died when Kathy O'Brien said one day: 'You, sir, eat too many of those damned roast-beef sandwiches and you drink too much coffee. Why don't you come out to my house tomorrow night and I'll cook you a decent dinner?'

He was so utterly flabbergasted, he had just answered lamely: 'OK. What are you going to cook for me?'

The slender Kathy, sassy to the last, had called back 'Roast beef' as she swung out the door.

That had been a year ago, and since then the admiral had discovered that this lady – who had her own money and did not particularly need the job – offered him what he had never been given by either wife. She offered him total respect for what he did. In her heart Kathy O'Brien worshiped him – although she was not anxious for that aspect of their relationship to become known. Unlike the wives, she had seen him operate at first hand – talking to the President as an equal, or laying down the law to people of incredible status on the international stage. She had seen high officers of the CIA tremble before his wrath. She had seen top brass from the Pentagon arriving at the White House just to hear his opinion. She had fielded calls for him from the heart of the Kremlin. Even from Beijing.

As far as she was concerned, this powerfully built 5ft 8in military dynamo was the most important man in Washington. He was important not for his family background and not just for his job, nor even for the fact that he had been one of the US Navy's best nuclear-submarine captains. No, in Kathy's mind, Admiral Arnold Morgan was important for his towering intellect and his equally towering personality. He was the biggest medium-sized man she had ever seen.

So naturally she never minded if he was late: *Christ, he's probably saving the world.* She never scolded him when he forgot a gift, or failed to thank her, or was suddenly unable to accompany her to her mother's house in northern Maryland. Because she knew him. If Arnold could cram those little matters into his crowded life for her, he would do so. If not, he was probably in the Oval Office or the Pentagon, or visiting Admiral Morris at Fort Meade. He could be anywhere. How many girlfriends could say that? Not many. And, above all, he was most definitely not a womanizer. As his secretary, Kathy *really* knew that.

And now, as she waited at Le Champignon, nursing a kir royale, she smiled at how she knew he would look when he came in the door: flustered, irritated, preoccupied, worried he had forgotten something, a look like thunder on his face, frightening the maître d' to death, telling him to get someone out there to park his car . . . until he saw her. And then the pent-up fury of Admiral Morgan would evaporate as she watched; his face would light up and he would lean over and tell her that he loved her above all else. She almost wept with joy at the very thought of him.

He finally arrived at twenty-five past eight, having fought his way up Pennsylvania Avenue in the pouring rain, cut across M Street and into Georgetown along 29th Street. As she had expected he told Marc, the maître d', to 'Get someone to get rid of my car, will you?' But he was too late. Like Kathy, Marc was honored to be in the great man's presence and had had someone out there waiting under the awning ever since Kathy was seated. Morgan always just jumped out on arrival, right outside the door, leaving the car running, with no thought for the two slightly confused secret-servicemen who followed him everywhere in another vehicle. One of them would drive them both home to Mrs O'Brien's house later.

Arnold greeted her with enthusiasm, it having been all of three hours since they had seen each other. He ordered the same drink as Kathy. One of the curious dichotomies in his character was that, for a man who professed to distrust all foreigners, he had developed the most cosmopolitan taste in food, thanks in part to Kathy, who had lived in Paris with her former husband for almost three years during the 1990s.

Tonight they chose pâté de foie gras, followed by sole meunière for her and coq au vin for him. He selected a bottle of 1995 Puligny Montrachet to share as they ate the first course; Kathy could finish it with her fish while he drank the half-bottle of 1996 Château Talbot he ordered to go with his chicken. It was an expensive dinner; they tried to have one like it twice a week.

Admiral Morgan was financially better off than he had ever been: his job as National Security Advisor to the President carried a salary of almost $200,000, and under a new law he was also entitled to collect half his admiral's pension while he still served in the White House. The President himself had pushed that law through because he believed it was absurd that top military people were being lost to the government simply because their pensions were suspended while they worked as senior public servants. 'The pensions have been earned, over years and years of service,' he had said. 'I expect these outstanding men to be paid entirely separately should they choose to enter another important job in government when their days in the armed services are over.'

All of this had been outstandingly good news for Arnold Morgan, because his two former wives had both remarried, his children were grown and earning, and anyway his daughter, like his ex-wives, was not actually speaking to him right at this moment. His obligations were minimal.

This evening Kathy was noticing that her admiral was not actually speaking to *her* much at the moment, either. He was very within himself as he munched contentedly.

'Is there anything the matter?' she asked.

He looked up suddenly. 'No, no . . . I'm sorry. I was just thinking about something . . . kinda bothering me.'

'What kind of thing? Not me, I hope.'

'No, no. You don't look anything like an Upholder-Class submarine. Entirely the wrong shape. And you're faster.' He grinned his lopsided grin.

'What submarine?'

'Oh, it's just been announced the Brits have lost a submarine in the English Channel. It's on all the news channels and it'll be in every newspaper tomorrow. It's the first time they've lost one for over 50 years. There's a real fuss going on over there. Right now, as we sit here, half the Royal Navy is trying to find it, but they've found nary a sign.'

'Oh, how horrible. Do you think it's on the bottom somewhere, and the crew're all still alive? How long have they got before the air runs out?'

'Not long – 48 hours at most. And the guys in Plymouth last heard from them about 20 hours ago. They're gonna have to move very quickly to have any hope of saving them.'

'Look, darling, I know how awful it is and everything. But why is it giving you such concern?'

'To tell you truth, I'm not sure. There's just something in the back of my mind that's bothering me. I think it's because there's been no sign of any wreckage – no oil, no buoys, nothing. Which means it went down intact. Now there coulda been a complete electrical failure, I suppose, but the Brits are damned good at this sort of thing and modern sonars are damned good at sweeping the ocean floor. Chances are she's still got some power, but no one's heard anything. Her area of operations wasn't that big and they've got God knows how many ships in there. It all suggests to me that the submarine ain't in its ops area. For some reason it went outside the "square." '

'Is that so bad?'

'Only because it's missing. But, if it did go outside the "square," there are five clear reasons it might have done so.'

'Tell me.'

'One, they got confused, made a mistake. Two, they got careless, weren't paying attention. Three, there was a catastrophic mechanical failure. Four, the submarine was hijacked by persons unknown who forced the crew to drive it somewhere. Five, the submarine was stolen, and the crew are all dead.'

'Jesus. Are you serious?'

'Kathy, let me tell you something. When we lost the *Thomas Jefferson* nearly three years ago the whole darned thing started with a missing submarine. And a navy that simply did not know where it had gone.'

'I notice you always get very jumpy when there's any kind of a problem with a submarine.'

'That's because I know what a menace they are in the wrong hands. And I'm not going to be all that relaxed until I know those guys in Plymouth have found it, either in good shape or wrecked. I just hate *not knowing*.'

'You haven't spoken to anyone over there?'

'No. Not yet. But I was thinking about having a chat to FOSM tomorrow. He's an old friend.'

' "FOSM?" '

'Sorry. Flag Officer Submarines. Dick Birley. He and I were in London together for a few months. Haven't spoken to him for a while. But he always sends me a Christmas card.'

'Do you send him one?'

'Well, I don't really do Christmas cards.'

'Perhaps we should think about rectifying that this year.'

The admiral smiled. 'Yes,' he said. 'I think we should. Perhaps it's nearly time we shared one.'

'Then you'd have to find yourself a new secretary – and I'd be the one waiting at home like all your other wives while you ran half the world. No thanks, Arnold Morgan. I'll marry you when you retire. Not one day earlier.'

'Jesus Christ. It's like trying to negotiate with the Russian Navy. I'm not *ready* to retire.'

'And I'm not ready to stay home waiting. Besides, I like to keep a careful eye on you. And I couldn't do that if I were Mrs Arnold Morgan. I think things are just fine the way they are.'

'I guess I love you, Kathy O'Brien. Don't ever go away.'

'No chance of that. We going home, or have you got to go back to the factory?'

'We're going home.'

310500MAR05. 47.02N 08.49W. Course 225. Speed nine.
HMS *Unseen* ran steadily southwest, almost 300 miles from Plymouth, 250 miles from the massive air–sea search being conducted by four nations on her behalf. The submarine had snorkeled for much of the night, so her battery was well topped-up as she made her way across the western reaches of the Bay of Biscay toward her first refueling point – out in the Atlantic, 500 miles off the Strait of Gibraltar.

Right there, two days from now, she would locate the *Santa Cecilia*, and the crew could hardly wait for that moment – not because they were worried about any shortage of fuel but because the 42 bodies piled in the torpedo room, zipped up in their bags, were decomposing. Lt-Commander Pakravan was in favor of firing them straight out through the tubes with the garbage, but that was principally because he had not given the matter much serious thought. When he mentioned the subject to Commander Adnam he quickly realized just *how* little.

'No, Ali. Wouldn't work. Every time you use a torpedo tube

to get rid of loose stuff – like an ill-fitting body-bag – something always gets caught up. Then you have to send someone into the tubes to free it all up. It's more damned trouble than it's worth.

'I worked out our plan of action long before we left Bandar Abbas – I anticipated we'd have to dispose of at least 40 bodies, because that's how many Brazilians I knew there would be. The problem is this: they need to be weighted down. Decomposing bodies blow up with gases and float to the surface. Someone would surely find one of them. So I decided we'd have to be very thorough.'

'You mean we have to get them up onto the casing?'

'We do.'

'But they're heavy as hell.'

'Yes, I know. We'll rig up the small stores davit, with a block and tackle right above the hatch. The blocks need to be eight feet above it, so that each body can swing out onto the deck. There'll also be a big canvas bag, the one they use to catch seawater coming down the tower in rough weather on the surface – looks like a huge spinnaker bag from a sailboat, but it'll do fine for us. All we need to do is get all the bodies into it, then haul away.'

'Sir, what about the weights? We don't have anything like that.'

'I never thought we would, which is why the freighter is bringing us a little gift, like 50 cubes of specially cast concrete, each one weighing 80lbs, with a steel ring and long plastic belts to attach them. They were aboard when we first left Bandar Abbas.'

'I didn't see them.'

'They don't take up much room, just a space eight feet by five feet by five. We stored them aft on the middle deck. No problem.'

'Why do you want to tie them on? Why not just unzip the bags and shove a cube inside each one?'

'Have you ever smelled a five-day-old body, Ali? I wouldn't wish that on any of you. Specially times forty plus.'

'No, sir.'

Adnam took her deep at 0600, just as the sky began to brighten over the Bay of Biscay. They would run all day 250ft below the surface and then come to periscope-depth to snorkel again through the night. The same would apply during the following

84

24 hours. Ben expected to make his rendezvous with the *Santa Cecilia* in the small hours of the next day, April 2.

011200APR05. Submarine Staff Office, Royal Navy Dockyard, Devonport.

Lt-Commanders Roger Martin and Doug Roper were absolutely baffled. Not a sight, not a sound, not a fragmented sonar bleep. No wreckage, no buoys, no signals. Nothing. HMS *Unseen* had simply vanished. Whatever air had remained in the lost diesel–electric boat must have long since run out, and there was now no possibility of survivors.

The situation was officially SUBSUNK. The chilling Royal Navy signal, reserved for use only when a submarine is known to have gone down, had been put on the nets the previous day at 0900. The urgency had gone out of the search because there was no longer any need for life-or-death haste to get surviving crew off the bottom of the sea.

Right now everything was going strictly by the book. But HMS *Unseen* still had to be found, and so the area of search was being extensively widened, it being clear that the submarine had gone beyond its quite small exercise area. Three Royal Navy frigates and Captain Mike Fuller's *Exeter* were methodically sweeping the bottom with sonars, as were the two minehunters. Eight times they had sent divers down with TV cameras, but there had never been so much as a hopeful sign.

Meanwhile the press were laying it on the Royal Navy. 'Experts' were demanding to know how such a thing could have happened. There were already distant allegations about bad training and poor discipline. 'What on earth was the Navy thinking of, allowing a bunch of Brazilian rookies to drive this boat underwater . . . *when it was known they were behind schedule in their training, and presumably competence*? Is it not a fact that Lt-Commander Bill Colley was unhappy with their progress? Was this not an accident waiting to happen?'

Every day now the Navy was being bombarded with these simplistic questions about what was a wildly complicated problem. The Public Relations Department was on duty 24 hours a day. And Captain Charles Moss knew that his days in the Royal Navy were probably numbered: someone was going to be blamed for this, and there was no one else available. He could imagine

what the admirals would say: 'Captain Moss should have initiated
SUBMISS earlier, when it was perfectly clear there was no communication of any kind from *Unseen*. And the question of the
Brazilians' competence must come into the matter. Did he or did
he not know that Lt-Commander Colley was concerned? If not,
why not?' Captain Moss, aged 47, was already considering his
future career opportunities out of uniform.

020230APR05. 35.22N 14.46W. Course 180. Speed nine, 240
miles due west of the Rock of Gibraltar.
HMS *Unseen* continued south through the darkness, snorkeling.
Commander Adnam took a sweeping all-around look for the
lights of the *Santa Cecilia*. They still had ample fuel, but Adnam
was as anxious as anyone to get rid of the bodies in the torpedo
room.

At 0240 they spotted the freighter's navigation lights out on
the southern horizon as she completed her journey from the
North African port where she had refilled her massive converted
diesel-fuel tanks in case *Unseen* was getting low. A half-hour later
Ben ordered the two ships together on the surface of a calm,
moonlit sea. He explained to *Santa Cecilia*'s officers that he did
not require fuel at this point but would like to make a new
rendezvous, 18 days hence, down in the Doldrums, the hot
windless seas around the equator. For now *Unseen* just needed
food and water – and the concrete weights to be lifted over. Ben
had no intention of telling anyone on the freighter what he
wanted those weights for, and no one asked. There was something
about Benjamin Adnam. He was not a man for idle chatter. If he
wanted you to know something he would tell you.

He stood up on the casing watching as the hydraulic lifting
arm of the *Santa Cecilia* hoisted and lowered the concrete cubes
in a heavy-duty tarpaulin, ten at a time. His crew stacked them
neatly on the unlit deck, and within a half-hour the freighter
captain waved them goodbye and turned back to the south.

At this point Ben's crew went to work. The davit was unbolted
from its stowage in the casing and slotted into its sleeve in the
deck, the block and tackle rigged ready. Down below the crew
were dragging the sealed bodies from the torpedo room to the
point where the big hoist bag rested on the lower deck. Six men
worked on the relocation and positioning of each bagged body

inside the bigger bag. Two more hauled it up and out of the hatch. Then three men lashed a concrete weight to the body with a few turns of the plastic belt and heaved it into the water. The first four out of the torpedo room and to take the 10,000ft drop to the floor of the Atlantic were Lt-Commander Colley and his men, the last ones to die.

The average time per body worked out at six minutes, so that the entire exercise took a little over four hours. It was a long and tiring task, but worth it: the bodies would never be seen again. There was a thin, self-satisfied smile on the face of Commander Adnam as he turned south and took *Unseen* deep once more, just as the sun began to lift up above the eastern horizon.

031100APR05. Office of the National Security Advisor, the White House.
'Hi, George. Anything happened?'

'Nothing in Plymouth. But we just got a new set of pictures from Bandar Abbas. I can reveal that that damned great building is definitely not a football stadium. They just flooded it up. It's a drydock for sure. Here, take a look – right here. See where they moved that beach in front? The water just flows straight in now.'

'So it does. And we can't see in from either of the Big Birds, can we?'

'No, sir. The angle's not good and the Iranians keep the door shut – no way we can photograph inside. Also, sir, we don't know much about the other building, the one constructed hard against it. I suppose it might be just a big storage area, but there must be something in it. Beats me.'

'Hmm. Guess so. What are they saying in Plymouth?'

'Not much. There's a few reports, just detailing what the submarine's program was for the day. Funny, they were scheduled to work on emergency maneuvers – you know, system failures, mechanical, electrical, hydro, fire drills, flooding drills. Also, they were out for 36 hours, practicing night snorkeling.'

'I'll tell you something, George. She'd have been a hell of a submarine to steal, if the guy doing the stealing was familiar with the Brits' work-up routine, knew how to read the signals off the Squadron Orders.'

'How do you mean?'

'Well, if he sent in his signals on time at 12 hours, and then

24, then missed when his diving time expired, Christ – he'da been about 300 miles away before he was missed. In another 24 hours, while the Brits were groping around his ops area, he'da been maybe 200 miles further on.'

'Sir, are you sure you're not letting your imagination run riot?'

'No, George, I'm not sure. But what I just said is *possible*. Sherlock Holmes would not have dismissed it. Neither should we, however remote it might be.'

'Arnold, they did have the signals in.'

'I know. But signals don't tell you where they began. Either by radio or satellite, he coulda sent in a signal to the operating authority from wherever he wanted and the Brits wouldn't have had the first idea whether it came from Plymouth Sound or Plymouth Rock. Signals are signals. No one would bother to check, because they all thought they knew where the goddamned submarine was – in its ops area, right?'

'Right.'

'Wrong. I do not believe the sonofabitch was in its ops area, because the goddamned British have been combing that for five fucking days with half the Home Fleet and they've found nothing. The chances are it's not there. So where the fuck is it?'

'I'm not sure, sir.'

'I know you're not fucking sure, George. Now let me ask you this. If you had to stake ten grand of your hard-earned personal money on a bet, would you bet, Yes, it's in its ops area, but the stupid Brits can't find the bastard? Or would you bet, No, it's not in its ops area, it's somewhere else, either by accident or design?'

Admiral George Morris thought carefully and then he replied, 'My ten grand says it's somewhere else, beyond the ops area.'

'Exactly. So does mine.'

CHAPTER FOUR

April, 2005.

COMMANDER ADNAM DROVE *Unseen* down the coast of North Africa, running southwest for 1600 miles past the long hot coastline of Mauritania, where the shifting sands of the Sahara Desert finally slope to the shores of the Atlantic Ocean. Right there, just north of the Cape Verde Islands on 17.10°N, 22.40°W, he changed course to the south, still running at nine knots at periscope depth, all the way down to the Sierra Leone Basin.

He made his final course change there before the refueling stop, and now he headed southeast for another 800 miles. *Unseen* crossed the equator at 1500 on April 20, moving silently through the lonely blue waters of the Guinea Basin toward the rendezvous point at 04.00°S 10.00°W. There was 17,000 feet of ocean beneath the keel.

The *Santa Cecilia* showed up right on time, at 0300 on the morning of April 22. They were 3600 miles and 18 days from their last meeting point, west of Gibraltar, and the submarine was low on diesel.

It was a stifling hot night; and there was no wind whatsoever. No waves either, but the swells were deep, and the great, flat, moonlit waters of the Doldrums rose and fell between the north-flowing Benguela Current, surging up the coast of Africa, and the south-flowing Guinea Current.

The fuel transfer was not easy and took four hours. The good-byes were brief. Before the two ships turned south once more, they arranged to meet again in 32 days' time east of the island of Madagascar.

May 10, 2005.

Admiral Arnold Morgan was going to break the habit of a lifetime tomorrow: he was going on vacation. And, as a further split with tradition, he was taking his secretary with him. In the White House secretaries normally remain in the office to cover for their vacationing bosses, but this time the violation of standard practice caused no consternation. Everyone knew about Admiral Morgan and Kathy O'Brien – had known for the past six months, ever since the National Security Advisor had decided to keep their relationship a secret no longer. He had even touched base with the President, informing him of the liaison on the basis that the Chief Executive ought rightly to be the first to know who the third Mrs Arnold Morgan might be.

The President was delighted for them both, but accepted that Kathy would, for reasons of propriety and professionalism, have to leave the White House once they were married. He also made one strict condition: he was to be invited to the wedding.

Since then every young stud on the presidential staff had refrained from asking Mrs O'Brien out for dinner – which was just as well since she always said 'No' anyway. But the subject of her discreet romance became unaccountably off-limits. No one ever mentioned it, and certainly no one risked a joke about it – possibly because there was the unseen threat that anyone who really pissed off the severe and autocratic ex-nuclear submariner might find himself on the wrong side of 100 lashes. Admiral Morgan had a way of exuding authority.

Two weeks ago, he'd talked to the President about the vacation, telling him he'd like to take Kathy to the Western Isles of Scotland. Since he'd be there anyway, there were a couple of people he wanted to talk a little business with in Britain. He'd be happy to confide in the President about his reasons, but would prefer to leave that until after he returned.

'Arnold,' said the great man, 'however you want to play it is almost certainly the right way. However, and for security considerations I'd prefer you to travel in a US military aircraft, and for personal considerations I hope you can make it back in time for my birthday on May 24.'

'No trouble, sir. I'll be gone ten days max., leaving on the 11th. But I might have a little interesting stuff when I get back.'

'OK, Admiral. Stay cool. We'll talk soon.'

And now Morgan was ready to leave, and two White House secretaries had been detailed to stand guard over Kathy's executive domain while she was gone. The admiral and his distant brideto-be would fly in a USAF modified KC135 jet, the military equivalent of a DC10, manufactured by McDonnell Douglas and fitted with a secure, ultramodern communications system in case the President should wish to speak to his security advisor in-flight.

They took off from Andrews Air Base at 0700 sharp on May 11, and came in to land at the Royal Air Force's Lyneham base in Wiltshire at 1800 local time. A US Navy staff car met them and drove them 50 fast miles to a beautiful private hotel–restaurant, the Beetle and Wedge, on the banks of the River Thames at Mouls-ford, Oxfordshire. The car which followed them contained two secret-servicemen plus the high-security communications system which could patch the admiral directly to the Oval Office should it be necessary. The hotel owner had previously worked at 10 Downing Street and understood the intricacies of such matters – though her ex-boss, the pedantically polite and careful Prime Minister Edward Heath, might have found little in common with the irascible right-wing American NSA.

Arnold Morgan and Kathy O'Brien checked into separate but adjoining rooms – 'Just in case those assholes from the London tabloids have planted some ugly little bastard with a camera up the goddamned chimney.' Later they dined by the river, looking out at one of the most perfect stretches of water on the Thames. They ate fresh grilled fish which the landlord prepared for them personally, and they sipped glasses of golden Montrachet Chevalier 1995. The admiral's long-suffering secretary had rarely, if ever, felt so happy.

'Why won't you tell me where you're going tomorrow morning?' she asked just before they retired for the night.

'Because tomorrow my private thoughts and fears suddenly become business. And that's classified, even from you.'

By eight o'clock the following morning Morgan was gone, being driven through the little towns of Wallingford and Thame to the Oxford–London motorway, the M40. His chauffeur sped him in the direction of Northwood, home of the Flag Officer of the Royal Navy's Submarines (FOSM). A young submarine officer met them at the main gate and hopped into the car for the short downhill drive to FOSM's lair. Morgan was escorted immediately into the inner sanctum, where he was greeted per-sonally by Rear-Admiral Sir Richard Birley, a lean, slightly built man with smooth-combed fair hair who walked athletically and whose frequent smile had caused deep wrinkles at the sides of his eyes. He had not smiled much lately, however.

'Arnold! How terrific to see you! It's been too long – actually, it's been ten years. Come and sit down.'

'Hey, Dick, good to see you, old buddy. How're Hillary and the girls?'

'Well, the girls are both at university now, but basically everything's fine. Bit quieter without them.'

'Guess so. I forgot to tell you before but I'm thinking of getting married again myself, 'cept she says she won't do it 'til I retire.'

'Christ, that probably won't happen for about 30 years since you're (a) indestructible and (b) wedded to the security of that country of yours.'

'Heh, heh, heh. I'll talk her into it.'

'Bully her into it!'

'Heh, heh, heh.'

'Want some coffee?'

'Good call, Dick. Black with buckshot.'

'Black with what?'

'Buckshot. That's what I call those little white bastards that make it sweet. I always forget the proper name.'

'Oh, I see. Well, I'll pour it while you tell me what you want to talk about. I'm assuming this isn't purely social.'

'No, it's not. I came to see you because I wanted to have a chat about HMS *Unseen*.'

'Uh-huh. I've been doing quite a lot of chatting about that particular submarine just lately. Not more than maybe 700 times a day, though.'

The British admiral poured the coffee, invited his lieutenant to locate 'buckshot' – which caused huge merriment among the US secret-service detail sitting in the outer office. They were very used to seeing people scurrying around looking for Hermesetas for the Big Man.

'Dick,' Morgan began, 'we're old friends. I want you to answer me straight. Was there a real problem with the Brazilians? Were they really as incompetent as the newspapers are suggesting? I mean, the general impression we're getting is that your department somehow allowed a bunch of lunatics to go out and kill themselves in a Royal Navy submarine.'

'Arnold, how confidential is this conversation?'

'Totally. I just want to get filled in privately. Nothing will go beyond these four walls. Not even to the beautiful lady who won't marry me yet.'

Admiral Birley chuckled. 'Arnold, the Brazilians weren't wonderful, but they weren't that bad, either. They were a little behind in their training, but only about a week, and I had four Sea Trainers on board, men who we think are the best in the world.

'The Upholder-Class boats are very good. We spent a year ironing out all the initial difficulties before we were forced to put them out of service and into reserve. HMS *Unseen* was completely sound mechanically. As a matter of fact she was in excellent shape, and with four of our best trainers on board it's very hard for me to accept the Brazilians did something so absurd that it sank the bloody boat.'

'But what about all this newspaper stuff?'

'Christ, you of all people know what they're like. Give them just a sniff of the possibility of incompetence and they move in like vultures, regardless of the damage they might be doing, regardless of who might get irretrievably hurt. Regardless of whether they're right.'

'I suppose that's the difference, Dick, between proper executives and media executives. The proper ones have to be right or they're likely to suffer horrendous consequences. The media guys can more or less get away with anything.'

'That's how it feels from here at the moment. We've been hunting that sub for six weeks now and we've found absolutely nothing. And the search is bloody expensive in time and money. It preoccupies the submarine service, in return for which all we're getting is pilloried on a daily basis. The training captain in Devonport knows his career is on the line – and I have to say I think mine is as well. The Royal Navy hasn't lost a submarine since the *Affray* in 1951.'

'Yes. It's a goddamned bad business. You guys only took five weeks to find the *Affray*, and that was with equipment half a century behind what we have now.'

'And, Arnold, it's all made worse by the unmistakable fact that we haven't found her when we ought to have. Privately, truly between you and me, I'm beginning to think something pretty bloody odd might be going on.'

'I've been thinking that since about April 5.'

'You would, cynical bastard. But I couldn't allow myself that luxury – not with my whole department under fire. And of course we've had all this grief from the Brazilians. "Where's our submarine?" "Where are our people?" "What kind of an operation are you running?" "This is a disgrace – we hope you don't expect us to pay for this." Not that they paid much for her anyway – 50 million dollars for a submarine that cost 300 million.

'Of course the damned media don't understand anything about a deal like this, and how bloody difficult it'd have been to stop the Brazilians going to sea if they'd wanted to. It was their submarine after all, and it's awfully hard to tell a foreign navy their chaps are incompetent, even if they are – which in this case they actually weren't.'

'Hm. Let me suggest something to you, Dick. I expect you know that when we lost that aircraft carrier, the *Jefferson*, in the Arabian Gulf nearly three years ago we had reason to think it was hit by a nuclear-headed torpedo delivered from a Russian Kilo.'

'No, I didn't know that.'

'Then I must ask you in turn to please make sure this conversation never gets repeated. That particular Kilo was in effect stolen from the Russian Navy, although there'd been no major act of violence. For weeks the Russians swore it had sunk in the Black Sea, and they were telling the truth as they knew it. But when the dust cleared it became obvious the boat hadn't sunk: it had been removed. And I'm very afraid we might be looking at something similar right here.'

'Jesus, Arnold, my heart's telling me that such a thing couldn't possibly happen to the Royal Navy in which I've served all my working life. But there's a still small voice in my brain which is saying, Yes it could.'

'I've been hearing that same voice for several weeks, Dick,' replied the American. 'Just because I know how good you guys are. I know how thorough a job you're doing. I know that modern sonars are excellent at sorting out what's on the bottom. Add to all that the fact that you're telling me you had your own Sea Trainers in that boat and the Brazilians weren't so bad anyway . . . So where *is* the sonofabitch?'

Both men were silent.

Then Morgan spoke again. 'Dick, this is the most secret information I have ever uttered to a foreigner. When we ran the mystery of the *Jefferson* to ground we came up with an Arab terrorist, trained as a submarine officer in Israel and in Scotland, where he passed your Perisher with flying colors. He was a submarine genius, and he obliterated a United States aircraft carrier.

'According to the Mossad, he's dead. But I couldn't place my hand on my heart and say I *know* he's dead . . . and I suspect neither could the Mossad. I'm scared shitless the bastard's still alive – scared shitless because he's familiar with the Upholder-Class, and extra scared shitless that he's out there driving HMS *Unseen*.'

Rear-Admiral Sir Richard Birley sucked in his breath involuntarily at the enormity of the American's words. 'Where do you think he's going?'

'That I don't know. But if he's taking weapons on board somewhere I guess we have to face up to the possibility that he might be planning to slam a few more warships – ours, yours, whoever's. Assuming he's the guy I'm thinking of, he's a fundamentalist, working for Iraq. He hates the West – he'll do anything to strike against us. We already established that. Hmm. But I can't see him taking the boat home to Iraq – they don't have deep enough water to operate a submarine.'

'Should we begin a search?'

'I don't know how. Your *Unseen* is like the Kilo, only even quieter. Can't hear it. Can't see it. I wouldn't know where to start. And I'm afraid to instigate anything myself. I can't advise the President to start looking for a submarine all over the god-damned oceans of the world when it might just have had a battery explosion and destroyed itself in the English Channel.'

'No, I suppose not. But it didn't, did it?'

'No, Dick. It didn't. And the only ray of light we have is that there's not really much he could do with it.'

'No.'

'I presume she has no weapons on board?'

'True.'

'And the Iraqis have nothing that would fit?'

'I very much doubt it. Nor any trained crew to drive it, much less handle weapons.'

'Then there's not much left. I guess he could fill it with explosive and blow it up somewhere it could hurt America.'

'You mean something like the Statue of Liberty?'

'Well, I dunno, really. But I guess he could make a hell of a big bang somewhere.'

'Seems a hell of a lot of trouble to go to for a bomb. There are plenty of better ways, easier ways to make a major bang. I must say, it's a baffling scenario.'

'Which means, Dick, we better think about it real deeply, right? Keep me posted, won't you?'

Three hours later Admiral Morgan and Kathy O'Brien arrived back at RAF Lyneham, where the KC135 was ready to fly them to Prestwick, on the western coast of Scotland, just south of the great championship golf links of Royal Troon. They arrived there at half past three in the afternoon, and Morgan insisted on driving the navy staff car himself, with just Kathy as his passenger. The four secret-servicemen with the communications equipment rode in a separate car right behind. Traveling, as the admiral put it, 'line astern', they headed north up the A78 coast road which winds along the spectacular shoreline of the Firth of Clyde until heading back toward Glasgow along the south bank.

But the admiral was not going that far. He drove 42 miles along the water's edge and then pulled into a small country hotel on the outskirts of the small commercial port of Gourock, which stands on the headland where the Clyde makes its great left-hand swing down to the sea. 'We're anchoring here for the night,' he told Kathy. 'The guys in the back have already made their security arrangements. Soon as we've checked in, you and I are going for a little walk. Been sitting down all day.'

They were shown immediately to their suite, which had a sensational view right across the water to the point of land where the Argyll Forest reaches down to the sea at the tiny fishing port of Strone. They watched a ferry moving lazily across the calm surface, and out beyond it there was a big sailing yacht, heading northeast with a light, chilly southwester billowing the mains'l. Further east, a black-hulled freighter steamed steadily toward Glasgow. Arnold Morgan stood before the window, staring distractedly at the idyllic scene before him.

They pulled on big sweaters and walked out into the late-afternoon sunlight, making their way along the shore for about a half-mile before Morgan stopped and pointed directly across the now deserted water. 'See that gap over there, between the town on the left – that's Dunoon – and the headland. There on the right?'

'Uh-huh.'

'That's the entrance to the Holy Loch, the old American submarine base. That's where we ran a Polaris squadron from, straight up there. Kept the world safe for a lotta years, right through the Cold War.'

'You were there for a while, weren't you?'

'Sure was. Must have been 30 years ago. I was the sonar officer in a nuclear boat. We were here only a couple of weeks. Went right out into the Atlantic, right up to the GIUK Gap. It was deep, cold water. We were watching for the Russian boats – tracking 'em, recording 'em. None of 'em ever got far without us knowing.'

'What's the GIUK Gap?'

'Oh, that's just the narrowest part of the North Atlantic – the choke point formed by Greenland–Iceland and the United Kingdom. The Russian Northern Fleet boats have to go through there to get out into the rest of the world, and they have to go through there again to get back. That's why we patrolled it all of the time.'

'Why were you so anxious to track them?'

'Because submarines are very, very dangerous, and very, very sneaky. You just don't want 'em wandering around on the loose when no one knows where they are. You have to keep an eye on them. If there's one thing that makes me real nervous it's a submarine that's somehow gone off the charts.'

'Like that British one?'

'Well, not really,' he said quickly. 'The Royal Navy thinks that one is wrecked on the bottom of the ocean. And we have to accept that. But I'd still like them to actually find it.'

Kathy looked at him quizzically. 'Well, my darling, I don't know who you were seeing this morning but I'd say your private thoughts had most definitely become business.'

They both laughed. He put his arm around her shoulders as they strolled leisurely the rest of the way to the harbor and watched the gulls wheeling in a noisy cloud at the stern of the departing evening ferry to Helensburgh.

'That's where we're going tomorrow,' he said. 'On the new car ferry. We're visiting an old friend of mine. We'll sleep late in the morning, then spend the afternoon getting there.'

The weather suddenly changed, and clouds began to roll in from the southwest, right across the Mull of Kintyre and the Isle of Arran, darkening the waters of the Sound of Bute, Rothesay and the Clyde. By the time Arnold and Kathy reached the hotel it was raining lightly and the water seemed misty.

It was not much better the next day – in fact, probably worse. The rain was steady as they sat in sweaters and raincoats under an awning, on the upper deck of the ferry.

'This is a most beautiful part of the world,' said Kathy. 'Is the weather always so miserable?'

'Mostly,' replied Morgan. 'A lot of people have summer homes up here on the lochs, but you couldn't *give* me one. I remember the time I was here. It wasn't much different from this the whole two weeks. And that was summer.'

'But it's so beautiful. I expect they forgive the climate.'

'I expect they do. There is a certain way of life up here – you know, golf, sailing, shooting, fishing. And there is a kinda cosiness about log fires and whisky, which is what they love. But it's goddamned hard work, if you ask me. Just a place to visit. Give me a warm sunny bay any time.'

'So speaks world beach expert, who hasn't had a vacation since 1942,' said Kathy, giggling.

'Jesus. I wasn't even *born* in 1942.'

'Precisely.'

'It's unbelievable, the insolence I have to put up with. You sure we oughtn't to get married? So I can keep you in order.'

'Quite sure, thank you. Unless you want to use that contraption in the leather case that Charlie's carrying over there and tell the President you've decided to bag his job and take to the hills.'

'Heh, heh, heh. Come on, we're outta here. This is Helensburgh. Let's get in the car . . .'

They drove the black Mercedes off the ferry into the rainswept streets of the little Scottish town, with the secret-servicemen right behind in the big Ford Granada. The admiral did not require a map to pick up the A814 road, finding it with the ease of a man who had done this before. They headed north up the eastern bank of the Garcloch. 'This is British submarine country,' he said. 'Right there, that's the Rhu Narrows. Used to be a very narrow channel leading up to the base at Faslane where the Brits kept Polaris. They widened it for Trident.'

Kathy stared out at the black waters. Just the thought of a submarine running down there gave her the creeps, and she imagined what Arnold must have looked like 30 years ago, perhaps standing on the bridge in his uniform, bound for the dark, cold wasteland of the North Atlantic.

Morgan, too, was preoccupied in looking at the waters of the loch. But he was wondering about a trainee submarine commanding officer who had also spent time here, learning the skills which had caused the US Navy so much heartbreak. *I just wish I knew whether that little bastard was alive or dead*, he thought. *That way I might have a better idea whether* Unseen *was alive or dead.*

They drove on in silence for a while until they reached the small town of Arrochar, way up at the head of Loch Long, fifteen miles from Helensburgh. There Morgan announced a course change onto the A83 through the forest, all along the foothills of The Cobbler, a craggy mountain which has marked the way home for submariners for generations.

'We're making a westerly course now,' he told Kathy, 'for about 16 miles, then we run down the coast of Loch Fyne to Inveraray. I'll show you a castle there which belongs to the Duke of Argyll. We'll go and take a look at it while the guys check into The George – that's a local pub.'

They took about an hour driving around to find a suitable vantage point from which to see the famous four round towers of the castle, and the secret-servicemen took even longer to organize their phone link-ups. The men decided to have dinner at the pub restaurant in two shifts, one at 1800 and one at 2100, since there would be two of them on duty at all times of the night.

Kathy and Arnold finally arrived at the big white Georgian house on the shores of Loch Fyne at half past five in the afternoon. It was still raining. They were greeted by a tall, elegant-looking man in his mid-sixties, with graying hair and a beautifully cut country suit. Impeccably mannered, he turned to Kathy and said: 'Hello, I'm Iain MacLean, and I am delighted to meet you.'

99

'He sells himself short, Kathy,' interjected Morgan. 'He's really Admiral Sir Iain MacLean, former Flag Officer of the Royal Navy's Submarine Service, and in the opinion of some people the best submariner this country has ever had.'

The two men shook hands warmly. They had not met for several years, not since the Scotsman had served a stint in Washington. But they had been in phone contact during the *Jefferson* investigation, in which the retired Royal Navy officer had played a pivotal role as the person who had once taught Benjamin Adnam how to command a submarine.

At this moment the introductions were cut slightly short because the front door was opened by a classic-looking Scottish country lady, just as an explosion of black energy burst around the side of the house in the form of a rambunctious trio of tail-wagging labradors. The first two, Fergus and Muffin, charged forward and climbed all over Kathy, but the third one, not much more than a puppy and with feet like saucepans, took a cheerful rush at the American admiral, leaped up and planted his muddy paws right in the middle of his white Irish-knit sweater.

'Iain! Iain! For God's sake get those bloody dogs under control. They're supposed to be trained gundogs, not street hooligans,' called Lady MacLean, but it was too late for that.

By now Morgan had decided to grab the puppy and lift him up. That way he could get a better grip on him, even though it meant getting his face licked. Kathy, who had dogs of her own, coped extremely well, and Sir Iain apologized.

'Don't bother apologizing to me,' said the NSA. 'I love these guys. What's this one called?'

'He's new. I call him Mr Bumble. Annie thinks he's an absolute bloody menace.'

'Well he *is* a bloody menace,' said Lady MacLean. 'This morning he went into the loch and then rushed through the drawing room straight over one of those sofas. It took me an hour to clean it.' Then she laughed, adding, 'By the way. I'm Annie MacLean. Arnold, lovely to see you again. And you must be the beautiful Kathy.'

It was second nature to this very senior officer's wife to put younger people totally at their ease. She had spent a lifetime doing it – as a captain's wife, then as a rear-admiral's wife, and finally as a vice-admiral's wife: being charming to the wives of lieutenants, knowing their husbands were terrified of Iain.

The butler, the red-bearded Angus, came out and took the luggage before showing the secret-servicemen to a small downstairs room next to the kitchen where they could have some tea and watch the television during the early part of the evening. Annie took Kathy into the big kitchen with her while the two retired admirals made their way to the great wide drawing room with its perfect southern aspect over the loch.

'Christ, Arnold, she's an absolute stunner,' said Sir Iain softly as they settled into the sofa Mr Bumble had done his resolute best to destroy that morning. 'Matter of fact, I'm slightly afraid she might be a bit too good for you.'

Morgan chuckled. He had always been extremely fond of the droll, aristocratic Scotsman, and he had much to talk to him about. Iain MacLean was one of the very few people in any navy to whom he was prepared to defer in matters of strategy, history and intention. They were both thoroughly learned men in the art of naval warfare, its execution, and its prevention.

Dinner that evening was substantial. They began with wild, local smoked salmon served with a white burgundy. Then Angus brought in a large, hot, baked Scottish game pie which Kathy thought was about the best thing she had ever tasted. She couldn't identify its contents, but according to Sir Iain neither could anyone else. 'I've always thought it was grilled stag with slices of barbecued golden eagle,' he said. 'Annie's got a warlock in the village who makes them.'

'Don't listen to him, my dear,' said Lady MacLean. 'It's a perfectly normal game pie, made by Mrs MacKay. She also makes them for The George. I expect some of the meat has been frozen but it's got pheasant, grouse and venison, and I think a few oysters.'

'Well, I say it's delicious,' said Kathy. 'And so does Arnold. I think that's his twelfth slice.'

'Eighth,' muttered Admiral Morgan, chewing luxuriously and sipping a glass of velvet 1990 Château Lynch Bages.

Sir Iain went out and produced a bottle of chilled Sauternes, a 1990 Château Chartreuse, which they sipped with the poached pears Lady MacLean served for what she described as 'pudding.' Her husband took pains to point out this was a 'particularly bloody silly English word for dessert used mainly as a way for pretentious middle-class snobs to identify the riff-raff.'

'Well, I'm not a pretentious middle-class snob,' said Lady MacLean with an edge of indignation.

'No. I know you're not, since your father's a ninth-generation Scottish earl. That's why I said *mainly*. I mean, "pudding"! What kind of a word is that? Bloody ridiculous.'

'Well, that's what our schools taught us. That's what everyone I know says.'

'Most of 'em probably only say it because you do. That's what snobbery is. Kathy, how about some Sauternes with your . . . pudding?'

By half past ten the party was drawing to a close. Lady MacLean announced that she was on her way to bed, and Kathy said she thought that was a sound plan. Admiral MacLean said he was thinking he and Arnold might wander over to the study for a medicinal glass of port before retiring, and to chat about old times for a half-hour.

They walked across the hall together and Sir Iain closed the door behind them. He put another dried log on the dying embers of the fire, and poured them each a glass of Taylor's '78 port from a decanter. The log crackled into life, and they sat in deep leather armchairs surrounded by the admiral's collection of books. Sir Iain touched a button on a music system to his left, and the unmistakable sounds of Duke Ellington drifted around the room.

'Goddamned Brits,' said Rear-Admiral Morgan. 'You guys have a real way of living life which I sometimes think we haven't quite mastered in the States.'

'We've just been at it a bit longer,' said the Scotsman, smiling. 'Probably learned a bit more about what's important. A person isn't here on earth that long, you know.'

'We're too busy being successful,' said the American. 'Still, I guess we might get there in the end.'

'Actually, I'd rather like you to get there now,' said Sir Iain, consciously changing the subject. 'What is it, Arnold, that really brings you here? As if I don't know.'

'If you do, tell me.'

'It's that damned submarine, isn't it?'

'Yes, Iain, it is.'

'And what is it you want from me? I'm long retired, as you know. Very out of touch, really.'

'I know one thing: your brain's no more out of touch than mine is. I just want to find out what you think. Is the boat still floating? Or is it history? Is everyone really dead?'

'Well, Arnold, I thought that they would find it within two weeks. Now I'm drawn to the conclusion that it isn't there. Look, they found the bloody *Affray* after five weeks, without any modern equipment. My opinion is that *Unseen* is not wrecked and did not destroy herself, and no one hit her with a torpedo – otherwise the searchers would most definitely have found something.'

'Well, where is she, then?'

'Three possibilities. The crew went berserk and stole her to get away from their wives. But you would think they'd have run out of fuel by now. The second is that the ship was hijacked for political purposes. The third is that she was stolen.'

'Which one do you like best?'

'Don't like any of them. But I don't believe she's sitting undiscovered somewhere in the English Channel. And, if you press me, the third. If she'd been hijacked for some political end we'd have heard by now. So I think she was boarded and stolen, that her own crew are dead, and that she's out there. I do not believe Lt-Commander Colley would have left the training area, but I am 99 percent sure that submarine is not in the training area any more. So someone else must have driven the submarine out.'

'That's precisely what I think, Iain, so my real first question is: who? Who's driving her with such skill she hasn't been caught in nearly two months? And where has she been getting her fuel from?'

'We're dealing here,' replied Sir Iain, 'not just with a competent submariner. We're into the realm of sheer daring, ruthlessness, originality, illegality and, not least, specialized competence in the Upholder-Class. There's only one man in all the world who fits that list. But, if I'm to believe my American friends, that man's dead.'

'If I believed that I wouldn't be sitting here with you, Iain. I think he's still alive, and I think he's out there, driving *Unseen*.'

'So, since you mention it, do I. Have done for some time now. Fancy another glass of port?'

'I think we may *need* another glass of port – since we've more or less established that an Arab homicidal maniac is riding around in a silent submarine waiting to do something big. I cannot tell you what it'll be like back home if he strikes again. It would finish this Republican administration.'

'Shouldn't wonder. Trouble is, Arnold, I don't know how to catch him. We have no idea where he is within 10,000 miles. Still, she was only on safety work-up – she wouldn't have had much on board in the way of serious weaponry.'

'Yeah, I guess so. Dick Birley and I came to much the same conclusion. But it's kinda tiresome, just sitting still waiting for something to happen.'

'I don't really think you have a choice, Arnold. What can anyone do? Unless he makes a mistake. But judging by his track record he's not especially prone to those.'

'I can at least get the US Navy to put everyone on a heightened alert – I can think up some spurious reason. But my fear remains that, despite the apparent lack of weapons, Adnam plans to hit another aircraft carrier.'

'You think his luck might hold that long? I doubt it. I think, if he tried again, you chaps'd probably get him. Nonetheless, it's a worry. But there's not much to be done – we just have to hope to God he makes a mistake.'

The two admirals retired for the night at half past eleven. Arnold Morgan lay awake next to the sleeping Kathy much later than that, trying to think of the glorious stretches of water they would see tomorrow on Sir Iain's boat. Trying to cast from his mind the specter of Ben Adnam at the helm of another rogue submarine.

201200MAY05. 15.52S 55.10E. Course 360. Speed 9.
The *Santa Cecilia* refueled *Unseen* for the final time shortly after midnight, 200 miles off D'Antongil Bay on the northern coast of Madagascar, close to the remote French Island of Tromelin. There remained just 17 more days of the journey back to Bandar Abbas, traveling deep, up the Indian Ocean to the Arabian Gulf. The submarine had run perfectly all the way, but they had been getting very short of food and water, and Commander Adnam was pleased to restock the galley.

Back at Bandar Abbas, eagerly awaiting their arrival, was Admiral Mohammed Badr. His plans to install the submarine in her new home without the prying eyes of the US satellites seeing it were well in place. He was confident no one would spot *Unseen* enter the new drydock, and confident no one could possibly photograph her once she was inside.

The Iranians had a very good hold on the US satellite patterns and were able to predict accurately enough the gaps in overhead cover. The submarine must start its 14-mile surface run across the shallow water to the harbor at 0130. That way she'd be in by 0245, 30 minutes before the next satellite would pass overhead. That was how they'd been able to land the Russian weapons system in total secrecy when it had arrived in March. The freighter had waited in the strait, right off the eastern tip of the island of Qeshm, then run in fast across the shallows, right between the satellites' windows of observation.

Admiral Badr was amused at the success of the earlier operation, but seethed inwardly at the humiliating fact that he and his navy had to behave in this way because of the Great Satan. It was, he said, unconscionable that a foreign nation should threaten the ancient rights of Iran to defend herself in any way she chose.

But all was going well. One complete Russian Grumble Rif missile system was safely installed in the workshop area at the deep end of the drydock; the other three were being set up as part of the naval air-defense system. The new dock's cranes were in place now, as were the long galleries which would afford engineers easy access to the submarine. High heavy-load lifting apparatus criss-crossed the upper airspace, right below the thick concrete ceiling. There were 50 guards on duty outside, night and day. The barbed wire had been brought in closer now. And a second noticeboard had been erected right outside. It read, like the one near the main gate:

AUTHORIZED PERSONNEL ONLY
INTRUDERS WILL BE SHOT ON SIGHT

Rear-Admiral Badr's missile engineers had checked the system right through and, as far as they could tell, it was flawlessly constructed. It was brand new, tried and tested over many months by the Russians in the Black Sea in their 10,000-ton guided-missile cruiser *Azov*. All that was needed now was Ben's safe return with the submarine.

The Russian freighter had delivered a stockpile of 96 weapons, which ought to be ample for their purposes, since Commander Adnam had said he would require only six. Badr looked forward to the Mission of Justice with great anticipation.

070100JUN05. 26.57N 56.19E. Speed 2.
Following a racetrack pattern in 150 feet of water *Unseen* slowly moved 50 feet below the surface, through the warm waters of the Strait of Hormuz just to the east of Qeshm, waiting for the American satellite to slide away through the heavens.

At 0130 Commander Adnam issued the orders to surface and head up to Bandar Abbas at 12 knots on course three-three-eight. The ex-Royal Navy submarine came barreling out of the ocean, shaking the blue water from her decks in a cloud of white spray, the batteries driving her forward on her single shaft, the fastest she had moved since leaving Plymouth Sound 68 days previously.

Adnam and his navigation officer, Lt-Commander Rajavi, stood on the bridge as they raced across the bay, the hot night air in their faces. Up ahead they could already see the lights from the Iranian Naval Station, and soon they could spot the green light high on the right-hand wall of the harbor. Adnam ordered a reduction in speed just outside the entrance, and at 0245 *Unseen* ran fair down the northerly channel into the arms of her new Iranian masters.

They made a hard 90-degree turn to the right at the end of the harbor wall, and two small tugs maneuvered the 230-foot hull toward the drydock. Adnam stayed on the bridge, checking the tugs. At 0256 the submarine slid into the new dock, far in, safely away from the vigilant photographer which would drift silently past, 20,000 miles above, in 19 minutes' time. The massive steel double doors, constructed to be able to take the full force of an incoming cruise missile without caving in, were now closed across the entrance to shield the lights inside, where a small team of naval personnel was waiting to welcome *Unseen*.

Ben Adnam walked across the gangplank onto dry land for the first time in four months. Badr was waiting and the two men embraced, kissing on both cheeks several times in the old Muslim way.

'How are you, Ben?' asked the Iranian submarine chief.

'I'm tired,' he replied. 'It's been a long haul.'

Badr led him out through a small side door to a waiting staff car, and they drove to the Iraqi's house. The journey took only six minutes but the commander was asleep by the time they arrived. Badr awakened him and carried his sea-bag past the six patrolling guards. Once Adnam was inside there were four young Iranians to assist him. They removed his Brazilian uniform, the only kind of clothes he had worn since March 29, and carefully placed his knife on the table. Then they led him to a hot bath full of exotic restoring oils. Ben managed to wash himself with a bar of jasmine soap, but fell asleep three times in the bright steamy bathroom. Two of the servants shaved the rough dark stubble from his face and finally let the water out and helped him to his feet, drying him off with big soft orange towels. They sprayed him with scented water, dusted him with jasmine talcum powder, and helped him into a freshly pressed white cotton robe.

Adnam fell into bed in the large air-conditioned room and slept for 30 hours, guarded like a *pasha*, protected like Fort Knox.

When the submarine commander finally surfaced it was ten o'clock on the morning of June 9. Rear-Admiral Badr had issued orders that he was to be informed as soon as Ben returned from the undead. Shaved and sharp now, the Iraqi was ready to come out at the bell, and he greeted Badr in the private dining room.

'We followed much of your progress through the English news-papers,' Badr said. 'Benjamin, you may leave no footprints, but you are very adroit at causing chaos.'

'I hope so, sir. By the way, under the terms of our agreement I am now owed three-quarters of a million dollars, which I shall require before we move further.'

'I am aware of that. The wire transfer was made yesterday morning to your numbered account in Switzerland. I have here the document of confirmation, signed by the bank. You are at liberty to check with your own bank now if you wish, on that telephone, to insure I am telling the truth.'

'That will not be necessary, Mohammed,' replied the com-mander, nodding. 'And I thank you for your meticulousness and your punctuality.'

'As indeed we thank you, Benjamin,' said Badr with a smile. 'Did you have any problems with the boat? All of our engineers report her in excellent shape. Just routine maintenance, a minor leak in the seal around the shaft. Electronically she's perfect, as far as we can tell.'

'She ran fine all the way. The operation was conducted with the utmost professionalism. I expect the Royal Navy was quite confused by the entire thing.'

'They have not said so, Ben. Indeed, the search still goes on in the English Channel. But I hear some rumblings that senior officers are beginning to wonder if she is there at all. However, nothing has been said publicly.'

'No, they won't do that.'

'Ben, what I really want to discuss with you is the Russian missile system. It's very large and very complicated to fit on a submarine. We could be refitting for a year.'

'Look, Admiral, if we were trying to fit a medium-range SAM system for use against military aircraft you'd be absolutely correct. Because we'd need large, complicated radar and control systems to cope with military aircraft – trying to evade, ducking and diving, using decoys and jammers. But we're not doing that. We're dumbing down a very sophisticated system. We can actually just bolt the parts we need onto the submarine, right up on the casing behind the fin. Our targets are much simpler, highly predictable, holding a steady course, speed and height. No defensive systems.

'We'll make one modification as I mentioned before, to ensure simple, active radar homing – just enough to allow front-lobe approach to the target. We can't rely on something like infrared rear-lobe homing. This weapon has to go to the height we tell it, then turn to meet its target head-on. It must acquire the target with its own radar homing system, then lock on and hit at a closing speed of perhaps Mach 4.'

'Hmm. Still, I've never seen so many radar systems as these.'

'But we don't need them on the submarine. Those are intended to give the weapon all sorts of guidance-update information from its surface-firing platform while it's in midflight. I intend to feed it all the information it needs to find its target before it's fired. I'm after a sitting duck, not a swerving teal. We're going to mount our missile-launcher in a specially constructed pressure-tight box and bolt it onto the rear end of the fin. The submarine's regular radar will have to be tweaked up for long-range aircraft detection, and we need it to provide basic preflight guidance instructions for the missile. After that, in trade terms, we just "fire and forget."'

If the target's not too fast we should have time to get a second bird away if the first one fails.'

'Ben, I've mentioned this before: you're a very clever man.'

'Still breathing, Mohammed. In my game that's a major plus.'

'I have a distinct feeling you're likely to go on breathing for a long time. So long as you always stay a couple of steps in front of the enemy.'

'I hope to, but right now I'd like to conclude this topic by making certain you follow our principal problem – that is, fitting the "box" to the submarine without dangerously reducing her surface stability. Like, she might become so top-heavy she rolls right over. But that should be easily solved with a couple of buoyancy tanks, regular saddle tanks on either side of the hull.

'Our only other problem is we have to build our own fairly simple fire-control system to work from inside the hull. Then we need just to connect things up so that the system is permanent and reliable, despite the difficulties of the underwater environment.'

'And you truly believe we can manage all that?'

'Certainly I do. Otherwise I'd never have begun the project.'

'But it's never been done before, has it? Not by *any* navy?'

'No. But only because there's never been an operational requirement for it. If there had been, every major maritime power would own such a system. It's just that submarines have never been sufficiently under threat from aircraft. They still aren't.'

222000JUN05. 30.30N 49.05E. Speed 2. Course 90.
The big Iranian Navy barge, edged along by a following tugboat, had reached its destination now, 600 miles north up the coast from Bandar Abbas in the Gulf of Iran, a little more than 40 miles offshore. Commander Adnam, Admiral Badr and the missile director from *Unseen*'s crew were all on the barge, on the bow of which was bolted the modified version of the Russian Grumble Rif missile system, securely covered, and surrounded by four engineers. Tonight was the night, clear and moonlit, with the stars shining brightly above. The test site was close to perfect.

They took the covers off the consoles, which were situated right back on the stern, and the missile director sat in the bolted-down chair in front of them. There was little swell in the ocean on this hot Arabian night, and everyone was in shirtsleeves. The radar on the barge scanned the skies for aircraft but found nothing within a radius of 100 miles.

Ben Adnam checked his watch, which now showed 2025. He knew the pilotless target aircraft was off the ground now, above Bandar Abbas, banking out over the Gulf then back along the coast, climbing all the while to the huge altitude of 60,000 feet. Soon it would head north for about 100 miles, or 17 minutes, before turning south for the final time and coming racing back at 600mph toward the skies above the barge.

They picked it up on the search radar on the southern leg of its journey, and the missile director found it again when it was 40 miles out, incoming. His fingers flew over the keys as he programmed the information into the missile's guidance system.

'Climb out position in.'

'Target course and speed set.'

'Target height preset at 60,000.'

'Weapon One ready.'

At two minutes before 2100 he called: 'Stand by!'

Then he hit the launch key and the big Russian Grumble-class SAM missile ripped out of the launcher in a thunder of flame and exhaust, dead vertical, and screamed straight up into the sky like a huge firework. Everyone watched it as it changed course after 25 seconds, reaching its 11.5-mile altitude. They saw it swerve north, still making 1700mph, toward the target. And they watched as it obliterated the incoming empty aircraft in dark but crystal-clear skies more than 20 miles from where they stood. A great sheet of flame semed to light up the universe.

It was a perfect front-lobe attack of such awesome speed and power that no one felt able to say anything for a few moments.

Except for Commander Adnam, who spoke crisply. 'Thank you, gentlemen. That will do very nicely. I think we can go home now.'

Fifteen minutes later the 275-ton Kaman-Class fast-attack craft *Shamshir* came alongside to take off the admiral, the commander and the missile officer. The engineers and the naval guards would remain on the barge for the slow journey home.

Admiral Badr and his submariners would be in Bandar Abbas in 20 hours. They dined on board while the German-built Iranian ship sped through the Gulf at 30 knots all the way. Conversation at dinner, during which Badr and Adnam sat alone, had an edge of elation to it. The system had worked – which, of course, for $300 million was only to be expected. But the question of time was important. HMS *Unseen* needed to be back in the North Atlantic by early January, which meant that work here on her had to be completed, all tests done, by late October.

Ben's view was sanguine. 'I can't see it taking that long, sir. The hardest part is behind us. The modifications to the submarine are comparatively simple. It's just a matter of ordinary submarine engineering, nothing very complicated.'

'And the dates, Ben, are you happy with them?'

'Well, I'm happy with one, January 17, the 15th anniversary of the day the allies attacked Iraq for the first time. But thereafter I think we'll avoid anniversaries. I'm afraid it might look too obvious that Iraq was being set up. And that would lead the Americans right to us. The missing submarine, the big new submarine drydock in Bandar Abbas into which they cannot see, three hits against the West plainly designed to get Iraq blamed.

'No, Admiral, I think January 17 would be nicely subtle. It might take everyone a while to figure the relevance out, but there are few better ways to persuade the Americans that Iraq is responsible. Incidentally, we mustn't forget to put the Kilo back in the new dock as soon as I sail and make sure we're *seen* doing it, for a few minutes right at the beginning of a satellite pass.'

241000JUN05. Bandar Abbas Navy Base, Special Ops Room
Commander Adnam had drafted the totally bogus signal that Navy Headquarters in Bandar Abbas was transmitting to an Iranian Navy patrol craft in the northern end of the Gulf. The message ran: *'Intelligence received of Iraqi surface-to-air missile test in area east of Qal'at Sālih. Four missiles flown. One at fast high-altitude airborne target – apparently successful at time 222101JUN05. Launch platform unknown. Investigate. 240100JUN06.'*

Encoded in only a comparatively low-level operational system it was, as Ben Adnam had anticipated, intercepted by local US radio surveillance at the time of transmission. Fort Meade had it decrypted within three hours. Langley had a copy one hour later. And the CIA's chief field officers in both Jordan and Kuwait had it soon afterwards.

Ben's plan was as usual proceeding with the inevitability of sunrise over the desert. This was not made to seem a particularly important message, just one of several reports sent out on a daily basis. And it scored a bullseye, ending up in the hands of Chuck Mitchell, an Arab-speaking American from Boston who operated under deep cover in the main telegraph and fax office on the east side of Rashid Street, Baghdad.

Mitchell had two messages that evening. The first was from Kuwait and quoted an inquiry about missile test-firing in the Marshes, east of the Tigris. The second message was from the CIA man in Jordon, asking baldly if he had anything on Iraqi missile tests in the Marshes near Qal'at Sālih. It added that there had been an inquiry from HQ.

Mitchell had heard nothing – but that did not mean nothing was happening. He contacted another CIA field man in Baghdad, Hussein Hakim, a recruit of some 12 years, and they arranged to meet, both wearing Arab dress, at 8pm in a dingy coffee house in the poor southern part of the city.

Hakim was late because he'd thought, neurotically, there might be a tail on him; that turned out to be a false alarm but by a quarter to nine, when he finally found Chuck, the American too was getting nervous. They had no wish to spend long together, and the conversation was terse. Yes, the idea of a big missile-testing program somewhere new was serious. But no, neither of them could work on it specifically. Best just to keep their ears to the ground and hope the satellites found something.

Mitchell sent a signal back to confirm he was on the case and ask for a better idea of the urgency involved and/or the need to substantiate the reports. He was not optimistic.

His communication reached the desk of the CIA's Middle East Chief, Jeff Austin, shortly before lunch. As Austin read it he ruminated on the endless problem of Iraq. If it wasn't one thing, it was another. That damned nation had practically caused a world war 15 years ago, and since then there had been nothing but problems – possible nuclear weapons, possible chemical weapons, possible use of nerve gas on the Kurds again. Not to mention, of course, the vaporizing of the *Thomas Jefferson* in the high summer of 2002. This had been plainly the work of Baghdad, and as yet had gone unpunished. Now the Iraqis were testing, apparently in secret, new anti-aircraft missiles down in the Marshes. There were two big questions: Where did they get them? And what did they plan to do with them?

Jeff Austin's antennae were up. He hit the secure line to Rear-Admiral Morgan's office. The two men talked for about ten minutes without reaching any major conclusions, save to keep a very careful watch on any activities by the Iraqi military in the Marshes and to be extra-vigilant with the satellite cover of that area.

'Fucking towelheads,' Morgan growled as he replaced the telephone. 'That's all we need. The Marsh Arabs with a nuclear deterrent. Holy Shit. How about the fucking Incas? What about the Eskimos?'

What Morgan did not know was that the only missile of any significance to have been fired in the Middle East this year was the big Grumble Rif in the Gulf of Iran a few days previously. Adnam had chosen his site well, way offshore, hundreds of miles from any city and fairly close to the Iran/Iraq border. And it had all been over in 70 seconds. There might somewhere have been an amateur astronomer who saw a flash in the sky, or possibly a group of tribesmen in the hills had thought they'd seen a herald of the end of the world, but no country had reported a downed plane and none had observed the missile taking off. No one had reported anything.

Meanwhile, back at the Bandar Abbas Naval Base a team of engineers was working on the new weapons system for HMS *Unseen*. Commander Adnam intended the system should be fitted as a self-contained unit, possibly as high as the top of the fin, bolted into place in an airtight and waterproof 'box,' and then connected by wires to the fairly basic control system already installed in the submarine. The set-up was cumbersome but ingenious, and Adnam had already proved, to himself at least, that it would work – to devastating effect. Inside the huge drydock the boltholes were being drilled into the casing and the stern end of the fin. By late August the missile system would be completely modified for its new and relatively simple task. Not even the Russians had the remotest clue as to what was happening in the drydock. No one knew what the thick rubber cable-connectors were for as the engineers gunned them into place on the aft section of the deck.

Adnam and Badr were constant visitors, waiting for the day when when the heavy load lifting apparatus would hoist the massive 'extra fin' into place. That happened on September 14;

when it was completely fixed, five days later, the engineers pumped the water-level as high as possible and then submerged *Unseen* to the bottom of the deep dock. Even though the water covered the fin by only about eight feet, this was enough to check over several hours that everything was watertight at periscope depth – this was as critically important as the test results at greater depths, because at such depths the whole system would be pressurized from the inside.

The seals held perfectly; not a drop of water entered the 'box.' Then the Iranians deliberately overpressurized it internally, pumping the air pressure up to two atmospheres. No bubbles emerged. The result brought a smile of satisfaction to the face of Ben Adnam.

The workshop became quieter after that. Only the electronics engineers continued working, calmly checking circuits as the system depressurized.

Later the same afternoon, as they walked into the dock, Commander Adnam said softly to Rear-Admiral Badr: 'Soon, my friend, both your revenge and mine will be complete.'

And he gazed with the utmost satisfaction at the submarine he had personally stolen from the Royal Navy – the submarine which would very soon launch an attack the like of which had never been seen in the entire history of naval warfare.

He did not, however, linger for very long. He had been busy all day, and tonight he wanted to pray, to ask the forgiveness of his God.

CHAPTER FIVE

January 16, 2006. Baku, the capital city of Azerbaijan.
The goodbyes were cordial, but no more. The six-man negotiating team from Russia had been noncommittal throughout.
The Chinese were polite but remote. The Iranians wore the
complacent smiles of those who hold all of the aces and three of
the kings. Four visiting Arabian sheikhs – an Al-Sabah from
Kuwait, a Salman from Saudi, Hamdan Al-Maktoum from Dubai
and a representative of the Emir of Bahrain – had been essentially
uninterested in the outcome of the meeting.

Bob Trueman, the 6ft 5in Texan leader of the US delegation,
had rarely attempted such an uphill struggle. At 384 pounds and
with a tendency to sweat like a wild boar, he gravitated toward
flat, even ground both physically and mentally. Mountainous roads
were not his line of country unless he was in his Lincoln Conti-
nental. He even made his home in the great flatlands of the
eastern shore of Maryland, where he remembered once taking
his wife Anne for a walk along the sprawling goose-hunting
marshes – ''Bout 30 years ago I think . . . before the boys were
born, anyway. Probably the last real exercise I ever took.'

And Baku, this strange half-Muslim city which sits on the
south shore of the great beak-shaped Apsheron Peninsula on
the Caspian Sea, had proved to be a pinnacle too far for the
mighty Bob Trueman. In his opinion there was no way the United
States was going to win the mounting global struggle for the vast
oil reserves which surround the region.

It was all too damned late. That was the trouble. The goddamned White House and Congress and the Senate had fiddled
while Central Asia had, in a sense, burned – right in front of
their eyes. And, in Bob Trueman's opinion, 'That damned President with the loose zipper ought never to have been elected. Just
sat there, that sonofabitch, attending to his personal problems

while the rest of the industrialized Western world edged closer to the brink. And now look what's happened.'

In Bob's view, the entire idea of this three-day conference had been nothing less than a Sino-Iranian strategy to humiliate his country. The Russians, the Chinese and the Iranians, thrown together now as never before in the entire history of Asia and the Middle East, formed a lethal oil cartel which had effectively shut the West out of the second largest reserves on earth. 'All we need now is for the Iranians to have another shot at blockading the Gulf with their fucking Russian mines and there could easily be a war,' he muttered. 'A real shooting war. Because if we can't tap into the Caspian reserves and the Gulf gets closed, even for a month, the whole fucking place is going to grind to a halt – Japan, Europe, the States . . .'

But these were personal fears; Bob's mission in Baku was public. This huge, bearlike, but deceptively cunning American smiled and shook the hand of his Russian host. He wished a warm farewell to his old and trusted friend Sheikh Hamdan, and to young Mohammed Al–Sabah. To the Iranians he was courteous, wishing profoundly there was some way, somehow, that the United States could participate in the marketing of the Caspian oil. But, as he knew only too well, the pipeline across Iran would be financed essentially by China. The only other pipeline was going *to* China. In brief, the Iranians had gone for the shut-out and they'd made it.

The problem was, how to get back in. So now Bob Trueman faced the smiling head of the Iranian delegation and the two men shook hands. They both knew there was a price the United States might have to pay, and they both knew it would almost certainly be way too high – like financing a whole pipeline in return for access to a mere 20 percent of the crude oil. Only Bob knew that Congress might just have to bite the bullet on that one and pay up. The balance of oil supplies these days was just too delicately poised.

He told the Iranian that he had greatly enjoyed his visit to the old Persian city of Baku, and that the mild winter climate had been more than agreeable. He thanked him for the tour of the historic Muslim part of the city, which dates back to the ninth century. And he remarked how impressed he had been at the smooth working of this, the largest cargo port on the Caspian

Sea. 'Just wish you guys could find a way for us to help out somehow,' he said.

'Mr Trueman, as you well know there were many years between 1996 and the new millennium when we would have welcomed your help. But your administration chose not even to speak to us. I am sure you, of all people, must understand we had to turn elsewhere.'

'I do understand, and I'm sorry the old enmities should have lasted so long. I guess we just had a President who thought he was still trying to get the hostages free in Tehrān, 18 years later.'

'We thought it showed a lack of foresight, Mr Trueman. There were so many people in my country who wanted a partnership with the West, so many who wanted to join in the prosperity of the West. But your people would never listen to the voices of reason which have always existed here in Persia. We're not all Muslim fundamentalists, you know.'

'I do know that, and I just wish things could be different. But, well, you hold the aces. The best way out to the marketplace for that oil is straight across Iran to a Gulf port, and we coulda built that pipeline quicker and better than anyone . . .'

'If, Mr Trueman, you had condescended to speak to us.' The Iranian smiled. 'By the way, when do you leave? I have much enjoyed talking with you.'

'We got a US Air Force plane taking us to London in two hours. Then we're flying Concorde home tomorrow morning – new service, nonstop London–New York, then on down to Washington. Probably takes that sucker about 16 minutes to get there.'

'It's a beautiful aircraft, Mr Trueman. I have always wished to fly on it one day myself.'

'Mr Montazeri, if you can come up with a way to bring my country into the marketing of the Caspian oil, I will have my government hire one of those babies just for you, and fly you from Tehrān to Washington to celebrate.'

'I will continue to think about it,' replied the Iranian, laughing. 'But the Chinese are very well entrenched now. As we both know, they invested billions and billions of dollars into acquiring the oil, helping us finance the pipeline . . .'

'Guess so. And, of course, they need so much oil. What's that statistic again? By the year 2012 they will require 97 percent of all the oil in the Gulf?'

'So the economists say, Mr Trueman. And, since Beijing cannot have all of that, I suppose they will have to purchase it from somewhere else.'

'I'm a little afraid they've already done that,' said the American. 'So far as I can see, the entire production of Kazakhstan is on its way to the east. And there's not a thing we can do about it . . . thanks to the shrewd and farsighted way our last President helped to make China the second richest country in the world.'

'No, Mr Trueman. I do not believe there is.'

Everyone was standing, making their farewells in the tall ornate government conference room, and Bob Trueman's men were beginning to move toward the massive bulk of their leader. His assistant, Steve Dimauro, the physical opposite of his boss, was whipcord slim, a former All-Star college baseball shortstop out of Vidalia, Georgia. Made it to the Yankees AAA in a big hurry, but lacked the patience and maybe the size for the final journey to the Bronx. Steve, with his degree in economics, had quit in his third year as a pro and joined the oil giant ARCO, where Bob Trueman was already a towering hero, having masterminded the huge strike in the desert of southern Dubai back in 1980.

Now, seven years later, the 30-year-old Dimauro was one of ARCO's young tigers, and his association with the formidable ex-VP, Trueman, leader of all current presidential missions to the Middle East, was powering him ever onward and upward in the corporate structure. ARCO was more than happy to lease him out for a year to gain priceless knowledge of the Russo-Sino-Iranian cartel which today had so much influence in the running of the industrial world. When Steve returned to the company he would do so as a vice-president.

Bob and Steve were accompanied by four US Republican congressmen: Jim Adison (California), Edmund Walter (New Hampshire), Mark Bachus (Delaware) and Dan Baylor (Texas). En route to the airport they traveled in two separate limousines, one for Bob and Steve and the former oil professional Dan Baylor, the other for the other three congressmen.

There was no particular hurry, but the driver was surprised at Bob Trueman's instruction for a first stop at the new McDonalds which had opened in downtown Baku. 'Just wanna pop right in there for a coupla of Big Macs,' he said. 'I often do that in the midafternoon, kinda stabilizes my weight, keeps it right where it is. At my age you don't wanna start losing, suddenly. That ain't real good for you.'

'You mean between lunch and dinner?' inquired Congressman Baylor.

'Right. You see, I'm a guy with a big bulk,' said Bob seriously – and unnecessarily. 'At my pressure of work, that bulk is under attack from my own body. Which means in about eight hours I could be undergoing some weightloss. Now that wouldn't affect a little guy like yourself,' he added, staring at the beefy six-foot Texan's 225-pound frame, 'but a big man's gotta do what a big man's gotta do. And right now, that's weight maintenance. McDonalds, driver.'

Bob Trueman was munching cheerfully as they arrived at the airport and boarded the USAF jet for the six-hour flight which would get them in to London at 1900 local, in ample time for dinner before spending the night at the Connaught Hotel, breakfasting with four US oil execs based in London, and then driving out to Heathrow for the 1100 departure of Concorde. By the time they boarded the jet he was still chewing and still grumbling about the shocking lack of foresight the West had demonstrated with regard to the Caspian oil. 'Even back in 1997,' he was saying, 'it was known that the Caspian reserves in Azerbaijan, Kazakhstan and Turkmenistan added up to a vast field second only in capacity to the big one in Saudi Arabia. With the Chinese desperate to plug into it what does the West do? It does four things.

'One, our President decides to do everything he possibly can to make the Chinese even richer – Most Favored Nation status, allows 'em to export anything they want to the States, hands over key aeronautical technology to them in return for our being allowed to export to them. Whatever makes them happy.

'Two, he decides not to speak to the Iranians, thus denying us a partnership in the best oil route out of the Caspian area.

'Three, the Americans determine to expand NATO east but not allow Russia in, thus driving China's traditional enemy straight back into her arms, now as a friend and vital trading partner. Not to mention the head honcho in the Caspian oil cartel – China's new best friend is in the precise spot we don't want her.

'Four, the Europeans, with a blinding flash of brilliance, decide to refuse membership of the European Community to the Turks, who, because of the Bosporus, own the only *other* way out for oil tankers from the Caspian.'

He stared at his five-man audience. 'Is there anyone here who can enlighten me as to where precisely we get these fuckups who are supposed to be looking after the interests of the West. Anyone? Please?'

There was no response but five grim smiles, as the bludgeoning words of the massive Texan struck home. The lethargic behavior of the Western powers had been close to blind neglect, as China, in partnership with Iran and the Russian oil corporations, had placed a deadlock on the Caspian oil. It was not as if there had been any secrets. There had been a huge public announcement when Iran had bought into a ten percent share, back in 1996. In 1997 there was another press announcement that China had wrapped up a deal with Kazakhstan for future exploration of the apparently endless oilfields in the western part of the country. The Chinese National Petroleum Company (CNPC) under this agreement immediately invested over four billion dollars in the 'exploitation' of the Aktyubinsk field – principally for the construction of a pipeline to ship oil from western Kazakhstan to Turkmenistan and, potentially, further on to Iran. Earlier that same week China had signed *another* four-billion-dollar deal for the exploitation of the nearby Ozen field. 'This arrangement,' Beijing suggested, 'may even conclude with a new pipeline direct to China, because of our determination to find secure oil supplies to meet soaring domestic demand.'

'Right there a three-year-old panda could've worked out what was happening,' grunted Bob Trueman. 'And right in the middle of it we have an ever-aggressive Iran, not just threatening but *actually telling everyone* they plan to blockade the Gulf with mines because the seaway belongs to them. So there we have it. The Gulf might close altogether, at least until we and the Western Allies can blow the bastard open again. And now we're locked out of the other big world oil supply. Everyone in the industry could see it coming. And what did we do? Nothing. A great big zero. And now this . . . Fuck me!'

The interesting part of this discussion was not that Bob Trueman had shed the light of a prophet upon the subject.

Bob was not renowned as a major intellect, even in the higher reaches of the ARCO boardroom. He was just a professional oil man, with a voracious appetite for knowledge. His staff referred to him as 'The Bear,' and his office was referred to as 'The Cave.' He usually carried three briefcases, and he read, according to Steve Dimauro, 'about 3000 magazines a day.' He was a likable character who tended to drive his colleagues crazy because he believed there was no group of people on his staff who could provide him with as much information as he needed. His intake of both knowledge and calories, on any given day, was inclined to the high frontiers of supply-side economics. Above all, however, he was quick to recognize a fool. And he definitely recognized one in a position of power. Bob Trueman had been voluble in his condemnation of the White House in the dying years of the 20th century. And he worked for America's current Republican President with all the energy of a true zealot. The cool rejection of his proposals in Baku by the new men in charge of world oil – or at least a significant piece of it – had frustrated him almost beyond tolerance.

'And it was all so goddamned simple,' he growled. 'All we had to do was cosy up to Iran, mend a few bridges, offer them some assistance. Then finance a US–Iranian pipeline with a big fat ARCO refinery, right at the end, bang on the Gulf. That way everyone would get rich, the world would keep turning, and Iran would lose its fanatical desires to close it all down. *Goddammit!*'

The final word offered the clue to the scope of his abilities. Bob did not come up with solutions. He was not a creative thinker. He was an oil-industry computer with a giant database of knowledge, honed after a lifetime in the world's oilfields. He was a man who ought to be listened to, but there were two reasons why he was never going to be President of ARCO: one, he might not find the decisiveness to move forward in a crisis; two, he did not look like a natural candidate for long life.

0950, January 17, 2006.
Bob Trueman and his colleagues were ensconced happily in the big Concorde lounge in Heathrow's Terminal Four. All six men were sipping coffee, and the team leader had helped himself to a couple of Danish pastries. Steve had made an unusual request. Lunch was to be served two hours into the three-hour flight.

However, he wondered of Julie, the Concorde flight attendant, if shortly after takeoff the chief US oil negotiator could have a couple of cheeseburgers. Steve thought he might have to explain the mysteries of his boss's weight-maintenance program, but Julie smiled sweetly and immediately replied, 'Of course, sir. I'm quite certain we can manage that.'

Meanwhile Captain Brian Lambert, in company with Senior Flight Engineer Henry Pryor and First Officer Joe Brody, was in the cockpit, running through the long prestart checklist which accompanies the still superb achievement of flying a 200-foot delta-winged aircraft at a speed of Mach 2, twice the speed of sound, right out on the edge of space with 100 people on board being variously served filet mignon, roast grouse and salmon.

Pryor had already walked around the aircraft for almost an hour making his standard visual external check. Now he sat in his seat in the cockpit running through all the preflight tests and checks in strict accordance with the minutely ordered written procedures. No details were skimped, no minutia was so small it could be ignored. Before takeoff Henry always operated by the well tried book.

The two pilots had studied the flight plan and the en route chart, and, with 50 minutes to go, the flight engineer handed over his documents to the captain, who signed the log and formally accepted control of the aircraft. Now both pilots had a copy of the flight log clipped to the front of their boards. They were concerned at this moment with waypoints, altitudes and radio frequencies.

Flying Concorde is like flying no other aircraft. Everyone is always busy, such are the terrific speed and height. The supersonic empress of the North Atlantic is a demanding mistress, and the degree of care required to bring her safely home remains the leading edge of crew diligence and perception. Her altitude is governed by barometric pressure rather than actual feet above the ocean, and, as she burns fuel at a terrific rate, becoming lighter in weight, she constantly rises and then corrects, maybe through 500 feet over a couple of minutes.

Right now Captain Lambert was feeding the 'waypoints' into the computerized inertial navigation system. These were the milestones they would call out to air-traffic control all the way over the Atlantic, every ten degrees of longitude – or 450 miles. They would check in with Shannon/Prestwick (SHANWICK) oceanic control about 30 minutes after takeoff, then make another call at 4°W, at the acceleration point above the Bristol Channel. This would confirm Concorde's route, which is not the same as that taken by the other big commercial jets heading west across the Atlantic.

Concorde flies alone for several reasons, the first being that all populations in all countries must be protected from her big sonic double-boom as she races through the sound barrier. Accordingly, her course takes her straight down the middle of the Bristol Channel toward southern Ireland, where she begins to wind up her speed to supersonic. Then she streaks southwest, climbing to her cruising altitude of approximately 54,000 feet – more than four miles higher than other jet aircraft – throwing her boom behind her across the ocean.

Out over the Atlantic she leaves the coastline of County Cork 45 miles to starboard, sticking to a course far south of other airliners. Concorde flies over no land between Somerset, in the West of England, and the immediate precincts of John F. Kennedy Airport, Long Island, east of New York City. The 3500-mile journey is accomplished in three hours. At supersonic cruise speed she makes 1330mph, covering a mile every 2.7 seconds, 22 miles every minute. She drops a little time climbing out over southern England, where her speed is strictly restricted to just under Mach 1 but still makes her more like a guided missile than an airliner.

Flying her today was 44-year-old Brian Lambert's second choice. His first would have been to watch his son Billy play rugby, captaining from the front row of the scrum for his prep school's first XV. They were up against the tigerish lineup of Elstree School in Berkshire, who traditionally won the game by about 20 points but were perceived as vulnerable in the new season of 2006. Still, his wife Jane would be going, and Brian would be thinking of them both at 1430 when Billy would lead the team out for the first time. The Concorde pilot would be in New York by then.

Bearing in mind that this was January, it was a good day for rugby: cloudy, not too cold, with a softish pitch thanks to three days of almost nonstop rain. Driving from Surrey to Heathrow on still wet roads, Brian had already noted the westerly wind and layered banks of cloud, assembling in his mind a picture of the kind of weather he would encounter as he flew the takeoff. He wondered which particular aircraft it would be today. Not, he hoped, the one which had developed a shaky gauge in number three fuel tank last week.

Now, with 45 minutes still to go before the 1100 departure time, he was familiarizing himself with his two-man crew. Henry Pryor he knew – they'd flown together in December – but Joe Brody, the First Officer, from West London, was a mere acquaintance. It was standard British Airways procedure to select random crews, mainly to avoid the obvious problems of overconfidence, slackness and bad habits which occasionally evolve among men who work together all the time. Thus the standard procedure is that the three personnel assemble as a flight crew for the first time a couple of hours before departure in the operations office, where they go over the flight plan and study the detailed weather information provided in a folder by the airport meteorological office. Every possible contingency is provided for here: temperatures, pressure systems, winds, potential areas of turbulence, possible icing areas – all laid out in a coded format, incomprehensible to a layman.

In the cockpit, preparing to leave, the planning schedules concentrated the minds of each of the three crew. The fuel tonnage, which insures they would have sufficient to land in the event of an engine failure, is critical. Because Concorde cannot fly at Mach 2 on only three of her Rolls Royce engines, neither can she remain at her great height under such circumstances. And, when she slides down to a lower altitude, her fuel efficiency is cut by about 25 percent, which may force her to land in the Azores, or Gander in Newfoundland, or Halifax in Nova Scotia. Henry Pryor was watching with a beady eye the steady filling of those tanks, each with a 95-ton capacity.

The trim of the aircraft is also a vital part of the preparation, because the center of gravity must be spot-on right. As Concorde carries a grand total of 185 tons, getting this correct is more complicated than on any other aircraft because of fuel being constantly transferred from one tank to the other during flight and the consequent redistribution of the tonnage. Most of the passengers are sitting in front of the center of gravity – indeed, the pilot works 38 feet in front of the nosewheel and 97 feet in front of the main wheels. The loading officers, in collaboration with the crews, often make keen judgment calls, but they miss nothing – and the 384-pound bulk of Bob Trueman had been taken into account along with everything else.

They called the flight shortly after 1015, and the passengers were all on board by the time the fueling was complete at 1028. The computerized loadsheet showing the final weight and balance of the aircraft was checked carefully by Brian Lambert, who signed it. The ramp coordinator reported formally to the cockpit, and then left, securing Concorde's door behind him.

Lambert and Brody set the white markers to the takeoff speed and pitch angles of the nosecone for the climb-out.

'Start clearance,' said Lambert.

Joe Brody contacted air-traffic control, requesting permission to start the engines. 'London Ground. Speedbird Concorde 001 on stand Juliet Three for start-up.'

'Speedbird Concorde 001, clear to start. Call on 131.2 for pushback.'

Henry Pryor made two further entries on his checklist. Then he started Concorde's number three engine.

171054(GMT)JAN06. 19.76N 32.03W. HMS Unseen *in the North Atlantic. Speed 5. Periscope depth. Course one-eight-zero.*
Linked now to the commercial satellite international communications system MARISAT, the ex-Royal Navy diesel–electric ran silently. The special submarine antenna had worked perfectly when they had accessed just before first light this morning. The message from Bandar Abbas Navy HQ had been succinct: *'King Birds on board Supersonic Flight 001, ETD London Heathrow Gate 1045 (GMT), scheduled 30W 51N app. 1219(GMT).'* Commander Adnam, standing in the control center with his navigator, had raised his eyebrows and murmured: 'Hmm. An interesting first test. The highest and the fastest.'

Now, four hours later, he checked for surface ships, found none, and ordered *Unseen* to remain at periscope depth in readiness to receive the next satellite communication. He also ordered the ESM mast raised; he listened to the hiss of the hydraulic rams as the big radar interceptor mast slid upwards, then checked the immediate horizon through the search periscope.

★

Flight Engineer Pryor now had all four engines running. Concorde's nose and visor were set in the five-degree position for the taxi to the runway, during which time 30 more checks would be undertaken by the flight crew. This morning Concorde would take off from runway 27R, heading 274° magnetic. The final checks completed, the big plane taxied into her holding position to await her turn to leave. The cabin staff were strapped in; the flight engineer had moved his seat forward and was looking over the pilot's shoulder, his left hand on the back of the captain's seat.

The word came over the intercom at exactly 1100. 'Speedbird Concorde 001 cleared for takeoff.'

'001 rolling.'

Brian Lambert opened the throttles. The afterburners kicked in, increasing the acceleration.

'Airspeed building.'

'One hundred knots.'

'Power checked.'

'V1, Captain.'

'V1' meant 165 knots, the point of no return. Any faster and the aircraft could no longer stop in time to abort the takeoff. Now she was hurtling forward, building to her ground-leaving speed of 250 knots.

'Three, two, one, noise . . . Cut the afterburners.'

Brian Lambert, husband of Jane and father of 13-year-old Billy, gunned Flight 001 westward, the airplane shrieking into the skies above London's premier airport, climbing quicker and steeper than any of her bigger, heavier Boeing counterparts.

Concorde was watched, as always, by a breathless crowd of onlookers in the Terminal Four departure lounges. But she was watched also by the naval attaché from the Iranian Embassy, who stood silently behind the glass staring west, speaking crisply into his mobile phone.

'Concorde takes off 1100,' he said softly.

171104(GMT)JAN06. HMS Unseen *at periscope depth. Speed 5. Course zero-two-eight.*

Commander Adnam held in his hand the printout of the brief satellite message, direct from the Iranian Embassy link: *'Flight 001 chocks away 1045, probable takeoff 1100.'*

One hour and ten minutes from now, he thought, Concorde will be a couple of hundred miles out. It was not a particularly clear day – visibility was only about three miles – but his radar would take care of that, and so far the sonar sweep had found no noises to suggest any ships within a 12-mile radius. The seas around the submarine were clear. No one about – perfect conditions in which to commit the ultimate sea–air atrocity of the 21st century.

His team was highly trained. When he gave the word to the radar operator to begin the tracking, his men would slip into well oiled routines they had practiced a thousand times. He felt relaxed and unemotional, as he always did when the pressure went on. And right now the Iraqi-born CO was in his rightful element, commanding a top-class submarine with two miles of water beneath the keel, out here just west of the Mid-Atlantic Ridge, watching and waiting, intending as usual to outwit his enemies in the most holy name of Allah.

171104(GMT)JAN06. Concorde. West of Reading.
Brian Lambert had Concorde at almost 400 knots and, with the nose now raised, they were climbing at about 3000 feet a minute. Joe Brody had received clearance for 28,000 feet, and the captain had turned off the seatbelt sign. The weather up ahead looked gloomy but settled. In any event, Concorde would be racing four miles above the nearest clouds once she reached her cruising altitude.

Still traveling at Mach 0.95, fractionally less than the speed of sound, the supersonic British Airways flagship thundered across western England. At 1124, high above the Bristol Channel, just before longitude 4°W, her oceanic clearance came through: *'Climb when you're ready. Cruise between 50,000 and 60,000 feet on track Sierra November.'*

Flight Engineer Pryor began the rearward transfer of the fuel in preparation for supersonic flight, and Brian Lambert pushed the throttles hard forward on full power. The afterburners were fired up two at a time as Concorde streaked through the sound barrier, smoothly accelerating to Mach 1.3.

Many passengers felt the two gentle nudges as the afterburners were ignited, and still others paused from scanning the morning papers to listen as the sounds of the big engines changed slightly in tone. Bob Trueman wondered if he might hear the sizzle of his two cheeseburgers deep in the galley. He cared about sudden loss of weight much more seriously than sudden loss of altitude.

He and his team occupied a block of seven seats close to the front of the cabin – two doubles on either side of the aisle, row four, one aisle single right behind in row five, and on the other side another double for Bob and his briefcases, row five C and D. Immediately in front of them was the unmistakable figure of the 1970s British pop icon Phil Charles, who was still recording at the age of 55 and had a reputed net worth of $300 million. The small, balding, unshaven figure sat unobtrusively with his pony-tailed manager. Both men wore T-shirts and leather jackets. Steve Dimauro had recognized the star immediately and nodded a greeting, which was returned with a grin. 'Sonofabitch can still sing,' he muttered as he took his seat on the aisle opposite the chief.

Way back in the aft section of the cabin was another pop singer, also British, the piano-playing rock star Shane Temple. He and Phil Charles wore nearly identical clothes, and they sang a lot of the same music. The difference was in the bank balance. Whereas Phil had never stopped being successful, deftly changing his style with the moment while retaining his individual sound, Shane had floundered in the 1980s, and even more in the 1990s, being reduced to working on the northern circuit of nightclubs – Skid Row to a pop icon. His career had begun again with a sensational rock-opera revival in the opening months of the new millennium. But times had been hard for a long time before that, and Temple was still a few hundred thousand pounds light of his next castle.

The Concorde trip was a big event for him; a major recording session in New York might see him right back on top this year, and so he had spent at least ten minutes cooperating with the airport press corps. Nonetheless, as they boarded the flight, his long-time manager Ray Duffield had groaned when he saw Phil Charles slumped in his seat reading the sports pages of the *Daily Mail*. 'Son,' he had growled to Temple, 'I've got bad news. If this fucking thing crashes, you're not gonna be the one getting the ink.'

Concorde reached 50,000 feet at longitude 10°W. This is the north–south meridian which cuts through the westerly isles of Connaught, bisects the Dingle Peninsula in County Kerry and runs to the east of Mizen Head. Brian Lambert's plane crossed it at 1136.30secs flying at Mach 2 at latitude 50.49°N. First Officer Brody reported their waypoint to Shannon, and the air-traffic control center made a note to expect Concorde to come in again 450 miles later, at 1157 at the 20°W waypoint.

The air routes were, as always, busy at this time of the day, and to the north of Concorde's flight path there were no fewer than six westbound air tracks in operation, with big passenger jets running through them 100 miles apart but flying in eight layers of aircraft 'stacked' at different altitudes. Only Flight 001 made her journey in solitary splendor, moving nearly three times faster than any of the others.

Bob's burgers arrived at approximately the same time as First Officer Joe Brody checked in to Shannon from waypoint 20°W, at 1157 (GMT) precisely. Out of range now for VHF, he used the High Frequency radio, confirming that the next communication would be their last before handing over to oceanic control Gander, Newfoundland, when they were 1350 miles out from Heathrow and approaching the midpoint of the oceanic crossing.

Shannon 'rogered that' and signed off. Henry Pryor checked the fuel tanks of Speedbird Concorde 001, and the First Officer confirmed the precise distance to waypoint 20°W – just a little more than 450 miles now, since they were running slightly south, and the lines of longitude were edging fractionally further apart.

171210(GMT)JAN06. 49.00N 30.00W. HMS Unseen *at periscope depth. Speed five.*
Commander Adnam's radar was searching the skies to the east, the operator paying particular attention for long-range air detections. 'Just keep looking,' said the CO. 'Anything at over 1000 knots, that's the target.'

The first detection found Concorde 210 miles out, at 1210.33secs.

'New target, sir. Moving very fast.'

'Must be an aircraft.'

'Fits Concorde's route plan, sir.'

'SURFACE. BLOW ALL MAIN BALLAST. I want a good blow – maximum buoyancy right away. Officer of the Watch, keep her headed into the swell. Avoid surface rolling as much as possible.'

The jet-black submarine erupted out of the icy depths of the winter Atlantic, water cascading off her casing. Deep inside the hull the Russian missile system's computer established the critical data for a surface-to-air missile attack.

'Speed 1300 knots plus, sir.'

'Approximate course two-six-zero.'

'Range now 188 miles.'

'OK, team,' said Ben Adnam calmly. 'Check the surface picture visual. No hurry, chaps. What do you have? Fine. Just those three civil airliners eighty miles to the north. No problem. Let's just relax and do it right.'

By 1213 all the known data, the radar range and bearing, had been fed into the computer. And now they had refined the target. Adnam had an accurate course, speed and closest point of approach. The range was now 153 miles. The closest point of approach (CPA) would be four miles. Every 5.2 seconds *Unseen's* radar completed a sweep, and each sweep informed them that Flight 001 was two miles closer.

'Officer of the Watch, sir. Submarine at full buoyancy now.'

'I have an adequate firing solution within the parameters, sir.'

'We have set the pressure height: 54,000 feet. CPA remains four miles.'

'Computer estimates time of launch 1216.'

1214: 'Target holding course and speed, sir. CPA same. Predicted time to enter the missile envelope 1218.12secs.'

1215: 'Computer in final pre-firing sequence, captain! Countdown now 60 seconds.'

Commander Adnam betrayed nothing. He stood motionless in the control center, awaiting the information which would confirm he had not crossed the Iranian border from Iraq in vain.

At 1216 it came. *'Missile launch!'*

And up on the casing, in the huge box situated right behind the fin, there was a searing burst of fire and fury as the Russian-built SA-N-6 Grumble Rif guided missile blasted into the empty skies above the ocean, making a course straight up through the thick gray cloud to 54,000 feet. The ten-and-a-half-mile journey took it a shade less than 30 seconds.

Once there – guided, like Concorde, by its pressure-height barometer – it leveled out and its preprogrammed computer brain changed its course, sending the fiery weapon four miles across the no-man's-land of the upper stratosphere right to the CPA of Flight 001 out of Heathrow. Again the Russian rocket swerved, making a final course change so that it was now aiming east-northeast.

The radar beam which lanced out of the head of the missile made a long, unseen cone shape in the sky, and it was straight into this that Concorde was heading. At this stage, barring a spectacular malfunction, Ben Adnam's killer Russian SAM could not miss.

In Concorde's cockpit First Officer Brody checked in to Shannon, again reporting his position on the primary band of the HF radio. They were now approaching the 30°W waypoint, and Joe Brody made his radio switch, changing to the secondary band to make contact with the air-traffic controllers at Gander. '*Good morning. Speedbird Concorde 001, flight level five-four-zero en route to New York. Mach 2. Three-zero west five-zero north at 1219 GMT. ETA Forty West 1241(GMT). Over.*'

'Roger that, Speedbird 001. We'll be waiting 1241. Over.'

On board HMS *Unseen*, tension in the radar room was beginning to mount.

'Missile on height through CPA, heading out to target. It's looking good.'

The words of the radar operator hung in the air as the SA-N-6 streaked along course zero-eight-zero, down which Brian Lambert's oncoming aircraft was a mere 78 miles away. Concorde and the Grumble Rif were closing at a colossal speed of more than Mach 4, 3000mph, a mile every 1.2 seconds.

1217: 'Holding missile and target firmly on radar, Captain. If the bird's on the right height, it's looking good.'

Commander Adnam moved into the radar room, gazing at the screen over his number two operator's shoulder. His fist clenched on the back of the chair as Concorde entered the firing envelope at 1218.12secs.

At 1218.18secs the operator called: 'Target and missile returns merged, sir.'

At 1218.20secs, Brian Lambert saw it, a bright glinting in the sunlight, with fire rampaging in its wake. He opened his mouth to speak, but had time to utter only the sound 'Miss . . .' before Adnam's radar-programmed warhead smashed into the underside of Concorde's nose, blowing off the entire front end of the aircraft and leaving the fuselage to rip back from the structural frame like a peeling banana.

The total disintegration of the aircraft was over in a split second. Death came instantly to the one hundred passengers and crew as they blew into the silence of near-space, their bodies exploding as suddenly the 15 pounds per square inch of external pressure that normally accompanies human life disappeared. The gigantic detonation of the fuel stored in the aircraft's wings blew even the wreckage to smithereens.

Bob Trueman died with a cheeseburger in his hand.

171219(GMT)JAN06. The radar room, HMS Unseen.
'No contacts on radar bearing, Captain. Just three civil aircraft to the north.'

Commander Adnam turned away from the screen and walked back to the control center. Once there he ordered the submarine dived. 'Open main vents. Slow ahead. Ten degrees bow down, 17 meters.' As HMS *Unseen* disappeared beneath the surface again he ordered, 'When you've checked the trim, go to 100 meters. We'll clear the datum to the southward at nine knots. Thank you, gentlemen. Thank you very much.'

The world's first disaster involving a supersonic aircraft had taken place. But at that stage, as the burned-out pieces of wreckage tumbled in an eerie silence down over a wide area of the wind-swept North Atlantic, no one apart from the perpetrators knew anything. And it would be a while before they did.

It would not take so long as it had taken last spring for the great naval brains to work out that HMS *Unseen* had vanished, but it would be another 20 minutes before an unnatural silence in one small corner of the great aircraft-control room at Gander would alert the world to the shocking truth that the unthinkable had indeed happened.

'*Last known position 50.30N 30.00W . . . British Airways Concorde Flight zero-zero-one.*'

There were few ships in the area on this freezing January day, but two Japanese trawlers began to head south out of the Labrador Basin toward the position in which Concorde might have come down. It was a forlorn hope, because survival was unlikely, to say the least. There's no question of slowing down to a reasonable landing speed on the water when your cruising speed has been 1330mph.

In the Canadian Naval Base in Nova Scotia the Commander Maritime Forces Atlantic, Rear-Admiral George Durrell, ordered two of his 4800-ton guided-missile frigates, the Halifax-Class *Ottawa* and *Charlottetown*, to make all speed to longitude 30°W on the 50th parallel. Each warship carried a Sea King helicopter. For good measure Durrell also sent in his massive 14,500-ton Heavy Gulf Icebreaker *Louis S. St Laurent*, turning it east-north-east from 500 miles off the coast of Newfoundland. With a crew of 59 plus 38 scientists, this ice-busting giant had been the first ship ever to reach the North Pole. Its three-shafted props could drive it through a big sea at 18 knots. The chances were the *Louis S.*, carrying two helicopters, would arrive at 30°W before the frigates. But, even so, it would take the icebreaker a day and a half to get there.

Admiral Durrell's aircraft would be quicker. By 0830 two Lockheed CP-140 Auroras were up and out of Greenwood, Nova Scotia, making 400 knots toward the Concorde crash area. They were scheduled to arrive by 1230.

In London, news of the lost supersonic jet broke before the end of the BBC's 1pm bulletin. The bald information was imparted in tones of pure disbelief by the newscaster, who also announced that the BBC2 television channel would follow the story day and night for the next 24 hours, all other programming being canceled. Not since the death of Diana, Princess of Wales, more than eight years earlier had the BBC been moved to give such extensive coverage to a single news item.

The trouble was, of course, that there was almost nothing to report. The great airliner had merely vanished: there one moment, gone the next. In the aftermath of its demise there was, so far, not one shred of wreckage, not one suggestion as to the whereabouts of the black box flight recorder, not a word for the viewers from anyone except Bart Hamm in Gander, who was quite prepared to confirm that he had heard precisely nothing.

Television, radio and newspaper reporters possessed three facts: one, Concorde had reported its height, speed and position at 30°W; two, it had failed to report in at its next waypoint, 40°W; three, there was a passenger list, and it was publicly available.

Ray Duffield had been right. His man Shane Temple drew

133

almost a blank. Phil Charles got the ink. The London tabloids unanimously led their front pages with variations on the same headline: 'PHIL CHARLES DEAD IN CONCORDE MYSTERY CRASH' or 'CONCORDE CRASH KILLS PHIL CHARLES.'

British Airways announced late in the afternoon that Flight 001 had been commanded by Captain Brian Lambert, 'one of the most senior and respected pilots on the North Atlantic route.' His co-pilot had been First Officer Joe Brody, 'an ex-Royal Air Force fighter pilot who had been with BA for 12 years.' Flight Engineer Henry Pryor was, according to the BA press release, 'shortly to have been promoted to the most senior engineering position in the entire Concorde fleet.'

Jane Lambert, who heard of the catastrophe during the half-time of Billy's rugby match against Elstree, was taken to the headmaster's study where she reacted with immense bravery. 'I've been Brian's wife for 18 years,' she said. 'I've always been prepared for something like this . . . every time he's left the house.' They didn't tell the boy until the game was over.

In Washington the loss of the government's oil negotiating team, including four congressmen, was a major story. The evening television newscasts, which had much more time to prepare than their British counterparts, were concentrating on a report from a Northwestern Airlines pilot whose plane had crossed 30°W around the same time as Concorde, some 80 miles to the north. 'I thought,' said Captain Mike Harvold, 'I saw a small fireflash in the sky south of my aircraft. I'd say just about on my ten o'clock. I was heading two-six-zero at the time for the coast of New-foundland.'

Questioned further, he confirmed he could not make out the shape of any aircraft so far away. 'I guessed it might be Concorde, but I couldn't be sure, and I just made my report of a possible explosion in an unknown aircraft. But there's nothing else up that high, so I guessed it had to be Concorde. Looked to me like it just blew right out of the sky. I suppose you couldn't discount the possibility of a bomb, but the security surrounding that thing is unbelievable. In the trade, a bomb in Concorde is regarded as just about impossible.'

By the late evening the 'experts' were in, expounding their opinions to a shocked audience. The possibility of a bomb was chewed over in much detail, but not with the same degree of seriousness as with other airline disasters. Concorde was too well managed, too small and carried too few passengers; its security was legendary for being as near to watertight as any security can ever be.

'Experts' who had never traveled on Flight 001 pronounced that they thought it was possible to plant an explosive device on board. 'Experts' who had actually flown supersonic thought the opposite. Some suggested Concorde might have blown up because of a fuel leak. One 'expert' even mentioned the possibility of a missile strike, assuming at this stage it could have come from a surface ship.

But checks were made over the next 48 hours and it became clear that, in the vast wastes of the North Atlantic 10 miles below Concorde's flight path, in waters so lonely the nearest land is over 1600 miles away in any direction, there was simply no platform for such an attack to be launched. No land, of course. No warship. Not even a decent-sized merchant ship. No one could have loosed off an accurate radar-guided missile at the supersonic passenger jet because no one had a place to put the launcher. In any event, even if there *had* been a launching pad, hitting an aircraft traveling that fast and that high was way beyond the capacities of 90 percent of the world's guided missiles. The possibility seemed so utterly unlikely that it played no part in any of the discussions at the highest levels – not in the Pentagon, and not even in the White House by the zealously suspicious Admiral Arnold Morgan, although he was heard to mutter cynically to Kathy O'Brien that evening, 'Goddamned Brits are getting a little careless, hmm? First a three-hundred-million-dollar submarine which is never seen again and now a supersonic aircraft. That's not like them. Not like them at all . . .'

By midday on the morning of January 18 it was decided that since the accident had been to a British Airways aircraft, built in Great Britain and flown by British pilots, the entire thing had little to do with the United States – at least, not in formal terms. Certainly the Federal Aviation Authority was more than interested in how the world's most famous aircraft had come to hit the Atlantic en route to New York, but the actual investigation into the causes of the destruction of Concorde would be undertaken by the Air Accident Investigation Branch of the Department of

Transport in London. The crash had in any event occurred slightly nearer to Britain than to the shores of either America or Canada.

Two Royal Navy warships were already on their way out to the seas which roll over 30°W around the 50th parallel, where at first light that morning Canadian Navy surveillance planes had spotted wreckage in the water. The big icebreaker was still 12 hours away from the spot, and the frigates were even further. So the searchers would just have to hope the lighter material would keep floating. The planes had seen no sign of any bodies.

The loss of Concorde very quickly became one of the great mysteries of modern times. British Aerospace and Rolls Royce engineers dismissed out of hand the possibility of the fuel leaking and igniting. The security dragnet which surrounds all Concorde flights similarly discounted as absurd any possibility of having planted a bomb on board.

Indeed, there had been only two comparable air disasters in recent years. The first was US Air's Flight 427 from Chicago to Pittsburgh in 1994: the Boeing 737 plunged 6000 feet and nose-dived into a ravine at 300mph, killing all of the 132 passengers and crew. The black box explained nothing, and no one had ever offered a satisfactory reason for the crash. The second was TWA's Flight 800, an aging Boeing 747 which burst into flames and plunged into Long Island Sound off East Moriches in July 1996. To this day there were those who swore the aircraft was hit by a guided missile – particularly three commercial airline pilots who reported seeing at least one missile in the air while flying over the same New York airspace where Flight 800 exploded. The pilots, from Northwest, Delta and US Airways, were all headed westward over the city toward Philadelphia, and they reported their missile sightings separately. The US Navy replied that they might have sighted two D5 Trident missiles being fired at the time from a submarine, USS *West Virginia*, off Florida, the night being very clear. However, those missiles were being launched toward the Azores, and the launch-platform was close to 2000 miles away; it was not terribly likely that all three of the commercial pilots could have made such a colossal error of distance judgment, especially since, anyway, they were all flying in the wrong direction to have seen the Trident missiles. Pierre Salinger, once press secretary to President John F. Kennedy, was convinced the US Navy shot had down Flight 800 by accident with a missile which somehow 'got away'; he went so far as to call a press conference in Paris four months after the crash to present his findings, but none of it ever came to anything.

The only truth was that no one had ever explained conclusively what happened to put US Air's 437 at the bottom of the ravine nor TWA's 800 on the bottom of Long Island Sound.

By the afternoon of January 19, Concorde 001 had joined that select pair of great modern aviation mysteries. No one was able to offer one single clue as to what had brought down the Mach-2 thunderbolt which had flown alone on the frontiers of space.

What everyone required were Concorde's two black boxes – the CVR (Cockpit Voice Recorder) and the DFDR (Digital Flight Data Recorder). But the aircraft had gone down in such diabolically deep water – possibly almost three miles deep and right on the far northwestern edge of the Mid-Atlantic Ridge – it might prove impossible to retrieve anything from the bottom.

The British would no doubt bring to bear the most modern sonar systems and diving machines, and the Americans would no doubt find a way to assist. But for their efforts to be successful they would have to surpass the finest feat of recovery ever, so far as black boxes were concerned. That took place in February 1996 when a Turkish-based Boeing 757 from the Dominican Republic plunged into the Caribbean, killing all 189 people on board. On that occasion four or five nations jointly financed a contract for the US Navy to dive to more than 7000 feet. On the first day the divers discovered that the black boxes were still emitting signals from their underwater locator beacons, which led the men immediately to them.

To this day airline investigators discussed the operation with awe, but one had to remember that it had been carried out in warm water, in bright conditions – a far, far cry from the black depths of the rough, storm-tossed North Atlantic in January. Even if Concorde's black boxes were still emitting signals, it would be from an ocean floor more than twice as deep as the one in the Caribbean.

The media's big problem in covering the news story soon became apparent: there was no one to blame. Certainly not the pilot or his crew, who (a) were dead and (b) had been flying Concorde for years. Certainly not the Shannon Air-Traffic Control operators, who had already said goodbye to Flight 001.

And certainly not those at Air-Traffic Control, Gander, who were 1600 miles away at the time, and reported no unusual weather conditions for any flight all day, particularly conditions that might affect a plane flying four miles above the weather, where the wind rarely exceeds 40 knots.

The tough, hard-eyed security chief on duty in the Concorde area at Heathrow made a bomb inquiry from a reporter from London's Channel Four Television look ridiculous. He gruffly informed her that, if she cared to put an unauthorized suitcase anywhere near Speedbird One's loading bay, she would probably be torn to pieces by guard dogs; failing that, she would be shot on sight.

He was only half-joking.

201100JAN06. 43.00N. 38.25W. Speed 5. Depth 100 meters. Course one-two-zero.
HMS *Unseen* was running silently and deep. Her Commanding Officer was sipping Turkish coffee in the control center as he sat in conference with his Navigation Officer, Lt-Commander Arash Rajavi.

'I think we were correct, Arash. It was wise to clear the datum and make nine knots away from the firing area for a day. Now I think we are also correct to continue at five knots. At this depth and speed we are completely safe from detection. But tonight we shall have to snorkel for a few hours – our batteries are getting low. I just don't want to come up before dark.'

'No, sir. I agree. The Americans are very vigilant around here. They have that big surveillance station at Halifax, as you know. That SOSUS could be very dangerous to us but, if we stay dead slow, they'll hear nothing, right?'

'That is correct, Arash. That said, though, we'll have to snorkel by 1800.'

'Then where, sir? Where do we go afterwards? What's our next mission going to be?'

'We'll stay on the westerly edge of the Mid-Atlantic Ridge for the next 12 days. Detection is nearly impossible here. That way we can be back in our old position on 30 degrees West at the 50th parallel in perfect time.'

'We're going to fire again, sir?'

'Yes, Arash. We're going to fire again.'

Day after day they cruised quietly, snorkeling for very short periods by night but always keeping the batteries well charged, just in case *Unseen* should need to get away from a pursuing American or British warship. It was impossible for Commander Adnam to know whether or not the military had yet been called in to assist with the investigation into the crash of Concorde, but certainly they would come in the end.

He sensed that he had, somewhere inside the US military, a very determined opponent – someone who, he had no doubt, would one day find out who was the maestro who had sunk a carrier and now downed a supersonic jet, both times using a submarine. Ben Adnam had no false modesty about his own cleverness, but he was equally sure there was at least one person, just as cunning and just as brilliant, operating on the Satan's side of the fence. It was this sort of assumption that kept him alive, he reckoned.

The submarine stayed silent in the deep water, occasionally monitoring the satellite transmissions for news or orders from Bandar Abbas. The Iranian crew waited patiently for the next instruction from their Iraqi captain. But for eight days he revealed nothing. They all understood that the next mission would be essentially the same as the first, but that was all. Then, on January 26, HMS *Unseen* received a terse signal: '*PR campaign launched.*' Adnam briefed his crew on what this meant.

Two mornings later, on January 28, a highly exclusive photograph appeared in the international Iranian daily newspaper *Kayhan*, which is the much harder-lined English-language edition, designed for an overseas readership, of the *Tehran Times*. The picture, in color, covered four columns at the top of page five. It showed two army trucks full of heavily armed Iraqi soldiers driving through the streets of the little marshland town of Qal'at Sālih, east of the Tigris, some 30 miles from the Iranian border. Behind one of the trucks was a trailer on which was some kind of a rounded cargo covered by a tarpaulin. The caption beneath it said: 'Iraqi Army personnel on the move near our frontier. Fears of major garrison being built at Qal'at Sālih.' The credit line beneath the picture read, '*Agence France Presse.*'

None of this was particularly interesting in itself. However, deep in the background of the photograph, slightly hidden behind the trucks, was what appeared to be a wall with some writing on it. In daubed Arabic lettering could be made out the slogan, 'DEATH TO THE OIL THIEVES.' Beneath the lettering was the unmistakable pterodactyl outline of Concorde coming in to land, nose angled down.

It really required a magnifying glass to figure out the exact message, but in Paris that morning there just happened to be someone with a magnifying glass – Ross Andrews, the CIA's chief field officer in France – who just happened to be now staring at the picture on page five of *Kayhan* with profound interest.

Andrews called Franc Gardu, the veteran picture editor at *Agence France*, and wondered if he could purchase a copy which might be clearer. Such requests from US Embassy staff officers were not unusual, and Gardu said he would call back when he had located the negative. But, unhappily, he could find no trace of the picture – not in the printing rooms, not in the wire room. Not wanting to call back the US Embassy and admit failure, he placed a call to the offices of the *Tehrān Times*, whose picture editor he had spoken to often before, especially during the various Middle Eastern conflicts of the past 30 years. Now he asked him: 'Are you certain you got that picture from us?'

'Of course I'm sure. It came in by wire yesterday morning. I just signed the credit to your account. It's a nice shot.'

'Does it have our stamp on it? Top left.'

'Wait, please. I'll check . . . Absolutely. It's right there.'

'You wouldn't be good enough to wire us back a copy, would you? I can't find the neg.'

'Sure – be happy to.'

With that Karim Meta wired a copy of a perfectly exquisite forgery to Paris – a forgery so beautifully worked that no one barring a military scientist would ever have been able to tell that the trucks and the soldiers and the trailer had been superimposed onto a photograph of a painted wall in a backstreet of south Tehrān.

That morning Franc Gardu received several other requests for the photograph, including one from the *Kuwait Times*. By the evening – midday in Washington – there were two wired copies of the picture on the desk of the CIA's Middle East chief, Jeff Austin, one direct from Paris and the other from the field officer in Kuwait.

Each was accompanied by a similar memorandum, remarking

how odd it was that a few remote people deep in the territory of the Marsh Arabs in southeastern Iraq had reason to be cheered by the loss of the American negotiating team which had died in Concorde. 'No secret about the deaths, every paper in the Middle East carried the story. Here in Kuwait City there was even an interview with Mohammed Al–Sabah about his friend Bob Trueman. Just seems a bit strange that way down there in the Marshes there should be people who're pleased the Americans died . . .'

Jeff Austin's mind buzzed. This was the second time he had seen the name Qal'at Sālih in the past six months. The first time had been back in the summer, when there had been a couple of mild alerts about Iraqi missile-testing in the Marshes, though nothing had ever come of it. And now there was this. Cheers from the Marsh Arabs about the Concorde disaster and the Americans who perished in it. Austin called Admiral Morgan in the White House on the secure line and recounted his thoughts. The National Security Advisor was very reflective.

'How'd we get the picture?' he asked.

'Apparently with some difficulty. Two of our guys spotted it in the Tehrān paper, and then had to negotiate with the French picture agency to buy it. I'm sending a copy over to you right away. You'll see, it's not that easy to read the graffiti right away, and anyway it's in Arabic. It's the drawing that grabs you – the drawing of the aircraft I thought both of our guys were pretty sharp to notice it – Ross Andrews in the Paris Embassy was first.'

'Uh-huh. Yup, Jeff, I'd like to see it. By the way, did we get any more confirmation on that missile-testing business we discussed before?'

'Not a word, sir. Not another word.'

'Qal'at Sālih. That's a goddamned funny place to be associated with world atrocities. Fucking Marsh Arabs splashing around with guided missiles hidden up their goddamned *galabiyyas* . . .'

CHAPTER SIX

February, 2006.

THE LOSS OF the 30-year-old Concorde, the sixth of the production models which had arrived on-stream between 1976 and 1980, occurred at a poignantly significant moment for the aircraft industry. At the time of the disaster Concorde's natural successor had been undergoing its final trials out on the West Coast of America. The Boeing Starstriker, as it was called, was in the opinion of its designers the last word in supersonic flight; it was twice the size of Concorde, had three times the passenger capacity, and was 350mph faster across the ocean. But, more significant than that, so far as its makers were concerned, was that it heralded the reclaiming of the high aviation ground by the United States after 35 years of European domination.

Those 35 years had never been easy for the American plane-makers to accept. Way back in the early 1960s, when President John F. Kennedy had been determined that the United States would lead the way in the production of supersonic passenger planes, Boeing had been at the very forefront of the design developments. The great swing-wing Boeing 2707–100, built to fly at Mach 2.5 with 300 passengers aboard, had seemed set to blow the Anglo-French Concorde right out of the game, just as the Boeing 707 had outcommercialized Vickers's beautiful, quiet VC10. 'But then had come the fashionable clamor for a cleaner, less noisy and less polluted world. America's East Coast liberals had waged a six-year campaign to have the supersonic transports killed off as 'too costly, too noisy, too threatening to the environment, totally unacceptable to anyone living anywhere near the airports of New York and Washington.'

With JFK gone, men like Senator William Proxmire rallied support against the US Government continuing to fund Boeing's 2707–100. There were Harvard scientists founding outfits like

Citizens' League Against The Sonic Boom. All over the country the hysteria grew ever stronger. The East Coast press printed every form of outlandish claim: that the great sound-barrier boom of the supersonic airplane would obliterate houses, destroy the American wilderness and wipe out entire species of life on this planet – birds, insects, domestic pets . . . possibly even liberals.

By the mid-1960s, it was clear that Concorde was ahead of the Boeing 2707–100 in its development. Nevertheless, most experts believed that, while the great SST from Seattle would come in late, it would have a more realistic economic base and take over the world's most expensive passenger flights without much trouble. Poor little Concorde would be stampeded aside in the rush.

However, the more pressing stampede was that of the abolitionists, and by the late 1960s the tide had turned. Pan-Am and TWA, the two US airlines which had offered supersonic transport such vociferous support, canceled their orders for Concorde. A shiver of apprehension was felt in Seattle.

And there was no help forthcoming from the military, which has traditionally stood behind major aircraft development. In the old days – back in the early 1950s – any new American SST program would have been for the development of some huge manned bomber for the Air Force, and money would have been made available from the Defense budget. But that game too was now changing drastically: big manned bombers were becoming obsolete in the new age of guided missiles.

Which left the Boeing Corporation in Seattle to fight a lone battle for its supersonic passenger jet – an aircraft totally impracticable without Government funding; an aerial wagon around which the Indians were already circling. On the night of May 17, 1971, Congress finally killed it, voting 49–47 to discontinue funding the project. The men from Seattle were devastated. Three years later they could only watch helplessly when a cheering crowd estimated at 250,000 surrounded Los Angeles Airport to witness the spectacular landing of Concorde prototype 002 as it came howling out of the skies, on its triumphant US Pacific Coast tour to sell the concept of supersonic flight.

There were many designers, engineers and test pilots at Boeing who never quite got over the political killing of the 2707–100, an aircraft equally as dramatic as Concorde and probably many times more financially efficient. One of them was a 28-year-old design engineer named John Mulcahy, an ex-Boston College football star with an engineering doctorate from the Massachusetts Institute of Technology.

Today, February 2, in the deep winter of the year 2006, the 63-year-old John Mulcahy, now President of the Boeing Corporation, sat at the head of the long table in the rarified corporate conference room and listened with unashamed satisfaction to the latest reports of the tests on Starstriker. This was indeed the aircraft to dominate the world in the field of high-speed business travel – trans-Atlantic, trans-Pacific, trans-*global*. Concorde had proved conclusively there was a market for executives who needed to move across the world in a big hurry and the hell with the expense. Now the giant Boeing SST was ready to put the corporation right back in the driving seat of world aviation. Where, John Mulcahy fervently believed, it had always belonged.

Certainly, in the years since Concorde had first taken flight, the Boeing Corporation had dominated the world of commercial aviation. Boeing 707s, 727s, 737s, 747s and the rest had been unrivaled in their volume, their safety and their efficiency. But Concorde, although nothing like so commercially successful and a financial failure on many routes, remained the glittering flagship of air travel. She was the capricious high-speed record holder of the airways, the passenger jet all the world loved to watch. She had always been to aviation what the Cowboys were to football, what the Yankees were to baseball, what Arnold Palmer was to golf, what the Princess of Wales was to fashion. Concorde was the supersonic jet everyone wanted to travel in, preferably in a window seat, sipping champagne trans-Atlantic style.

It made many Boeing execs consider the world a cruel and unfair place. They had designed an SST that was just as glamorous, even more spectacular-looking and considerably faster. Yet Government officials more than 3000 miles away – *American* Government officials – had destroyed her.

But now, Mulcahy thought with profound pleasure, things were going to be very different. Basing their work on those long-shelved plans and designs the Boeing people had re-created it all 35 years later. They had advanced the systems and, working in conjunction with Pratt and Whitney, refined the engines. From the old stillborn 2707–100 had sprung the 21st century's

2707–500, the Boeing Starstriker. Now the world's hotshot travelers would see what American excellence really stood for. And, in a sense, the men from Boeing would stand vindicated for all the millions of millions of dollars they had spent and all the thousands of man-hours they had expended back in the 1960s.

Starstriker represented living, growling proof that, where politicians might be quite happy to squander colossal amounts of money (which wasn't even theirs, anyway), America's heavy industry was not so inclined. Their knowledge and their research and development records had been meticulously stored over the years, then distilled, cultivated and improved. And the East Coast journalists who had gleefully added up the costs of the old 2707–100 and pronounced Boeing money-managers 'guilty of extravagence beyond words' throughout the first SST program – well, they could now go chew on their own long-dead, ill thought-out feature articles . . . in the unlikely event they would ever be able to comprehend the depth of their own misjudgments.

John Mulcahy beamed with good humor. He sat next to his chief engineer and long-time vice-president, Sam Boland, whom he had first met at MIT and subsequently lured from another major US plane-maker. To his left was the top test pilot in the United States, Bob 'Scanner' Richards, Boeing's near-mystical project manager, whose instinct for the smooth running of a revolutionary design venture was fabled throughout the industry. Scanner had just declared the titanium-bodied Starstriker, 'about as close to perfection as anyone's gonna get an SST in this lifetime.'

Mulcahy had also just listened to a speech by his public relations chief, Jay Herbert, who had described in barely controlled excitement the events which would unfold in Washington, right there in Dulles International Airport, on February 9 when Scanner Richards would take Starstriker on her maiden trans-Atlantic test flight in company with all of the top Boeing technicians who had worked on her for so long – there would be no passengers other than the high-tech aircrew and staff. The guest list for the celebrity breakfast and reception was as glamorous as anything seen in the nation's capital since the Reagan years.

Ten minutes earlier Jay had revealed that the President of the United States would be there at Dulles in company with his wife and his National Security Advisor, Admiral Arnold Morgan, plus the Secretary for Defense, Bob MacPherson. The Chairman of the

Joint Chiefs, Admiral Scott Dunsmore, had accepted his invitation, as had the heads of all three armed services, leading senators, congressmen, state governors, the titans of corporate America, media tycoons and Wall Street giants, plus a smattering of showbiz lightweights – actors and singers who would probably claim most of the headlines.

The upcoming maiden transoceanic flight of Starstriker had captured the attention of the press and television as few technological subjects normally do. Orders and inquiries from at least eight different airlines, four of them American, were already being dealt with by the marketing department. Mulcahy had known some great days as the man at the helm of the world's greatest aircraft production corporation, but February 9 promised to be his finest hour.

He was a tall craggy man, inclined to look a bit disheveled even in a brand-new expensive suit. His much younger wife, Betsy, fought a losing battle to make him look like the President of the Boeing Corporation, but she could never persuade him it was important to get his shoes shined. And no matter how many times she bought him a tie from Hermès he always managed to knot it badly – somehow too thin, and rarely hiding the top button of his shirt.

That said, there was an aura of power about the man. He stood 6ft 3in and his iron-gray hair was thick. If he laughed a lot, he also frowned a lot, and he ruled the corporation from a stern hands-on position. Only his true friends understood that behind this forbidding, somewhat severe exterior there lurked a wild Irishman, dying to break cover. No one who was there had ever forgotten John's 60th birthday party in a private room at the most expensive hotel in Seattle, when he'd stood on a table at 1am and insisted on singing a succession of traditional Irish revolutionary battle hymns. Upset a few local matrons, but Senator Kennedy had seemed wryly amused.

Mulcahy's great-grandparents had come from County Kildare in Ireland, and he treasured his roots in the old country. Each year he and Betsy flew to Shannon and drove up to the family village of Kilcullen to stay at the home of one of Ireland's major industrialists, Brendan Sheehan. On the way, they would stop and play golf for two or three days at Mount Juliet in County Kilkenny. In Kildare they played Michael Smurfit's magnificent golf course at the K-Club. One day John Mulcahy intended to bring Starstriker to Shannon, which housed, after all, a section of the oceanic control center which would soon be guiding the new supersonic aircraft safely across the eastern half of the Atlantic.

He found the very prospect of his great aircraft descending through the mists of the Shannon Estuary enthralling, its landing wheels reaching out for Irish soil a century and a half after the penniless Seamus and Maeve Mulcahy had fled the famine, survived the voyage to America, and set up home in Boston, where, three generations later, John had been born.

He was a true romantic, an Irishman of the blood, and his contract with Boeing stipulated in italicized letters that he was *never* to be required to attend the office on March 17 of any year, save for an outbreak of war, fire or mutiny. He did not miss many of the other working days, however, and he held the daily operations of the corporation in what some people believed was an iron grip. Boeing had never had a better president.

The meeting today found him in expansive mood. The Concorde disaster had of course played into their hands. While no one wanted to gloat on any airline's catastrophe, particularly if the airline were an important customer like British Airways, it was impossible to smother the thought that Concorde's calamity was, inevitably, Starstriker's good fortune.

Nonetheless, the specter of that splendid airliner coming apart at the seams way up in the stratosphere hung heavily over the table.

'What do you think happened to it, Scanner?' asked Mulcahy.

'I'm completely bewildered, to tell you the truth, John,' said the ex-USAF fighter pilot. 'I mean, what could have happened to it? There's nothing up there to hit, and nothing known to man that could have hit it. Except maybe a meteorite, or a chunk that fell off a satellite. But the odds against that have gotta be millions and millions to one.'

'Then what?' persisted the president.

'Well, we do have that other pilot's assertion, the guy from Northwestern, that he saw fire in the sky right where Concorde must have been. But I don't know about that . . . Guess we must be left with internal failure of some kind.'

'Yeah, but what kind of failure?'

'I can't imagine. Both British Aerospace and Rolls Royce say a fuel-leak fire is absolutely out of the question, so we have to forget that. And no one thinks it remotely possible a bomb could have been planted. Which really leaves not much, except an engine fire which somehow got to the fuel. But to me that doesn't really ring true. Without the fire observation from the other pilot, I'd be inclined to think in terms of metal fatigue or a structural failure at Mach 2. But I don't think either of those things would set the sonofabitch on fire. Beats the hell out of me, John.'

'And me. Just doesn't add up, does it?'

'Not in this life.'

'Anyway, gentlemen, we better get on. Now, when are we moving to Washington?'

'On schedule, John. The aircraft departs on the afternoon of February 7, subsonic from Seattle to Dulles, leaves at 1600, arrives in secret and in darkness 2220 local. She's being towed straight to a hangar, kept under wraps for the night, and serviced thoroughly the next day ready for the 0830 departure for London on the 9th.'

'OK. The rest of us leave here at 0800 on the 8th, arriving Washington 1630. Reception and dinner beginning 1900 at the Carlton. That's industry-only except for three senior senators.'

'Good. Kennedy coming?'

'Yup.'

'That's better yet. He's still the best we have. Knows more. Thinks more. Does more. Even though he's a Democrat. Plus he's funny as hell. Put him near me, willya?'

'How about John Kerry?'

'Yup. He's coming as well.'

'Excellent. Am I going to be speaking?

'Yes. First draft's ready tomorrow. I believe you're working on the departure speech yourself.'

'Yup. Don't want any help with that one.'

Friday, February 3, London.
Great Britain's Minister of Transport, Howard Eden, was under pressure. Every day he faced a barrage of criticism over the Concorde air disaster. The media were demanding answers, the opposition benches in the House were demanding answers, and now the Prime Minister was demanding answers.

'Jesus Christ,' he told his secretary in their besieged private offices in Westminster, 'you'd have thought I was *driving* the bloody thing.'

He had just returned from a bruising session of questions in the House during which there had been calls for his resignation. He had been publicly described as the Minister Without A Clue – a crib from a recent tabloid headline – and variously as 'incompetent,' 'uncaring,' 'witless' and 'Ti' – the latter, the Tory shadow minister had explained, was short for '*Titanic*,' which everyone knew had been a total bloody disaster.

Howard Eden was the latest in a long line of British Government ministers who seemed fine while the winds were fair but came unbuckled at the first sign of trouble. This was undoubtedly because the ruling parliamentary party too often appoints ministers to areas where their degree of knowledge and competence is near zero. In recent years they have made bankers and lawyers into Defence Ministers and appointed all kinds of political misfits into the other great offices of state.

Eden, in office now for only 18 months, still knew very little about modern air transportation, and he was little better on road and rail. His current job was regarded as merely a stepping stone to higher office. Which was why he was all at sea in his current predicament. And now he had to report to the Prime Minister who had made him transport minister in the first place to explain precisely why his department was being made to look absurd on a daily basis, right out there in front of the entire world.

He had no answers. Everyone knew that. The search for wreckage was going especially badly in mountainous North Atlantic seas almost three miles deep. The only glimmer of hope was that, on the tenth day of the operation out on 30°W, a Royal Navy sonar operator had thought he'd heard the locator beam of one of Concorde's black boxes. Whether or not they could ever get down there to retrieve it was highly debatable, but arrangements were being made for an unmanned diving submarine to give it a try.

The Prime Minister's concern was a sharp lessening of public confidence in air travel. Being an instinctive politician, he understood that the reason for this was the lack of an explanation as to the cause of the disaster. What he needed was someone who could step forward and say, 'Prime Minister, we are almost certainly dealing here with an instance of metal fatigue, and we are examining every aircraft in the fleet for any further signs of it. Concorde was lost due to a structural failure and we are making absolutely sure that such a failure can never, ever happen again.'

The public could come to terms with an identifiable problem which was now being fixed. They had proved that years ago when there had been a succession of accidents with the Comet airliners. But what the public could not cope with was uncertainty, especially when the government's own experts were plainly without clues. The British Airways Board was beside itself with worry. Three of its members would be in Washington five days from now to see the fanfare of publicity surrounding the departure of the big Boeing superstar which would, expensively, put their beloved Concorde out of the business of supersonic flight forever.

It would of course be churlish for the Prime Minister to sack Howard Eden for his current role in one of Britain's worst ever crashes – one which had killed four US congressmen. But it might look a whole lot better if Eden resigned of his own accord. There's nothing quite so good as a scapegoat to take the heat off everyone else.

However, in this instance the public outrage, fanned by the press, was so intense that it seemed nothing but a sacrifice could diminish the clamor for heads to roll. As if 115 lives lost on board Speedbird One were not sufficient.

Eden had no intention of going to Washington to attend the triumphalist ceremony staged by the American plane-makers. It was with a weary step that he headed downstairs toward the ministerial limousine that would take him to 10 Downing Street for possibly the last time.

Not far away, there was equal depression in the offices of the Air Accident Investigation Branch of the ministry. With every day that had passed the number of clues had lessened. There had been pieces of wreckage on the surface, but only from the cabin: all of Concorde's heavy-duty components – like the four engines, the tailplane and undercarriage – were on the bottom of the Atlantic. The wings seemed to have been blown into shards by exploding fuel, and the shards did not float. The Navy's searchers had found no sizable pieces whatsoever.

The other problem was the height. 'Normal' air disasters, taking place at the regular cruising altitude of above 30,000 feet, can scatter debris over an area four miles square. But in this case, given the altitude of ten miles and the terrific speed at which Concorde had been traveling, the wreckage seemed to have been scattered across a square of ten miles by ten miles. From the searchers' point of view, the task of combing a hundred square miles was made infinitely more difficult because no one actually knew for certain precisely where Concorde had been when she'd come apart.

Each day the department tried to assemble a report to demonstrate that some progress was being made. But it was almost impossible. Although they were assisted by the senior brains of British Airways and the British Aircraft Corporation, even by experts from the French Aerospatiale, there was nothing to piece together – not unless they could find a way to reclaim the critical parts from the bottom of the Atlantic. And no one seemed very optimistic about that, particularly since it would cost a king's ransom even to attempt it. No one had ever conducted a search for wreckage at anywhere near that depth. Not even the *Titanic* had rested in water *that* deep.

Friday, February 3, Office of the National Security Advisor, the White House.
Admiral Arnold Morgan was taking his 'break.' This was a 20-minute hiatus he tried to take each morning at about 1100 so that he could check through newspapers and magazines 'just to make sure no one's done anything absolutely fucking ridiculous.'

He was sitting at his big desk, perusing the national weeklies, chatting to Kathy O'Brien and sipping black coffee. 'This Concorde thing's like a timewarp,' he said. 'Remember last spring when the Brits were searching for that submarine? Well, they're still doing the same thing now – groping around the bottom of the goddamned ocean, and both times they're finding nothing significant.'

'I could remind you,' said Kathy, 'that despite your fears the submarine has never been seen again, and neither has it blown up another aircraft carrier. Most reasonable people believe it must be on the bottom, wherever that may be, a tomb for all the crew, whoever they may have been.'

'You could remind me of that,' replied Morgan. 'And you

could remind me that in your view I suffer from incurable paranoia, which I do.'

They both laughed. But Arnold Morgan became quickly serious once more. 'All through my career in the intelligence agency I tried to connect apparently disconnected facts. And a lot of the time I was very wide of the mark. But not always. And I got it right more often than anyone else, which is why, I guess, I'm sitting in this chair. And I'm now pondering three totally disconnected facts.

'One, that British submarine is *still* missing, and I, in company with a very few like-minded paranoids, think it might be out there plotting and planning a strike against the West. I think it is possible that Commander Adnam may be alive, and that, if he is, he's driving HMS *Unseen* . . . somewhere.

'Two, a brilliantly maintained aircraft, flying high enough to be completely out of harm's way, suddenly falls clean out of the sky for no discernible reason.

'Three, in the intelligence community there are deep suspicions that Iraq, possibly assisted by the Russians, is testing SAMs, surface-to-air missiles, down in the Southern Marshes – a strange and remote place where we know that by curious coincidence there was also some elation over the Concorde disaster.'

'Hold on one moment, Arnold. Are you trying to tell me we have this homicidal maniac, who's *stolen* a Royal Navy submarine, somewhere on the loose in a sub which can shoot down supersonic airliners at will? Isn't that a bit far-fetched?'

'Probably. At least, it would be if his name weren't Benjamin Adnam. But the most far-fetched part is *where Concorde vanished*.'

'How do you mean?'

'Kathy, over 94 percent of all air crashes take place on landing or takeoff. Just go over the disasters you remember: the one in the Florida swamp, the one in the Potomac, the one at the end of the runway in Boston, the one up the mountain near Tokyo, the TWA bird off Long Island, the one near Paris, the one that fell short of Birmingham airport in England . . . All near airports. Passenger aircraft hit mountains as they come in to land, they misjudge runways in bad weather, or they take off when something's not quite right – but they hardly ever blow up of their own accord, or fall apart when they're cruising through empty skies, because there's nothing else up there.'

'No, I suppose they don't . . .'

'Just think about it for a minute. Here we have this beautiful aircraft, powered by four Rolls Royce engines that the Brits check thoroughly about every two days. Its safety record is immaculate, and its pilots and flight engineers carry out five times more safety checks than any other aircraft requires. When that baby takes off, every working part is as close to flawless as the Brits can get it. The safety procedures are sensational – they even make sure they have sufficient fuel with them to be able to land on a single engine anywhere during their journey.

'And yet, halfway across the ocean, in light winds, flying clear at 54,000 feet, not a semblance of a problem, something happens that is so sudden, so utterly drastic that the sonofabitch just self-destructs, all on its own. Neither pilot apparently had time to yell to Gander Control on the radio so much as a "We're in trouble!" Not even "Holy Shit!" Nothing. Kathy, that aircraft was taken out at the speed of light, and even the terrorist community would have to reckon it'd be impossible to get through the BA security to plant a bomb. The Concorde team give a detailed security check to the baggage of *every goddamned passenger*. No, Kathy, even in the absence of the black box, I'm saying that something's going on.'

'Do you think someone fired a missile at it? Like they say happened to the TWA flight.'

'Kathy, I can't say that. There's nowhere in that part of the Atlantic from which to fire a missile.'

'How about if there had been . . . a nearby island, maybe. Or a cruising foreign warship? What would you say then?'

'I'd have been pretty goddamned suspicious that's what, Kathy. I'd have been drawn to the conclusion that someone had knocked Concorde right out of the sky.'

'Which leaves us where?'

'Nowhere, basically.'

'How about Adnam?'

'Well, no submarine, in *anyone's* navy, has ever possessed the capacity to fire a surface-to-air guided missile that high, that fast and that accurately – not even us. And Adnam is an Iraqi, working for a kinda technologically primitive regime. I suppose the Iraqis might have bought and tested a Russian missile which could have done the job. But it would have needed refining. And their submarine would have required major surgery as well – so far as we know they don't even *have* a submarine. They don't have any water deep enough to float it in. Hell, the Iraqis don't know how to *service* a submarine, never mind turn it into the most advanced underwater weapons system in the world.

'The trouble is, Kathy, if we accept there is even a possibility that Concorde was hit by a missile, we have to accept that that missile must have come from a vanishing submarine. Because there was nowhere else it could have come from. Barring outer space.'

Monday, February 6, Office of Admiral Joseph Mulligan, Chief of Naval Operations, the Pentagon, Washington.
'Arnold, as I live and breathe! To what do I owe the pleasure of this unexpected visit? Good to see you.'

'I just wanted to have a chat to one of the very few people operating in this neck of the woods who has an entirely sane mind.'

'You might have the wrong office. Three years in this place can really test your powers of logical thought.'

'Not yours, Joe. How 'bout some coffee? You might need it when you hear my latest theory.'

'Good call. Lemme order some. Then we'll talk.'

Five minutes later the two men settled into more comfortable chairs and began a discussion which might have sounded eccentric had it taken place between other naval officers. But not between this pair.

Admiral Morgan cited the two entirely separate circumstances which had seen 'the Brits groping around on the bottom of the ocean.' He outlined his view that the apparently deceased Commander Adnam might not be quite so dead as all that, and added that it was his opinion, shared by some very influential others, that the Iraqi commanding officer might right now be at the helm of the lost HMS *Unseen.*

He then cited two other circumstances which he considered to be absolute impossibilities. The first was that HMS *Unseen* had somehow been undiscovered by the Royal Navy even after an exhaustive ten-month search, assuming she had in fact sunk. 'Not possible, not even likely; she's out there somewhere. Stolen.'

Admiral Mulligan nodded gravely. And then he nodded some

more after Morgan explained that to him Concorde's disappearance was, if anything, even more mystifying than *Unseen's*. The question he wanted to run by the professional head of the US Navy was this: 'Do you think it's possible that the fucking Iraqis have somehow converted a submarine into an anti-aircraft guided-missile boat which knocked Concorde out of the sky, bang in the middle of the North Atlantic?'

Morgan waited for the big ex-Trident commanding officer to laugh. But Joe Mulligan did no such thing. He stood up and walked around the room, a deep frown on his face. And then he said: 'If it was any nation other than Iraq – they know zero about submarines – I'd have to say yes. But, Arnold, they don't even own one, and never have. They couldn't possibly produce a team capable of operating one. And certainly nor could they manage the modifications . . . Hmm. But have you considered the possibility that they might have had someone do it for them? This is just a simple missile system we're talking about. It's not brain surgery or anything.'

'Joe, I had, but I came up with no answers.'

'Well, let's think of it now. But, just before we do, let me run this by you. Anti-aircraft missiles on a submarine are not entirely unknown, although there's never been a diesel boat with the kind of firepower you're talking about. But there was such a sub, back in the 1970s.'

'There was? Who did it?'

'The Brits.'

'They did?'

'Uh-huh. It was kept very low-key. But it was carried out by an old friend of mine, Royal Navy two-and a half, Harry Brazier, Lt-Commander H.L. Brazier to you. Lovely guy, smart as hell. Painted his submarine, an old A–Class boat, with "SSG 72" in white letters on the fin.'

Morgan chuckled, slurped his coffee, and said, 'Go on.'

'Well, the Royal Navy converted some boat – HMS *Aeneas*, she was called. They somehow fitted an old Blowpipe system to the front of the fin. Harry told me all about it. They called it SLAM – Submerged Launch Air Missile. They had to come to just above PD and then the captain aimed it through the search periscope. Fired it from a mounting that was like a kind of big, bulbous tower which came above the height of the fin. I remember he once showed me a photo – told me they had to remove the gun on the forecasing because of the top-weight.

'There were four missiles inside that tower, pressurized to keep out the water. It was only a modification to the land-based, hand-held Blowpipe. And it didn't pack that much of a wallop. The missile went only about 3000 yards, but they thought it might knock a helicopter out of the sky. Harry told me it was dead easy to do the conversion. The only difficulty was making it sea-tight. But the Vickers engineers did it, and it worked. That boat could come up, slam a helo out of the sky, and vanish without trace. So far as anyone else was concerned it was like a guided missile had been fired from nowhere.'

'Do you think the Iraqis could have stolen *Unseen* and made such a conversion some other place?'

'I very much doubt it. A missile system which would launch a weapon ten miles into the air and still keep going, maybe for a total of 40 or 50 miles, would need a pretty good-sized launcher and a very sophisticated fire-control system. To fit it you'd need some serious engineering, and deep skills. You'd have to have high-tech workshops and heavy lifting gear – all the trimmings. But if you had the system on board a big supply ship, and you had a place to work, I don't think it'd be impossible. Assuming you could find a way to engineer it into place in secret.'

'As I recall, Joe, the Iraqis still have that Stromboli-Class replenishment ship they bought new from the Italians. I forget her name, but she displaced nearly 9000 tons loaded; she was pretty useful. I suppose a rendezvous between the Stromboli and the submarine wouldn't be out of the question. It's just a matter of where they could have got the conversion done.'

'Guess so, Arnie. But it's still a hell of a long shot. I assume you've checked the Stromboli's whereabouts and activities.'

'Yes – she's out of it. And I know it's a long shot. But there ain't no short shots right now, so I'm into long shots. Maybe they got ahold of another ship.'

The CNO laughed, but he was still very serious. He was about to speak again when the President's National Security Advisor stood up and said swiftly, 'Joe, I don't wanna waste your time. But let me ask you one final question, bearing in mind that I think we have just outlined the merest possibility that Ben Adnam might be out in the Atlantic with the most lethal submarine ever built – the world's first terminally deadly anti-aircraft submarine.'

'Well, *you* have, Arnie. Go on.'

'What's the worst thing that could ever happen, this week?'

'Dunno.'

'Come on, Joe. Think. Right now let's assume Commander Adnam is moving east across the North Atlantic, where he's been hiding. And say he's on the move, heading for the Mid-Atlantic Ridge, out by 30 degrees West. He's running slowly, 500 feet below the surface. What's the most terrible thing he could do?'

'You mean, start knocking passenger airliners out of the sky . . . ?'

'No, Joe. Not any old passenger airliner.'

The big man hesitated for a few moments before saying quietly, 'Jesus Christ! Starstriker . . .'

'Yes, Joe. Starstriker.'

'My God, Arnie. That's a big ole bone to chew on. You think it's possible?'

'Not really. I'm still hung up on the sheer unlikelihood of Iraq being able to make that missile conversion. Besides, there's not a damn' thing we could do about it. The Royal Navy's Upholder is like the Russians' Kilo: you can't hear it at all, unless it's careless. So what could we do? Send out the whole Atlantic Fleet to hunt it down? They might try for a year and *still* not find it. No, Joe, I'm afraid it's too way-out – no facts, just supposition. And you and I can't operate like that, not on blind guesswork involving a 1000–1 shot.'

'Guess not. But it's sure as hell been an interesting discussion. You leaving now?'

'Yup. See you Thursday, Chief, bright and early. And, by the way, it might not be that bad an idea to fire up SOSUS to keep a wary eye out for the lost British Upholder. You never know – they're pretty good up there in those waters.'

'We've done all that, and we've got the Brits to hand over *Unseen*'s signatures. Hey, before you go, there's just one thing else I recall about *Aeneas*. That Blowpipe program wasn't done for the Royal Navy. It was for the navy of some other nation. Paid for the whole development in cash. Harry says the Royal Navy merely lent the submarine for the missile-firing trials and took the money.'

'You don't happen to remember which nation that was, do you? Maybe they could have passed along the plans to someone recently.'

'No, Arnie, I don't know who it was. Harry was never told. But he always thought it might have been Israel.'

0700, Thursday, February 9, Dulles International Airport, Washington DC.

Marie Colton, the svelte, dark-haired 45-year-old deputy head of Boeing's Public Relations Department, had been in action since five in the morning overseeing the transformation of the biggest room in the airport. The deadly serious, inwardly driven Californian divorcee must have walked about 300 miles throughout the first-class area before her boss, the tall, laid-back Midwesterner Jay Herbert, arrived on the scene at five past seven.

At this point Marie was ordering a group of flower arrangers around as if she were in an armored Panzer division moving forward on Leningrad. You couldn't see the carpet for blooms, petals, leaves and cut stalks. In the background, a six-strong team of long-haired electrical madmen were wiring up an interplanetary sound system to a couple of speakers the size of the Lincoln Memorial.

'Jesus Christ!' said Jay, protecting his ears from a high-pitched shriek which threatened to render everyone deaf from one end of Fairfax County to the other. To Marie he added, 'Everything under control?'

He intended the question to have an edge of irony to it. But Marie had never been terribly into irony. She possessed the quintessential literal mind. Jay had a policy *never* to waste a good joke on the female *Obergruppenführer* of the PR Department, but occasionally, in the face of chaos too great to bear, he caved in and let one slip.

She turned to face him, her quick deep-red smile designed to betray the put-upon hurt of early-morning martyrdom. 'Perfectly,' she replied. 'I wish you had been here a little earlier.'

'Oh really?' he replied, caving in to his own sense of humor yet again. 'I'm sorry, Marie. I had no idea you'd be so occupied.'

Thus began the busiest, most important day in the entire history of the Boeing PR Department. 'Sometimes I think you say things just to upset me,' said Marie. 'Which is very unfair when you know how difficult this has all been. And how pressed we are for time.'

'Ah, but I have inordinate faith in you,' said Jay. 'And I know we're going to see order spring from this chaos inside the next 30 minutes. Either that or we're all fired.'

Exasperated, Marie turned back to the flower arrangers. Jay moved toward his technical director, who was testing the television satellite hook-up which would relay live from the cockpit the entire flight of Starstriker 001. 'We in good shape, Charlie?' he asked.

'Yes, sir. Looking good. Here, watch this. See that picture there, looking out at the maintenance area of the airport? That's being filmed right through the cockpit windshield of Starstriker. We got a ship out there off Long Island recording the sonic boom from below. We got the black box wired up to the satellite link. Everyone in this room's gonna hear every word while they're watching the big screens. These guys are gonna think they're *in* Starstriker, not just listening and watching.'

'Looks terrific, Charlie. Sound effects OK?'

'You bet. We got the full Dolby wrap-around digital system installed. When that baby blasts off the runway, this room is going into a gut-rumbling shudder. Just like in a movie. The earth will move. When she breaks the sound barrier that sonic boom is going to rattle the cutlery in here. Then we're switching right back to the main cabin where there'll be total silence. The pilot is going to mention the boom right before it happens. Then he'll explain how it slips away and how no one inside the aircraft can hear a thing.'

'Perfect. No glitches, Charlie, for Christ's sake. We got the President in here and God knows who else. Right now the future of the entire corporation is in your capable hands.'

'Yes, sir. Don't worry. We're not going to have a problem. Everything is very routine. And we're well organized. Just sit back, eat your breakfast and enjoy.'

'You do good work, Charlie. Keep going.'

Jay Herbert held down one of the biggest PR jobs in the United States because he never wasted his time on details. His job was too diverse for that. He delegated carefully, picked his employees well, and edited the minutiae out of his life on a daily basis. He did not much like her, but he had hired the

Obergruppenführer because he'd sensed that painstaking detail – the feverish pursuit of the apparently unimportant – was her forte. She never forgot anything; her desk was a symphony of lists, and she walked around with a clipboard containing the key ones, checking off, adding to, adjusting, arranging, adjudicating . . .

'Marie Colton,' Jay would whisper conspiratorially to senior colleagues, 'lets nothing through the cracks, and I mean that financially, socially, academically and probably sexually.' It always got an inexpensive laugh, which was after all a part of the corporate PR head's job.

There was just one area of his duties which caused Jay Herbert to become marginally bogged down, and that was copywriting. An ex-Chicago newspaperman, the 48-year-old Jay had been out of journalism for almost 20 years now but he still had the editor's dire compulsion to cut, change and rethink other people's words. He always said it had to do with the natural literary rhythm that ran through his soul, and he found it impossible to deal with any writer who did not march to the beat of that precise same drum. Accordingly, he drove a succession of advertising agency executives almost crazy with his insistence on passing, personally, every sentence of every Boeing brochure – every headline, every cross-head, every descriptive word. He would pore over submitted copy, cutting, editing and improving, and forcing the advertising men to wonder why the hell he had hired them in the first place since he plainly wanted to write the stuff himself.

Today's brochure, produced and designed using the most expensive color printing it was possible to find, had taken six months to put together. Jay regarded it as his masterpiece, and it probably was. He walked outside into the corridor, to where the big boxes were being opened. Four female assistants were in the process of placing one brochure at each table-setting. Another pile was being set up at the entrance table where each guest would also receive a metal Starstriker badge engraved with his or her name.

Jay could see the front cover of the brochure, glossy white except for the words: 'STARSTRIKER – Stairway to the Future.' It was illustrated with a thin line of shooting stars which swept away toward a rendition of Old Glory fluttering in the heavens. The PR chief thought it was a knockout.

It was almost half past seven now, and Marie Colton had the

flowers under control. The horticultural mess had vanished and the room was spectacular. The miles of electrical wires which had traversed the floor a few minutes ago had also vanished. The two big cinema-sized screens were in place, set diagonally across two corners of the great room to insure that everyone could see everything.

Jay had a quick conference with the catering boss to make certain absolutely anything anyone could desire for breakfast was available. On the top table, laid with a milk-white tablecloth, were placed jugs of orange juice and bowls of fruit. Baskets for toast, hot rolls and Danish pastries were everywhere. All of the waitresses were dressed as international airline stewardesses, the waiters as pilots. An Air Force band was tuning up in a corner of the room. A 25-foot model of the new supersonic aircraft was suspended from the ceiling.

The 16 guests at the top table would be the President of the United States, John Mulcahy and Senator Kennedy with their wives, plus Admiral Arnold Morgan and Secretary for Defense Robert MacPherson; interspersed among them would be the Chairman of the Joint Chiefs, Admiral Scott Dunsmore, plus the three separate service chiefs, including of course Admiral Mulligan, all with their wives. The other two main tables, each seating 48 people, were placed at right angles to that of the VIP group, and everyone was seated democratically: senators, congressmen, business leaders, potential customers and show-business personalities. Behind these was a long narrow press table on which, facing the screens, were to be seated 24 media heavy-hitters: a half-dozen top columnists, six stars of television news, six editors and six proprietors, all hand-picked by Jay Herbert.

Outside, beyond the doors of the great room, was another press area with its own screens and tables, buffet refreshments and a zillion telephones and computer terminals. The press and public launch of Starstriker would bang a hole in a million dollars. The place was already crawling with secret-servicemen.

Shortly after twenty-five to eight the guests began to arrive. As they did so the cinema screens came to life, the one on the left showing the scene outside the door with a detailed account of who each person was: 'Ladies and gentlemen, we are pleased to welcome now Sir John and Lady Fredickson, the Chairman and Chief Executive of British Airways and his wife Georgina . . . arrived last night from London . . .'

The big screen on the right, meanwhile, was relaying the scene from the cockpit, where Scanner Richards and his co-test pilot, the Yale graduate Marvin Leonard, were running through the checks with Senior Flight Engineer Don Grafton. As with Concorde, the procedures would take more than an hour; the men had already been working on the task since seven o'clock. The audience could see them in the dark cockpit, following the list on Engineer Grafton's board as he studied the cathode-ray tubes which contained the critical databank which would alert the crew if anything was even remotely amiss. The 'Glass Cockpit's' instrumentation panel, with its six big CRTs, made Concorde's bewildering mass of conventional dials and switches seem like something out of the Dark Ages. In the deep background, caressed by symphonic Dolby sound, the late Frank Sinatra sung alternately, 'Fly Me to the Moon' and 'Come Fly with Me.'

He sang until eight o'clock precisely, when the presidential motorcade arrived, the first car bearing the President and his wife with Admiral Morgan and Robert MacPherson. In two cars following came the service chiefs and a posse of secret-servicemen. Everyone was greeted by John Mulcahy and his wife and the party walked into the big room while the Air Force band robustly played 'Hail to the Chief.'

The Republican from Oklahoma occupied a very special place in the hearts of almost all the Americans in this room, and they stood and clapped in time to the old familiar music. As they did so, a giant Stars and Stripes slipped down from the ceiling and fluttered perfectly in the controlled breeze of a secret fan set in the fuselage of the model Starstriker. As the music ended, the entire gathering was on its feet to clap and cheer the right-wing President from the southwest, a man who loved the military, who loved big business, who would not permit one dime to be cut from the Defense budget, and who had twice reduced corporate taxation.

Insiders, of whom there were many in this room, were still talking about a story that had been making the Washington rounds in the past few days. A national news magazine had planned to write a humiliating cover story involving a very minor indiscretion by a senior, highly decorated army officer who had twice been cited for gallantry in the Gulf War.

The publisher of the mag had, apparently, been marched into the Oval Office, where the President had told him that he 'would not tolerate one of my most trusted Commanders-in-Chief being held up to ridicule in front of every tinpot fucking dictator in the world because of your goddamned desire to sell magazines. Run that story and I will use my executive power to have you charged with treason against this nation – and don't think I wouldn't do it. Try to remember one thing: you happen to be an American, no matter how hard that may be for the rest of us to believe. Try to behave like one for a change. Now, get out.'

The publisher was apparently shaken visibly – had to be given a glass of water right there in the West Wing. But the story was canceled, and the publisher now sat subdued at the long press table. Everyone in the room noticed he alone did not applaud the great man when the music died down.

It was fourteen minutes past eight now and Starstriker was moving out to the taxiing area. The big screens were showing views from outside and inside the cockpit, every touch of the throttle eliciting a deep grumbling roar from the Dolby sound system as all four engines responded slickly. Everyone saw the ground engineer disconnect the tug. The nose and visor were lowered, and Scanner Richards headed her out to the takeoff point.

Now, for the first time, Boeing's supersonic aircraft could be seen in her entirety, a sleek, white 300-foot-long delta-winged giant. Its body was wider than Concorde's, but not noticeably so because of the extra length. Passengers would ultimately sit in thirty-six rows of eight seats, each row widely separated into four pairs. The pilot was almost 60 feet in front of the nose wheel.

The Dolby sound system was still picking up the words of the flight engineer as he ran further safety checks while heading out toward runway 19L, nearly two miles long.

Starstriker arrived at the takeoff point three minutes early, which gave the restarted Sinatra time for another couple of verses of 'Fly Me to the Moon' and John Mulcahy time to stand and welcome everyone all over again, asserting what a very great privilege it was for him to host such an august gathering of dignitaries, all of whom, he hoped, would shortly be paying customers on his aircraft, no matter which airline's livery Star-striker carried.

Everyone heard the Dulles Tower clear the aircraft to enter the runway. And then the voice came through again: 'Tower to Boeing 2707–500. Starstriker 001 cleared for takeoff.'

In reply Scanner Richards's echoing words, mundane as they were, sounded on the Dolby system as if he were intoning Shake-speare: 'Zero-zero-one rolling . . .'

The assembled dignitaries heard Marvin Leonard, inside the cockpit, counting: 'Four – three – two – one – *Now* . . .'

They watched Scanner Richards smoothly extending the throttles forward as Boeing's supersonic flagship powered out of the starting gate.

'Airspeed building.'

'Afterburners. One hundred knots.'

'Power checked. V1 . . .'

At 200 knots the nose wheel lifted off the runway, and Star-striker seemed to hang at an angle of ten degrees as her speed built.

Inside the VIP room the big hitters held their breath as Marvin Leonard said, 'V2, sir. 221 knots.'

And Starstriker rocketed off the runway, accelerating to 250 knots, climbing into the cold clear skies above the Washington suburbs, tracked by the television cameras as avidly as any launch in the space program.

Scanner Richards had taken off to the northeast, and now altered course to due east for the 135-mile flight to the Atlantic coastline. There he would accelerate again, climbing the plane to her cruise altitude of 60,000 feet, where her engines would settle her into traveling at the fantastic speed of Mach 2.5 – close to 1700mph.

Starstriker had to fly southeast for 50 miles before adjusting through 90 degrees for the Atlantic crossing. Boeing's supersonic masterpiece made short work of that, and the VIP room sat spellbound, listening to the pilot call the waypoints. From the moment of the major course change to the northeast, Starstriker, still accelerating, devoured the 300 miles up to Nantucket Island in 15 minutes.

'Nantucket abeam, sir. 39.50 North, 69.00 West. Mach 2.5.' The words of Marvin Leonard, magnified by the sound system, electrified the gathering. The President looked over at Admiral Morgan and shook his head in sheer wonder. This thing was not a spaceship on its way to Mars. This was a regular passenger jet aircraft, the herald of the way ordinary men and women would be able to travel in the 21st century, exactly as Jay Herbert's carefully crafted sentences pointed out in the Boeing brochure.

Jay himself had pulled up a chair to the press table and was talking some of the newsmen through the flight, explaining how Captain Richards would shortly come under the guidance of Oceanic Control, Gander, checking in every ten degrees, or 450 miles – or, incredibly, every thirteen and a half minutes.

Right now Starstriker was at full throttle. She checked in at the 50°W waypoint, right on 42°N, ten miles above the great swells of the Atlantic flowing over the freezing Grand Banks. Relaxed now, Scanner Richards faced the camera while Marvin Leonard flew the aircraft; Scanner told everyone back at Dulles what a truly fantastic machine this was and what a great privilege it was for him and his crew to make the first trans Atlantic test flight. He wished everyone good morning, and jauntily asked John Mulcahy if it would OK for him to have a quick cup of coffee. It was mild little joke by Scanner's normal standards, but it laid 'em in the aisles in the VIP room, such was the depth of admiration for the job he was doing.

As the guests continued with their eggs, scrambled with smoked salmon, accompanied by Krug champagne and orange juice in Waterford crystal glasses, the minutes ticked by. Starstriker ripped across the clear northern skies, the throaty crackle of her four engines lost out here on the frontiers of space.

The waypoint at 40°W was passed right on the 45th parallel, and ATC Gander, in faraway snowbound Newfoundland, checked them in. Starstriker thundered on toward the next waypoint, the one right above the Mid-Atlantic Ridge, where Richards and Leonard would alert ATC Shannon in Southern Ireland that his supersonic aircraft was checking in from 60,000 feet at 30°W. That would be thirteen and a half minutes from right now. Speed was steady at Mach 2.5.

Marvin Leonard said goodbye to Gander, and made the 30°W contact with Shannon right on time, reporting height, speed and position. The deep southern Irish brogue that marked the distinctive tones of a Kerryman came in immediately: 'Good morning, Boeing Starstriker zero-zero-one. Roger that. Talk to you in minutes thirteen. Over.'

At which point there came the first glitch of the morning. Both the big screens illuminating the flight at the VIP breakfast banquet went blank, fizzing noisily through the mammoth Dolby speakers. A collective groan went up, just as if these were the early days of cinema and the reel had run out. Before the fizzing died away, two things happened. The chief electrician headed across the room toward the control panel, and Admiral Arnold Morgan leapt to his feet, knocking his chair flying, and yelled: 'Jesus Christ! Oh no! Jesus *Christ.*'

To his fellow guests it seemed like an outpouring of fury and disappointment at the failure of the system. A few people laughed.

The President's wife grabbed his hand and said, 'Come on, Arnie, it's not that bad. They'll have it going in a few minutes.'

But her husband's National Security Advisor was completely distraught. *'No . . . no they won't! Goddammit! Goddammit! That bastard! GodDAMMit!'*

Those closest to him could see tears of anger and frustration streaming down his craggy face. A further clue that this was no ordinary outburst was perhaps the fact that the Navy's Chief Operational Officer, Admiral Joe Mulligan, looked positively ashen. He excused himself from those sitting to either side of him and came round to Morgan, placed his arm around the admiral's shoulders, and muttered, 'Come on, old buddy. I guess we got work to do.'

Everyone saw the two military men leave the room, walking quickly out toward the office where the presidential communications were located under guard of six secret-servicemen. There were three telephones in there. While John Mulcahy was standing up to apologize to the VIPs for the technical interruption, the President's chief military advisor was already on the secure line to the White House, instructing them to patch him through to Air Traffic Control, Shannon.

That took less than 30 seconds because Kathy O'Brien had the numbers right in front of her. When Morgan made contact, announcing himself as the senior military representative of the President of the United States, the operator put him through at once to the ATC supervisor.

Who had no idea what the fuss was about. 'Sir, Starstriker

zero-zero-one made contact at 30 degrees West nine minutes ago. She's not due in for another four minutes. How can I help?'

'Go to SELCAL. Bombard the cockpit with signals. *Get 'em on the line!*'

'No problem, sir. I'm sitting right here with the operator now. We're going through on her private call-sign HF band. We just lit two warning lights in the cockpit and right now we have four warning bells ringing.'

'Are you getting any response?'

'Not yet, sir.'

'Hit 'em again, for Christ's sake!'

'No need, sir. These systems operate nonstop. It's happening over and over.'

'Are they coming in?'

'No, sir.'

'How long before they're due?'

'Two minutes, sir.'

'Keep hitting 'em!'

'I'm doing it, sir. But they're just not answering. It's very unusual . . . very, very unusual.'

'Gimme the time again!'

'Starstriker's due in 60 seconds, sir.'

Arnold Morgan waited. He waited next to his trusted friend Joe Mulligan for a full minute, then another.

Finally the Irish ATC supervisor said: 'We're on the line. You can probably hear our operator right next to me.'

In the distance Admiral Morgan could hear a disconnected voice. The tones were somehow hollow. 'Starstriker, Starstriker, this is Shanwick. This is Shanwick. Go ahead with your position report. Starstriker zero-zero-one, please go ahead with your position report.'

The two admirals, both in mild shock, stood in silence, still listening for the words of the Irish supervisor to confirm that it had all been a mistake, that the Boeing supersonic was still racing through the skies.

But at 1001 (EST), the operator came back on the line and delivered his message. His words were softly spoken but they had the impact of a jackhammer. 'I'm sorry to inform you, sir, that we are now certain Starstriker is down in the North Atlantic, somewhere east of 30°W. Her last known position was 50.30°N

167

at 60,000 feet. We are alerting all ships in the area as well as the appropriate United States Agencies.'

Admiral Morgan replaced the receiver, looked at the professional head of the United States Navy, and said, 'He's got her.'

Mulligan found it hard to speak. Their conversation of just three days before would haunt both men for years to come. And still the question remained: was Ben Adnam really out there in a stolen diesel–electric submarine, silently slamming passenger jets out of the Western skies of behalf of Islam?

'Well,' rasped Morgan, 'with two supersonic aircraft down in roughly the same patch of water in three weeks and for no discernible reason, an accident looks pretty goddamned coincidental.'

They walked back to the main room, uncertain what to do or say. But pandemonium had already broken out. After Shannon put out the announcement to the international air–sea rescue services it took just a few minutes for the news to reach the BBC and subsequently to be released in a newsflash on the BBC's television and radio networks. This meant, broadly speaking, that within 20 minutes of the crash the entire world news media knew that Starstriker was down.

The television people at Dulles could not believe their luck. Here was one of the great stories of all time, and here they were in a room with the President of Boeing, his PR chief and other executives. Add to that the President of the United States, the head of the United States Air Force, the Chairman of the Joint Chiefs . . . They even had the Chairman of British Airways, who had lost a Concorde a mere 20 days ago. These journalists were involved in the News Nirvana of the century.

In the opinion of Arnold Morgan, nothing useful could possibly be achieved by any of the presidential party, and he recommended that everyone leave immediately, an evacuation facilitated by the Secret Service. Admiral Mulligan made the same suggestion to Scott Dunsmore, and the military top brass were also out of there in record time, leaving Jay Herbert to protect John Mulcahy as best he could. The electronic satellite links to the great aircraft were switched off now, since it was plain there was nothing to which they could connect. Starstriker was history.

The Pentagon staff car dropped Admiral Mulligan at the White House. There, in the West Wing, behind the locked doors of the office of the NSA, the only two men in the United States who had even a partial – however outlandish – theory to explain what had happened tried to assemble their thoughts, tried to decide what to do about the menace that might be lurking 500 feet below the surface anywhere in a million square miles of the North Atlantic.

'The trouble is,' said Mulligan, 'we still don't have a shred of evidence, and I can't just order a fleet to take off on some wild-goose chase. It would cost a fortune, which is not in our budget, and we'd hardly know where to start looking. Plus the operation would have to be "black," since we can't alarm the populace. We'd need a dozen warships, which would alert the entire armed forces that something suspicious was going on out there where the two jetliners went down.'

'I know, Joe. Don't I just know . . . I think the best way forward is for us to carefully intellectualize the whole scenario – just to get it clear in our minds. Which means we ought to assess the similarities between the two disasters – should be simple enough.

'Both aircraft were maintained to the highest possible standards. Both of them just vanished off the airwaves around 30°W. Neither pilot, so far as we know, had time even to utter the word SHIT. Which means they both blew up internally, or fell apart for unknown reasons, or they were hit by a big guided missile, capable of perhaps a 50-mile range, at a speed somewhere between Mach 2 and Mach 3. Because of the heavy security surrounding Star-striker there can be no question of a planted bomb – and neither does anyone think that was possible with Concorde. Which leaves us with the possibilities of metal fatigue or structural weakness.

'But for two aircraft built 30 years apart – one of which had been flying perfectly all its life and the other judged to be the very last word in supersonic travel by every single one of the many, many world-class engineers at the Boeing plant – to be suffering the same problem seems impossible.'

'I agree with all that, Arnold. Which leaves only the missile.'

'Right. And the difficulty with that is simple: there's nowhere to fire it *from*. No land. No nearby ship – certainly not a warship. Unless the missile was delivered from space, which is not within present-day technology for us so almost certainly isn't for anyone else, it must have been fired from a submarine. A specially fitted submarine, one with a sizable surface-to-air system out there on its casing, probably in front of the fin like your man Harry's Blowpipe, only a lot bigger.'

'Right, Arnold. And we have a missing submarine, nearly brand-new, whereabouts unknown, somehow taken beyond the very capable reach of the Royal Navy.'

'Correct. Add in that we have the possibility of one of the most dangerous submariners who ever lived being at the helm. I've spoken to David Gavron in Tel Aviv and he admits, very frankly, that when you get right down to it they can't be absolutely certain whether Commander Adnam is dead or alive. They never saw the body before it was cremated by the Egyptians. They only had his papers. Could have been anyone. They could even have been forged, probably by fucking Adnam himself.'

'Plus, Arnold, we have the irritating possibility – likelihood, in fact – that the plans for Harry Brazier's Blowpipe system are in the archives of the Israeli Navy. If they are, it's dollars to a pinch of shit that Adnam has a copy of them. Christ, he served as commanding officer of an Israeli submarine. I bet he knew every inch of those drawings.'

'Could be. If your Harry's best guess is correct, Ben Adnam would have known how to make that conversion. The only gap in an otherwise reasonably logical progression is that we don't know how the goddamned Iraqis did the engineering or where they found a trained submarine crew.'

'No . . . no, we don't. And it's a big gap. But Adnam's fixed big gaps before. I think we're going to have to assume they did it. And I think we have to consider ways of catching this submarine before he strikes again. I'm just not sure where to start. SOSUS came up with nothing. Do you think we have to talk to someone? Like Scott, or the President? Maybe Robert Mac?'

'I don't know. For right now I think we ought to wait 24 hours and see if anything comes out in the media or in from the searches going on out there. I think if we're going to propose a truly bizarre course of action we need the boost of the continuing mystery. That way people will be a bit more ready to listen to us.'

'OK. Shall we regroup late afternoon tomorrow, compare notes? Here?'

'Yes. 1700 hours.'

'You got it.'

The Navy chief walked out, still frowning. As he did so, Morgan picked up his secure line and dialed a number on the other side of the world. Seconds later the telephone rang in the big white mansion on the shore of Loch Fyne.

'Iain?'

'Speaking.'

'Arnold Morgan here.'

'Good afternoon, Arnold. How nice to hear from you. I'm afraid to say you have the most terrible problem.'

'I know. It's him, isn't it? Banging out airliners from a submarine.'

'Yes, Arnold. Yes it is. It's him.'

CHAPTER SEVEN

February 9, 2006. 1500, the Oval Office.
Admiral Arnold Morgan had just walked through the door and the President was waiting for him, sitting quietly with the Secretary of State, Harcourt Travis. Before the admiral could utter even a word of greeting the Chief Executive said curtly, 'National Security Advisor, you are holding out on me.'

'Sir?'

'You are holding out on me. When Starstriker was lost this morning you were the only person in that room who knew what had happened. You were expecting it. You reacted in about a half-second. Too quick to absorb a mere possibility. And you were right, a full 15 minutes ahead of the rest of the world. You said, "That Bastard." I heard you.

'Arnold Morgan, I am sufficiently presumptuous to regard you as a true friend. And I'm not accusing you of anything. Not yet. But you better have a real good explanation for your apparent foreknowledge.'

Morgan nodded to Harcourt and said, 'Sir, I do have some theories. And I won't pretend I didn't have a gut feeling this *could* happen. But when it actually did I was as shocked as the next man. Just a bit earlier. And you know me well enough, Mr President: I tend to react quick. If there was anything I coulda done to prevent that disaster, you know I'da done it. With or without your permission.'

Over two cups of coffee in a talk which lasted almost 30 minutes he recounted to his President and the United States Government's senior foreign-policy executive every one of the thoughts he'd had on the subject, from the moment HMS *Unseen* went missing to the moment Starstriker was apparently blasted out of the sky.

He fitted the pieces together and plotted the progression of his ideas, making particular reference to the fact that he had no explanation as to how the Iraqis could have converted the British submarine into an anti-aircraft weapon. In particular he pointed out the real gap in his argument: the question of *where* the Iraqis could have carried out the work, given the impossibility of their own situation – no deep water, no submarine base (and thus no home for *Unseen*), no expertise, not many friends. He pointed out also that, though the US surveillance system was all-seeing, it was not fireproof, and the Iraqis had shown before they were capable of extraordinary cunning.

Finally he talked about Benjamin Adnam and his belief that the presumed-dead terrorist *must* somehow be involved.

'I did not, sir, want to alarm you,' he said, 'because I did not have one shred of proof. I still don't. It's all just my own thoughts. But when you think and then half-believe something, and along comes a hardass fact which slams it all together . . . well, right then you start to believe you may be right. Which I now do.'

The President nodded. 'Very well, Arnold. I understand. A few questions. One, how did Adnam know our oil-negotiating team were going to be on board that particular Concorde flight?'

'That's easy. Any one of those Arabs could've found out and Bob Trueman certainly knew at least two of them pretty well. I am sure they just asked politely about his long journey home and, being a civilian, he told 'em he was flying Concorde tomorrow morning out of Heathrow.'

'Right. And Starstriker?'

'That was Adnam's real objective, and it was one of the most publicized flights in history. Even Scruff, Kathy's highland terrier, knew Starstriker's ETD from Dulles this morning.'

'Hmm. I guess he did. How about the missile? Heat-seeking?'

'No, sir. Both aircraft were going too fast to risk chasing from anywhere astern. They were also damned high and there are very strict range limits on these highly accurate SAMs. You'd get only one shot at a supersonic. My guess is that the missile was launched vertically, with preprogrammed radar. It adjusted trajectory and course automatically – the system is called "fire-and-forget" in the trade. Came in from dead ahead and smashed straight into the nose.'

'Jesus. But, Arnold, ought you not to have mentioned this to me beforehand?'

'Sir, for the past ten months I've been pondering the possibility that Adnam might be driving a stolen submarine. Naturally my thoughts were that he might take another shot at us, even though I knew he had no major weaponry on board. But I didn't have the remotest idea where he was. I wasn't even confident enough to talk to the Navy. It was just a theory – mostly intuition, no facts. Then Concorde goes down. Do I connect my off-beat military theory with a crashed British passenger aircraft? Maybe. But not strongly enough to start alerting the Navy to take action. Certainly not to bother the President of the United States.'

'No. I do see that. In the light of this latest tragedy, though, when *were* you going to speak to me?'

'Probably tomorrow evening. I told Joe Mulligan that, before I said anything, we better wait to see there was nothing from out of Starstriker's cockpit like a simple "We just ran out of gas." But, not for the first time, you pre-empted me.'

The President relaxed. 'Guess I did. And you're a pretty hard guy to pre-empt. But Jesus, Arnold, I never saw a public over-reaction like yours this morning. People thought you'd lost it.'

'Not quite, sir.'

'No, Arnold, not quite . . . And now what? What do we do?'

For the first time now, the refined, scholarly Harcourt Travis spoke. But first he stood up and walked, thoughtfully, the length of the Oval Office and back. 'Arnold,' he said, 'the trouble with theories is that they take on a life of their own. And if the very basis of their premise is wrong in the first place, they waste a thunderous amount of everyone's time. Also they have a way of quite unnecessarily annoying foreign governments with whom we are compelled to deal.

'Greatly as I respect your instincts, I'm obliged to remind you that a couple of air crashes do not necessarily give credence to a scenario from a Bond movie . . . mad underwater terrorist running amok with the world's airlines.'

'No, Harcourt, I know they don't.'

'Plus the fact that your villain (a) is supposed to be dead, as far as anyone knows, and (b) is from a country that does not even own a submarine at all, far less the most lethal anti-aircraft boat ever built.'

'I know that too, Harcourt.'

'When I listen to you fit some of the pieces together, I do accept there is a remote chance you may be correct. But by God, Arnold, it's so remote. *If* the British submarine was not sunk, *if* it was somehow stolen, *if* this Adnam character is somehow still alive, *if* Iraq was somehow able to get it, hide it, convert it, man it, and operate it, *if* this same country was able to buy such a missile system from someone and fit it to a submarine, *if* this Adnam was able to conceal himself in the North Atlantic, *if* he was able to fire two untried SAM missiles from some kind of a jury-rigged launcher, and actually hit two of the highest, fastest aircraft ever built . . . *If*, Arnold, your auntie had balls I guess she'd somehow be your uncle. Count me out, pal. At least until you can provide me with one solitary shining F–A–C–T.'

The President shook his head. Then he repeated his last question. 'Well, what do we do?'

'I honestly don't know, sir,' replied the admiral, ignoring the onslaught of skepticism displayed by Harcourt Travis. 'I suppose we could accept my theory and obliterate Baghdad in retribution. But we'd look pretty fucking silly if a different kind of truth came out about the crashes. So that's out. At least for the moment.'

'You can say that again,' interjected the Secretary of State. 'Do you have any idea what an uproar something like this could cause. Really, Arnold, even *you* have to get real on matters of this scale.'

'Harcourt,' replied Morgan wearily, 'you don't have to keep reminding me of my shortcomings, mainly because I might have to remind you of a few of yours. Lemme just run this technical detail past the Chief . . .

'Just assuming my unsupported theory is largely correct, the search area for the submarine is, by now, massive. Take the spot around 30 West where the two aircraft vanished. It's at 50.30 North. By the time we get out there with search aircraft, Commander Adnam could have been moving for 24 hours, leaving us a search area of at least 30,000 square miles – expanding with every fucking minute that passes. By the time we get ships out there three days later, the target could be virtually anywhere.

'If you take 30 West, 50.30 North as the search's center, he could be anywhere in an 800-mile radius circle, or, stated another way, in a search area of over two million square miles . . . and that two million square miles is all water. Because the crashes happened bang in the middle of the ocean – by design, one suspects.

'HMS *Unseen* could have gone north, toward the coastal area of Greenland; west, way off the coast of the USA and Canada; east, toward the west coast of Ireland; or south, to absolutely nowhere. Adnam could be *anywhere in that area*. We'd have only one chance – that he got careless and SOSUS picked him up, held him long enough for MPA to get a fix . . . Sir, whatever, we're still looking for a poisoned needle in the Sahara Desert.'

'Supposition, supposition,' said Travis. 'The entire theory is one of supposition. We're not just looking for a needle in the Sahara, we're looking for a needle that probably doesn't exist. And in my book that's probably a needle not worth looking for.' He was on the verge of exasperation.

But the President wanted to proceed. 'Arnold, how would it have been if we'd sent a fleet of nuclear submarines out there the moment we knew about the crash?'

'Better, but not much. They'd want three days minimum to get to the crash site. HMS *Unseen* would still be more than 600 miles from the datum. That's a 600 mile radius circle, or one million square miles. We'd still have to trip over the sonofabitch – and we'd be just as likely to trip over ourselves.'

'Who else knows your thoughts? Just Joe?'

'And our old friend Admiral Sir Iain MacLean. As you know, I visited him in Scotland. And I spoke to him again about two hours ago. He agrees. Adnam is on the loose, and he will almost certainly strike again. But Iain has a thought which could be useful: refueling. HMS *Unseen* has a range of about 7000 miles. He thinks it likely that Adnam was topped up say 1000 miles out from the datum before Concorde. That means he's probably used up more than half his fuel just running back and forth.

'Joe's activating a search for any suspicious-looking tanker in the North Atlantic, any tanker which is apparently going nowhere, Iraqi or otherwise. If we find one, I guess we could have 'em tailed by a nuclear boat. That's how the Brits caught the *General Belgrano* off the Falklands. Tracking the refueling ship.'

'You want Harcourt to call some kind of a council of war?'

'Not yet, sir. We better wait to see if anything whatsoever shakes out of the crashes in the next two or three days. I really think it would be crazy to start sending the Atlantic Fleet out right now. We've told 'em to maintain overhead surveillance in the immediate search area, and SOSUS has been briefed to be more than usually vigilant for *anything* that might be an Upholder-Class signature anywhere in the North Atlantic. Meanwhile I think we better keep our powder dry – the last thing we need is coast-to-coast panic because an unseen enemy is wiping out international air traffic.'

'No. We wouldn't be thanked for causing that. But, Jesus, what if he hits another airliner?'

'Sir, I think we have to brace ourselves for that. But we'll be much more alert, and I think we should quietly send a carrier battle group into the area – they're pretty good at finding sub-marines. Usually. Then we can keep land-based Maritime Patrol Aircraft working as well. Make it a general area search. But we should keep the SSN force well clear – otherwise we'd end up with a Blue on Blue. If we stay with surface-and-air search only we can say they're just looking for wreckage.'

'Arnold, as always our conversation has been instructive in the extreme. Keep me well posted, will you? I agree we ought not to make an early, rash move. But please, if you have any thoughts whatsoever, make sure I know about 'em. Real early.'

'Absolutely, sir.'

Morgan stood up and walked to the Oval Office door. As he opened it the President spoke again. 'That, by the way, was not an admonishment – just my way of congratulating myself on my choice of a National Security Advisor.'

'Thank you, sir.' Morgan left.

Turning to his Secretary of State, the President said, 'You were pretty hard on him, Harcourt. I know I told you to bounce him up and down a little, find out how strong his theory was, but you came close to making him look a fool.'

'Men like Admiral Morgan cannot be made to look very foolish,' replied Travis. 'He's too damned clever. Also, he happens to have the only theory in town about the crashes. But it *is* so far-fetched – more Hollywood than Washington – and I still do believe it will be completely discredited in the end.'

Harcourt Travis stood up, gathered up his documents, and made for the door. But he was leaving behind a man in a mammoth quandary. The President had always recognized the admiral's paranoia about submarines, and he did not want to be sucked into some drastic action against an enemy which might not exist. As Morgan himself had pointed out, he had not one shred of proof that this Adnam was out there – no proof that he was even alive, never mind at the helm of a rogue submarine. Certainly there was nothing but a bunch of circumstantial evidence to back up a truly majestic theory of international terrorism on an unimaginable scale. Travis, by contrast, offered the easy, do-nothing, political solution, the cynical, lethargic stance of the international statesman: never get into a fight you might not win.

Maybe the admiral's losing it, the President thought. *Maybe he's just worked this one out a step too far, since, by his own admission, the Iraqis seem incapable of operating the submarine, much less making the missile conversion on the stolen submarine. And yet . . . being right has a virtue of its own. And with my own eyes I saw that Morgan was the only man in the United States this morning who was right, who was half-expecting Starstriker might not make it across the Atlantic. What do they say in horse-racing: keep backing him until he loses? I guess he's my man, for better or for worse.*

By now Admiral Morgan had quickened his stride as he marched back to his own office, head thrust forward, his mind locked on one unnerving fact. *I have to get this whole fucking scenario right out of the hands of civilians and under the control of the military on both sides of the Atlantic. I just can't have some fat, dumb, happy asshole in a Savile Row suit making some loosey-goosey remark on the BBC which is gonna send half the world into a fucking tailspin. And that is highly likely to happen. 'Specially if they find one of the black boxes.*

He walked into his office, closed the door, kissed Kathy, told her he loved her, and then ordered her to snap her ass firmly into gear, and get Admiral Sir Richard Birley on the line in London right now, if not sooner. 'He's probably at his residence – it's 2100 over there. He lives right near the base at Northwood. The number's on file, comes under "FOSM." '

Before Morgan had finished yelling his instructions, Admiral Birley was on the line.

'Arnold, hello. I was half expecting you to call. If our last conversation had any basis in truth, we are, shall we say, in the deepest possible trouble.'

'Dick, we have more or less accepted here the truth of our last talk. I am presuming there has never been a squeak from *Unseen*?'

'You presume correctly. And we both know why. We have to ask ourselves, what now?'

'Well, I had a purpose in this call. I think circumstances have thrown the Royal Navy and the United States Navy together. What might appear at first sight to be a civilian problem is now no such thing.'

'Correct. I had absolutely the same thought myself.'

'Are the search ships for Concorde all Royal Navy?'

'Yes. Two frigates and a destroyer. We're running a deep unmanned submarine from a civilian mother-ship as well, but I can keep the lid on that.'

'Great. Because we're sending three US Navy ships out there to search for the wreckage of Starstriker. Also, I wanna get a CVBG into the area as soon as possible. And, even quicker, some MPA. The thing is, we have to keep all news of any black box we find under very tight control.'

'We realize that over here, too. If the recording has the pilot shouting out that he was about to get hit up the arse by a guided missile . . . well, we won't want the media getting hold of that too soon. Because they'd go instantly berserk. God knows what would happen. I suppose all trans-Atlantic flights would be in chaos, but also Adnam would know we were onto him – he might make a bolt for it and disappear for good, knocking down a sodding aircraft whenever he felt so inclined.'

'That's it, Dick. We have to keep this very, very tight. What I need to know is this how can our two organizations keep a handle on it? The black boxes must be kept out of careless hands. I'm assuming your investigators wouldn't just unpick the box and issue a press release?'

'Good God, no. We're probably as tight with this information as you are. The box, assuming we find one, will be dealt with in secret at the laboratories of our Air Accident Investigation people. Nothing will be released to anyone until our chaps are sure of their ground. But in this case I think there should be a formal military representative on the team as well.'

'Right. I was going to suggest our CNO talks to your First Sea Lord – just to insure that, if either you or we get ahold of any one of the four boxes, we share whatever information we have. The idea is to catch this bastard, not sell fucking newspapers.'

'Absolutely. I'll tell you what, I'll speak to someone in the ministry right away and brief them as to our thoughts. Basically, I think the way forward is for our Air Accident Investigation people to lock in with your Federal Aviation Administration. I'll call you back.'

'OK, I'll be waiting.'

All through the small hours of the night, the Navy chiefs conferred. The First Sea Lord arranged for representatives of both the Royal Navy and the Royal Air Force to attend the black box recordings at the headquarters of the Air Investigation Authority. Admiral Joe Mulligan, through Admiral Dunsmore, received similar clearance from the Oval Office, and by 0400 London time the deal was done. The Royal Navy and the United States Navy would operate in tandem, expense no object, in order to bring up the black boxes.

It was as well they had all worked so quickly. At 1340 (GMT) the following day the Royal Navy's deep-submerged submarine found one. It was still transmitting its locator signal, and HMS *Exeter* had detected it on passive sonar. The box itself was three miles down, but they grabbed it with the aid of a television monitor, two floodlights and a special small bathycaphe lowered from their mini-submarine.

Back on board *Exeter* they identified the black box, which was in fact orange, as the Concorde's CVR (Cockpit Voice Recorder). In accordance with the latest orders, a satellite signal was sent to both Northwood and the Pentagon. Then the box was sealed and *Exeter* made all speed due east toward the English Channel, where she would come within the range of a Royal Navy Sea King helicopter.

The box was ultimately flown straight to the Royal Navy Air Base at Culdrose, Cornwall, and on from there by fixed-wing military aircraft. It was a long, costly mission for one single word. The only sound to be heard from the cockpit – beyond the reams of regular flight recordings, was just one short shout from Captain Lambert. It sounded like 'miss,' but there was a lot of interference. It could just as easily have been 'kiss,' or 'bliss.'

That part of the recording was relayed to the Pentagon immediately, where Admiral Morgan and Admiral Mulligan were waiting. Arnold Morgan suggested, 'The guy either wanted to take a leak, or he was requiring, or getting, a blowjob from the stewardess.'

He caught Mulligan in mid-swig, and the CNO did his best

not to laugh or blow coffee down his nose, but failed on both counts. While the towering ex-Trident commander mopped his mouth with a big white handkerchief, the NSA moved into serious mode without missing a beat.

'Joe,' he said, 'Captain Brian Lambert saw it, didn't he? Not once in the whole recording, all the way from Heathrow, did we hear him even raise his voice for emphasis. That loud shout of "miss" was entirely out of character. In my opinion the captain meant to say "MISSILE!". Poor guy never got the chance to finish the word. The bastard was coming straight at him, closing at Mach 4, nearly 2700mph. If he'd spotted it in clear skies even as much as four miles away, it would have hit him in five seconds. And that'd be my rough assessment of a totally lousy equation.'

'Sounds right to me, Arnold. There is no other word which fits the pattern, especially the ones in your sexually explicit theory. He was trying to shout "missile," all right. This recording has been very useful . . . it's just about confirmed our original thoughts. And it emphasizes that, if the Brits can find a small box in the middle of the Atlantic, they sure as hell could have found a fucking great submarine in the English Channel.'

Just then the telephone rang on Admiral Morgan's desk. It was a call that had been intercepted and passed on by Kathy, so it was plainly important. The NSA picked it up and was connected with Admiral George Morris, calling from Fort Meade.

'Arnold, hi. One of my guys just got something which might interest you. We've been running routine date checks on the computers, seeing if anything interesting correlates. And he's come up with this. January 17 – the day Concorde and our oilmen were blown out of the sky – it was the 15th anniversary to the day of our opening shots in the Gulf War. January 17 was the day we unleashed the first barrages of Tomahawk cruise missiles at Baghdad. It's not that much of a coincidence, but it's a bit of a one.'

'Yes, George. Yes, it is. The odds against it are 364–1, and it might be a pointer. I thank you and your team.' Click. As ever, Morgan had no time to say goodbye. Ostensibly civilian problems crowded in, unsolved, on his military mind.

That evening he and Kathy O'Brien dined together in Georgetown. Despite all of his efforts to make the occasion cheerful and pleasant, the silences were too long and the admiral's preoccupation was almost total.

'You always take these matters so personally,' she said, holding his hand, looking into his eyes, confirming unknowingly that she was easily the most beautiful woman in the room. But he kept repeating over and over, 'Darling, he's going to do it again. I know this bastard.'

'Would you like to go home?'

'No. We better hang around for a bit and then get the driver to swing back through the city and pick up the first editions, see if the Fourth Estate have stumbled on something I've missed.'

'Would that be a first in your long career?' she asked sweetly, fluttering her eyelashes.

'Maybe a second,' he growled. 'But I don't remember the other occasion.'

They sat companionably sipping amaretto on the rocks, while Morgan tried to cast from his mind the all-too-real vision of a missile closing at Mach 4, as the one which hit Starstriker would have been. 'Imagine that,' he said. 'You could see it four miles out, perhaps a glint in the sunlight, thin contrail behind. Now count to five . . . that's it. One. Two. Three. Four. BAM. And it's gotcha. Wouldn't that be a bitch?'

'Oh yes, I think it would,' she replied. 'A real bitch.'

Even Admiral Morgan smiled, just once.

An hour later the newspapers were in the back of the White House car, displaying practically nothing else but the Starstriker story on the first ten pages. The headlines were varied, from the staid *New York Times*'s 'US Supersonic Crashes in North Atlantic' to a local tabloid's 'Starstriker Strikes Out.'

Inside the papers were columns and columns of news and speculation, the disaster having taken place so early in the day there was ample time to interview all manner of 'experts,' especially those who had been captive at the VIP breakfast banquet.

Every one of the publications on Arnold Morgan's lap connected Concorde and Starstriker, speculating on the proximity of the crashes in terms of both position and time-frame. Somewhat to Morgan's relief, no one discoursed on the possibility of a missile having been the culprit, because the Federal Aviation Administration had stamped on that from a great height. 'You would need a certain type of high-accuracy missile to achieve such an objective,' their spokesman had said. 'The best of them have a range of only about 50 miles, and at that point in the Atlantic Ocean there is simply nowhere to fire from – no land and, the satellites confirm, no ship. We regard a missile as impossible.'

Every newspaper carried that quotation, and none of them carried the theory any further. Instead they concentrated on the risks of flying that high and that fast in anything except a spaceship.

Two of them, the *Washington Post* and the *Philadelphia Inquirer*, went into the possibility of a stratospheric Bermuda Triangle, trying to compare the fickle atmospherics ten miles above the earth to the strange volcanic eruptions under the sea near Bermuda, which 'experts' believed released gases into the ocean water, reducing its density and causing ships simply to sink.

The *Post* hired an expert from the Woods Hole Oceanographic Institution to explain how this theory concerning the reduction in water density depends on the principle of Archimedes that a ship displaces a weight of water equal to its own weight, and will thus stay afloat only if its average density is less than that of water – 'Therefore, if the ship is designed to float 50 percent underwater, but the water here is 50 percent less dense because of the gases, then the ship will just go straight down . . .'

The general drift was that, somewhere up there in the final layers of the earth's atmosphere, there was just such a hole, and the two supersonic airliners, traveling on almost identical flight paths – one heading east, one west – had just charged straight into it, spun, and powered into the ocean, with no time for anyone to correct anything. 'It takes,' the 'expert' wrote ominously, 'only 27 seconds for Concorde to travel ten miles, probably faster going straight down . . . Starstriker could have hit the ocean from that height in 15 seconds.'

Spokesmen from the Green Party had a field day, citing the hole in the ozone layer as the likely culprit for the crashes. 'With the atmosphere noticeably thinner in certain areas, it seems probable that the air density may be reduced sufficiently to make the flight of a high-altitude delta-winged aircraft impossible. It is therefore our view that all such flights should be suspended pending a scientific investigation of the atmospheric phenomena ten miles above the earth.'

'Do you believe any of this stuff, darling?' asked Kathy. 'I mean the hole in the stratosphere, like the hole in the ocean near Bermuda.'

'No,' said Morgan brusquely.

'Why not? It makes sense to me.'

'Because it's aerodynamic bullshit,' he replied unexpansively.

'How do you know?'

'Because Concorde has been flying through it eight times a day for 30 years and hasn't ever fallen out of the sky before. Now we have two planes doing it in three weeks.'

'Maybe the situation is worsening. Maybe it's been worsening for several years, and suddenly reached a critical point.'

'Maybe. But Concorde has not suspended flights. In the 23 days since Captain Lambert's aircraft hit the ocean there've been nearly 200 supersonic flights from Paris and London to New York and Washington, going right through, or damn' close to, that flight path. You know why they didn't flip and plunge into the sea? Because Ben fucking Adnam did not fire a guided missile at 'em, that's why.'

'Oh,' said Kathy, with an air of finality, 'you mean he's kinda on his break?'

'No. He's just pretty selective. And I have no idea where he will strike next. But he will. Mark my words. He will, if he can. I know him.'

'Oh, do you? I didn't realize. Perhaps we should have him over for dinner . . . How about next Wednesday, with the Dunsmores?'

Admiral Morgan, despite himself, caved in and laughed, really laughed, for the first time that evening. 'It is my unhappy lot to be contemplating marriage to a complete dingbat,' he said. And then he softened even more as he added: 'Without whom the sun will never rise for me again.'

Kathy O'Brien had, however, learned from her man the joy of pressing on with a winning line. Now she had a small gold pen in her hand and was writing in a small leather-bound notebook. 'That'll be seven now, won't it? I do hope he likes swordfish – some people are funny about it. Oh my God, he's not a vegetarian, is he?'

'Thank you, Katherine,' said Morgan, still chuckling. 'I think

I'd prefer we gave him a nice little serving of grilled cyanide, since we're on menus.'

By now it was almost midnight, and the car was turning into Kathy's wide tree-lined drive. The second car, the one with the secret-servicemen and the communications system, came in right behind them. Another secret-serviceman, driving the admiral's own car, brought up the rear. Both Arnold and Kathy were used to traveling in convoy by now, and Charlie, Arnold's chauffeur, never worked nights.

The three secret-servicemen on duty spent the night watching television in Kathy's basement study, taking turns to walk around the grounds in pairs, sidearms drawn, in contact with their colleague by radiophone.

Arnold Morgan's was the best-known relationship in the White House, but no one had ever tipped off the press. Not a word about it had ever appeared in any tabloid publication, possibly because both Kathy and Arnold were unmarried, so there was no scandal involved, but perhaps because of the reason offered by Charlie himself: 'Ain't no one never gonna gossip about that admiral, because of one good reason. Terror, man, sheer fucking terror. Trust me.'

HMS *Unseen*, running deep at eight knots in the early hours of February 10, was making a northeasterly course right above the submerged cliffs of the Rekjanes Ridge in 2000 feet of water. She was on longitude 29°W heading for 51°N, 500 feet below the surface. She left no trace, and nor would she unless she ran right into the path of an American nuclear boat. Three days from now she would slow down and remain totally silent, except when she was snorkeling. On this particular night she would not even come to periscope depth.

Twenty thousand miles above her the satellites scanned the Atlantic Ocean, still searching for the surface ship which could have fired the missile that had downed Starstriker. Below them, the search aircraft laid and relaid their buoy patterns. But there was nothing to show for all this. And Commander Adnam was heading for shallow water, where he would be even more difficult to locate – shallow water where his snorkel mast could more easily be lost in false echoes on searching radars.

He stood quietly in the control center with Lt-Commander

Arash Rajavi. They were looking at a screen showing a North Atlantic chart.

'Right there, Arash. I want to stay right above the Ridge in the shallowest possible water. We're much easier hidden that way. So let's make our course three-one-five for another 500 miles, then switch to zero-four-five all the way up to the Icelandic coast for the refuel. How far does the Rekjanes stretch? 'Bout 1200 miles?'

'Bit more, sir. More like 1350. We ought to be off the southern coast of Iceland by February 15 – that's five days from now.'

'What's our position for the course change, Arash?'

'We'll be at 37 West 54 North . . . That's when we swing northeast at last.' Rajavi indicated the shape of the Ridge, like a big, broad V facing west. 'It would save a lot of trouble to go straight across the gap between the arms rather than follow the line of the Ridge,' he observed for the thousandth time.

'Not if someone picked us up in deep water. We stay right over the Ridge all the way.'

'Aye, sir.'

'You have our destination plotted. See, right here – this big fiord way east of Reykjavik. We'll still be 175 miles south of the Arctic Circle, so there's no danger of our getting frozen in. Also, the bay I've chosen is very quiet and shallow, though deep enough for us to hide, and almost landlocked, so it's hell for a searching radar or sonar. I once went up there with the Royal Navy. It's where one of the big Icelandic rivers flows in . . . Dammit, what's its name again? Ah, right here on the map. The Thjorsa. Flows right down from the central mountains to this place Selfoss.'

'Will they be looking for us yet, sir?'

'If they are, they'll be in the wrong place. That's why I struck twice from exactly the same spot. That's where they'll concentrate their search. We'll be hundreds of miles away by the time they arrive. My only worry would have been if they had gone looking for our refueling tanker . . . but we don't have a tanker, do we, Arash? We have the beautiful *Santa Cecilia*, registered in Panama, just an old coaster running along the shores of Iceland. They won't give it a second glance.'

'You think of everything, sir.'

The CO grinned. 'Still breathing, Arash. That's the test. Officer of the Watch, hold our speed at eight knots for another 20 hours.

We come to periscope depth then, access the satellite, then snorkel for three hours. That's all.'

February 11, the White House, Office of the Vice-President.
Martin Beckman was not the kind of Veep normally associated with a right-wing Republican administration. At age 62 he was a totally unreformed environmentalist, a throwback to the anti-Vietnam marches of the 1960s, a man whose secret patron saint was John Lennon. They had both wanted, with great passion, to Give Peace a Chance. Beckman still did.

He had been selected as a running mate because he was prob ably the most left-wing member of the Republican Party and it was widely believed he might scoop up a few million votes on the college campuses, campaigning on the hot environmental issues of the day. Beckman was also one of those liberal thinkers who, if he could, would have presented every last American dollar to the weak, the sick, the hopeless, the impotent, the pathetic and the poverty stricken. Tough-minded, hard-working successful Americans were not Beckman's game. He believed they could get on with it by themselves.

He was a wealthy man, the recipient of a huge trust fund from his father, an old-time investment banker from New Jersey who had made millions and millions of dollars but had successfully sired only one child. From birth, Beckman Junior had been on the hog's back.

And he had a following. There were people all over the country who believed in and liked the tall genial Easterner who looked very like Franklin D. Roosevelt and displayed similar perfect manners, kind smile and large fortune. Like FDR, Beckman had never done anything in his life except to run for office and to try, instinctively, to make things better for the less fortunate. However, the mere sight of the great liberal, Martin Beckman, working in the clever, cynical, realistic setting of this American presidency was a total incongruity. Like seeing Stormin' Norman Schwarzkopf in a gay bar.

But he was an important Vice-President, because the Chief Executive had made him so. He had handed over for his attention every single left-wing issue that needed addressing. The Veep was the main man in matters of welfare, black education, urban improvements, the environment and peace talks in all their forms, especially if they involved the Third World. The President was not afraid to delegate, and in Martin Beckman he had an extremely capable, loyal man who willingly represented him at all the solemn, tiresome gatherings he wished to avoid.

Beckman, who had never married, was tireless. He sought no glory for himself, and briefed the President often and meticulously on all matters he thought required the attention of the top man. Which was basically why this presidency had steered clear of almost all trouble for the past five years. And why Martin Beckman was about to charge off, with a full staff, to a world peace conference being held in London between many nations – including Iraq, Iran, Libya, Syria and China. This was a group the President could just as easily have hung up by the thumbs, never mind talked peace with.

But it was a highly acclaimed achievement by the British to have organized such a conference. Basically it included the major Commonwealth countries plus the nations of Europe, the Middle East, the old Soviet Union, the United States, Japan, Brazil and Argentina. Third World countries were not included, but all the Arab nations were because this was essentially a discussion about money and oil and trade. It sought to clarify the idea of peace based on economics. More cynically stated, it represented the oldest bedrock of modern civilization: how can the rich keep the poor under control without going bust in the process?

Martin Beckman had been nominated to chair the conference, and he rightly regarded this as a great honor. The President was delighted, and his second-in-command would travel to London with the kind of backup usually reserved for a presidential state visit. Beckman would travel with a major staff of twenty-four, plus two Democratic congressmen, one from California and one from New York. Their London headquarters was already in place at the US Embassy in Grosvenor Square. It was the most widely publicized gathering of international statesmen for years.

The entire US team would make the journey together in the brand new intercontinental Presidential jet, *Air Force Three*, a lavishly modified Boeing 747. Colonel Al Jaxtimer, a former B-52 Air Force pilot in the Fifth Bomb Wing, out at Minot Air Base, North Dakota, would fly the aircraft, assisted by his long-time co-pilot, Major Mike Parker and his regular navigation officer, Lieutanant Chuck Ryder. The three had flown many missions together, and in accordance with the new US Air Force policy would fly the presidential jet as a team for a period of two years.

For the peace mission they would fly from Andrews Air Base direct to London Heathrow. They would be met by the US Ambassador to the Court of St James, who would travel to the embassy with Martin Beckman in an open limousine, assuming a clear day. It was anticipated that a vast throng of British peace marchers would line the route to the left of the north-running road through Hyde Park, to clap and cheer the Vice-President of the United States, the man upon whom so many hopes were pinned, the farseeing man who seemed to hold the hope of the modern world in his hands.

The President of the United States himself, not to mention his National Security Advisor, privately considered the whole lot of them, including the Arab-sympathizer Martin Beckman, were out of their minds.

But, sane or not, the US delegation to the four-day Peace Conference of Nations took off in *Air Force Three* on the morning of Tuesday, February 21. And the journey was everything Martin Beckman had hoped, a beautifully smooth Atlantic crossing, an impressive reception at the airport, and a rapturous welcome among the cold green lawns of London's Hyde Park, where thousands turned up and lined the route.

The great swelling sound of their anthem, 'Give Peace a Chance,' could be heard a mile away. Martin Beckman waved in greeting, visibly moved by the far-lost sounds of his younger years as the haunting bittersweet words of the song drifted up through the bare trees. He found himself thinking, irrationally, 'My God, I just wish John Lennon could be with me right here. What a moment for all of us who believed then, when no one else did.' He was right, too. It was the highest moment in a privileged life. Martin Beckman, the world's best-known liberal, might even take a run at the presidency in 2008.

During the conference, London was a city under martial law. The delegates used the great forum of the Guildhall for their deliberations, and thus more or less brought the financial district to a standstill twice a day, since the Prime Minister had authorized the army to throw a cordon around the building in readiness for a threatened terrorist attack by the Irish Republican Army. In

London this was a likelihood as powerful as ever after the total failure of the latest round of peace talks and, in the IRA's view, the total failure of the British Prime Minister to control the intransigence of the Ulster Unionists.

All the major embassies in London were under guard by the police and the military, as were London's leading hotels. You could have mistaken the Connaught for Catterick Barracks. There seemed to be enough uniformed soldiers outside the Savoy Hotel and the Grosvenor House Hotel in Mayfair for a winter Trooping the Colour. The US military, in plain evidence on the great steps of their own embassy, made the west side of the square look like West Point.

No one could remember security like it. But Britain's Anti-Terrorist Squad believed an attack was not only possible, it was likely. And their general view was that if any delegate, *anyone*, from any nation was injured by a bomb, the reputation of the capital city of the United Kingdom would be forever tarnished. Worse yet, the Anti-Terrorist Squad would get the blame. Thus no chances were being taken. The world's delegates for peace would carry out their duties protected by those who believed that real strength came from hardassed military training, top-class battle equipment, wary eyes and a big stick.

The conference itself was a brilliant success. The press reported it nonstop. It led on every television newscast, the newpapers were filled with interviews from delegates, and the discussions which took place in the great forum were reported diligently. Even the private deliberations between individual nations were followed almost immediately by a press release. All over the world, the firm but understanding voice of Martin Beckman was heard. Matters of great moment for the Third World – and indeed for the survival of a free world without war – were debated long and hard.

The delegates tackled the most vexing subjects of the previous decade, such as the crippling burden of Third World debt, which, at the turn of the millennium, meant that every single person in the Third World owed a total of $400 to the Western banks. For three years now there had been suggestions that the Third World countries must ultimately be forgiven these debts, in some way, because most of them simply could not pay – not if they were also to run their countries. There were penniless African nations whose repayments each year added up to more than their GNP.

Naturally the question of corruption came up – how these African dictators were running around in Rolls Royces and stealing Western aid to hide it away in Swiss banks. But Martin Beckman stood up in his seat for the first time in the conference and made a highly impassioned plea, almost begging the richer nations to force their banks to forgive at least half of the debt. He ended his speech with words that were heard around the world: 'It is not just a matter of corruption, it is a matter of humanity, a plea for someone to listen to their plight, a plea to someone to respond to the heartbreaking conditions, a plea to end, in the name of God, these areas of stark, human misery.'

He got his way, too. The delegates agreed unanimously to recommend that their governments attack the problem, forcing the banks to listen to reason: that it was not all the fault of the poor nations. Much of the problem could be laid at the door of the banks themselves, for making highly injudicious loans to those who plainly could not repay – worse, who did not understand the terms correctly. Martin Beckman was on the verge of reserving himself a significant place in modern financial history.

The delegates also worked on the problem of the burgeoning grain mountains, examining ways to ship the vast tonnage of surplus cereals from Europe and the United States to the Third World. They hammered out a rota system whereby other nations would contribute the shipping and freight costs to match the contributions of the governments which supplied the wheat, oats and barley.

They tackled the world oil-distribution problem. At least, they tried to. But there was a certain reserve among the Middle Eastern nations, most of whom had recently mortgaged years of 'futures' in order to buy warships and aircraft. China, whose voracious appetite for automobile fuel was reaching gluttonous proportions, stayed out of this discussion despite Martin Beckman's assertion that they were currently using more refined oil than the United States.

Nonetheless, it was tacitly agreed that all the nations represented at the conference would resolve to insure that the world's tanker routes would remain open for free trade, for the greater good. Iran, the nation which strategically controls the Strait of Hormuz, voted in favour of this only after Martin Beckman made another speech suggesting that any blockade of the Gulf would cause untold hardship to the sick, the elderly and the children of the poorer European nations.

'This is a conference about humanity, for humanity,' he said. 'I am quite certain that all the nations here would wish to proceed in that spirit . . . I do not think anyone in this room would approve any nation making oblique threats to cause hardship to any of our fellow men. Not here, Iran. This is a forum for peacful coexistence among nations, and I defy you to vote against a resolution for the sustainment of the peaceful trade routes of the world's principal fuel.'

Thus the guardians of the Strait were shamed into joining the unanimous vote for free and open tanker routes, wherever the tides ebb and flow on the planet earth.

Martin Beckman had arrived in London a hero of the left. As he prepared to depart for Washington on Sunday morning, February 26, he was a hero of the people – and not just the people of Great Britain and the United States. He was a hero of the people of the world. His was the voice of decency and reason, a man whose clearly defined basic goodness came through to all the delegates who dealt with him.

Certainly the world leaders present recognized that he spoke with enormous authority, as the Vice-President of the world's most powerful nation. But Beckman never specified what that nation itself might or might not do. He came to the conference with an air of modesty, and, despite being lauded by the international press on an almost hourly basis, departed with the same humility. Which was a considerable achievement, because it seemed that every person in the crowd which had thronged the eastern edge of Hyde Park to see him arrive now swarmed into the precincts of Heathrow Airport to see him depart.

The security was massive as the US delegation arrived at Terminal Four, but thousands and thousands of students nevertheless packed the viewing galleries and the fences along the perimeter to watch the gleaming new Boeing of the US presidency take off for Washington. And, as it did so, above the roar of the four giant Pratt & Whitney engines there could still be heard the anthem of the doves, swelling out across the airport. The unforgettable words of the slain John Lennon rose into the winter sky, lilting, beseeching, over and over, turning the commercial sprawl of Heathrow Airport into a sacred cathedral on this cloudless Sunday morning: 'All we are sa-a-ying . . . is give peace a chance . . .'

260900FEB06. 53.20N 20.00W. Course 180, speed 9, depth 300. HMS *Unseen*, fully refueled and stored, had been running quietly south from the frozen shores of Iceland for four days, snorkeling for the shortest possible periods. And now, 470 miles due west of Galway, Commander Adnam ordered the submarine to periscope depth once more.

They raised the big communications mast and sucked down the critical message from the satellite. *Unseen* was back underwater, cruising south, by the time the commanding officer decrypted it. *'Target 3.* Air Force Three *VP–US aboard. ETD/LHR 1100GMT. En route Washington direct, GCR, via waypoints Bravo, Golf, Kilo, November, Papa, Quebec, and X-Ray. Squawking IFF Code Three, 2471.'*

The Sunday morning air traffic was busy, but not so busy as on a weekday. Trans-Atlantic jetliners were using four of the northerly routes across the ocean, stacked four high. This meant that on average every nine minutes a big passenger aircraft from one of the European capital cities would be passing overhead, flying at about 420 knots at a minimum altitude of 33,000 feet. Sometime after 1210 (GMT) HMS *Unseen* would begin her target search – for the only one using IFF Code 2471.

The time passed slowly in the black submarine, but at last the boat came back to periscope depth, going to full alert shortly after 1200 (GMT). At 1233 the radar screen detected IFF Code 2471 for the first time.

'Squawk Code 2471, sir. Bearing one-zero-zero. Range 224 miles.'

1235: 'Range 204 miles, sir. Track and CPA assessed. Distance off-track 34 miles.'

'That's too tight. I'm going to make a fast run south,' snapped Ben Adnam. 'Ten down . . . 150 feet . . . make your speed 18 knots. I want to be back up and looking by eight miles to CPA.'

The submarine drove down under the Atlantic waves, leaving no mark on the choppy surface. The planesman leveled off at 150 feet, and then *Unseen* accelerated, running flat-out through the deep, eating up the distance, but risking detection as her electric motors powered her forward.

At 1245 the Americans picked her up on SOSUS, the great underwater electronic network which scans the oceans on behalf of the United States. It was a quiet day at the US listening station at Keflavik, way out on Iceland's southwestern peninsula, and the urgency in the voice of the young operator was surprising. 'I'm getting something, sir. Not engine lines, but it's a noise source of some kind, probably flow noise. I don't think it's weather.'

His supervisor moved swiftly over to check it out. There were still no machine-originated lines coming up, but it was a very definite noise. And it was not a fish. That left the only other fast-moving creature under the sea . . .

The supervisor strained his eyes for five minutes, searching for a clue. Shaft count? Blade count? Not a whisper. No tell-tale pattern came up on the screen.

At 1256 the marks faded, then died altogether as HMS *Unseen* slowed right down and began to head back to the surface.

The supervisor moved away, told the operator to stay sharp, and immediately sent a signal to Fort Meade, Maryland. 'Eleven-minute transient underwater contact at 1245GMT. Position 50N 20W – accuracy plus/minus 200 miles. Insufficient data for classification other than possible flow noise. Zero correlation on friendly nets.'

The signal was on Admiral George Morris's desk by 0800 (EST). The Director had been there since 0700, and he read the message carefully, simultaneously hitting the secure line to the White House, directly into the office of the President's National Security Advisor.

At 1258 the radar operator in *Unseen*, now at periscope depth, was scanning the skies to the east. Within 30 seconds he had re-established the track and the CPA. 'Target approaches 49 miles. Distance off-track 20.'

'Surface! Blow all main ballast.'

HMS *Unseen* climbed malevolently out of the Atlantic, smashing her way through the waves, green water surging over the casing, the missile launcher stark against the empty skyline as the radar tracked the incoming *Air Force Three*, bearing home the champion from the Peace Conference of Nations.

'Speed 420 knots, sir.'

'Range now 42 miles, sir.'

'Check surface picture. Anything out there, inside 12 miles? . . . Nothing? Perfect.'

'We have an adequate firing solution within the parameters, sir.'

'Target holds course and speed. CPA unchanged. Entering the missile envelope, sir.'

Commander Adnam nodded, checked his watch. 'Countdown?'

'Sixty seconds, sir.'

1302.20secs: *'Missile launch!'*

HMS *Unseen's* third SA-N-6 Grumble Rif blasted off from the deck of the ex-Royal Navy diesel–electric. With fire roaring from behind, it streaked into the skies, climbing to 2000 feet in three seconds, where it should have accelerated. Instead, it abruptly blew itself to smithereens, showering the ocean with flame, sparks and shrapnel.

'Malfunction, Sir! Missile has self-destructed!'

But the CO had seen the sudden, unaccountable destruction and the heavy cloud of smoke which hung high above his ship. With the launch aborted, he ordered the fire-control team to program and launch missile four.

At 1303.20secs the replacement weapon fired, screaming into the sky with a perfect vertical takeoff to reach 33,000 feet in under 20 seconds, angling across to the CPA , toward which *Air Force Three*, still 15 miles out, was making 420 knots.

Colonel Jaxtimer saw it through the clear skies, or at least he saw the vertical smoke-trail way out in front. The ex-USAF bomber pilot reacted instantly. He was trained for this, and he was ready, and he knew what he was seeing. His broadcast waveband was open to Shannon, ready for the 20°W waypoint, and he hit it instantly. 'Missile! This is a guided missile!'

As he spoke the SA-N-6 changed course and came straight at the presidential Boeing. Al Jaxtimer, still on the line to Shannon ATC, saw it. He hit the decoy button, knowing it to be near-useless in a head-on attack, and then hauled on the stick, trying to evade. But the big Boeing was not built to be a fighter plane. The Shannon operator heard the colonel cry out, *'Jesus! Mike!'* as the big Russian-made weapon came screaming in, smashed into the area right below the nose, exploded, and blew apart *Air Force Three* along with everyone who flew in her.

In the control center of *Unseen*, the words that signified a task accomplished were simple. 'No contact on radar bearing, captain.'

'Thank you, gentlemen. Nice recovery. Open main vents. Take her deep – 300 feet. Make your speed nine when you're down there. Course zero-four-five.'

It was precisely 1305 (GMT).

0805, Office of the National Security Advisor, the White House.
Arnold Morgan gazed at the communication from the Icelandic listening station; George Morris had faxed it over from Fort Meade. Morgan looked at the time the US surveillance team had picked up the transient contact. Twelve forty-five. 'Jesus! Twenty minutes ago. Not bad.' He walked over to his big sloping chart desk, whose light was permanently on, and checked the position.

He took his calipers and made some measurements, muttering to himself constantly. 'Something out there on 20 West, way south, opposite the west of Ireland . . . could *he* be out there? And, if he is, what the hell's he doing? It's 17 days now since Starstriker went down, but this signal is telling me the guys at Keflavik think they may just have detected a diesel–electric, and that bastard's in one.

'Let's see . . . Uh-huh, he could be in that position very easily. But why's he in such a goddamned hurry? What's he doing running his boat at a speed like that for eleven whole minutes? He must know we might get onto him. Beats the hell outta me, but he must think it's worth it.

'He's too far north to be after another supersonic airliner. And there's not many warships out there. It beats the hell out of me. But what do I know? Not a lot, except he got two supersonics and he might be after a third. That's still not much, but it's a whole lot more than some of these other assholes around here know.'

He buzzed Kathy and asked her if there was anything he could reasonably offer her to acquire a cup of coffee. 'I'm up for anything – dinner tonight, marriage, undying love . . . whatever pleases you. But – black with buckshot, dingbats!'

Kathy shook her head, fixed him some coffee and walked into

his office. There she found her boss and future husband hunched over a map of the North Atlantic, pressing the buttons of a small calculator. 'He coulda got there – no doubt about it. And, since George couldn't find a trace of another diesel–electric boat within hundreds of miles, and since even the Brits haven't the first idea who it might be, I guess that's gotta be him, right?'

'Right,' said Kathy. 'Here, drink this. Will I presume you are still searching for your phantom Arab submariner?'

'I'm not sure I haven't *found* the sonofabitch,' Morgan growled. 'At least, a very sharp young man in Iceland may have found him.'

'Iceland!' said Kathy. 'I thought he was an Arab, not an Eskimo.'

Morgan smiled. 'No. They just caught a noise they thought might be a submarine up there. Pretty vague, but plausible for the man I seek. He gives away nothing if he can help it. And he ain't given us much this time, either.'

By 0820, he had finished his coffee and was preparing to attend a meeting in Bob MacPherson's office when the phone rang. It was Admiral Morris again, from Fort Meade.

'Arnold? George here. *Air Force Three*'s down in the Atlantic. No survivors. Hit by a missile. The pilot saw it, and he had time to broadcast it. I gotta recording. Last known position 20 West 53 North. I'm sticking right here.'

Admiral Morgan felt the blood draining from his face. His mouth went dry, and there was a tremble deep within him. He could find no words. He just stood in the middle of the room in total shock.

Kathy O'Brien came back through the door and she thought he was having a heart attack. 'My God! Arnold, what's the matter? Here, come and sit down.'

Morgan walked to his desk and sat down with his head in his hands. 'Just please tell me if you're ill,' she said. 'Shall I get a doctor?'

'No. No. I'm OK. But I just heard *Air Force Three* has been hit by a guided missile, right where I'm guessing Adnam is on the chart. The Boeing's down in the North Atlantic. No survivors.'

'Holy Mary, Mother of God,' said the Irish redhead. 'Please tell me this is a joke. Was Martin on board?'

'The whole team was on board. Al Jaxtimer had time to broadcast. He saw the missile which killed everyone.'

Just then the admiral's private line to the Oval Office lit up red, the signal for the NSA to report to the President immediately. He pulled on his jacket, grabbed the chart he had been working on and walked swiftly to the private office of the Chief Executive.

The great man was alone, pacing the room. His face, like Morgan's, displayed only numb shock and sadness. However, he had not summoned his senior military advisor merely to join him in grief, and Morgan knew that. Before the door was closed he heard the President say, 'Well, Arnold, that's that. You were right. That theory of yours has panned out. There's someone out there shooting down airliners. I don't think any reasonable person could arrive at any other conclusion.'

'No, sir. And they have to be doing it from a submarine. And there's only one submarine which could be doing it, and that's the one missing from the Royal Navy. As you know, sir, in my opinion there's also only one man who could be doing it. And he's not as dead as we thought.'

The admiral laid out his Navy chart on the table and pointed at longitude 20°W. 'Twenty minutes before *AF3* was hit, sir, right down here, our listening station in Iceland picked him up on SOSUS. They couldn't be accurate about position and the boat was too far away to put up engine lines, but they thought it worth reporting as a possible submarine running through the water – quite fast, I should think. It was for 11 minutes only. It had to be him, sir . . .'

Just then one of the private phones rang and the President picked it up. Then he handed it to Morgan. 'It's for you . . .'

'Morgan. Hi, George. Yup. Yup. What was it? Merchant ship. Jesus Christ! We're gonna have trouble keeping this one quiet.'

He replaced the receiver and said to the President, 'This is developing into an even bigger horror story. A British merchant ship in the area, running 20 miles due south of the datum, reported in on the air–sea rescue band. They saw the smoke-trails from two missiles. The first seemed to explode right above the water. Then they saw a much longer trail going very high. After that they thought they saw fire and wreckage falling toward the water. They're heading into the area right now. That means the Irish and the Brits already know something diabolical has happened.'

'They're right, too. It has. But you and I alone, Arnold, cannot have the luxury of grieving. Not right now. We have to get this into line. And we have to stop this sonofabitch. I mean – Jesus! – he can't just park himself in the middle of the Atlantic and keep firing missiles at passenger jets.'

'Yes he can, sir. He can in that submarine. It's just like the Russian Kilo. If he stays deep and slow we might not find him in a year. Not if he can discover a way to refuel without us catching him – which he obviously has, because he must have refueled several times already. If he can find his way to relatively shallow inshore waters – which is what that submarine was designed for – we might *never* find him. The ocean's just too fucking big, and that boat is too damned stealthy.'

'Arnold, there has to be a way.'

'Sir, whether there's a way or not we sure as hell have to try. I was about to call Joe Mulligan and give him the new search datum. I'm assuming the Royal Navy is sending in a couple of ships to try to locate whatever floating wreckage there may be. I'm afraid we're running out of deep-submergence submarines. At this rate we need a new one every couple of weeks.' He paused, then added: 'Do you have to broadcast, sir?'

'I'm not certain. But I guess so. Tonight.'

'Well, sir, I better go and establish who knows what, and who has already said what to whom. Will we reconvene in, say, one hour?'

'Yes. Come right back here – make it ten o'clock. Give me a little time to chat to Dick Stafford, and Harcourt . . . Jesus, this is unbelievable!'

The admiral's inquiries seemed to be overtaken by a new development every five minutes, but he noted the hard, salient facts down in his log in the characteristic manner of an ex-nuclear submarine commander:

1. 261304(GMT)FEB06. 53N, 20W app. *AF3* hit by guided missile fired from sea level. Destroyed. Plainly no survivors.

2. Oceanic Control, Shannon, has tape of Col. Jaxtimer's voice

199

confirming missile sighting. Tape removed by Station Chief in accordance with international airline agreements. Now held securely, pending arrival of US Ambassador from Dublin and US Naval Attaché from London.

3. Shannon alerted all air–sea rescue networks to crash. They estimate it took place 470 miles due W of Galway.

4. Irish and UK press found out that *AF3* was down app. 1330 (GMT). US press picked up newsflashes 1340 (GMT), 0840 (EST).

5. Gander ATC not involved. *AF3* had not yet checked in.

6. One Irish operator and one supervisor heard Col. Jaxtimer's last words. Both men reputedly senior, reliable, bound by classified-information rules inherent in their job. But they know and are not under our control.

7. UK merchant ship saw two missile smoke trails. Broadcast this information on air–sea rescue networks. May have been heard by several ships, but we have not located *any* other ships in the area. UK captain bound for Cardiff docks, S. Wales.

8. MOD, Whitehall, unhopeful of castiron secrecy even if no one else heard merchantman's broadcast. But captain will be met in Cardiff by MI5, plus reps from US Embassy, London. Captain ex-RN, former surface ship Lt, which is hopeful.

9. Assessment of chances of keeping missile attack secret: not high. Must plan for it to leak out inside week.

10. Assessment press angle when they find out: they'll go for terrorism since we're not at war.

At this point Morgan closed his book and called Admiral Mulligan for the third time in 45 minutes.

'Hi, Arnold,' Mulligan said. 'We got two LA-Class boats up that way, both attached to the *John Stennis* CVBG. They've been heading north up the Atlantic for a few days now, but they're within 12 hours of the datum. I put the whole group on high alert. But we've no idea which way the submarine will run – north, south, east, west.'

'I know. It's a fucking frustration, right?'

'Yeah, that and the fact that in 12 hours, even if he's making only five knots, deep and quiet, he's still going to be anywhere in a circle radius of 60 miles – somewhere in the middle of over 10,000 square miles. If he makes a fast run for it, which I don't think he'll do because of SOSUS, you could very quickly double that.'

'Why do you think they heard him, Joe, just before he fired?'

'I'd say he wasn't happy with his position off–track, and with the Boeing charging in toward him he had to make his adjustment very fast. He took the risk and ran the boat flat out to get into the best firing position, and they caught him. But then he went slow again, so they never heard him again.'

'You know the problem with this bastard, Joe? He's a perfectionist in a submarine. Hardly ever takes a chance, never makes a mistake. I must say I'm filled with foreboding about this. But we have to catch him, Joe.

'I'm just afraid he'll strike again before we do.'

CHAPTER EIGHT

THE DEATH OF Martin Beckman was a staggering blow to the morale of the Western world. The United States was stunned, coast to coast. This was the kind of public grief hitherto reserved for John F. Kennedy, for his brother Robert, and for Martin Luther King. For men whose vision had given great swathes of the populace a reason for hope and optimism. No vice-president in the entire history of the nation had ever come close, in death, to causing such a widespread outpouring of mass despair. In London, the former New Jersey senator had touched a chord of high, unselfish principle and reasoned promise, just as the Kennedy brothers and the Reverend King had done, almost every time they spoke publicly.

On this late Sunday afternoon, in churches of every denomination all over the United States, services were concluded with renderings of John Lennon's everlasting song. And all through this night thousands and thousands of ordinary American people would keep a candlelit peace vigil outside the White House. By 6pm the vast crowd was already massed all the way back to the Washington Memorial. Huddled together in coats, parkas, scarves, gloves and fur hats, they crowded the icy acres of West Potomac Park, along the Reflecting Pool right to the steps of the Lincoln Memorial. And each time the bells of nearby St John's Church behind the White House tolled out the hour, a thunderous chorus of the dead Vice-President's beloved anthem lifted up through the black winter skies of the American capital: 'All we are sa-a-ying . . . is give peace a chance.'

Martin Beckman had touched the soul of a nation. These people, gathered on this freezing evening, believed that somewhere out there, perhaps now on the mystic foothills of heaven's Mount Olympus, the Great Champion of Peace still stood tall. And they believed that his voice would never be silenced, just as the voice of the Reverend King had never died away. They believed the memory of Martin Beckman would always remind the most powerful nations of an ironclad world to listen to his plea for the plight of the Third World poor . . . in the name of God, to look on the plain, heartrending face of stark human misery.

Perhaps in death the Vice-President's avowed cause would grow even greater. But back in the Oval Office, where the President, his NSA, Bob MacPherson and Admirals Dunsmore and Mulligan racked their collective brains, the talk was not of peace. It involved the massed resources of the United States Armed Forces taking up secret battle stations against the great underwater terrorist from a distant desert.

It was Secretary of State Harcourt Travis who brought the voice of the cold-blooded detective to the meeting. Appraised once again this evening of the suspicions of Admirals Morgan and Mulligan, this time he did not dissent, but suggested an organized shortlist of suspects be produced, just to demonstrate, if necessary, that things were not being run in a haphazard way.

Morgan's face betrayed a hint of irritation as he replied, 'I got it right here, Harcourt. Been updating it every four hours for three weeks. I'll read it to you and give you a copy. Sometimes I forget that politicians spend at least one-third of their time covering their asses. In my game you don't always have time for that.'

'If this situation should somehow get out of hand, you might be grateful to me,' replied the Secretary of State, smiling thinly.

The NSA grinned back, no more warmly. 'Goddamned bureaucrat,' he muttered. In a louder voice he continued: 'Now, pay attention. There are four nations which have submarines out there that we cannot locate at present, and have not located during the entire period of the three crashes.

'One, a French strategic-missile boat, the 14,500-ton *Le Temeraire*, commissioned in 1999, based in Brest. She's probably on patrol in the Bay of Biscay, but anyway we discount her as a suspect. We'd have picked her up if she'd been in the middle of the Atlantic.

'Two, the Royal Navy has a Trident SSBN out there somewhere, HMS *Vengeance*. She's bigger, 16,000 tons, and also was commissioned in 1999. If we ask the Brits where she is they'll tell us, but I don't think that's necessary in the light of our close association with them in this matter.

'Three, the Russians have two which we cannot locate. The first is TK-17 – that's one of those 21,000-ton Typhoons out of the Northern Fleet, Litsa Guba. She was damaged by fire in 1994, but they repaired her. She's a strategic-missile boat. Most unlikely, but possible, although I'm damned sure we'd got her if she'd been in the area. The other is a Delta IV, K-18, 13,500 tons, out of Saida Guba, again the Northern Fleet. We'll probably pick her up in the next few days. She's another strategic-missile boat, and no more likely to have avoided detection than the Typhoon. But I'm planning to touch base with Moscow tomorrow, just to check.

'Four, China has one missing, her newest, 094. She's a medium-sized, 6500-ton strategic-missile boat developed from the old Xia-Class. Received a new missile system up in Huladao back in 1998. But she's based on the other side of the world. I suppose she's a possibility, but highly improbable. That Chinese boat is way behind Western technology, and would be even less likely than the Russian Delta to avoid SOSUS. And I doubt the Chinese would wanna operate so close to us and so far from home. Remember, in the past two or three years, they have, er, lost some of their, er, top guys.'

Admiral Morgan paused and peered over the half-spectacles he now used for reading. He was staring at the Secretary of State. 'The other possibility, Mr Travis,' he said elaborately, 'is called HMS *Unseen*. And for me she's fucking well named.'

'Thank you, Arnold. Just checking,' Travis responded brightly, still smiling.

The President asked the critical question. 'How long do you think we have to locate and destroy this fucking submarine before the world starts to speculate, and then finds out about it?'

'Not long, sir,' Admirals Morgan and Mulligan answered in unison. The NSA added, 'In my view, probably less than two weeks. I think the media will stick to their theory that there's a "Bermuda Triangle" out on the edge of space until it finally sinks in that *Air Force Three* was downed from a much lower altitude in a very different place. Then they're going to try and connect all three crashes in some other way, all related to big US interests. No other nation harmed except the Brits, who are anyway considered by our enemies to be the 51st state. All the flights were easy to locate through their known departure times, etc.

'Then there's going to be one tiny whisper out of somewhere that the Concorde pilot tried to shout "Missile!" After that there'll be a tiny leak of the last call from *Air Force Three*. Then there'll be a barrage of inquiries demanding to know if there was *anywhere* the missile could have been fired from. Then the captain of that merchant ship will sell his story to a tabloid and the headline will read: "WERE ALL THREE AIRCRAFT SHOT DOWN BY MISSILES?" Then one of the defense correspondent guys will actually wonder whether it could have been launched from a disappearing submarine.

'At which point we would have to run the risk of looking very, very foolish if we dismissed it as a possibility. That's a "worst case" scenario, but we want to be ready.'

'That, Arnold is not good. Not good at all.' The President was frowning deeply, his face displaying profound worry. 'The ramifications are simply horrific. Imagine the press arriving at the conclusion that there is a rogue submarine, undetected, out in the middle of the Atlantic, knocking down passenger airliners. The mere fact that they got to that conclusion apparently before we did would make us look criminally careless.

'Then they'd go after us – dumbass military, dumbass politicians, the usual. Then there'd be a real crisis of confidence. Calls for my resignation, and probably all of yours, too. Then there'd follow a world airline crisis, with some passenger carriers refusing to make the North Atlantic run. That kind of stuff can bankrupt airlines, and passengers would be canceling flights wholesale.

'That would cause a stock-market crash of every industry connected with airlines. You'd see big publicly held stocks cave in, and corporations who build planes and aircraft parts would suffer staggering losses. Banks owed big sums of money from airlines and plane-makers would go into a collective tailspin, if you'll excuse the pun. The whole thing could turn into your worst nightmare.'

''Specially if that bastard Adnam bangs out another one,' growled Morgan.

'Jesus Christ,' groaned the President. 'And you know the media are gonna just love it. They'll come at us like a pack of starved dogs. And they'll demonstrate all their familiar traits –

ignorance, naivety, innocence – dressed up as ferocity. I guess they'll never learn that the games governments play are usually much more complicated than the games they *pretend* to play.'

'No, sir,' replied the NSA, 'they won't ever learn that. But they'll always love wading in and upsetting the applecart. Despite the obvious fact that any damnfool hack can upset an applecart. That's easy. It's understanding the entire picture and then acting carefully that's hard. And, anyway, the press don't have time for that.'

Admiral Dunsmore, the Chairman of the Joint Chiefs, spoke next, in his usual calm and thoughtful way. 'Despite our general disapproval of the way the media are about to behave,' he said, 'I think we can be sure they won't do much tomorrow. They'll be too busy handling the news story. But we should take very definite steps to keep the lid on this for as long as possible. No good can possibly come out of a public uproar.

'So far as I can tell, we have two objectives. One, to seek and destroy HMS *Unseen* before she strikes again. Two, to bottle up the situation, tight, until that's done. Even then we might never be able to announce what has happened.'

'Expertly stated, Scott,' said the President. 'Please continue.'

'Thus I think we should have patrols organized around Iceland and right across the GIUK Gap. We should keep the *John C. Stennis* group in the area and have them work east from 30 West, then move south for maybe 200 miles before heading west again. That way we might just push *Unseen* into an area covered by SOSUS. I would also like to see three more frigates up there, and I suggest Joe Mulligan and I have a strategic meeting as soon as possible.

'In regard to keeping the story tight, I think we should have our ambassador in Dublin pull a few strings to ensure the Irish understand that it was *our* Vice-President who died, *our* two Congressmen who were lost, that the aircraft was US military, and that the entire matter is regarded as classified by both ourselves and the UK.

'I think we should also prevail on the Brits to shut up that merchant-ship captain. That may take a threat, but Whitehall is very expert at this sort of thing. I believe we have the black box recording from Concorde under tight control. So, if we're careful, we might be more successful than Arnold believes at shutting this story down.'

'Christ, I hope so, Scott,' replied Morgan. 'To get back to the search operations, I've instructed George Morris to beef up our satellite surveillance of that part of the Atlantic, and SOSUS is already fully in the picture. Trouble is, *Unseen* is undetectable if she stays slow and deep. Even when she snorkels she's a whole lot quieter than a Kilo. And if she's being driven by Adnam there's gonna be no mistakes. He won't even snorkel in good SOSUS water if he can help it.'

'What are your instructions to our commanding officers, Joe?'

'Uncompromising and closely controlled, sir. If they locate a diesel–electric boat showing an unequivocal Upholder-Class signature, anywhere near the area, to sink it.'

'Christ, what if they sink the wrong one? The owners will be seriously pissed off.'

Admiral Mulligan chuckled. 'Sir, the Royal Navy have no diesel–electrics at sea. They only owned four of these boats. They sold one to Israel and we know that's in Haifa. Two are out of commission in Barrow-in-Furness. The last of the four is *Unseen*. I've already spoken to the First Sea Lord. The Royal Navy have their own frigates out there as well. If they trip over a diesel–electric with a U-Class signature, *they*'ll sink it.'

Morgan interjected: 'Sir, it would be better to hunt the boat to exhaustion, then capture it on the surface. That way we could catch Adnam and his crew and hang the fucking Iraqis out to dry. That way no one would object to whatever reprisals we might wish to take. But we may prefer not to risk that with this bastard, sir. He's too slippery. We just might lose him.'

'Yes, Arnold. I do see that. By the way, what precisely do you mean by "hunt to exhaustion"? I'm not familiar with that.'

'It's a submariners' phrase, sir. It means setting out a kind of dragnet on the surface, using a mass of radar, and keeping the target sub submerged, with his battery getting lower and lower. Every time he comes to periscope depth he picks up a surface ship or aircraft ready to detect his snorkel mast. He has no option but to go deep and hope that the coast will be clear when he comes up later. But his battery will eventually get very low, and he'll have to come up again. He may get lucky, may be able to snorkel for 20 minutes, except then he's caught again. But 20 minutes isn't enough – he can't submerge for long enough to get away because someone's bound to catch him on radar. Then the real hunt is on. You bring in a surface ship real close, something which can knock off his snorkel mast and cut off the air-supply to the engines.

'Right then, he's nearly finished. He has to surface. And that's when we bang a couple of shells through his sail as a gesture of our interest. Then we accept her surrender, board the submarine and interrogate the crew.'

'Well, if I was driving the submarine, gentlemen, I'd sink the surface ship with a torpedo,' said the President.

'Sir,' said Admiral Mulligan, 'we have many ways of avoiding torpedoes if we have good prior warning. Especially if we know precisely where our enemy is located. In such a case, if our CO believed there was a real danger from the submarine, we would simply attack first. Those are the orders my men have at this moment. And to me they make military sense.

'However, Arnold has political obligations. He wants to find out who the hell these people are. And he's right. I'll change the orders to my COs. Delete "Sink on Sight," substitute "Hunt to Exhaustion." '

At that moment the President's private phone rang and confirmed he would be broadcasting briefly to the nation at 9pm. Giant television monitoring screens were being erected all through the parkland to the south and southwest of the White House, where there were now an estimated half-million people gathered in tribute to the dead Vice-President and his staff.

Dick Stafford, the Press Secretary, was waiting outside the Oval Office, preparing to go over the speech with the Chief Executive. Clearances were being requested for the forthcoming memorial service for Martin Beckman, which would be held in the massive graystone edifice of Washington's National Cathedral, three miles to the northwest of the White House. The great bells of the Cathedral Church of St Peter and St Paul would toll for Martin Beckman throughout this night.

The President called his meeting with the military to a close, thanked everyone for their efforts, and approved their recommendations. He went on to say he wished he were leaving with them to work on the plan to eliminate, finally, the specter of Commander Adnam. But that was impossible. As the President phrased

208

it, 'Guess I have to stay right here and mind the store.' And as Bob MacPherson added, lingering behind for a few moments, 'Minding the store might be a lot better than helping these guys. They've got an uphill struggle. And if they fail to catch him, and he hits again, heads are gonna roll.'

Meanwhile the three admirals were all headed in different directions – Morgan to Fort Meade, Mulligan to COMSU-BLANT in the Norfolk yards, and Dunsmore to his house along the Potomac.

Arnold Morgan would spend the entire evening with Admiral George Morris, watching the satellite reports and praying for a breakthrough, just a sighting of the missing British diesel. They would also watch the presidential broadcast and then, sometime after midnight, the NSA would call his old sparring partner in the Kremlin, Admiral Vitaly Rankov, Chief of the Main Staff, the third most powerful man in the Russian Navy. It was a call to which he was not looking forward.

The evening passed swiftly. Morgan and Morris pored over charts, studied photographs, and tried to get into the mind of Ben Adnam. Which way would he go? Or was he still lurking 500 feet below the surface, right above the Atlantic Ridge, where SOSUS's detection efforts would not be quite so efficient? Every two hours, satellite reports came in to Fort Meade. At 2035, shortly before the President's broadcast, a picture from Big Bird confirmed that Chinese submarine 094 was cruising east through the Shanghai Roads. Neither of the American admirals was surprised.

The presidential broadcast was the highlight of the television coverage, which was relaying routine messages of condolence from heads of state all over the world. They were all sympathetic, all complimentary, all despondent about the future of world harmony without Martin Beckman. But none of them contained the pure cry from the soul that was echoed in the words of the President of the United States. No one would ever forget his unscripted concluding passage.

'I never once briefed Martin on any issue which involved the poor and the underprivileged. There are no words to convey to such a man the depth of the despair of the Third World. He needed no words, no paper, no files, no parchment, no rules to play by, because his rules were written on his heart. I don't know quite what we'll do without him.'

On the following day, no fewer than eight major East Coast city tabloids printed their front page edged in black. The tone of the media was, for once, pure shock, as if none would dare to offend a single citizen with a smartass tasteless headline. The *New York Times* led the way with two massive lines straight across the top of page one reading, 'MARTIN BECKMAN, OUR MAN OF PEACE, DIES IN MYSTERIOUS CRASH OF *AIR FORCE THREE*. The *New York Post* stated simply, 'DEATH OF THE PRINCE OF PEACE.' Almost all of the broadsheets divided the front pages into two stories. The first dealt with the actual demise of the aircraft, the evidence, the height, position and speed, and whatever quotes there were. The second, much bigger story was devoted to Martin Beckman, and how a huge, dangerous shadow now hung over the world because of his death.

Arnold Morgan had to wait until 0800 (EST) to reach Admiral Vitaly Rankov in Moscow. He made the call from his office using the old secure line into the Kremlin. The Russian officer greeted him in English with polite reserve, concerned as he always was that, when Morgan called, there was trouble, somewhere, for someone.

'Arnold, a nice surprise to hear from you. And how are things at the hub of the world's last remaining superpower? Not so good today, ha? I am very sorry, Arnold. He was a very special man.'

'Yeah, Vitaly. It's too bad. Left a big gap here. Everyone liked Martin.'

'But what about the aircraft, Arnold? My God, it was nearly new, wasn't it? What went wrong?'

'Who knows, old buddy? Damn' thing just crashed.'

The American was struggling to get out of this drift in the conversation. He wanted only to check on the whereabouts of the two missing Russian submarines. But Rankov was making that awkward. 'But how did it crash? There's nothing up there to collide with, right? That's three bad crashes, all unexpected, in the past five or six weeks. All unexplained. What's going on, Arnold? Is that what you called about?'

The admiral knew he was starting into a route which would cause him to level with Vitaly Rankov; although he did not particularly wish to do so, he was not unduly bothered by the prospect. Rankov was the former head of Soviet Naval Intelligence, and he knew about secrets. Also, he might be able to help. The two men had cooperated before. Nonetheless, Morgan elected to keep his powder dry. 'It was not exactly what I called about, Vitaly. But I would appreciate you marking my card, if you could.'

'Very well, Arnold. How can I help?'

'According to our surveillance, there are two Russian submarines we cannot see or hear. I don't want to know *specifically* where they are or what they're doing, but I want to ask you to tell me *roughly* where they are – unless it's a state secret, and then of course I'll understand.'

'I doubt it'll be a secret, these days. Which two?'

'Northern Fleet Typhoon TK-17. Northern Fleet Delta IV K-18.'

'Wait a minute.'

Admiral Morgan held on, drawing little submarines on his writing pad, as he usually did in times of stress.

In less than four minutes the Russian was back. 'The Typhoon's in the Pacific, way south of the Bering Strait, heading for Petrapavlovsk. You'll probably pick her up there on overheads tomorrow. The Delta IV's in refit in the Baltic. Covered drydock in St Petersburg. That's why you can't see her. What else? I am anxious there should be no misunderstanding between us.'

'Not much, really. Pretty routine inquiry.'

'Arnold, dear Arnold, on the day after your Vice-President is killed in the crash of no less an aircraft than *Air Force Three*, probably the best-maintained passenger jet in the world, you get up at God knows what time to call me to ask about a couple of submarines which are doing no harm to anyone, especially the one that's in hospital? I have leveled with you, my friend. Now you must level with me, otherwise a very useful friendship for both of us will begin to lose its foundation.'

'Crafty Russian motherfucker,' murmured Morgan, but not quite softly enough, not on the new crystal-clear international phone lines. He heard at the other end a roar of laughter from the giant ex-Soviet international oarsman.

They both laughed now, and Morgan knew he had to say something, although he was not sure precisely what that ought to be.

Admiral Rankov saved him a lot of trouble. 'Arnold, you don't think someone shot those aircraft down, do you? And if the answer's yes, you couldn't possibly think it was us, could you?'

'Vitaly, I do think someone shot them down. But I never thought you had anything to do with it. I now know you *couldn't* have had anything to do with it.'

'Why? Because the two submarines are now accounted for?'

'Yes.'

'Then you believe the aircraft were shot down by a missile launched from a submarine?'

'Yes.'

'Jesus. Who has such a submarine? Not us.'

'Nor us. But someone has. You haven't fitted a surface-to-air system on someone else's boat, have you?'

'If we have, no one's told me.'

'Well, Vitaly old buddy, the last time there was an almighty calamity, the one involving our aircraft carrier, you'll recall it all started with a missing submarine of yours.'

'I'm unlikely to forget that.'

'Well, if you have anything in the North Atlantic and it happens to trip over a diesel–electric boat with engine lines from a couple of British Paxmans, do me a favor, will you? Sink the sonofabitch before it knocks out another airliner.'

'Arnold, is this classified information? I presume you do not wish a word of this to get out?'

'Vitaly, it's as secret as any secret I have ever confided in you. Don't let me down, will you?'

'I would not dream of it, my friend. Basically you are telling me that someone stole or hijacked the Royal Navy's Upholder-Class boat that went missing a year ago? Is that what you're saying?'

'Correct.'

'And he's somehow converted it to carry an anti-aircraft missile launcher, and now he's out there, causing havoc?'

'Correct. And remember, if they can hire one of yours, they can surely steal one from the Brits.'

Admiral Morgan could not of course see it, but there was a broad smile beginning to decorate the Russian's face. 'Arnold, what kind of security do you have on *Air Force Three*? You do of course have missile jammers and decoys, and not just some kind of chaff?'

'No, we never went that far.'

'Arnold, I'm surprised. You really want to get that security beefed up. It's a damned dangerous world out there. As *you* once told *me*, old comrade, stuff happens.'

'All right, Vitaly, all right. I'm hearing you. Don't give me a difficult time. I've got enough troubles. But if you should see or hear anything around the area of 20–30 West on the jet flight paths, lemme know, will you?'

'Absolutely. I'll put our two North Atlantic patrol submarines on alert right away. Just one thing though, before you go.'

'Uh-huh?'

'Remember, stuff happens.'

012130MAR06. 57.49N 09.40W. Speed 8. Course 90. Depth 300. HMS *Unseen* was running quietly eastward in deep water. Commander Adnam's task for his Iranian paymasters was over, the revenge of the Ayatollahs on the Great Satan complete. Three strikes. An eye for an eye. And now the former Israeli commanding officer was alone in his cabin, wondering whether he would find his reward of the final $1.5 million in his bank account. The Iranians had paid the first $1.5 million in three installments without a murmur. The question was, would they now cut him loose? Or, more likely, have him assassinated and save the cash? *I know what I'd do, if I were the head of the Iranian Secret Service,* he pondered. *I'd execute Benjamin Adnam forthwith.*

He sat with his loaded service revolver on the small table before him, his big desert knife sheathed on his belt beneath his jacket. He was writing a letter to his trusty navigation officer, Arash Rajavi. It read as follows:

My dear Arash,

We have traveled far together in the short time of our acquaintance but, as you know, for many reasons I have to leave you. This letter is to confirm what you already know, that I enjoyed serving with you, and regard you as potentially a great submariner. I do believe this is a very good boat and will do much to further our cause.

During your long journey home, please try to remember all

213

that I have taught you. Keep your speed down to less than eight knots all the way, run close to the coast of Ireland, and then get into the Bay of Biscay, staying inshore all the way round. Then run down the coast of North Africa to your refueling point. Your next stop is at Code Point Delta, two hundred miles off the east coast of Madagascar, and after that I want you to make slowly for the coast of Somalia and Oman, and stay inshore where you will be much safer. In so doing you will be well clear of the American CVBG.

Until we meet again, my friend, may Allah go with you.

Commander B. Adnam

He took the letter and sealed it in an envelope, on which he wrote carefully, 'To be opened by Lt-Commander A. Rajavi after my departure. Commander B. Adnam.' It would not be long now.

The telephone on his desk rang almost immediately he had finished. It was the navigator, reporting their position; Commander Adnam ordered the Officer of the Watch to take *Unseen* to periscope depth. He put down the telephone and began to change into the wetsuit he'd kept from their swim in Plymouth Sound. Over that he put on extra layers of the cold-weather clothing provided for the bridge watch-keepers in the North Atlantic. The gear rendered him as close to immune from cold, wind, rain and snow as made no difference.

The commander placed his belt, with its sheathed knife, around his waist, and stored in the zipped pockets of his jacket a large envelope of cash, his revolver, his compass, his hand-held GPS, a small chart and his paperweight, the one he had used to stun the would-be assassins before fleeing Iraq. He carried two sealed bags in which were stored civilian clothes and shoes, his passports, papers, a substantial supply of food and mineral water, his binoculars and a flashlight. Then he pulled on his fur gloves; he had no need of a hat, the jacket having a tight fur-lined hood rolled into the collar. He concluded he could survive for several days in the open, should that become necessary.

Adnam picked up his bags and made his way to the control center, where there was already activity. The fishing boat was signaling about a mile off their port bow. Ben ordered them to surface and make their way toward the boat. The night outside was frigid, but the sea was calm and the skies were clear. 'We'll make a straight ship-to-ship transfer,' he said. 'Put the fisherman on your starboard side. Deck crew to their stations.' He turned, removed his right glove and asked his senior officers to enter the control center.

He told them that he had been privileged to fight with men such as they were. 'And I believe you will all become very fine submariners. You have learned thoroughly and learned quickly, and I shall miss each one of you, although I have high hopes that we shall meet again.'

He paused, and an immense sadness settled upon him as he prepared to part from the men with whom he had lived and worked for so long. For a moment he scmed lost for words, but then he extended his right palm, and, echoing the words of another commander, he said softly, 'I should be obliged if each of you would come and take me by the hand.'

As they did so, they each understood the true meaning of camaraderie as perhaps only fighting men can – those who have faced danger together but somehow come through it. Most of these young Iranians had been with their Iraqi-born leader for well over a year. Most of them had gone into the water with him in the outer reaches of Plymouth Sound on that black night when they had stolen the submarine. It was not yet clear in their minds that they were the most hunted men in the world. But they knew the drama was not over yet.

By now the deck crew was preparing to secure *Unseen* alongside the still-moving, aged, rusting 200-tonner *Flower of Scotland*. There was urgency in their every move. Out there were the search ships of both the United States Navy and the Royal Navy. The Iranians intended to be on the surface for the minimum possible time. It was understood among them that they would dive the submarine, if necessary, leaving the commander in the water should they be threatened.

The fishing boat lowered big fenders close to the water's surface, its engines reversing, as the captain himself threw a looped continuous line over the rail to the submarine for the CO's bags. Adnam had his life-jacket on now, and his men were hitching two life-lines to his belt. Transfers of this type can be extremely dangerous in the dark in midocean, and there was tension in the air.

The wide gangway was pushed out from under the rail of the

fishing boat, and the submarine's deck crew hauled it over. They had just made it secure when, somewhat to Adnam's surprise, a submarine officer he had seen several times in Bandar Abbas walked across and joined him on the casing. 'Good evening, Commander,' he said. 'I am Lt-Commander Alaam. I was responsible for hiring the boat; you will return in it to Mallaig. The skipper knows the way.'

'But I understood you were coming back with me,' replied Adnam.

'Change of plan, sir. I am taking over *Unseen*, all the way home.'

'I see. But I have not briefed you.'

'I presume you have briefed someone, sir.'

'Of course. The Navigation Officer, Lt-Commander Rajavi, is in a position to take command. But the matter has nothing more to do with me. I should speak to him immediately if I were you.'

'Yes, sir. Goodbye, sir.'

Commander Adnam turned once more to face his deck team for the last time. 'Allah go with you,' he said.

'And also with you, sir,' replied one of them.

With that Benjamin Adnam walked across to the *Flower of Scotland*, where he ordered the skipper to let go all lines and head due east at full speed. The Iraqi stood on deck in the biting wind and watched *Unseen* pull away, running south. One minute later she was gone, beneath the dark waters of the North Atlantic from which she had caused such havoc.

Then he turned and went immediately to the bridge, where he asked Captain Gregor Mackay to join him alone on the deck. His request was simple. 'I want you to stop this ship immediately and hand over to me the rigid inflatable you have on the stern. I want her filled with petrol and ready to go in five minutes. Also, put a full four-and-a-half-gallon jerry-can in the boat. Do it yourself – no one else.'

'I canna do that,' said the captain in a broad Scottish brogue. 'I dinnae even own the ship.'

Ben smiled at the old familiar accent he had heard so often during his time training at Faslane. He pushed away a million memories of the Scotland of his younger days and returned quickly to business, a subject he knew sat easily with any

Scotsman, especially a fisherman. 'How much is the Zodiac worth? She's a 15-footer, right? With a 60hp outboard?'

'Yes, sir. I suppose six thousand pounds, sir.'

'Then if I give you ten thousand in cash you'll be very well placed, correct?'

'Yes, sir.'

'Then hurry, man,' snapped the commander, reaching into his bag for his stash of British money and watching with some satisfaction as the fisherman from the Western Isles moved aft and began to fill the tank with gasoline.

Seven minutes later the ship was stationary and the Zodiac was in the water, secured by a painter to the portside rail. Commander Adnam handed over the money and Mackay counted it out very carefully. 'Aye, sir, I think 200 of these 50-pound notes adds up very nicely.'

Ben grabbed his bags and threw them down into the rubberized Zodiac. He climbed over the side, dropped onto the firm GRP deck, revved the engine, slammed her into gear and took off into the night. Captain Mackay watched him go, half in amazement, half in ecstasy. 'That young man is in a very great hurry,' he muttered. 'But it was a pleasure doing business with him.'

Ben Adnam moderated the speed as soon as he had put 200 yards between the Zodiac and the *Flower of Scotland*. Then he checked his global positioning system and the compass, and settled into a steady 15 knots, a speed he would hold in an easterly direction for a little over two hours. He did not yet refer to his map. Instead he made himself comfortable on the long rubber seat behind the wheel, pulled up his hood, and watched over his right shoulder as the lights of the fishing boat headed southeast.

The night was bitterly cold but still and clear as he moved swiftly across the calm sea. There was a slight swell, but the Zodiac rode that perfectly, the silence of the seascape broken only by the high-pitched whine of the well tuned outboard. So far as he could tell there was no other ship in the vicinity save for the *Flower of Scotland*, the lights of which he could still see two miles away.

He checked his watch, which was still set for Greenwich Mean Time, and saw that it was 2320. He glanced again at the running lights of the fishing boat, and then turned back toward the east, where a rising moon was casting a thin silver path on the sea, lighting his way.

The mighty red and orange flash as the *Flower of Scotland* and her three-man crew were blown to pieces by a bomb which detonated right behind her engine lit up the sky behind his right shoulder and turned the night into day. Two seconds later he heard the thunder of the blast, splitting the night air.

Ben Adnam turned to watch the burning wreckage scatter downward onto the water. Then he shook his head, shrugged and kept heading east.

He knew it had been a bomb. A torpedo from *Unseen* would have caused quite another kind of explosion – more muffled, less spectacular. And yet he was curious, because he could see in his mind's eye the tense, worried look there had been on the face of Lt-Commander Alaam. He remembered the way there had been no time for even the warm exchange of greetings so customary in the Muslim world. No time to discuss anything, not even to deliver the congratulations of their masters. Not a word about the success of the operation. Not even civility. Not even approval, far less warmth.

The Iranian, Ben had thought, had been a man on the edge of his nerves, fraught, dry-mouthed and desperate to get away. He had been too overwrought even to offer a reasoned explanation for the change of plan. In Adnam's view, Alaam might as well have carried a placard with him which stated he had just booby-trapped the *Flower of Scotland* in order to kill Iran's redundant employee, who now knew too much.

But Ben Adnam was still curious. 'I wonder why,' he asked the empty ocean, 'after all that I've done, some people still assume I might be a fool?'

So many lessons, for so many people. 'Especially Captain Mackay,' he mused. 'That was a hard way to learn that there's no such thing as a free lunch.'

His own situation was, however, only marginally better than that of the late master of the *Flower of Scotland*. He had been betrayed first by Iraq and now by Iran, and the horizons were closing in. He understood the reasoning of the Ayatollahs – that he, Benjamin, was just too much of a liability. If they offered him shelter and perhaps more work in Iran, it would be only a matter of time before someone put together the pieces which made up the picture of his murderous six-week reign of terror in the North Atlantic. The Americans were plainly not going to sit still and forget about the events he had perpetrated. There would be men in the Pentagon and the CIA, perhaps even in the White House, who would never rest until he was caught. He knew, too, the icy cunning of the British military, who would eventually learn of his whereabouts and come after him.

So the Ayatollahs would have been crazy to harbor him. He had always known that, but it was nonetheless an emotional if not an academic shock to him that they had attempted to execute him quite so summarily, within a couple of hours of his leaving the superb submarine he had acquired for them. *On reflection*, he thought, *I'm glad I played it safe. I just hope my crew are as lucky.*

He had experienced the same feeling of desolation when he had walked from Baghdad almost two years previously, but tonight it was a hundred times worse. Because now there was no way he could go back to the Middle East, where he was wanted as no Arab had ever been wanted. Three powerful governments – Israel, Iraq and Iran – had all made determined attempts to assassinate him. He had to face it. There was *nowhere* for him to go. He was, as usual, entirely on his own.

For the moment he must concentrate on survival in the short term. He could feel the chill of the night upon his face as the Zodiac ran on toward the island. He pulled out his chart and checked the GPS and compass. He held the little boat steady on course zero-nine-zero and, facing the east, prayed silently to his God to forgive him.

The trouble was, he needed to get into his bag for the flashlight and he needed time to look at his chart, just to check. Rather than attempt to hold his course during these routine navigational procedures, he switched off the motor and stopped. And there, solitary in the gusting chill of the Atlantic, Ben Adnam once more studied his bearings. He had already programmed in the waypoints; now, after two minutes of checking, he kicked over the engine and headed east again on course zero-nine-zero.

As expected, the GPS told him he was about 15 miles west of the four lonely, uninhabited islands of St Kilda. These sit in galeswept isolation, at the mercy of the open Atlantic, 50 miles west of the rest of the Hebridean Islands, and 110 miles from the Scottish mainland. They are the most westerly point of the British

Isles save for the great granite slab of Rockall, which lies another 180 miles closer to North America.

Adnam was headed for the largest of the St Kilda group, formally named Hirta but generally referred to simply as St Kilda; the trio of tiny neighboring islands are Soay, Boreray and Rona. The combined population of the four is easy to calculate. Zero.

Before the 1800s the only way out to St Kilda from the Scottish mainland was in a rowing boat pulled by the men of the Isle of Skye; the voyage took several days and nights. Even today it can be impossible to make a landing in the massive seas which have battered the islands since the dawn of time.

Ben knew the problems, and he knew how swiftly the weather could change out here. Even now he could feel the wind freshening a little from the southwest; he thanked God it was not from the southeast, because a gale from there renders the only landing place on the entire island, Village Bay, out of the question. He had been to St Kilda once before, during his submarine training with the Royal Navy, but they had not landed, and so far as he knew, no British Naval warship had ever put in to Village Bay, not even in the deep water on the outer edges.

Right now he just had to pray that the weather held and that he could get into shelter unobserved. Instinct was telling him to open the throttle full and go for it, but that would use too much gas; besides, much more important in his mind, it would betray panic, a lack of professionalism. Ben Adnam despised amateurs.

He shone the flashlight on the chart again and checked the depth of the water and the precise position of his waypoints along the route to the beach. He noted once more that the southeastern tip of St Kilda was separately named Dun; this high, jagged promontory was three-quarters of a mile long. The chart showed there was a channel between Dun and the main part of the island, but it was very narrow, and shallow at low water, strewn with rocks; at one point the chart showed zero depth at low tide. The former Commander of HMS *Unseen* had previously determined he would go right around the long headland, despite the extra 20 minutes' running time that would add to his journey into Village Bay. If he went through the Dun Channel and just once revved his propeller on its rocky floor, he knew he would be finished.

With the slight rise of the wind the night grew a little darker, as lower cloud drifted northeastward out of the Atlantic, a high thin layer of cirrus that veiled the moon. But the decreasing level of light did not worry Ben. He knew everything he would see in the dim, diffuse glow. And he recognized the cloud for what it was, the precursor of an Atlantic low, bringing rain on a southwest wind along with reasonably warm temperatures.

He was satisfied he had his mission under tight control, including the effects of the weather, his precise course and his position. Not for him the nagging dread of a less experienced helmsman at the dead of night, with no radar – that of being swept against the cliffs or the rocks in a following sea, which this had now become.

Adnam stayed deliberately on the southerly edge of his planned track, which would take him within a mile of the terrible black cliffs of St Kilda. But he would be able to see them in this light even if the GPS failed.

The Zodiac went on for another 50 minutes, twelve and a half miles of planing comfortably at just below 15 knots. Then Adnam cut back the engine and chugged forward quietly, just at idling speed. Suddenly he could see the shape of the island: bang in front, a monstrous cliff topped by a massive 1000-foot mountain peak, glowering out over a shallow bay. He could also see yet another peak, even higher, way back beyond the first one. He shone the light on his chart. 'That's it,' he murmured. 'I'm looking at the twin peaks of Mullach Mor and Mullach Bi.' He checked the compass and saw that his GPS had not let him down.

He stopped the engine and poured half the contents of his spare gas can into the fuel tank before setting off again at five knots. After ten minutes he slowed right down and turned inshore; there, about 100 yards off his port bow, he could see the great rock stack of Hamalan, close to the tip of the Dun headland. He ran on for another 200 yards through the dark before turning northeast, then right around into Village Bay, setting a course of three-four-two on his hand-held compass.

The bay itself measures a mile across, from Dun to the northern point. The British had built a military base along that northern shoreline, and used it spasmodically as a missile-tracking station for the rocket range at Benbecula on the main Hebrides Islands. According to Ben Adnam's guidebook, the British Army made a foray to their base every two weeks, when a couple of soldiers would land and stay for two days, checking over the island and particularly the electronic equipment.

Commander Adnam thus headed quietly into the western edge of the bay, where the chart told him he could land and secure his boat behind a rocky outcrop and out of sight of the north shore. He would then proceed on foot to the military base, which he hoped would be deserted and have a store full of gasoline. If there were soldiers in residence, he proposed to move into one of the original old islanders' cottages, currently being restored by the Scottish National Trust and the Scottish National Heritage during the summer months, and there wait out the soldiers' 48-hour tour of duty. He had sufficient food and mineral water to last him at least that long.

He got without incident to the dark shore of Village Bay. Given the calmness of the sea, he was surprised at the rough water breaking onto the shore. He steered the Zodiac right in, but heaved the engine up as the bow hit the shingle. As it clicked into its secure position, he darted for'ard with the painter in his right hand and jumped off the bow into a few inches of water.

He waited for the next wave to come in and lift the much heavier stern, and then moved left, heaving the stern right around, so that the raised rubber bow now pointed out to sea. He knew from long experience that even the smallest waves could wash right over the stern of a boat like this and quickly fill it with seawater and weed. The problem was that the stern, with the suspended engine, was very heavy, and that was the part he had to pull. So he attached the anchor line to the wooden transom and, every time the sea lifted the boat, hauled on that line until the Zodiac was on relatively dry shingle. Then he wrenched the little craft around and dragged it further up the beach into the shadow of the rocks, where it would not be seen unless someone fell over it. It remains a sailor's mystery why it is so difficult to haul a 15-foot rubber hull backward but hardly any trouble to pull it forward.

He leaned on the rocks and opened one of his bags, devoured a chicken sandwich and swigged greedily at a bottle of water. He was in the lee of the wind now but it was still cold, and he pulled on his hood again as he set off in the direction of the military camp. He moved quickly over the beach toward the old church and manse where St Kildans had often spent nine hours a day on

Sundays before, in 1930, they finally evacuated the place after a thousand years.

The old white-painted church, standing just beyond the camp, would provide excellent cover from which to observe the military buildings. The submariner stayed low, finally coming off the beach some 40 yards beyond the Army huts on the north shore. He reached the moonlit shadows of the church and edged around them until finally he faced the camp.

There, to his irritation, he saw lights in two rooms. As he drew nearer he could hear the unmistakable hum of a generator. As if to confirm his worst fears, an Army Landrover was parked right outside the door. No doubt about it: there were at least two soldiers in that building.

Ben swiftly reassessed the military options. (a) He could check out the building, break in and kill both men right now, drive his boat over, fill it with gas and leave. But that would be messy and, as soon as the landing craft returned, probably tomorrow, the discovery of the murder of two British soldiers would quickly cause an uproar he did not need. (b) He could hide his boat and himself until they all went away in a couple of days' time. Then he could break into the store and steal the gasoline. But that ran the small risk that the Army landing craft, which would probably come in during daylight, might spot his boat as it crossed the bay. Alternatively, the soldiers in residence might find his boat. So (b) was no good either. Too slow. Too many risks.

He looked again at his watch. It was 2am. He moved back into the shadows, checked his chart and went to Plan (c). He would make his way back to the boat, deflate the sides and pile shingle over and around it to disguise it from anyone approaching by water. Then he would find the main street, to the north of the camp, and get into one of the houses for better shelter overnight. Tomorrow he would get around to his boat before it grew light, at about 0900, and wait out the few hours of daylight until about 1500. Then he would go to work.

By 0300 the boat was adequately concealed and, carrying his two bags, Adnam found his way to the line of village houses, shown clearly on the map, and shoved open the door to the one with the freshest paint. It was cold inside, but at least it was out of the wind and there was a sofa set in front of the fireplace. He decided not to risk a fire, but he spread out luxuriously upon the sofa and soon fell asleep, his big desert knife clutched in his right hand, which rested on the floor.

He wakened at 0800, ate a sandwich, drank more mineral water, and slipped out of the house into the chill of a March morning in the Outer Hebrides. He pulled up his balaclava and left the road, moving cross-country back to the boat, staying out of sight and range of the Army buildings. Nothing stirred save a gaggle of puffins on the beach and a passing gannet, which had been fishing in the shallows.

At 1100 he heard the Army Landrover rev up and drive away. He could see two soldiers occupying the front seats. After they had left, driving to the west, Ben carefully headed for the camp. There, near the church, was the building where the lights had been on. Now there was nothing. Just silence. No sign of life.

'Just the two of them,' said Ben to himself. 'Excellent.' He made his way back to the boat and there waited out the daylight hours, eventually watching the jeep return at about 1400.

1700, St Kilda.
Lt Chris Larkman and the burly Corporal Tommy Lawson, both of the Royal Army Service Corps, were playing cards in front of the electric fire which warmed their spartan room. The young officer put down his losing hand and walked slowly over to the north window.

'Anything the matter, sir?'

'No. Nothing. I just thought I caught a glimpse of a light, way up there on the headland, the Oiseval side.'

'Well, sir, unless there's been a plane crash, I'd judge that as totally unlikely.' The accent was flat, East London, in contrast to the harder public-schoolboy tones of the commissioned man.

'Very unlikely, Corporal Lawson. It must have been a reflection through the window.'

'Yes, sir. As a matter of fact I'm very pleased it was nothing because I'm about to take command of this game.'

'I wouldn't doubt it, Corporal. Nor would you if you could see the load of rubbish I'm playing with.'

'Right, sir. How about this?' Lawson laid down the ace, king, queen and jack of spades, plus the other three kings.

'Christ, Corporal, that's a lot too good for me. Hey, wait a minute! I could have sworn I just saw that light again.'

224

'Where, sir? Let me have a look.'

The 32-year-old Lawson joined the 25-year-old officer at the window. In the way of the British Army, the young elite was assisted by the old stager, a combination upon which the Army was built. Chris Larkman, whose grades at Bryanston had not been good enough to put him through a top university, had struck up a lasting friendship in the Army with the former failed bricklayer who now shared this remote island with him. And they represented a formidable fighting unit, Larkman and Lawson, should push come to shove. The slim, athletic, former Hampshire County rugby full-back and the rough Eastender with iron in each fist.

Lt Larkman's wealthy parents have been bitterly disappointed that their son should have ended up in the RASC – 'So much nicer in a good Guards Regiment' – but Chris was happy, and was considered by his superiors to be a man destined for higher rank. Lawson, by contrast, was going nowhere but was fine where he was, a natural-born corporal – tough, bossy, sharp, irreverent and a bugger when riled.

And now Lawson was standing by the window with his commander, peering into the black night, up at the great escarpment of Oiseval, which rose fairly smoothly on the landward side and then ended with terrifying suddenness to seaward, like a giant apple sliced in half. The black cliff plunged down 500 feet almost sheer to the jutting deep-water rocks below. It was only half as high as some of the other cliffs on St Kilda, but it was a hell of a sight from both top and bottom.

'There it is, Corporal. Look . . . up there. To the right, three flashes.'

'Where, sir? You mean, high up?'

'Right. Keep looking. Pretend you're staring up at the very top of the headland. Keep staring.'

Three minutes went by, and then Lt Larkman saw it again. 'Did you see it, Corporal? Three flashes.'

Tommy Lawson was silent, which was unusual and brief. But when he answered he was deadly serious. 'Yes, sir. Yes, I did. That was not some fluke of nature. Someone's up there, sir. And if he hasn't landed in a bloody parachute, quite frankly I don't know how the fucking hell he got up there, do I?'

'Do you think it is definitely a person? Not some sort of meteorite, or something?'

'That, sir, is a bloke. A bloke with a fucking light, right? Otherwise he wouldn't be shining it, would he?'

'No, I suppose he wouldn't.'

'Well, what's he fucking doing up there, then? That's what I wanna know, don't I?'

'Yes, that's rather what I want to know, too. We, Corporal, had better find out.'

'Well, sir, we've really got two choices. We can either take the jeep and get up there, with lights, and flush him out, or rescue him, as the case may be. Or we leave him up there all night to freeze his bollocks off.'

'I don't think we really ought to do the latter. We're in charge of this place. There's quite a lot of sensitive equipment here, and I'm inclined to think we should just go and sort the situation out.'

'I think that is the correct military assessment for an officer of your class, sir. And I'm here to do as you tell me. However, I must say, meself, I'd probably take the bollock-freezing option.'

'OK, Corporal. Coats on. We won't need weapons. Bring two flashlights and let's get out there. Warm the engine over, will you? I'll shove a petrol can in the back. You know the gauge has never worked on that bloody thing.'

'Right, sir.' Corporal Lawson headed for the door, jangling the keys of the jeep. He opened the vehicle on the driver's side, climbed in and kicked over the engine, which started with a roar. The lieutenant was right behind him with a gas can from the store.

The breath of both men was white on the freezing night air. The corporal glanced once more up toward the highest escarpment of Oiseval. And there it was again. Three short flashes. But this time it was followed by three longer ones, and then, immediately, by three more short ones. 'Sir, I think we're seeing an SOS up there,' said Tommy Lawson. 'Which means it's got to be an aircraft of some kind. There's no other way anyone could be up there. Might be a Navy chopper or something. But we didn't hear nothing, did we?'

'No, we didn't,' replied the lieutenant. 'Nothing at all.' There was a worried frown on his face as Lawson gunned the jeep over the rough terrain beyond the camp, heading northeast across the rising ground and up toward the light.

The total distance to the summit of Oiseval was less than half a mile, but the terrain was rock-strewn and Lawson had to pick his way through the boulders. They were making only about five miles per hour as the Landrover lurched and roared its way up the steep hill to the top. Every few moments they saw the flash of the light above. As they drew closer they had to make a wide detour around a sheer rockface which even this vehicle could not handle.

Finally they were within sight of the highest point, and they saw the flashlight again, straight ahead to the east, on the brink of the cliff. There was no sign of wreckage as the headlights of the Landrover shone out over the ocean far below.

'What I don't want to do is drive this fucking thing over the edge, right, sir?'

'Right, Corporal. Actually, I think we should stop here and wait for the light. Keep the engine running and the main beam up so that whoever it is can see us. He can't be far away, but it's so damned dark.'

'Yes, sir. And it's a bloody long way down if anyone misjudges it.'

They waited for five minutes. There was nothing. 'Perhaps he's fainted, sir or died.'

Chris Larkman was about to agree when the light flashed again, directly opposite the officer's left shoulder, not more than 30 yards away. Still there was no sound. Lawson heaved on the handbrake, took his flashlight, and opened the door. 'Hold it, sir. I'll come round.'

The corporal stood outside for a few moments fastening his big winter jacket and pulling on his gloves. Then he slammed the door on the driver's side and walked to the back of the Landrover. As he did so, Ben Adnam came out of the night like a demon and crashed his paperweight into the area behind Lawson's right ear, just as he had done so many months before, so far from this desolate rock, to the would-be assassins sent by the treacherous President to kill him. The big Eastender crumpled to the ground. Chris Larkman never heard a thing above the noise of the Landrover's engine. Through the steamy perspex of the rear window he never saw the Iraqi commander drag the corporal's body back around to the driver's side.

Larkman waited. Then he called out, 'Corporal Lawson? Everything OK?' But no reply came back. He tightened his belt and pulled down his hat, then opened the door and stepped out onto the frozen peak of Oiseval, instinctively moving to the back of the jeep in the direction he had seen the corporal walk.

Commander Adnam was waiting. The young lieutenant thought he saw a shadow and made to turn, but he was too late. The former master of HMS *Unseen* banged the paperweight hard into the area behind the officer's right ear and he, too, crumpled to the ground.

It took Ben Adnam a full ten minutes to haul both unconscious men back to the Landrover and into its front seats, but he managed it in the end, let go the handbrake, slammed the driver's door shut and heaved against the open window.

The Landrover began to roll forward, its headlights still on. It gathered speed slowly, and was traveling at no more than about 10mph when it plunged over the precipice, its engine still running as the vehicle plummeted all the way down until it crashed into deep water 500 feet below. Ben heard it hit the ocean, and doubted whether anyone would ever find it.

But now, alone at last on St Kilda, he had to become extremely busy. He checked his watch. The two soldiers had died at 1741. He turned back toward the military camp, far below, and, snug in his cold-weather gear and using the big flashlight he had 'borrowed' from Tommy Lawson, he made his way down to the British Army's fuel store.

It took him 15 minutes to get there, and he made a visit to the living quarters before he went to work. He noticed a label on a suitcase. 'Lawson T. 23082826. Corporal. Royal Army Service Corps.'

Ben stood by the electric fire for a few minutes and decided to make himself a cup of tea in the small kitchen. He sat down in the one comfortable chair and sipped the hot, sweet brew, thinking about the journey he must now undertake – 140 miles at 15 knots. Over nine hours' running time if he made no mistakes. At the moment the sea remained calm enough; perhaps the low front which he'd feared had just drifted by on its way to

Iceland and the North Cape. He'd need a lot of gasoline. But right now he *had* a lot of gasoline.

He returned to the kitchen and washed and dried his cup, carefully placing it back on the shelf where he'd found it. There were two dirty cups in the sink, and the arch terrorist considered a third might be a clue to the Army investigators. Also, he wanted no fingerprints left behind.

Leaving the lights and heater switched on, he went outside, still using Lawson's flashlight to save the battery of his own. The fuel store was open, and inside it there was a 1000-gallon diesel tank, its gauge showing half-full. This was only moderate news, since the diesel would not power his outboard, but then he found a stack of four-and-a-half-gallon gasoline cans in a lean-to shed at the back — the fuel for the Landrover, stored in the fresh air for reasons of safety.

Ben left immediately, heading along the shore toward his boat. Once there he cleared the stones away, re-inflated the buoyancy bays and hauled the boat the short distance to the water, where he manhandled her into the light surf breaking in from the Atlantic. He paddled out into deeper water, let down the engine and primed it using the rubber bulb on the fuel line. He hit the starter and Captain Gregor's Zodiac fired first time. Ben drove her easily across the bay to the flat landing place right below the church.

He raised the engine and beached her, then jumped out and spun the boat round, bow to sea, with the stern and raised engine hard aground. He guessed the boat would float and drift on the incoming tide inside 20 minutes, so he had to move fast. He jogged back to the store, in under 15 minutes returning more slowly with two heavy fuel cans. There was an extended tank beneath the seat of the Zodiac, and it took the whole nine gallons.

Two journeys later he had another three cans on board, giving him nearly 13 gallons more — plenty, he knew, to carry him over the water to the little Scottish fishing port of Mallaig. He still had six big sandwiches and three bottles of water left; he had not taken any extra food from the soldiers' kitchen, great though the temptation had been. Commander Adnam regarded himself as a professional military man, not a sneak thief, and so his principles did not permit him to take as much as a piece of cheese unless it were essential to his survival. He was curiously obsessive about the whole concept of acting professionally. Indeed he had his own private definition of the word: 'Professionalism has nothing to do with money. It involves the total elimination of mistakes.'

And, thus far, he considered he had made none. The Iranians hadn't come after him so they plainly believed he was now dead, an error of judgment which had also been made briefly by Iraq and for much longer by Israel and the United States.

The Army landing craft would arrive tomorrow morning, at the earliest, and the officers would be faced with the complete mystery of the disappearance of two of their soldiers, a lieutenant and a corporal, plus one Landrover, green in color, property of the Royal Army Service Corps. Unless they were prepared to spend years combing every yard of the treacherous, deep waters beneath St Kilda's cliffs, they would *never* know what had become of the missing men. Nor would they discover that Commander Adnam had ever visited the island. There was, he knew, no trail. There had been no fighting, no gunshots, no blood, nothing broken. No one had seen him – at least, no one still alive. And he himself was uninjured – better yet, he was mobile.

He paddled the Zodiac out into deeper water before lowering the engine and running swiftly to the east, across dark Village Bay, and out into the open North Atlantic toward the main Western Isles and, 100 miles beyond, the fishing village of Mallaig on the Scottish mainland.

CHAPTER NINE

B EN ADNAM CLEARED the outer reaches of Village Bay just before 2100 on the night of Thursday, March 2. It was still calm but there was now an unmistakable Atlantic swell. However, the waves rolling in from his starboard hip were fortunately long, with smooth tops, and the Zodiac could quarter across them with ease.

He was more than happy with the conditions, even though his full concentration would be required for hour after hour. He was, after all, warm, dry, relatively comfortable and, so far as he knew, not immediately wanted by anyone. It was his former submarine they were after. He himself had just to continue heading east in the dark, keeping a sharp eye out for fishing boats and restricting his speed to a relatively easy 15 knots. He was well practiced at keeping his speed down, and he wore a lean smile in the night as he steered along course zero-nine-seven, going for the Sound of Harris, some 40 miles distant.

The Zodiac was a very good boat, and she zipped effortlessly through the mild hills of the Atlantic. She steered easily, and Ben could check his GPS without cutting his speed.

At 2300 he ate another sandwich, leaning back in his seat, staring into the dark and listening to the perfect running beat of the outboard engine as the Zodiac climbed the retreating swells, flew along the tops, and then raced downhill into the troughs. Less than an hour away he would enter the central seaway through the islands which form the Outer Hebrides. This is the Sound of Harris, which divides the island of Harris to the north from the sprawling archipelago of North Uist to the south.

The Sound of Harris is about five miles wide at its narrowest point, but it is scattered with small islands and hunks of rock that are both too big to be ignored and too small to be named. Adnam would have to be very careful in here because, though the tide would be quite full, the chart showed the waters were studded with dangerous obstructions, difficult to see in the dark, particularly if just beneath the surface. The Zodiac drew only about a foot when it was running fast, on the 'stump' of the engine's wake, but he could not risk losing his propeller. He hoped to God there would be some moonlight south of Harris to help him through the rocky seaway.

In this he was lucky. The clouds had cleared and the moon was high at midnight, as his GPS flicked to 57.48N 07.15W. This meant that the tiny uninhabited island of Shillay, a 116-acre slab of granite which marks the southern entrance of the Sound, lay somewhere to starboard. He elected to run southeast for a further couple of miles in the hope of seeing it, and indeed, after eight more minutes, he picked it out on the freezing moonlit ocean a half-mile off his starboard beam, its vertical cliffs rising sheer out of the water.

He thanked Allah for the GPS and slowed the Zodiac to a halt. The three hours of running had used seven gallons; he tipped the entire contents of one of the Army's cans into the tank, knowing he could now go for another three hours before he had to refuel again. Then he pressed forward once more, heading due southeast now, toward where the northern headland of the island of Berneray awaited him six miles further on.

He passed Berneray shortly after 0030, and then braced himself for the really tricky part of the run through the sound: picking his way through the cluster of tiny islets which guard the eastern entrance, southeast of Killegray. There is often a buildup of ocean swell right here, and the islets are low and hard to see in the dark. Adnam elected to keep well southeast; even so, when the islands came into sight they were a lot closer than he had expected. He crept carefully past them, and met with relief the wide expanse of the Hebrides Sea which separates the Western Isles from Skye. Almost immediately the ocean seemed to flatten out.

He was not unfamiliar with these waters, thanks to his months near here in the Royal Navy, and he knew that the Hebrides influence the western coast of Scotland very much as the Great Barrier Reef does eastern Australia, sheltering the mainland from the winter rage of the open ocean. One way and another he was glad to be in calm seas with a full gas tank, west of the historically romantic Isle of Skye, headquarters of the powerful Clan

MacLeod. And, as he turned more toward the south, he found himself singing quietly that most haunting of Scottish airs, a song which he had once learned by heart from the local people around the Royal Navy submarine base at Faslane, which had been his home long ago.

> Speed, bonny boat, like a bird on the wing,
> 'Onward' the sailors cry;
> Carry the lad that's born to be king,
> Over the Sea to Skye.

And, like Scotsmen all over the world, he saw clearly in his mind the most famous image in the long and bloody history of that country – that of 24-year-old Flora Macdonald and her men rowing the Catholic Charles Stuart – Bonnie Prince Charlie – to safety across these very waters after the crushing defeat of the Jacobites at the Battle on Drummossie Moor, Culloden, in 1746.

From his position reading at 0100 he was 25 miles from the coast of Skye and he considered that if Flora and her men could row it, his Zodiac ought to make it without much trouble. He pulled down his hood, tucked himself behind the perspex windshield to shield himself from the wind, and pressed forward on a course of one-six-five. Two hours later he was right off Neist Point at the top of Skye's Moonen Bay, and so far he had not seen a ship.

He eased his speed and tipped the contents of both his remaining petrol cans into his almost empty tank. That would give him ten gallons for the final three hours it would take him to cover the 48 miles down to Mallaig, from where Lt-Commander Alaam had chartered the *Flower of Scotland* four days previously.

He'd make it, of that he was sure, and once more he pushed open the throttle and settled the Zodiac into its cruising position, beginning his run down the long dark coast of the sprawling 400,000-acre Isle of Skye.

It was 0500 when he crossed Soay Sound in the shadow of the towering Cuillin Hills, which rolled down to the sea on his port side. Adnam could barely see them, but he could feel them somehow blocking out the horizon to the northeast. Twelve miles ahead he would see the lighthouse at the Point of Sleat, and from there it would be a straight five-mile run across the Sound of Sleat to the port of Mallaig – which was, of course, right now one fishing boat light of its full contingent.

Ben knew there were clear identifying marks on the Zodiac which would link it to the *Flower of Scotland*, and consequently he wanted to make the port before daylight. For all he knew Mallaig might be crawling with police and coastguards in search of the missing fishermen. He picked up a red marker buoy a half-mile outside the harbor and followed the lights in, carefully filling his army petrol cans with seawater and lowering them over the side before he arrived.

Right outside the harbor wall he cut his engine, and thereafter rowed in using his paddle, staying right in the shadow of the moored boats. Then he made for a mooring at the far end which had a small rowing boat attached. He tied up the Zodiac and transferred his bags to the ten-foot wooden dinghy, jumped aboard and rowed the hundred yards to the stone jetty, fastening off the painter with a bowline on a ring-bolt.

Climbing some steps, he came onto the dockside, which was lit by only a single small streetlight. This was the first time he had stood on inhabited land since *Unseen* had left Bandar Abbas five months previously. Carrying his two bags, he found himself in an unspoilt little fishing port, a total jumble of fish-curing sheds, fishing baskets, herring-boxes, netting and gear.

Out close to the approach road was a big steel rubbish tip, half-full of cardboard boxes. Commander Adnam ducked in behind it, and with huge reluctance began to pull off the wonderful cold-weather Iranian Navy clothing which had protected him for the past four days. He doused himself liberally with deodorant talcum powder, which was all too plainly an essential part of his kit. In the other bag he had a dark gray, heavily wrinkled suit, a clean shirt, tie, socks and shoes. He had no coat, no scarf and no hat, and the temperature was only about four degrees above freezing, with a light wind. Nonetheless, he couldn't wander around this West Highland town looking like Scott of the Antarctic, and so he packed his foul-weather gear into one of the bags, jammed the bag into one of the cardboard boxes, and crushed it down to the bottom of the skip. Then he picked up the other bag and began to walk into the town, toward the railway station, hoping it was not a Sunday – he had lost count of the days of the week.

His guidebook told him there was a restored winter train service on weekdays leaving Mallaig for Fort William at eight o'clock, a little over one hour from now.

The walk seemed as cold as the desert at night at this time of the year, but Commander Adnam could deal with that. He quickened his pace as he followed the signs to the station, and was gratified to discover it was Friday morning, March 3. He was also cheered to find a low, hot radiator in the waiting room, and he thankfully sat on it, having purchased a single ticket to take him 130 miles south to Helensburgh. He would change trains 35 miles from here at Fort William.

At half past seven the train pulled into the station from a siding, Mallaig being the end of the line. Inside the train it was warm and, as passengers poured on, became quite busy, but Ben Adnam found an empty corner. He guessed, accurately, that the crowding would not apply for long: as it was a Friday morning, there were people on board who were plainly going to work in Fort William. With his dark beard, rumpled suit and lack of coat, he did not consider he much resembled the normal perception of a foreign terrorist who has just wiped out three of the world's most important trans-Atlantic jet aircraft on behalf of the Islamic Republic of Iran. Even so, he felt uncomfortably conspicuous.

Ben Adnam had never traveled this far north on the West Highland Line, but he had been to Fort William once with an old girlfriend. Actually, she was the only girlfriend he had ever had, and he remembered it as if it were yesterday. He remembered, too, the old Scottish garrison town, standing rock-steady in the shade of Ben Nevis, the highest mountain peak in the British Isles. They had stayed in a lovely hotel, Ballachulish House, which dates back to the 18th century and overlooks Loch Linnhe and the Morven Hills. Fort William held many memories for Ben Adnam, and he tried not to think of them, for they represented another world, one to which he no longer belonged. They were days of remembered laughter and love. But now, after a brilliant if unorthodox career, there was but one preoccupation for him and it overwhelmed every other emotion he had: survival. Nothing else.

The train pulled out of Mallaig on time and headed south, then east across the top of Loch Shiel and on into the Highlands. It reached Fort William before nine o'clock, and the Glasgow train was already waiting for them. Ben grabbed a copy of the *Scotsman* from the kiosk and found an empty compartment. The train left immediately, but he saw nothing of the first 15 minutes of the journey because it took him that long, searching the newspaper diligently, to ascertain that there was, as yet, no mention of missing trawlers or soldiers.

This task complete, he took the opportunity to clean himself up properly in the lavatory before going back to his seat. He was now free to stare out of the window at the breathtaking scenery as the train ran along the River Spean, with the great pinnacle of Ben Nevis 4500 feet above them to the right. After 15 miles they turned down the glen, all the way along the eastern shore of Loch Treig and through the mountains to Rannoch Moor. From there it was southward all the way, right along the northern end of Loch Lomond and past Loch Long to the Gareloch. The route took them past Faslane and the Rhu Narrows and into Helensburgh.

The final miles were laden with memories, and the submariner thought of his months there, of long-lost colleagues and, perhaps most of all, of his Teacher, Commander Iain MacLean, the cleverest man he ever saw in a submarine – the stern, beady-eyed martinet who had taught him how to sink a big warship and how to evade the most relentless of pursuers. He tried now, as he always tried, to fight away the memories of the great man's daughter, the soft-spoken Scottish beauty who, to his everlasting regret, he'd never had time to love, far less to marry.

Helensburgh Station looked the same as always, gray and dour. A few passengers were waiting for the Glasgow train, but other-wise the place was largely deserted. It was middday when his train arrived, and Ben was one of only five people disembarking. It was a little warmer here, certainly warmer than it had been out in the Hebrides Sea earlier in the morning, and Ben Adnam was determined to find what they still call in this area a 'gentle-man's outfitter.'

He stepped out into the small resort town sloping up from the Clyde, and the wide streets seemed little changed. He knew precisely the sort of shop he required, and he was inside and soon out again with two dozen pairs of undershorts and socks, plus ten shirts and a half-dozen ties. He then headed for a country sports shop down a small narrow throughway off Upper Colquhoun Street, and in there he purchased a thick Scottish sheepskin coat, two cashmere sweaters in olive green and dark red, a cashmere scarf and a trilby hat. To this he added two country tweed jackets, two pairs of dark gray trousers and two pairs of cords, one tan and one dark green. Shoes were more difficult, but he opted for a couple of pairs of brown loafers with thick leather soles and a pair of black brogues. He wore one of the sweaters, the sheepskin coat and the trilby, and, feeling considerably better, he stepped out again into the cold with his many bagged packages and headed for the Royal Bank of Scotland, having just punched a serious hole in his last fifteen hundred pounds. Right now he wished he had not been quite so generous to Captain Gregor – who had, unwittingly, wasted his payment anyway.

Ben had always retained a bank account in Scotland under the name Benjamin Arnold, and he had made a point of keeping a minimum of £20,000 there in case of an emergency, such as the one in which he now found himself. No one at the bank knew him any longer, and he had to provide identification in order to collect a thousand pounds. He checked the balance of the account to make sure it was correct, and inquired briefly if there had been any mail addressed to him in the past three months. There had not, and nor had he expected there to be. Since the Iranians had intended he be blown to pieces on board the *Flower of Scotland*, he considered it unlikely they would have deposited his final payment of one and a half million dollars. He was right about that. They hadn't.

He left the bank, once more feeling a sense of desolation, and wandered through the town in search of a cab. That took him ten minutes, and by the time he arrived to spend the weekend at an old haunt from his Faslane days, the Rosslea Hall Hotel in Rhu, it was almost one o'clock in the afternoon.

At that precise time, a Royal Army Service Corps Sergeant, George Pattenden, was stumping around the military camp on the island of St Kilda making one loud and noisy demand: 'Right, then. Well, where the fucking hell *is* everyone, then?'

Back on the beach, Captain Peter Wimble RCT was still holding the landing craft in the shallows near the church in readiness for Lt Larkman and Corporal Lawson to come down

237

the beach ready to be evacuated. This was unusual in itself, because everyone knew by radio the ETA of the landing craft, and thus far in his two-year tour of duty in the Hebrides Captain Wimble had never yet arrived not to find the two departing men already standing on the beach, ready to go.

On this Friday lunchtime Sergeant Pattenden had leapt onto the shore and yelled. When no one showed up he had, with considerable bad grace, walked up to the camp and been mildly surprised that the lights were all on and the generator was still running, but that the jeep had gone. Of the lieutenant and the corporal there was no sign.

'Funny,' he had muttered. 'That's bloody funny. Where the fuck are they?' His irritation had good cause, since it was obvious his landing party couldn't return to base at Benbecula without the men they had come to take off St Kilda. Larkman and Lawson could not just be left behind with limited supplies.

At its longest stretch, the southwestern shore, the island stretched for three miles, from Soay Stack to the tip of Dun. At its widest point, from Gob Chathaill on that long shoreline east to the Oiseval, St Kilda measured almost two miles. But its coastline was a largely unapproachable panorama of towering, cave-riddled black cliffs, with fairly high mountains in the interior. It was not a desperately difficult place to search, if you had a half-dozen Landrovers, but they didn't. In Army terms, that meant they would have to walk, and there were only two hours of daylight left.

The sergeant headed back down to the beach to report the situation. The young captain, a friend of Chris Larkman's, immediately ordered the landing craft to be made fast at the jetty further along the bay and detailed two parties of three men each to begin a search, one party on the Ruaival side of Village Bay and the other up on Oiseval.

They kept going until 1630, by which time it was becoming hopelessly dark, and then returned aboard, radioing to their Hebrides HQ the distressing fact that Lieutenant Larkman and Corporal Lawson were missing. Everyone knew their weekend was shot to pieces. There would be no going back until Chris Larkman and his corporal were found. They all had the most terrible feeling of foreboding, because there was really nowhere the two men could be unless they'd gone over the edge of a cliff.

Captain Wimble decided they would be more comfortable at sea, and all six men spent the first night in the landing craft, anchored off in the bay. In the morning, back alongside, they set out once more to scour the Atlantic island.

By lunchtime the situation was judged to be critical, and two Army helicopters were dispatched from Benbecula. They combed the area for two hours, searching above the walking troops, clattering along the shoreline and gazing at the cliffs through binoculars, using infrared sensors. By dark, which today fell at 1640 there was not a sign of the missing men or their Landrover, and the two helicopters had to return to base for more fuel.

The search party now had their sleeping bags, food and supplies back in the huts, as well as a new Landrover which had been brought over in a second landing craft. The Army also replaced the fuel cans that Adnam had taken. But, his heart heavy, Captain Wimble now accepted that Chris Larkman and Tommy Lawson were dead, although he had no idea what had become of them. But he knew Chris, and he knew that something terrible must have happened. The ex-rugby player from Hampshire was a very solid citizen in Wimble's view, and Lawson was a cool, experienced soldier. It was inconceivable that either of them would have done anything ridiculous. He just couldn't imagine what had happened. And neither could anyone else.

Monday morning, March 6, found Ben Adnam still ensconced in the Rosslea Hall Hotel, still resting, but shaved and comfortable. He was now operating under the name Ben Arnold. His plan was to lie low for a month. He needed to find a quiet place, miles from anywhere, where he could rest, think and walk, regaining his composure and fitness, because right now, with his mind in a turmoil, he judged himself to be no good to anyone. He couldn't even go home: he *had* no home. There wasn't even an office he could call. Any phone call, any journey, would be fraught with peril. All he needed was time to think, because he required, unlike other men, a completely new life. And that, he guessed, might be pretty hard to come by.

Five months in a submarine had played havoc with his sense of well-being. He was anxious to get into shape. He bought himself a new pair of training shoes, a tracksuit and sweat pants, and a guidebook to the Highlands. What he really needed was a guidebook to the universe, because the boundaries of this earth were extremely confining to an ex-naval officer with Ben Adnam's track record.

He studied the guidebook all through his dinner in the hotel, and by ten o'clock had drawn up a shortlist of things to do. Ben retired to his room at a quarter to eleven, poured himself a glass of whisky, and sat down to make a decision. Half an hour later he made it. He would hire a car for cash from a local garage and drive up to a little village named Strachur, on the Cowal Peninsula. There he would check into the renowned The Creggans Inn, right on the eastern shore of Loch Fyne. It was a place he had been to, long ago, and he remembered it well, with its awesome views across the lonely water. He and his girlfriend had dined there on the night he had passed his Submarine Commanding Officers Course. So far as he could recall it had been the happiest night of his entire life.

He was not experienced in matters of the heart, and every instinct he possessed told him there was no point ever going back. Nothing was ever, or could ever be, the same. There were so many things he had never said, wished he had said, and now would never say. Returning to the place where once the two of them had been so content would probably just make matters appreciably worse.

She had gone now. Had been gone for several years – five at least since they had last spoken. He knew she was married to a wealthy Scottish landowner. They had seen each other twice since then. Surely a return to The Creggans Inn could do nothing except enhance his sadness, and highlight the fact that his future life held little promise for him. The longer he was alone the worse the depression became. Few people had ever compiled such a personal record as he had . . . rejected and betrayed by the only three employers he had ever had – all of whom, now, had tried to assassinate him. He had no home, no future, no love, no relatives, no friends. All he had was a past that would surely devour him in the end.

Nonetheless, he picked up the telephone and booked himself into The Creggans Inn for a month. He informed the receptionist that he was a South African, mainly because he always carried a South African passport alongside his Iranian and Turkish ones; for this excursion he had also brought a four-year-old UK passport, although he had not as yet used it.

He checked out of the Rosslea Hall Hotel when the garage brought his rental car, for which he paid £300 in cash, the other £300 being due when he returned it in a month. It was a six-year-old metallic-blue Audi A8 with 70,000 miles on the clock, but it ran well. The mechanic didn't bother to check his British license, carefully forged for him in Egypt a few years previously under the name Benjamin Arnold, like two of his other passports.

It was a little over 30 miles around the lochs to Strachur, and Ben drove it slowly, especially the first part, running north up the east bank of the Gareloch, the dark familiar waters in which he had so often driven submarines. He ran much more quickly for a while through the Argyll Forest Park on the A83 before slowing down again, dawdling along the bank of Loch Fyne, looking for the big white house on the far bank where once, and once only, he had been a guest. That, too, he remembered as if it had been yesterday.

He checked into the warm, comfortable inn and sat by the fire in the bar. He had chicken sandwiches for lunch, sipping orange juice and reading the *Scotsman*. Now, on this misty Monday morning, he found two news items that took up a considerable amount of space.

The first was on the front page, from which the unsmiling faces of two soldiers stared out. On the left was Lieutenant Christopher Larkman, on the right was Corporal Tommy Lawson. The headline read, 'OFFICER AND CORPORAL MISSING IN ST KILDA MYSTERY.'

The story went on to detail the Army search of the island which had been going on all weekend. It quoted the officer in charge, Captain Peter Wimble, confessing that everyone was completely baffled by the disappearance of the two men and their Landrover. 'They didn't have a boat,' he was reported as saying. 'They can't have been kidnaped – it's more or less impossible to land on St Kilda at this time of year without a military landing craft. Which means they must be either on the island or in the ocean. And we now know they're not on the island. Which, I am afraid, leaves only the ocean. Though how or why or when we can't say.'

The story concluded with the statement that the Army did not believe either of the two men could still be alive, but that the search would continue along the shore, beneath the cliffs, so long as the weather permitted.

The second item, inside on page three, concerned a missing fishing boat, the *Flower of Scotland*. The newspaper treated it as another mystery. The harbormaster at Mallaig had lost contact with the boat in the small hours of last Thursday morning, March 2. This had not at first caused much concern since it was not altogether unusual – radio failures can occur any time. But there was now worry for Captain Gregor Mackay and his crew, even though the master was very experienced in fishing the deep, lonely waters out toward the Rockall Bank. The situation was regarded as sufficiently serious for a sea and air search to have been instigated, and the newspaper revealed that 'the Royal Air Force are expected to send out two Nimrods at first light on Monday morning.'

It was, however, a later part of the article which interested Ben Adnam. According to the harbormaster, the Zodiac tender from the *Flower of Scotland* had been discovered on the outer edge of Mallaig Harbor on Friday morning. It was parked on a mooring used by a lobsterman, Ewan MacInnes, for his small boat, and the lobsterman knew it hadn't been there when he'd left the previous evening. Adding to the mystery was that MacInnes, who had spent all of his life in Mallaig, knew Gregor Mackay well, and had seen him leave two nights previously with 'a foreign-looking laddie' on board. He had watched them clear the harbor, the stranger standing on the stern 'right by the Zodiac.'

Ewan MacInnes was not, apparently, regarded as the world's most reliable source. A cheerful, bearded man of 55, he had a reputation as a hard drinker and a bit of a romancer. But the coastguard had grilled him, the police had grilled him, and the reporter from the local newspaper had grilled him and still – despite the assertion of a local landlady that 'Ewan was half the day in here drinking before he sailed' – the lobsterman was adamant. No, the Zodiac had not been on his mooring when he left, 'for the plain and obvious bloody reason that it was on the bloody stern of Gregor's boat, where it always bloody well is.' He added that 'I saw it leave. And yes, the foreigner was standing next to it. And what's more I can tell you what he was wearing: a dark blue jacket, looked military, with a fur hat . . .'

The *Scotsman* plainly believed the fishing boat was gone. On an inside feature page the newspaper ran a big speculation piece on 'yet another disappearing trawler' and cited an ever-lurking menace to fisherman: Royal Navy submarines prowling beneath the surface. For the moment the newspaper was prepared to disregard a different sort of menace the Royal Navy itself had to deal with. The features department had instead concentrated on the age-old problem of an underwater warship hooking into a trawler's net and dragging it down, stern first, to the bottom.

The article named all the trawlers which had met this fate in recent years, and mentioned the Navy's reluctance ever to accept responsibility for these mishaps unless the evidence is overwhelming.

The problem is that no submarine can see the lines that hold the net. There is a regulation intended to counter the problem: all trawler captains are supposed to station on the stern a man with an ax while the boat is running through the submarine roads around the Clyde estuary. If the net snags on a periscope or a mast the drill is to sever the lines instantly and let the net go. The Navy, subject of course to an internal investigation, will bear the cost of new gear. But out at sea, in the open Atlantic, the issue is more complicated. The submarine involved might be owned by the Royal Navy, the United States or Russia, and no one would be any the wiser. It sometimes takes a full week before it is even realized the fishing boat has gone. This, the *Scotsman*'s feature writers asserted, was most certainly what had happened to the *Flower of Scotland*.

The *Scotsman* had a 'house list' of former Royal Navy commanders, retired but still Scottish residents, who were always good for a pithy quote. On this occasion they took delight in quoting the former Polaris CO Captain Reginald Smyth. 'Oh, Christ,' he told the reporter in his usual languid drawl. 'Another one? Bloody bad luck, hmm? That's the trouble with Scottish fisherman, they're usually drunk. Couldn't trust any of 'em to swing an axe straight – they'd probably chop their dicks off.'

Pressed further by the reporter, Smyth added: 'Seriously, the chances of a submarine catching a fishing net are millions to one against. The ocean's a very big place. But, until those trawlermen understand thoroughly that it *can* happen, there'll be accidents. If they want to avoid them, they *must* have an axe-man on the stern. The submarine can't see them, and it can't feel them if it snags the line. Only the trawlermen can tell something's wrong . . . and they've got about five seconds to swing the axe. It's damned rare, though. You can understand them not always bothering.'

Captain Smyth got his photograph in the newspaper for that piece of intelligence. The italicized caption beneath it was a simple 'quotation': *'Drunken fishermen have themselves to blame.'* Three weeks later, although no one could know it now, Reg Smyth would receive a mild rebuke from the Admiralty.

Ben Adnam was contemplative. He finished his chicken sandwich and ordered a cup of coffee. And he gave due consideration to the conclusions that might arise from the evidence of Ewan MacInnes. *If he's believed,* Adnam pondered, *it'll become obvious that someone got off the fishing boat and found his way back to Mallaig. But that'd be impossible given the petrol situation. Which means, I suppose, that MacInnes won't be believed. But a good detective would wonder. He might even wonder if there was a connection between the Zodiac and the missing soldiers . . . I hope not.*

He finished his coffee and then went up to his room to change into his get-fit kit. He was next seen pounding along the A815 main road along the loch, bound for the tiny village of St Catherine's, four miles away. Alas, he never made it – he blew up after two miles and was forced to lie down on his back on the wet grass. Once he'd regained his breath he walked slowly back, feeling sick and sweating like a Japanese wrestler. Five months with no exercise can reduce anyone to feeling middle-aged, even a man as fit as Ben Adnam once had been. And this manifestation of his poor condition made him doubly determined to get back into top shape.

Every morning for a week he rose at six, pulled on his trainers and tracksuit and pounded his way towards St Catherine's. Then he tried again in the afternoon. On the fifth day he made it the whole way. On the seventh he made it there and back without stopping. By the end of the second week he was running effortlessly to St Catherine's and back twice a day, timing himself.

He also took charge of his diet, eating only fresh fruit and cereal for breakfast, grilled fish and salad for lunch, and fillet steak or roast lamb with green vegetables for dinner. Temporarily he cut out all dairy produce, and drank nothing but fruit juice or water.

By Wednesday, March 29, one year to the day since he had stolen HMS *Unseen*, he felt that his body was back in shape. Today he had abandoned the soft option of running along the A815 and instead had taken to the hills, running for miles in the mountainous foothills of Cruach nan Capull, which rises 1700 feet above the loch, opposite the Duke of Fife's Inveraray Castle. For the first time in a year Adnam felt lean, hard-trained and ready to fight to the death if necessary.

And yet . . . and yet something had happened to the mind of Benjamin Adnam. For the first time in his life he questioned the things he had done. Had they been, in fact, *right*? Was he really the obedient instrument of Allah, fighting for a holy cause? Or was he just the pawn of power-crazed earthly leaders who answered to the same god as the citizens of the United States: the god of money and possessions?

He believed in the future triumph of Islam, and he believed in the cause of fundamentalism. And yet . . .

No man had ever done more than he had, risked more than he had, been more successful than he had. And where had it put him? Nowhere. He was regarded as a total outcast throughout the Middle East. His massive contribution to the *jihad* against the West had turned him into an Arab who was essentially stateless, with a price on his head in several countries. And the great State of Islam could, it appeared, offer him nothing – not even loyalty – except death: death by assassination, not death in battle or in glory, but death in some backstreet building at the hands of fourth-rate hired murderers. Was that a fit ending for Benjamin Adnam?

For the first time he began to reflect on the acts he had committed. He now asked himself, were they *crimes*, those massive blows he had struck against the Great Satan? Not if they were executed on behalf of Allah for the greater understanding of his Word. But how could he now think that? The rejection by Iraq and then by the Ayatollahs of Iran must surely mean that Allah was displeased with him. Otherwise his humble disciple Adnam would certainly have received some reward, some recognition, or even at least an *honorable* death and the eternal peace of the life hereafter.

But he had received nothing. Except treachery. And he had been responsible for the deaths of so many people, most of them entirely innocent. Thousands of American sailors and aircrew on the carrier, a packed Concorde airliner, Starstriker, the Vice-President of the United States plus his entire staff . . .

My God, what have I really done?

The darkness came blood-black for Ben Adnam on the night of March 29. For hour after hour, his dreams were interrupted by the searing crash of high explosives, and he woke frequently, cradling his own head against the pillow, sweating, trembling at the impact, haunted by his own most terrible actions against humanity. He was afraid to go to sleep, afraid even to close his eyes, because the images were too stark, too real. He could not look at the burning men of the ships he had smashed; the engulfing red tide of his dreams was not the heavenly sunset of his aspirations – it was too dark for that and the screams too loud. Twice he woke to find himself fighting to break free of the plastic body-bag that was dragging him inexorably to the bottom of the Atlantic, weighted down by a concrete block.

He got up, and drank some water, and mopped his face with a towel. Sheer exhaustion drove him back into bed and to fitful sleep once more. But unconsciousness did not last for more than a half-hour. Before dawn broke over the peaceful waters of Loch Fyne he had thrown himself violently to the side of the big double bed, gripping the sheet, trying desperately to break free of the army Landrover as it plunged toward the water . . . gaining speed . . . down . . . down . . .

. . . down . . .

At six o'clock on the morning of March 30, while the great terrorist Ben Adnam lay on his bed on the eastern side of the loch, breathless and shaking like a leaf, terrified he might be losing his mind, there was a flurry of activity on the loch's western side and about a mile-and-a-half to the north in the wide, sweeping front drive of the big white Georgian mansion owned by retired Admiral Sir Iain MacLean.

The admiral was making an early start, and had five passengers to fit into his Range Rover: his trio of black labradors – Fergus, Muffin and Mr Bumble – and his two granddaughters, Flora, aged six, and Mary, nine. The evacuation was not proving easy because the youngest of the quintet, the 18-month-old Mr Bumble, made a rush for the loch. The pup was pursued by Flora, who fell onto the wet grass and wrecked her trousers and coat while Mr Bumble carried on doing a fair imitation of Mark Spitz in the freezing water.

Lady MacLean arrived with towels, grabbed the dog from the shallows, carried him wriggling to the Range Rover, and threw him in the back with the others. Flora made her own way back, giggling and trying to restore her clothes – a plainly impossible task.

Sir Iain said he had no time to wait, because the plane would probably be early into Glasgow from Chicago. He told Flora that God only knew what her mother would think of her, covered in mud, but that her stepfather would almost certainly laugh. Lt-Commander and Mrs Bill Baldridge did, after all, live on a vast ranch in the state of Kansas, surrounded by grassland and miles and miles of the mud that goes with grazing pastures in winter.

This was the first visit Bill and Laura had made to Scotland since they had left together in the winter of 2004. Sir Iain had twice visited them in Kansas, but there had been terrible family scars caused by the brutal court battle which had taken place over his daughter Laura's children.

Laura Anderson, mother of two, had, at age 34, left her banker husband, Douglas Anderson, for the US Navy officer to whom she was now married. The MacLeans and the Andersons, lifelong friends, had banded together to make the girls Wards of the Court in Edinburgh, and absolute custody had been granted to their father. The judge had made it perfectly clear at the hearing that, if Laura insisted in running off with her American lover, it would be a very long time before she would see the girls again. As the Anderson lawyer had pointed out, these girls were daughters of Scotland, granddaughters of a famous Scottish admiral on one side and, on the other, descended from one of the most important landed families in the country. There were critical questions of inheritance to consider. No, the court would not permit them to be taken to the US Midwest, from where they might very well never return.

It was Iain MacLean himself who broke the deadlock. He told his disapproving wife, Annie, that he could not bring himself to turn his hand against the daughter he loved. He added that he didn't give a bloody fig for Douglas Anderson, whom he considered an extremely dreary man, and that he liked Bill Baldridge very much. He was determined to do something to resolve the situation.

Assisted by the fact that Douglas wound up in the London tabloids, having an affair with an actress from Notting Hill Gate in London, the Admiral moved to have the Court Order overturned, citing that Lt-Commander Baldridge was the son of one of the biggest ranchers in Kansas, that he had a doctorate in nuclear physics from MIT, that he had been one of the leading weapons officers in the US Navy, and that he was a personal friend of the President of the United States. 'And, perhaps more significantly, of mine,' MacLean added with uncharacteristic immodesty.

MacLean enjoyed firing a powerful torpedo, and the judge decided that, without the admiral's support for it, the Court Order was essentially worthless. Yes, the girls were free and entitled, and could by rights visit their natural mother in any and all school holidays. And now the imminent arrival of Bill and Laura was an occasion of great excitement, because they were staying for ten days and then taking Flora and Mary to Kansas for the first time, for the remainder of the Scottish schools' long Easter break.

The other objective to be achieved was a reconciliation between Laura and her mother. The two had hardly spoken since the custody case ended, since Annie MacLean felt that poor Douglas Anderson had been dealt a cruel and unnecessary blow. But now that the man had married his actress things were rather different, particularly since Douglas was fond of saying publicly, albeit self-protectively, that 'Natalie is a lot prettier than Laura, and a lot less bloody trouble.'

Sir Iain thought Anderson was a lousy judge of women and a man to be pitied. But his wife, on first hearing of the remark, changed her allegiance dramatically and leapt to the defense of her absent daughter like a tigress defending her young, and made no secret of the fact that she now supported every one of her daughter's decisions. Both Sir Iain and Laura were hopeful that in the next few days the deep family rift would be healed.

The Range Rover made it to the airport a half-hour early. They parked the car and headed for the international exit gate. Bill and Laura, traveling first-class, were among the first out, Bill wearing a big leather cowboy jacket over a dark gray suit and tie, his rolling gait, straight from the High Plains, unmistakable. Laura followed him through the door. She looked slim and quite stunning in a long, fitted, dark-green suede overcoat with matching trilby hat, and burgundy leather boots. Iain MacLean had never seen her look so well, nor so happy. The girls fell into her arms, and the two ex-naval officers shook hands warmly. 'She looks marvelous,' said the admiral quietly. 'I was quite worried about her a couple of years ago. Thank you, Bill . . . for looking after her.'

The Kansan grinned. 'And thank you, Admiral, for being so goddamned decent about the whole thing . . . Neither of us could help it, you know. It just happened, and it wasn't a mistake.'

'No. I know it wasn't.'

Laura introduced the girls to their new stepfather, and for a few moments they just gazed up into the deep blue eyes of the 6ft 2in Midwesterner who looked like a young Robert Mitchum. In the end, the elder daughter, Mary, asked earnestly, 'Sir, are you really a cowboy like my father says you are?'

'Yes, ma'am,' said Bill, grinning. 'I sure am. Ridin' them dogies home, out there on the prairie.'

This caused the little girl to fall about with laughter.

'And you're really my stepfather?'

'Guess so, Miss Mary. Sure hope we git to ride the range together some time.'

'Stop it, Bill,' said Laura, laughing. 'Mary, ignore him. He really doesn't talk like that at all.'

'Jest cain't wait to git back in the saddle agin,' added Lt-Commander Baldridge.

With the introductions complete, Laura kissed her father and they walked back to the Range Rover and the frenzied barking of the labradors. The 55-mile journey took them almost two hours, thanks to the morning traffic in Glasgow. Bill regaled the girls with tales of Wyatt Earp and the Dalton Brothers, never once dropping his cowboy act. He told them about the prairies, and the fact that his mother was on the board of the cowboy museum in Dodge City, 'where I'm sure gonna take both you girls, once I git you fixed up with a couple of six-shooters – jest in case we meet any cattle rustlers on the trail.'

Even Sir Iain was laughing by this time, and it was not until they headed north up the bank of the Gareloch that Bill suddenly offered his hand to Mary and told her, in a completely different accent, 'Just kidding, Mary. Lieutenant-Commander Bill Baldridge, United States submarine officer by trade. You can call me Bill.'

Mary looked quite disappointed. 'Hmm,' she said. 'I wish you were still a cowboy.'

'Well,' said Laura, 'I'm glad we got that little charade over. He's so silly, Daddy. He's actually been practicing his cowboy act in case we meet any of your stuffy friends.'

'Good idea, Bill,' said the admiral. 'Give 'em the full Wyatt Earp.'

It was just before ten o'clock when they arrived at the house, and the admiral moved in to deal skillfully with any tensions which remained between his wife and the visitors from the United States.

Bill did his part here, too. 'I just wish you could find some time to come over to visit us, Annie,' he said. 'I've always thought you would like it, and my mother would love to meet you at last.'

Lady MacLean smiled. It was a smile that did not quite ask for forgiveness, but almost. It had been so much easier for her husband, who had liked Bill from the very start and had indeed worked with him on a Royal Navy mission. And even she had to admit that Laura's second marriage had worked out well: she had never seen her daughter so happy, nor in such a bloom of health – at the end of the winter, too. 'Kansas certainly seems to agree with Laura,' she said to Bill. 'I'm sure it'll be fine for me as well. Iain loves it there, as you know . . . and I hope you'll find it in your heart to forget the bitterness of the past. It was such a shock for us all, you know.'

'As far as I'm concerned, the past is already forgotten,' replied the rancher gallantly. Turning to Mary, he added, with a conspiratorial wink, 'Yes, *ma'am*.' Which again reduced the little girl to helpless laughter.

'He's a cowboy, Grandma,' she said. 'That's how they talk.'

'Only sometimes,' said Annie. 'Don't forget, I've known him longer than you.'

'Yes, but he's *my* stepfather,' Mary said.

'And he's *my* son-in-law,' replied her grandmother.

'Easy, girls. Hold your fire. I don't want y'all to start fightin' over me.'

'*There!*' yelled Mary triumphantly. 'I told you that's how they talk . . .'

At this point Admiral MacLean assumed a loose command. He suggested Annie organize some coffee, and he sent Angus, the red-bearded butler, upstairs with the suitcases, calling after him, 'The blue room in the front!' Then, turning to Bill, he added, 'There's a big double bed in there now, so don't look too forlorn.'

'Oh, right. I forgot. That's my old room. I haven't been in there for what? Four years?'

'Must be. It was 2002, wasn't it, when he got the *Jefferson*.'

'It was also 2002 when we got him, wasn't it?'

'Well, it was 2002 when the Mossad *thought* they got him.'

'Oh, I think they did, sir. Did I ever tell you that the President presented me with Adnam's little submarine badge – the one he received from Tel Aviv?'

'No, you didn't. And will you *please* stop calling me "Sir" whenever we touch on Navy matters. I'm Iain – plain, simple Iain. Do you understand me, Lieutenant-Commander?'

'Yes, sir.'

'Excellent.'

Both men laughed easily. 'As a matter of fact, Bill,' MacLean continued, 'the President told me he'd given the badge to you. I talked to him at the wedding. I must say he was very impressed by the way you first identified the problem and then hunted the submarine down.'

'Actually it was the man I hunted down, rather than the submarine. We'd never have found that, not without a tip-off.'

'No. I suppose not. They are the devil to find, those diesels, eh?'

'Sure are.' Baldridge paused for a moment. 'I miss it all sometimes, you know, Iain. That's not a complaint, by the way. Laura and I are very happy running the ranch, and it'll be great having the girls there for a vacation. But there are times . . . times I see an item about the Navy in the newspaper and think about how I would tackle it. There's no better life when you're single, and free, and you feel you're helping run the world.'

'I know, Bill. I miss it too. I suppose we all do after we leave. But some of us never quite take off the dark blue, eh?'

'Not quite, sir,' said Bill to the senior officer, who this time raised no objection.

By midday, on the other side of Loch Fyne, Ben Adnam had somewhat recovered from his tortured night. He had opened the curtains wide at first light and slept in bright sunlight for most of the morning. Having missed breakfast, he decided on a quick cup of coffee, which he sipped downstairs in front of the fire. Then he decided to attack his all-time record of 51 minutes to St Catherine's and back. This required him to reach the halfway turning point in 24 minutes – six minutes per mile – because the second half was always slower. He set off along the loch, running hard on the flat surface of the A815.

The trouble was, his heart simply wasn't in it. He found himself dawdling, looking at the water rather than his watch. He jogged into St Catherine's five minutes behind schedule, which in his mind defeated the object of the exercise. So he sat on a stone wall looking across at Inveraray while he regained his breath.

Once more his thoughts returned to the darkest side of his life – to the monstrous acts of destruction he had perpetrated. And again he was haunted by the one question he could no longer answer: 'For whom did I do it?' And he was afraid there was no answer, because there was no one to whom he could defer in the matter of his deeply held religious beliefs.

He did not doubt Allah, nor did he doubt the Prophet, nor indeed the Koran. His worry was that he had performed his great tasks without Allah approving what he was doing. He had been taught that the senior clerics of the Muslim faith, the *mullahs* and the *ayatollahs*, were not in direct touch with God but were merely teachers, learned men who were there to study the Koran and to guide their fellow Muslims in the words of the Prophet Mohammed. He understood thoroughly that all Muslims must find their own faith, because there can be no shortcut such as direct word through the *mullahs* or the *ayatollahs*.

He could not possibly defer to the President of Iraq, for whom he had operated for most of his life. And, although he had felt very at home in Iran, the clerics of that country had not hesitated to cut him off from his reward immediately it suited them.

Who, then, *was* he? Just a terrorist who would operate for anyone? Just some kind of an international criminal? A hit man?

A mercenary? Because, should that be the case, he was uncertain he could live with it. Ben Adnam was a man who had believed in his own higher calling, but now that profoundly held philosophy was in ruins. He didn't know what to do, nor where to go. And there was one other problem that would not go away, a more mundane one: he was, without question, the most wanted man in the world.

He gazed across the flat, dark, shining waters of Loch Fyne. It was almost two miles wide right here. But it was a very bright, cold, cloudless day, and Ben was able to see for a long way. Snow still shone on the high peak of the 'submariner's mountain,' The Cobbler, which Ben could see nine miles to the east, up across the huge pines of the Argyll Forest. It reminded him, as everything here did, of days long past; especially those days when he had returned to the Clyde estuary in a Royal Navy submarine, watching for that mountain as a sign that they were almost home.

Home. Now he had no home. But The Cobbler was still there. And so was all the grand and glorious scenery on the other side of the loch, the steep lightly wooded foothills which slope up to Cruach Mohr, which looked back at him from where it towered over the land behind Inveraray Castle.

Directly across the water was the great white mansion of his Teacher, the father of the only girl who had ever loved him. Alone in his desolation, Ben stared at the far bank, trying to see the house where once she had lived, but there were trees to the north of the grounds, he remembered, and it would be hard to catch a glimpse of the building from where he sat.

It was strange how he was suddenly drawn to the memory of Laura MacLean, now that he was not only the most wanted but also the most *un*wanted man in the world. They say that men facing a firing squad or the noose or the electric chair often cry out 'Mummy!' as they go to meet their Maker. And Ben wondered if that might not be the reason he so yearned for Laura now. Was it just a helpless, despairing cry for unconditional kindness. He was not sure she could, or would want to, deliver that any more, but the brutal truth was there was no one else.

He sat on the wall, in the sharp chill of the early Highlands spring, believing that she was far away somewhere with Douglas Anderson, but unable to tear himself from the sight of the place where once she had lived. He felt like a jilted lover, the kind who cherish a masochistic desire to stand and secretly watch the home of their former wife or girlfriend – just for a glimpse, just for even a thought-flash of remembered joy, remembered passion, in the desperate million-to-one hope of a chance meeting, an instant reconciliation.

Wearily Ben picked himself up at last, and turned back down the loch, running hard now, trying to drive the demon of Laura from his soul, as if he ever could. But he had to get back to the inn. He had ordered lunch for 1.45pm, home-made soup and a grilled Dover sole, and he needed the fuel. This afternoon, before dark, he would attack his St Catherine's record again. And this time he would concentrate. If he could.

The bar was fairly empty, but the fire was crackling and the landlady was as always cheerful. They talked for a while about his work in the South African mining business. And he explained why he was here after a lifetime in the perfect climate of Pieter-maritzburg. 'My grandfather was a Highlander,' he told her. 'And my wife died recently. I just wanted to come here for a month and feel my roots, visit a few little villages in the area. Someone told me how beautiful Loch Fyne was, and someone else told me about this place. Here I am, for another few days . . . getting rested and fit. And I'm enjoying every moment of it.'

He liked the people who owned The Creggans Inn. They were never intrusive, and allowed him all the space he wanted. They worked on the old Scottish theory that, if a man wants company, he'll ask for it. There's never a need to intrude. To some visitors this private, standoffish view of the world is precisely what leads to the Scots being described as 'dour.' But to Ben Adnam this quality was a godsend. Soon he would vanish from this place for ever, to be remembered by, he hoped, very, very few people.

He decided after all to cancel his afternoon run and instead to take the car and drive the 28 miles up to the northern point of Loch Awe, the thin, 23-mile-long serpent of Highland water at the head of which stand the 15th-century castle of Kilchurn and the great brooding mountain of Ben Cruachan, which looms 3700 feet above the loch. Ben was resolved to walk to its peak some day to claim what is widely regarded as the best view in Scotland. Ben climbing Ben, as it were. But probably not today. He put his binoculars in the car in case he just wanted to look down at the magical waters of this heavily wooded, deep-water fisherman's paradise. In the back of his mind he also thought he might have a further use for the binoculars on the way back. But it was a thought he refused to acknowledge.

There was little traffic and the Audi made short work of the journey. Ben gazed at the towering bulk of the mountain, and decided to walk quietly around the castle instead. He climbed the stairs to the huge turrets and tried to imagine the force of the gale which had destroyed one of them on that terrible night after Christmas in 1879 when the Tay Rail Bridge in Dundee was also demolished. He inspected the turret, and then walked to see the view from atop the castle right down the long, straight waters of the loch. It was, as the guidebook had said, truly spectacular.

Afterwards he returned to the car to drive, he knew, to the east bank of Loch Fyne and look across the water to the house where Laura had once lived.

It was growing dark by the time he arrived at his observation post on the edge of the road. A soft tallow mist was already gathering in the central channel of the loch, and it would soon obscure his view of the grandiose MacLean mansion. But for the moment it was still pretty good. The high-powered glasses magnified the far bank many times, and Ben could easily discern the lawn running down to the water. He and Laura had walked along that bank before dinner on the one night he had been invited to her home.

Ben focused the binoculars, and now he could see the lawn clearly. He could also see two, maybe three figures moving across it toward the loch. But the distance was too great for him to make them out properly. He guessed they must be his old Teacher, Commander MacLean, with perhaps his wife and an early-arriving weekend guest – he remembered that the family did a lot of private entertaining. But what Ben really wanted to know was the whereabouts of Laura. And he had no way to cure the obdurate stupidity of that thought. His mind ranged over a succession of ludicrous options associated with such a reunion. *(a) Take out Douglas Anderson, and maybe she would come with me . . . but to where? (b) Try to charm her, persuade her to see me. No possibility. We both knew it was over the last time we met. (c) Kidnap her, and beg for a second chance. (d) . . . Forget it, Ben. It can't happen. But if I could just see her . . .*

He stared across the water at the green of the MacLean lawn

and wondered again where she was. Never had he known himself so acutely irrational. But he had nothing else to do, and he had no idea where to go.

The end of the afternoon on the other side of the loch saw the admiral, Bill and Laura, all three of them dressed warmly, strolling back across the lawn after a long walk down the shore. Both of the visitors had found the conversation riveting, because Iain MacLean had been telling them in a perfectly matter-of-fact way that he and Arnold Morgan both believed Ben Adnam was still alive. At that point in the talk, Bill Baldridge had almost fallen into the loch.

'*Alive?* How could that be? The Mossad took him out in Cairo, didn't they? Jesus, I've got his badge. Admiral Morgan's seen the documents, and so've the Israelis. They've got his passport. They have his personal Navy record, the one he owned himself, with his entire career on it.'

'All true,' replied Admiral MacLean. 'The trouble is: none of them have seen the body. You'll remember that Ben – or *someone* – was assassinated by two people who'd never laid eyes on him. They left with the dead man's papers, but the Egyptian police took the body and cremated it. As Arnold is rather fond of saying, the Mossad have no idea whether they took out Ben Adnam or Genghis Khan.'

Bill laughed. But then suddenly he became thoughtful. 'And what gave rise to this sudden desire to exhume the Israeli commander?'

'Ah, that's another story,' replied the admiral. 'I'll tell you at dinner. Come on, let's go in and have some tea – we've walked far enough for one day.'

'Do you really think he's still alive, Daddy?'

'Quite frankly, yes I do.'

'Try to remember, darling,' said Bill soothingly. 'Should he call, don't forget to let us know.'

Laura was pensive. She walked back to the house behind the other two. What a curious circle her world had turned in. The first man she had ever loved, Ben Adnam, had done something so terrible, so shocking, it had led her to the only other man she would ever love. For several long years she had believed Ben dead, but now . . . Her thoughts cascaded. She had walked on this lawn with him, held his hand, laughed at his jokes. Had it really been *that* empty? Or, with a man like that, did love ebb and flow? And how would she feel if she ever saw him again? – not Ben the mass murderer but Ben the gentle, handsome boy who was cleverer and nicer than all the others. The Ben she had loved for so long.

Laura looked again at Bill, her tall, wonderful US Navy officer. Ben had never possessed that kind of relaxed *savoir faire*. He was too hard, too busy, too preoccupied.

No, she'd take Kansas over the Middle East any time.

Dinner that night was a re-creation of the feast Bill had enjoyed when first he had come to visit the admiral's family, back in 2002 – the time when he had first met Mrs Laura Anderson. There was a magnificent poached salmon with mayonnaise, potatoes and peas. A bottle of elegant white Burgundy from Meursault and a superb bottle of Lynch Bages 1990 were set in the middle of the table. Bill remembered two things about his first dinner at the MacLeans – one, that the admiral never served a first course with salmon, because he believed everyone would much rather have 'another bit of fish if they were still hungry,' and, two, that Sir Iain preferred to drink Bordeaux with salmon, as did Laura, which left Lady MacLean to deal with the Meursault.

Of the many differences between then and now the most striking was the lack of a view through the windows. In that hot July when his heart had raced at the very sight of Laura he had been able to see right down the loch while they dined, and he recalled Sir Iain pointing out the little village of Strachur, over on the Cowal Peninsula.

Tonight everything was just as charming, but different. There was a glowing log fire in the 50-foot-long dining room, and the big patterned brocade curtains were drawn. Lights were switched on above the six paintings which hung from the high walls – three ancestors, one 19th-century racehorse, a stag (probably at bay), and a pack of hounds in full flight. Otherwise the only light in the room came from the eight lighted candles set in obviously Georgian silver holders which Bill thought probably came with the house.

As before, he sat next to Laura and facing Annie MacLean.

The two girls had had an early supper in order to watch television in Laura's old nursery.

The salmon was as good as the last time, when it had been the best Bill had ever tasted. The Lynch Bages was perfect, and the admiral was amusing them all with tall stories about Arnold Morgan's visit several months ago.

'What precisely did he come here for?' asked Bill.

'Well, I think he wanted to get away for a week or so with that extremely attractive lady he plans to marry.'

'Kathy? Yes, she *is* very beautiful, isn't she?'

'Absolutely,' said Sir Iain. 'I told him she was probably a bit too good for him, really. He took it very well, for him.'

'But what else, Iain? Tell me more.'

'Well, Bill, I suppose if anyone is entitled to know this, you are. And so is your wife. I've been wondering whether to break this to you gently or just to come straight out with it. And I've decided on the latter course. Arnold Morgan and I think that Ben Adnam has stolen and now commands the missing Royal Navy submarine HMS *Unseen*, and that he has been sitting underwater in the middle of the Atlantic banging out jet airliners, including Concorde, Starstriker and *Air Force Three*.'

As showstoppers go, that one went. Laura choked on her Lynch Bages, and Bill dropped his fork on the table with a clatter.

But Bill recovered quickly. 'Oh, I see,' he said. 'Nothing serious. I was thinking it might be something important.'

'Oh, no,' said the admiral. 'Very routine. Just the sort of thing he might do, don't you think?'

'Well, assuming he managed to jump off that Egyptian funeral pyre, I'd say most definitely. Right up his alley. Any evidence, or are you and Arnold going in for thriller writing?'

'Actually, there *isn't* much hard evidence, only circumstantial. But there's a lot of that – and, very curiously, Arnold and I stacked it up quite separately, on different sides of the Atlantic, and arrived at precisely the same conclusion.'

'Might I ask when Arnold arrived here?'

'Yes. Last May. A few weeks after *Unseen* went missing. He came here with a real bee in his bonnet about it. And his reasons, as you would expect, were pretty good. He was puzzled first that the submarine had not been found by the Royal Navy, despite the use of God knows how many ships, all the most modern sonar and underwater diving equipment in a relatively narrow, shallow section of the English Channel: the boat was obviously not there. He thus reasoned that it had left its exercise area, and inferred that it had been deliberately driven out of that area and by someone other than the British lieutenant-commander who was officially in charge.

'Therefore, Arnold considered, the ship had been either hijacked or stolen, and he went for the second option. *Unseen* had sent all the right signals back during the first couple of days after leaving Plymouth, therefore her CO knew what they were and he knew how to send them. Ben Adnam? I taught him all that – I even taught him how to drive an Upholder-Class boat, which *Unseen* is.'

'Hmm,' said Bill. 'And then . . . ?'

'Well, she vanishes and is never heard from again. But then Concorde falls out of the sky, for no known reason – the most brilliantly maintained aircraft on the North Atlantic suddenly disappears. Then, a matter of days later, Starstriker falls out of the sky on her maiden voyage. A brand-new, tried and tested proto-type which Boeing swear by, an aircraft that's been under guard for weeks, carrying no passengers, just crew . . . Starstriker falls straight into the Atlantic without a word. Same place – 30 West, right over the Mid-Atlantic Ridge, the very best place in all the ocean to hide a submarine.

'And then *Air Force Three*. Virtually new. Flown by one of the best pilots in the US Air Force. Gone. I hear on the grapevine there were smoke trails spotted of the kind that might fit the notion of a missile.'

Bill interrupted. 'One major point, Iain. *Unseen* has no weapon which would fire such a missile. Neither does any other submarine in the world. Such a system would have to be custom-made and fitted, wouldn't it?'

'Well, Bill, I think Arnold believes the Iraqis found a way and *did* fit such a system. I intended to ask you what you thought might be feasible.'

'I suppose one of those advanced Russian SAMs might do the trick – maybe the Grumble Rif. It'd have to be radar-guided – heat-seeking wouldn't do it, because the supersonics would be going too fast. Come to think of it, you could probably adapt the submarine's regular radar to just a part of the system: the launcher and the missiles. If you did that you could catch the aircraft coming in, in the normal way, then send the bird right off the casing to the correct altitude and let the missile's own nose cone radar do the rest. Couldn't miss, if you did it right.'

'One problem, Bill. I wanted to ask you about it. If Iraq was responsible – and we know Adnam is an Iraqi – then *where*? That's what's exercising Arnold and me, *where* they could have made the conversion. They've got no submarine facilities.'

'I don't see that as a major problem. I think such a system could be just bolted onto the deck, with most of the high-tech work being completed from inside the submarine. If you could hide her for a short while alongside a submarine workshop ship – well, what I'm saying is that you might get it done without even going into a drydock, so long as there was a crane on board.

'Hmm. Adnam got ahold of a submarine before when he needed it. I guess he could do it again. But I think his biggest problem would be getting a crew. There's no submariners in the Iraqi Navy, and there'd be no way to train them. Surely he couldn't have persuaded an entire crew of Brazilians to go along with the scheme. Did Morgan have any ideas on that, or did he just assume Adnam had found a way, like he did with the Russian Kilo?'

'He didn't mention any of that. I thought perhaps he might know something he wasn't prepared to share with me. Anyway, Bill, that more or less brings you into line with our thinking. But the problem of finding the sub is very tough. And there've been a few developments around here which I've been pondering, probably stupidly, just because I've got a bit too much time on my hands these days . . . Let's just finish our coffee, then we'll go over to the study and have a glass of port, and I'll show you a few things. Laura, you wouldn't pop across there and put a couple of logs on the fire, would you?'

'Only if I can come over with you and have some of that port,' she replied. 'How about you, Mum?'

'Oh, I won't, dear. I'm off to bed. It's been rather a long day. Don't keep your father up half the night.'

'No danger of that. Bill and I would like to be a–l–o–o–o–o–ne in the room where we first fell in love. I'll send Daddy packing, don't you worry.'

The others laughed, and they helped take the cups and dishes to the kitchen before crossing the hall to the book-lined study. Laura stopped blasting the fire with bellows as they arrived, and thoughtfully poured three glasses of Taylor's '78 before taking a seat in the left-hand chair, leaving Bill and her father to sit closer to the fire and study an atlas the admiral had obviously been making much use of recently.

Sure enough, when MacLean handed the heavy book to the Kansan he was holding it open to a map of the eastern side of the North Atlantic. 'You'll see on there that I've made a succession of crosses placed in circles. Well, the one on the far left is the place where the two supersonic jets went down. The next one, more easterly, is where you lost your Vice-President in *Air Force Three*. The next two are more recent – very up-to-date. You see the one about 35 miles west of St Kilda?'

'Got it.'

'Well, we have reports in the Scottish papers this month of a mysterious incident. A fishing boat just vanished somewhere out near there, and there were a few rather baffling circumstances. My next cross is exactly on the island of St Kilda, where, a couple of days later, two trained British soldiers – an officer and an experienced corporal – just vanished. The Army hasn't found 'em yet.

'My fifth cross is in the harbor of Mallaig, where there may be yet another mystery. The tender from the lost fishing boat, a 15-foot Zodiac, suddenly turned up on someone's mooring a couple of days later. Everyone is saying the lobsterman who discovered it is an habitual drunk and ought not to be listened to, but his story is that the boat had been on his mooring just a few hours, even though the police say, according to the newspapers, it must have been on the mooring for days.

'Bill, quite frankly, if you were a fisherman I don't care how tiddly you were: you'd *know* if someone had parked a bloody great rubber boat on your mooring four days ago or last night. I think I believe the lobsterman, not the police.'

'Hm,' said Bill, studying the map intently.

'And now I'm going to leave you with this thought. Follow my crosses, look at the dates, and see how the crosses move in a steady easterly direction. They're a chain of circumstances . . . but leading to what? Or who? Ben Adnam? I wonder.'

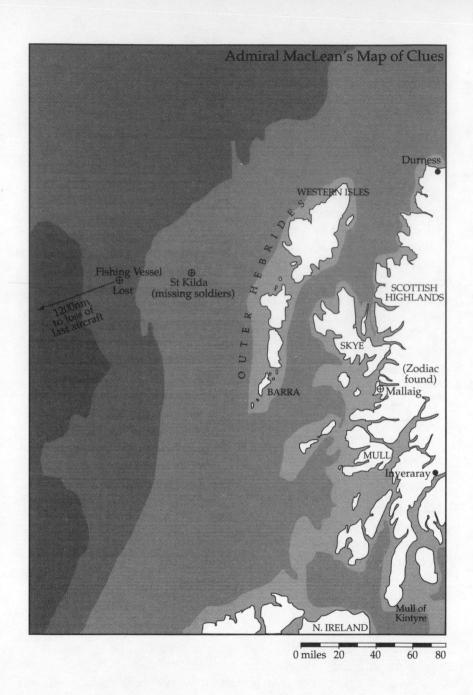

Admiral MacLean's Map of Clues

Durness

WESTERN ISLES

Fishing Vessel
Lost

St Kilda
(missing soldiers)

1200nm
to loss of
last aircraft

O U T E R   H E B R I D E S

SCOTTISH
HIGHLANDS

SKYE

(Zodiac
found)
Mallaig

BARRA

MULL

Inveraray

Mull of
Kintyre

N. IRELAND

0 miles   20   40   60   80

'Let's regroup in the morning. Breakfast at 0900, I think. Goodnight, you two. Oh, and Bill, have a look at the little book there, the one about St Kilda. I think you'll find it interesting.'

After Sir Iain had said his final goodnights, Laura walked across the room and removed the atlas from Bill's lap, folded it and placed it, with exaggerated firmness, on a shelf. She then took from a sidetable a CD, and walked over to the player and turned it on.

'*Rigoletto*,' he said.

'The first CD we ever listened to together, my darling,' she whispered. 'Right here in this room, nearly four years ago. Placido Domingo as the Duke, Ileana Cotrubas as Gilda.'

As the rhapsodic sounds of Verdi's overture rang out, dominated by the glorious violins of the Vienna Philharmonic, Laura walked over to her husband and sat on his lap and hugged him as she always did, as if she would never let him go.

'I love you,' she said. 'And it started in this room. When I had known you for about three hours. I've never doubted it, and I would change nothing.'

'Nor me,' said Bill.

'Nor I,' she corrected, laughing at his inability to deal with 'me' and 'I.' Then she kissed him softly, her hands in his hair. Her touch electrified him, as ever.

'Same bedroom tonight,' she said. 'How lovely. How unbear ably romantic.'

Neither of them knew that, beyond the deep red curtains of the study, out under the tall hedges beside the road near the main gate, was parked a metallic-blue Audi A8, its driver finding an unbalanced peace just in being there.

CHAPTER TEN

March 31, 2006.

BY ONE O'CLOCK in the morning the downstairs lights were out in the locked, silent MacLean household. The three labradors were asleep in the big kitchen near the Aga, but the dogs had, at the admiral's insistence, the complete run of the house during the night hours, just in case an intruder should decide to press his luck.

This had never happened. Most professional burglars are aware that the average labrador is a bit of a Jekyll and Hyde. Once darkness has fallen and a house is quiet, the cheerful, boisterous companion becomes a suspicious, growling watchdog, likely to go berserk at the slightest sound. That huge neck of his powers jaws that can snap a limb-bone in two. The reason the British police do not use labradors in confrontational situations is the dogs' instinct to go straight for a man's throat.

Ben Adnam was not a professional burglar and was unaware of these canine subtleties. Fifteen minutes after one o'clock he stepped out of his car and walked softly down the drive toward the house. Why he was doing this was beyond him: he just wanted to be near the building where once he had been near to Laura. Unfortunately, Fergus was unaware of the innocence of Adnam's motives. With ears that could detect a shot pheasant hit the ground at 200 yards, the burly black labrador heard a footfall on the gravel drive. He came off his beanbag barking at the top of his lungs and raced toward the front door, pursued now by the even bigger Muffin and by Mr Bumble.

The noise was outrageous. Upstairs the admiral wakened. He walked out into the corridor and found Bill already standing there in his dressing gown, with all the downstairs hall lights on.

'What's the matter with them?' he asked.

'I don't know, Iain, but when dogs react like that in the middle of the night it's always because they heard something.'

Even as they spoke they heard the unmistakable sound of a car pulling away, heading up towards the village of Inveraray, fast.

'Probably just someone who was lost,' said the admiral. 'It's pretty dark out there.'

Maybe. Hope so.'

The dogs were quietening now, and Sir Iain turned out the lights. 'See you in the a.m., Bill. 0900.'

'Yes, sir,' said Bill, against the house protocol.

Commander Adnam shot through Inveraray at almost 70mph, his headlights on full beam. He might not have had much success at beating his all-time record to St Catherine's and back, but he set some kind of a mark for the Scottish all-comers Inveraray–Creggans Inn run. Right around the north end of the loch he had his foot to the boards.

He used his key to slip in the inn's side door and went immediately up to his room. There he lay exhausted on his bed, wondering exactly who was at home in his former Teacher's house. Where was Laura? Could she be there?

Would he ever see her again? And what had he been doing, lurking in the night shadows like some burglar? He didn't know. All he knew was that there was nowhere else where he could connect with anyone, even in his mind. It was as if the aura of the MacLeans, a family which once had almost liked him, had created a room of memories. And even to sit in his cold car outside the house was to sit in that room. The alternative was so lonely, so frighteningly isolated, that he didn't believe he could face it for much longer.

He was certain of one thing, however. For the first time in his life, he was in danger of losing his grip – because *there was nothing for him to do*. He was friendless, stateless, and certainly homeless. And his ungrasped straw was Laura.

Ben didn't sleep at all that night – partly because the nightmares made him afraid to do so but mostly because he knew he had to move from here and seek out some direction in life. The problem was that he couldn't even make a phone call: there was no one he *could* call. One false move and he would be arrested and possibly deported to the United States, where he was undoubtedly

Public Enemy Number One. If the Americans nailed him, they would not, he knew, bother with a murder charge or a life sentence. He would face a charge equivalent to Treason Against the State, and that, he guessed, would mean the Chair.

For breakfast Adnam just drank coffee. His breakfast fare was in sharp contrast to the splendor of the spread which had been prepared at the MacLeans. The admiral loved fish for breakfast, so long as it was served after nine o'clock, and Angus had produced kippers and poached smoked haddock for two – none of the female members of the household had yet made an appearance.

Bill had never had fish for breakfast before but he entered into the spirit and tasted his first kippers. He ended up having two pairs of the rich, smoked Scottish herrings.

Over China tea and toast laden with chunky, locally made marmalade, he and the admiral settled down to chat about the Great Theory. The atlas was already open on the breakfast table. 'Well, Bill,' said Sir Iain, 'what did you come up with?'

'Not much, really. I was tired as hell, and Laura wanted to play some opera for sentimental reasons. By midnight I thought Rigoletto was driving HMS *Unseen*.'

His host chuckled and then produced some newspaper clippings. 'Here,' he said. 'Read this one. It's got the stuff in it from the lobsterman – the stuff they've all, apparently, dismissed as unreliable. I'd be glad if you'd give me your own impressions.'

Bill read through the piece slowly. 'Well, Mr MacInnes was pretty definite, wasn't he? I mean about the Zodiac suddenly showing up in the small hours of the morning. And he was also pretty definite about the foreign guy on the fishing boat, the one wearing the military jacket.'

'Wasn't he, though? *Very* definite. And I can understand why. That chap has lived all his life in Mallaig, where his father was also a fisherman. The sight of that harbor is unchanging. *Anything* slightly out of the ordinary would register, even on a man with a few drinks inside him. He's probably seen Gregor Mackay's boat pull out of that harbor a thousand times, but on this particular day he noticed something different – a new face, strange clothes, a man standing on the stern by the Zodiac, where MacInnes had never seen anyone before. To him, that would be a major departure from the norm. As if you reported to Boomer Dunning's *Columbia* and found a Zulu warrior at the periscope . . .'

Bill laughed, but his demeanor remained very serious. 'Like seeing a sheep on my land. We've never raised them. Just cattle.'

'Exactly so, Bill. That man, even through the alcohol, *remembered*. If I were the investigator I'd regard the drinks as a plus, not a minus.'

'I think I would too, Iain. So what you're saying is that someone got off the fishing boat in the Zodiac and drove it all the way back to Mallaig. Christ, it's gotta be – what? One hundred sixty miles?'

'At least. More like a hundred and seventy-five, I'd say.'

'It couldn't carry that much gas, could it?'

'Easily. If it had four of those four-and-a-half-gallon jerry-cans.'

'Well, let's assume it did. What does this have to do with our man commanding the rogue submarine?'

'Only that someone could have *got off* the rogue submarine.'

'Onto Mackay's kipper ship?'

'Possibly.'

'You think he was out there recruiting?'

Sir Iain laughed loudly this time. 'Bill, I love that American sense of humor. But that's not really what I meant. I meant maybe Gregor's boat was hired to go out and *take* someone off the sub.'

'But who could have hired it? The Iraqi Embassy?'

'No,' said the admiral with another chuckle. 'But how about the foreign-looking laddie in the naval jacket standing by the Zodiac?'

'Jesus, I've been so busy making jokes I never really thought about that.'

'Well, son-in-law, think.'

'Right. I'll do it. One question – how far from the place *Air Force Three* went down was the *Flower of Scotland*'s last known position?'

'I've calculated it, Bill. The VP crashed at 20 West 53 North. The *Flower* was last known to be in the vicinity of 09.40 West 57.49 North – about 490 miles from the hit on *Air Force Three*.'

'How about timing?'

'The Boeing was lost around 1300 GMT on Sunday, February 26. The harbormaster at Mallaig lost contact with Captain Mackay on the night of March 1.'

'So the submarine had six days to get there?'

'It would have had nearly that, my boy, if this were a leap year. Only 28 days in February, remember.'

'Christ, I'd forgotten about that! So it had only a little over three-and-a-half days?'

'Correct.'

'You got a calculation on that, sir?'

'Uh-huh. Four hundred and ninety divided by three-and-a-half is 140 miles per day. Divide that by 24, and you have a nice quiet little running speed of 5.8 knots. Just about reasonable for a submarine creeping away from the scene of a crime to a rendez-vous point, wouldn't you say?'

'Just . . . But then what? Ben gets off, pinches the Zodiac, and somehow sinks the fishing boat? I can't buy that. If Captain Mackay had come all the way out to meet him, why didn't Ben just travel to Mallaig with the boat?'

'Well, I agree, Bill, it's all a bit far-fetched. But in the middle of it all we do have one incontrovertible fact – that fishing boat *did* vanish. I suppose Ben, or whoever it was, could have shot the crew dead, left in the Zodiac and lobbed a hand grenade on board as he went. But that's unreal, reckless thinking. Not at all like him. Too noisy. Too likely to be discovered. What if someone had heard the explosion? He couldn't afford that.'

'And how about the gas for the outboard?' Bill said. 'There's no chance there was enough in it for 175 miles. And the trawler's diesel fuel wouldn't work in an outboard. Which puts Ben in the middle of the Atlantic in the middle of the night with no fuel – don't like it, sir. Doesn't stack.'

'Not quite. I agree. And the disappearance of the trawler is something I don't really have an answer for. But Ben would know how to sink a boat, *if* he were prepared to kill the captain and the two crewmen.'

'Only to be stranded himself, Iain. Stranded absolutely nowhere, and with no way to get anywhere.'

'Ah, but Bill, there's something you've forgotten. *Someone* did get *somewhere*. Someone rode the Zodiac back to port, right back to where it was found on Ewan MacInnes's mooring on the morning of March 3. That's when he says it arrived, and I believe him.'

'All true. But *how*? They don't usually run on air.'

'No, they don't. But it'd be nice to ask the two missing soldiers, don't you think? St Kilda is only 35 miles from the *Flower of Scotland*'s last known position. Ben could have made it to there easily enough.'

'Jesus, sir, so he could. I wonder if they've noticed any missing gas, or missing gas cans.'

'I imagine they're too busy looking for missing soldiers, but it's food for thought, don't you think?'

'It sure as hell is.'

'What I can't work out is what happened to the fishing boat? But I can conceive that Ben Adnam, having planned his evacuation from the submarine, might have been the man in that Zodiac, for whatever reason. So he goes to the military base on St Kilda, takes out the two soldiers, steals as much gas as he needs, and arrives in Mallaig a couple of days later, on the morning of March 3, which is when Ewan MacInnes noticed Gregor Mackay's tender on his mooring.'

'Admiral, for a story with as many holes in it as that one has . . . you make out a very good case. Tell me your conclusion.'

'I think Ben Adnam was in Scotland - I actually think he might still be here. And what worries me is what he might be planning next. I mean, it wouldn't be beyond him to take a shot at a Trident submarine. I just don't know, but Arnold Morgan and I both think he stole HMS *Unseen*, so God knows what he might do next.'

'Be kinda interesting if he stole a Trident and blew up half the world, wouldn't it?'

'Extremely. The trouble is that there are really only three people in this world who understand the man and his capabilities. Me, who taught him. You, who caught him. And Arnold, who's paranoid about him.'

'Hmm. One thing, though, Iain. Picture this yourself. You're in a 15-foot boat climbing through the Atlantic swell. It's freezing cold, you're all alone in the pitch dark heading for an uninhabited rock called St Kilda. According to your little book the place is surrounded by huge black cliffs and is just about unapproachable in winter. How the hell could you think you'd manage a safe landing under those circumstances? You'd get swept onto the rocks and drowned, and no one would ever know. You'd head someplace else.'

'Not Ben. He's been there before. At least, he's been close

enough to have a good look at Village Bay, in the southeast of the island. He's seen the place right from the fin of a submarine.'

'He has? How do you know that?'

'I was there.'

On Monday morning, April 3, Ben Adnam checked out of The Creggans Inn, and drove to Helensburgh. He paid his second cash installment on the car and asked if he might keep it another week. He'd pay £150 extra if it proved to be less than a week, £300 if it turned out to be more. 'As long as you like, sir. Just keep us informed if you want it more than two weeks.'

Ben picked up more cash at the Royal Bank of Scotland and requested they provide him with two credit cards, a Visa card and an RBS bank card, plus a couple of cheque books. He expected, he said, to be going on a journey, and he would be wiring £50,000 into his account today.

The bank was more than happy to oblige an excellent, if frequently absent, customer like Mr Arnold, and agreed that his business mail would be held here at the Helensburgh branch until further notice. They would deduct credit-card bills from his account automatically. He could pick up both cards in a few days.

The Commander then set off for Edinburgh, a drive of 70 miles, straight through Glasgow and on to Scotland's capital city along the M8 motorway. He located and checked into the Balmoral Hotel, at the eastern end of Princes Street, right above Waverley railway station. In the absence of a credit card he left a deposit of £500 in cash with the receptionist.

He checked into his room and then immediately left the hotel, walking swiftly up The Bridges to the nearby office of the *Scotsman*, with its computerized reference room in which, for a fee, readers could sit in a small cubicle and pull up on screen cuttings and pictures from any news event which the newspaper had covered, with a further charge for printouts and copies. The place is a fountain of information, and the Iraqi terrorist wished to bring himself up-to-date with world events which had taken place in the long months he had been at the helm of HMS *Unseen* – particularly those events in which he had personally been involved.

He began by pulling up the stories concerning the missing submarine itself. There were plenty of them from around the time Ben and his men had been running south down the Atlantic a year previously. But coverage of the sub's disappearance died out quickly, as the Royal Navy's search came to nothing. There was a routine 'WHATEVER HAPPENED TO UNSEEN?' But there was no further information, no progression of the facts. No one had speculated anything that came even close to the truth. At least, not in the *Scotsman* they hadn't.

He then pulled up the stories on the Concorde disaster and was shocked at the amount of coverage – reams of pictures and pages and pages of feature articles identifying the victims, their families and the crew who died out over 30°W in the North Atlantic. There were, in addition, sprawling two-page features on two separate occasions speculating about the 'Bermuda Triangle' out on the edge of space – detailing, for example, an eminent scientist's view that the hole in the ozone layer might make supersonic flight impossible in years to come. Ben permitted himself a thin smile at that one.

The Starstriker catastrophe received matching acreage, with a correspondingly generous rerun of the 'Bermuda Triangle' theme. One scientist felt that it was now more or less proven and agreed with the Greenpeace spokesmen that all supersonic flights should be suspended until a thorough investigation had been completed.

By the time Ben got to here in his reading it was 5pm and the reference room was about to close. He put on his sheepskin coat and stepped out into the chill Edinburgh afternoon, walking slowly back to his hotel, alone as perhaps he must always be – the great terrorist with nowhere to turn.

The following morning he was back in the reference room by 10am, reading through the accounts of the death of the Vice-President in the crash of *Air Force Three*. He found the account of the merchantship captain who has seen the wreckage falling from the sky, and who talked initially of smoke trails. But there was no follow-up to that. The captain, a former Royal Navy officer, had either not been pressed for more detail or, thought Ben, he had been told to shut up.

The fact was that, wherever he looked, there was no mention of missiles. No connection had been made anywhere with the possibility of something having been fired from a submarine. Ben had accomplished his task with the maximum of publicity and the maximum of terror, but the minimum of identification. He considered he had done his job for the Islamic Republic of Iran impeccably – and the best they'd been able to do in return was refuse to pay him and try to have him murdered. Ben shook his head.

Next he pulled up the cuttings on the St Kilda mystery. Still no sign of those two soldiers. But he was somewhat unnerved to discover the testimony of Ewan MacInnes, the man who *knew* someone had driven the Zodiac back from the *Flower of Scotland*, and who categorically stated that he'd seen that idiot Alaam standing publicly on the stern of the departing trawler. Adnam thought Alaam's slip in doing that was an example of amateurism at its worst. He was gratified to see that no one had expanded on the observations of the lobsterman. It seemed to Ben that no one believed the man.

In the next hour he pulled up everything he could find on the Iranian naval headquarters at Bandar Abbas. This was very little. Certainly there was no mention of the big drydock in which they had converted *Unseen*. No mention of terrorism, nothing on missiles, not a word about Iran purchasing new SAM systems from Russia. He checked, too, the military news from Baghdad, and found it was more or less nonexistent – just a small item about the Pentagon checking into the possibility that someone had been test-firing surface-to-air rockets somewhere down in the Southern Marshes.

So far as Ben could see, neither he nor any other individual was under direct suspicion for the atrocities which had taken place in the middle of the Antlantic. Which, all other things being equal, would have meant he could make a clean getaway; in his case, however he had nowhere to get away to.

His thoughts returned, yet again, to Laura MacLean.

He gazed at the computer, afraid to slide back down into the well of maudlin introversion which had consumed him for several days . . . but afraid more of being alone. He told himself to get up and get out and think, make a plan. Yet the memory of her perfect face stood before him still. He stared at the keys and willed himself to leave this building. But then he punched in the name MacLean, Admiral *Sir* Iain, by now, he guessed. Within seconds the file jumped onto the screen, and Ben scanned down its index. One item popped right out at him: 'Daughter's divorce and custody case.'

He ran the cursor down, and pressed 'Enter' to retrieve. A stack of reference material became available. Not quite so much as about the crash of Concorde, but more than he had found on the missing *Unseen*. Ben could scarcely believe his own eyes. It was all here. He scrolled down the computer pages, reading with amazement the story of Laura's split with her Scottish banker husband, Douglas Anderson.

He considered the entire thing so out of character. Laura? On the front pages of the newspapers in a terrible scandal which ended up in the High Court in Edinburgh? In his anxiety to devour as many facts as possible Ben had skipped over the part about the man with whom she had run off. It took him ten minutes of paging back through the reports to find his name, Lt-Commander Bill Baldridge (Retd.) of the United States Navy. 'At least I outrank him,' he muttered.

There was very little in the paper about the divorce itself, because that had been heard in camera, as such personal matters often are in Scotland. The newspapers printed the name of the man cited by Mr Anderson, but very little more. The real public uproar had erupted over the custody battle for Laura's two children. So far as Ben could tell, the American had come to the court and been photographed, but of course took no part in the custody case. The rights and future entitlements of the little girls were discussed by the judge, the lawyers and the two very influential families.

Laura's barrister had pleaded her case valiantly, but reading the reports in retrospect it was obvious that the judge was never going to allow her daughters to leave Scotland while they were so young. And, to Ben's amazement, Laura had left without them. In an unguarded moment, replying to a reporter's question about when she would return, she had turned around and snapped, 'I never want to lay eyes on this damned place, ever again.'

Douglas Anderson had been very dignified throughout the whole proceedings, and had said nothing outside the court except that he and his family, assisted by Admiral Sir Iain and Lady MacLean, had a duty to raise the little girls in the best possible way, and to insure their inheritance was properly managed.

So that was it. Laura was gone. And, save for a short mention in the *Scotsman* that the American had become a farmer in the Midwest after leaving the navy, there was no further clue as to where Mr and Mrs Baldridge now lived. Ben assumed they were somewhere together, and now married, since all of this had taken place in the winter of 2003/4, over two years ago.

An appalling melancholy swept over him. The United States was the most dangerous place on earth for him – he would be executed summarily if they found him there and discovered who he was. And Commander Adnam did not underestimate the men in the Pentagon. He knew they were incredibly smart and absolutely ruthless, and would think nothing of 'stringing up some towelhead terrorist.' He had met Americans, right here in Scotland, men from the Holy Loch Base. He knew how they talked and what they thought about serious enemies of the United States.

For the first time, ever, he began to believe he would never speak to Laura again.

It was with a sad heart that he turned off the machine. He walked out bareheaded into the cold streets of Edinburgh, not minding the steady rain that fell because it obscured the tears which ran silently down his face. It was the first time the 46-year-old Benjamin Adnam had wept since his childhood in the village of Tikrīt, on the banks of the Tigris.

He didn't want to return to the Balmoral Hotel, because that was just another prison: he would find there only his empty room, and he was frightened of the solitude. He actually thought he might break down completely.

And so he kept walking, heading, for no reason, toward the great ramparts of Edinburgh Castle, which glowers over the city.

It was a little after half past twelve when he turned into the High Street, walking west up the long rise to Castle Hill, which in turn leads up to the massive granite edifice which has symbolized the innate defiance of Scotland for over 850 years. Ben had been here once before, in 1988 with Laura. Now he stood staring up at the Outlook Tower. Just then the castle's one o'clock cannon shot crashed out over the city, as it did every day except Sunday.

There was a considerable crowd of tourists awaiting the sound of the cannon, which was greeted by a predictable number of oohs and wows. Ben, though, stood still and silent at the sound of the sudden shot, and his muscles tensed. His was the reaction of a military man in a military place. Although no armed forces have been garrisoned in the castle since the 1920s, it was once home to great Scottish regiments – the Black Watch, the Royal Scots, the Seaforth Highlanders.

In the Middle Ages the castle was besieged constantly, mostly by the English. It is impossible to remove the overtones of blood and valor from such places, and Adnam felt more at home here, in these stark, bleak surrounds with their redolence of distant courage and gallantry, than ever he had in the Balmoral Hotel. He was imagining the clash of steel and the thunder of guns as he walked slowly along the stone walkways to the 12th-century St Margaret's Chapel, the small stone-arched place of worship inside the castle. These days it was nondenominational and used only by visiting military, but once it had been an important Catholic church.

Ben opened the door and stepped inside, gazing at the five magnificent stained-glass windows behind the altar. Before him were images of St Ninian, St Columba, St Margaret herself and St Andrew. But Ben had no interest in them. He walked to the bright, beautifully colored window dedicated to Sir William Wallace, the great Scottish national hero of the 13th-century.

This, Ben knew, was a real man. William Wallace led his renegades to kill the Sheriff of Lanark, and then to defeat the English Governor of Scotland, Lord Surrey, in a brutal battle near Stirling. William Wallace, the man who temporarily drove the English out of Scotland altogether. Ben knew that in the end Wallace had been executed by the English for treason, but he had died a brave death, at the age of about 33. Commander Adnam stood in front of the window and bowed his head in front of Scotland's most noble terrorist.

He stayed just a few minutes longer before walking outside once more. It was still raining. He felt within himself the old resolve surge. He gazed out northward across the gray expanse of the city toward the wide waters of the Firth of Forth and beyond to the ancient kingdom of Fife. He thought back to the days of Wallace, and the undaunted fearlessness of the man – the audacity it must have required to move in and ruthlessly attack the enemies of his country.

Suddenly, for the first time in a month, Adnam believed he was thinking clearly again. The face of William Wallace had seemed to look kindly upon him, and the example of the long-dead martyr of freedom seemed to galvanize his spirit. In a flash of inspiration he knew where he must go, and what he must do. It was his only chance, and it was a chance that might at the same time lead him to Laura.

But first he had to find her.

He turned from the castle and headed back downtown, hurrying along the High Street and then back along The Bridges to his hotel. There he found a telephone book with listings for the border country. The *Scotsman* had always cited Douglas Anderson as 'Speaking from his estate near Jedburgh last night . . .'

'Anderson, Douglas R., Galashiels Manor, Ancrum, Roxburgh – that's him.' Ben Adnam wrote down the address and phone number. He debated the merit of making a call, then decided against it. The telephone had a distinct disadvantage, he decided. The person at the other end can say politely, 'No, I'm afraid I can't help, and I'm extremely busy at the moment. Goodbye,' thus effectively bringing the campaign to an end.

No, Ben concluded, *I'll go to Galashiels Manor and talk to Mr Anderson in person, if he's there. I'll make up some story to persuade him to give me Mr Baldridge's address.*

He had a quick cup of coffee in the downstairs vestibule, ordered his car from the garage, and set off out of Edinburgh toward the southeast, toward the Borders.

He drove quietly past the city limits and onto the A68. It was 28 miles to Galashiels, down a long winding road past the western edges of the Lammermuir Hills. Here on the high ground were some of Scotland's finest grouse moors, in particular those of the Dukes of Roxburgh, not to mention that of Sir Hamish Anderson, Douglas's magisterial father.

Commander Adnam sat behind the wheel glancing occasionally at the cold, bleak winter home of the game birds and reflecting upon his forthcoming tactics. He would pretend he knew nothing of the divorce, and had come to visit Laura and her husband in response to a longstanding invitation.

In the end he wanted just one thing from the banker: the US address of Lt-Commander Baldridge. If Mr Anderson proved difficult, it might be necessary to force the information from him, which would mean Adnam would have to silence him permanently before leaving. But that was a course of action Adnam was quite prepared to take – old habits tend to die hard among military terrorists. He knew that for the rest of his life, if he was to evade capture, he might have to take such actions. One witness to his possible identity was one too many. Discovery would signify, quite simply, the end of his life.

He reached the junction with the Selkirk–Kelso road and carried on straight ahead for the six-mile run down to Ancrum. The afternoon had turned suddenly bright, the rain clearing swiftly away to the northeast. After a couple of miles Ben stopped in a desolate stretch of green hilly countryside and checked his map. He was inside a triangle defined at three corners by Selkirk, Jedburgh and Kelso. Twelve miles away to the southwest was the cashmere and knitwear town of Hawick.

Right here he was in the heart of the great border tribes of Scotland, the men once known as the Border Reivers. For 350 years before 1600 their lawless reign of terror had flourished along these lonely hills, the English having decided the entire region was 'ungovernable.' Ben himself had just seen, over the past 20 miles, signs that remained of them still – ancient castles, stately homes, fortified farmhouses, ruins of historic abbeys, relics of watchtowers built as fortresses with walls seven feet thick . . . There were remnants of abandoned hamlets in remote valleys – remnants of a cruel and turbulent four centuries during which the warring tribes of England and Scotland had fought each other savagely. Many of their descendants still lived in the area – families with names like Nixon, Armstrong, Graham, Kerr, Maxwell, Forster . . . and Anderson.

But all was quiet here now as Ben Adnam continued to drive south, almost eerily quiet. For these borderlands represent the center of one of Britain's last wilderness areas, a land of vast moors, forests, hills, rivers and streams. The Iraqi carried on down to Ancrum, stopping just short of the tumbling River Teviot, a haven for salmon fisherman for hundreds of years. Ben actually drove past the village green and on out to the other side of Ancrum before realizing his mistake and turning back.

He parked in front of the village shop. Inside, he inquired where he could find the address of Mr Douglas Anderson. 'Take the road to Nisbet,' he was told by the tidy, gray-haired Scottish lady behind the counter. 'And on your left you'll come to a gray stone gateway with carved granite lions on the posts. Turn in there. The drive's about half a mile long. Mr Douglas is in residence, I believe. By the way, if you get to the Memorial, you've gone too far.'

The Commander found the road to Nisbet and drove out through the rolling country traditionally hunted by the Duke of Buccleugh's foxhounds, next to the vast lands owned by the Marquis of Lothian. He found the gates with their lions and turned into the drive, making his way between long lines of spruce trees that towered on either side. The house itself was likewise gray stone, and had four columns on the front portico. The oak doors stood 12 feet high.

He parked the car, walked up the four steps to the entrance and rang the bell. An elderly butler, dressed in striped trousers and a black jacket, answered, and Ben asked if he could possibly see either Mr or Mrs Anderson. His English was impeccable, and the butler invited him to step inside. Then he asked who he should say was inquiring.

'Tell them, Mr Arnold. Ben Arnold from South Africa.'

'Very well, sir.'

When the butler returned he was accompanied by a dark-haired, youngish woman of medium height and quite striking good looks. She wore a deep-red silk shirt, tight black pants and high heels. Her lavish lipstick matched her shirt. She looked the part of an actress to the tips of her dark red fingernails. 'Good afternoon,' she said. 'I'm Natalie Anderson. My husband is rather busy at the moment. I wonder if I could help . . . I don't believe we've met?'

The Commander smiled and offered his hand. 'No, no we haven't. I'm Ben Arnold, and this is all rather embarrassing.'

'It is?'

'Well . . . Yes, it is. You see, I thought Mr Anderson was married to a lady named Laura.'

'Not any more,' said Natalie, laughing. 'They were divorced two years ago. I've been married to Douglas for more than a year now.'

'Oh, I see. Then that makes it even more awkward.'

'It does?'

'Yes. You see my wife and I met and became quite good friends with Laura Anderson in Cairo several years ago. We live in South Africa, but we exchanged addresses with her and promised to meet again if we ever were in the same place. My wife arrives tomorrow, and we're staying in Kelso. So I thought I'd do a recce, and arrange a dinner or something . . .'

'Well, Mr Arnold, that sounds lovely. But since none of us knows each other it's probably out of the question . . .'

'Oh, absolutely. And I apologize for taking your time.'

Ben turned to leave, but he hesitated and looked back suddenly. 'I say, I'm sorry to be a bore, but do you think your husband would have Laura's address? At least then we could send her a Christmas card and let her know we tried.'

Natalie smiled. 'I'm sure he would. Let me go and get him. I have to go to Kelso myself just now, so I'll say goodbye and send Douglas to see you.'

Ben waited, feeling the hilt of his desert knife in the small of his back, wondering how he would feel when he confronted the man who had taken *his* Laura. In less than two minutes he found out. Douglas Anderson, a tall, heavily built man wearing a country suit with thick, long socks and plus-fours, came marching across the hall, the steel tips of his highly polished brown brogues clipping on the stone floor.

'Good afternoon,' he said, in an accent that betrayed every vestige of the polished, landed Scottish banker. 'I hear you've got your wires a bit crossed. I'm Douglas Anderson.'

The two men shook hands. Anderson immediately looked at his watch and said, 'What is it? Five o'clock. Tell you what, you've come a long way – how about a cup of tea?'

'Well, I hate to intrude . . . but that would be very nice.'

'Come on in here,' Anderson replied, leading the way into a warm, comfortable drawing room with a log fire. 'You can tell me about meeting Laura.'

Ben followed him in. 'Cairo,' he said. 'Maybe eight years ago.'

'Yes, I remember she did go there once for a brief holiday with a girlfriend. Annie, wasn't it?'

'Yes, I believe that was the name of Laura's friend. I'm not sure. Anyway, my wife Darlene got on very well with Laura. They went shopping together, and hired a couple of camels for a ride out around the Pyramids. I used to call her Laura of the Desert. We were all staying out at the Mena House Hotel near Giza.'

'Absolutely. I remember her telling me about the place.'

'Well, we lost touch, but we always kept her address, and now

I'm here on business for a few days and Darlene's flying into Edinburgh tomorrow. I thought we might all get together – but it really was a bit embarrassing meeting the new Mrs Anderson like that. I suppose I should have phoned ahead and saved everyone a lot of trouble.'

'Think nothing of it, old boy. I'm glad of the company. Natalie's gone to her bloody aerobics class, and I'm alone for a couple of hours.'

The butler brought in the tea, and Douglas Anderson poured it. 'Sugar?'

'No, thanks. Just a splash of milk.'

'And how about you, Ben? What's your line of country?'

'Mining. Copper and coal. We have holdings in both. I'm here to see several bankers in Edinburgh, but I thought it would be nice to stay out here for a few days in the country. I say, I'm really sorry about you and Laura – she seemed such a nice girl.'

'Oh, yes. She was. Damned nice family. Daughter of a very eminent admiral, you know. It all happened so damned quickly. I never knew what hit me. She suddenly met this bloody American, here in Scotland, and announced she was buggering off with him. Shook me up, I can tell you.'

'Well, Douglas, you look to me as if you've made a successful recovery,' said Ben, smiling.

'Haven't I?' said Douglas, laughing loudly. 'I was a bit bloody lucky really, landing a beautiful younger woman like that. She's only 28 now. I'm 45. She keeps me young, and I've taught her how to catch a salmon. Not much of a deal for her really. But she seems to like it up here, and we have nice holidays.'

'Where did this "bloody American" come from?'

'Well, that's all been a bit secret, Ben. You remember that US Navy aircraft carrier that got itself blown up about four years ago? Apparently the Pentagon thought it might have been hit by some fucking Arab in a submarine, and this Baldridge johnny – that was his name – was over here trying to find out who he was. Apparently Laura knew the chap they all suspected – an old boyfriend, I think – when he was training here. Nothing serious, of course – just some bloody foreigner learning how to drive a submarine. Her father was the Teacher at the base at the time.'

'Hmm. Did they find him?'

'Don't think so. I never heard any more. All I knew was that my wife had cleared off with the American investigator. Left me high and dry. My luck changed in the summer, though. My mother's on the board of the Edinburgh Festival and we had a group of the actors and directors out here for dinner one evening. Natalie was playing the lead in the main theatre. I was lucky enough to draw the seat next to her at dinner, and we've never looked back.'

'Well, Douglas, you've been very kind,' said Adnam, putting his cup down. 'The only thing I wondered was if you could possibly let me have Baldridge's address. I think my wife would like to send Laura a Christmas card or something, and let her know we did try to get into contact. Darlene'll be very disappointed to have missed her.'

'No problem, Ben. Natalie mentioned that, and I have it right here: Baldridge Ranch, Burdett, Pawnee County, Kansas, plus the zip code. My daughters are going over there in a few days for the first time. I did hear that Laura and her husband might show up here for a while first, but I think the plan is that they're bringing the girls back after the Easter holiday. No one tells me much – not now I've remarried. I believe American Airlines are in command of the outward journey.'

Ben stood up and offered his hand. 'Douglas, I'm sorry to have taken up your time. It has been most enjoyable, and I wish you every happiness. You have a very lovely wife.'

'Thank you, Ben. I'm glad to have met you. I hope you have a nice stay in Scotland, and please give my regards to Darlene, who I nearly met.'

They both laughed and Ben took his leave, walking out into the dark. He started the car and headed out through the spruce trees toward the A68 back to Edinburgh.

Admiral Sir Iain MacLean answered the telephone in his study just after six o'clock in the evening. 'Oh, hello, Douglas. How nice to hear from you.'

'Yes, well it has been a bit of a time, hasn't it? We don't seem to run into each other so often these days. How's Annie . . . and the American branch of the family?'

'Oh, they're all fine. Bill and Laura are here at the moment, actually.'

'Oh, they are? I thought the idea was that their mother would bring the girls back.'

'Well, it was. But they had a change of plan – decided to come over for a few days and take the girls back with them to Kansas. Then, after the holiday, they'll fly them up to Chicago and put them on the direct flight home to Edinburgh. You don't want to speak to Laura, do you?'

'I don't think so, Iain. Tell you the truth, I was just looking for an excuse to have a chat for a few minutes. Nothing very important. But I had a rather unusual visitor this afternoon, looking for Laura.'

Iain MacLean's voice went ice-cold. 'You did? Who was it?'

'South African chap. Nicely dressed, expensive sheepskin coat, driving an Audi. Told me he and his wife had been friends with Laura about eight years ago. But the address he had was mine. He thought we were still married.'

'What did he look like, Douglas?'

'What do you mean, what did he look like? Perfectly ordinary sort of chap – well spoken, something in the mining business.'

'No, Douglas. What did he *look* like.'

'Well, he wasn't all that tall. I'd say a bit less than six foot. Quite broad, well built.'

'What kind of coloring?'

'Oh, dark. I took him for a South African Jew. Black hair, curly, cut short.'

'Did he tell you his name?'

'Yes. But I can't remember it . . . the surname, anyway. His first name was Ben.'

Admiral MacLean's mouth went dry. He said, 'Just a minute, Douglas . . .' He poured himself a glass of mineral water and took a gulp before continuing.

'Was there anything else about him that you noticed?'

'No, not really.'

'Did he say where he and his wife met Laura?'

'Yes, he did. Cairo. Laura went out there with her girlfriend Annie about eight years ago. Stayed at the Mena House, out near the Pyramids. According to this chap, they all met there and exchanged addresses. I just thought it was a bit strange. You know, Laura never mentioned anything about a South African couple

282

to me, and I just wondered if the chap rang any sort of a bell with you.'

The admiral was silent for a few moments, hearing about ten thousand bells of pure alarm ringing in his head. But when he spoke it was quietly. 'No, Douglas. She never mentioned anything to me, either. I was just about to ask you if you'd told him that Bill and Laura were here, but of course you didn't know.'

'No. But I think I mentioned they were expected sometime soon. You know, bringing the girls back from America – that sort of thing.'

'Did he say how long he and his wife were planning to be here?'

'I think he said a week or so. His wife arrives in Edinburgh tomorrow.'

'Well, Douglas, I thank you for ringing. Sorry I can't help much. Hope to see you soon.'

They said their goodbyes and then, without putting down the phone, MacLean immediately made another call, this time trans-Atlantic – to Washington, direct to the main switchboard of the White House. 'Would you connect me to Admiral Arnold Morgan, please.'

'Certainly, sir. Who shall I say is calling?'

'MacLean. Admiral Iain MacLean from Scotland.'

A new voice came on the line. 'Admiral Morgan's office . . .'

'May I speak to the admiral himself, please? This is Iain MacLean in Scotland.'

'Morgan. Speak.'

'Arnold, it's Iain.'

'Hey, Iain, old buddy. How ya bin? Anything hot?'

'Hottest. He's here.'

'Who? No. Jesus Christ! You at home?'

Morgan knew the answer to that. He paused for a few seconds, gathering his thoughts: no secure line. 'When you say he's here, Iain, do you mean the "he" I think you mean? And do you mean he's in the country, in your house, or in your study?'

'In answer to your first question, the very one, Arnold. He's trying to find Laura. He turned up at her ex-husband's house this afternoon looking for her.'

'*Jesus Christ!*'

'Look, Arnold. I've been fairly certain for some weeks now

283

that he was in Scotland. Can you lay hands on a chart of the North Atlantic, the eastern side?'

'Yeah, wait a minute.' It took two. Then. 'I'm looking at it.'

'Right. Get a pencil and mark with a cross the following positions: two on 30 West, one of them on 20 West 53 North – right, where the airliners went down. Now put another cross at 09.40 West 57.49 North. That's it. Now one at 08.35 West, same latitude. Now one at the port of Mallaig on the coast of Scotland opposite the southwest corner of the Isle of Skye.'

Morgan's cartography done, MacLean pointed out the progression of his thoughts – the lost fishing boat, the missing soldiers on St Kilda, the Zodiac suddenly turning up in Mallaig. 'I believe,' he said, 'that our man got off *Unseen* at 09.40 West, made his way to St Kilda for petrol, and then got to Mallaig. I've no idea what he's doing right now – but today a man turned up at my former son-in-law's house looking for Laura. The description fitted Adnam as I remember him. This visitor claimed to have met her in Cairo, and she and Adnam once went there together. No one was supposed to know about it, and no one outside the family but Adnam *could* have known. It was him today, all right. He's on the loose here.'

'Did he give any indication how long he was staying in Scotland?'

'No. But my idiot ex-son-in-law told him Laura was expected at the end of Easter, so I imagine he'll stay around here for another couple of weeks. But you can never be sure, with him. For all I know he's going to go back to the submarine and hit something else. Anyway, I thought I'd better keep you up to speed.'

'Iain, I don't need to tell you I'm delighted that you called. I'm just wondering if there are any further checks we ought to make. Where are Bill and Laura now?'

'They're going to be here for another five days.'

'Let's get 'em the hell out. Back to Kansas. And I think I'd better put out a general alert to watch for Adnam at all airport entry points in the United States. I can't imagine he'd come here, where he's most wanted, but now he knows she's gone off with an American he might try to get to her in the States. Wish we knew what name he was traveling under.'

'Douglas – my ex-son-in-law – was told a name, but he's forgotten it.'

'Don't forget to congratulate him for me on that.'

'I won't. Do you have a decent picture of Adnam for your checkpoints?'

'I'm not sure, but I think I could get one OK from David Gavron.'

'All right, Arnold. I won't keep you any longer. If you don't have any luck with the Mossad, we have a good picture of him when he was here. It's 18 years old, but it might help.'

'Good. We'll talk later.'

As Commander Adnam drove north, back toward Edinburgh, his mind was churning. Laura was coming to Scotland, but what good would that do him? She'd be at MacLean's house, and the admiral would recognize him instantly. He couldn't keep the white mansion under surveillance, and she might be there for only a couple of days. No, if he wanted to talk to Laura and her husband, the place to go, perhaps during the next week, was Kansas, their permanent home.

The USA was also, he had now come to believe, the only place he *could* go – the one country whose natural self-interest might just make him too valuable to kill, if he played his many high cards correctly. Because Benjamin Adnam was not merely the most wanted man in the world, he was also one of the most knowledgeable. He knew many of the naval and other military secrets of Israel, Iraq and Iran. He understood their attitudes, hopes and fears. With him, Benjamin Adnam, on their side the United States would have a supreme strategic asset. Just so long as he could convince the Americans of this before they took him out.

He knew he would have to go in at the highest possible level, and that might not be too simple. He had not a single contact in the United States. Unless – and the thought struck him suddenly – a certain Mr Baldridge took him there. The man entrusted with running to ground the perpetrator of the *Thomas Jefferson* disaster would be a man in touch with the highest members of the current Administration in Washington.

The sheer simplicity of this trail to a new life struck Ben as so utterly transparent it must be impossible. But the logic was as straight as a line of longitude. If he could find Laura, he would find Baldridge, and if he found Baldridge he might be able to swing some kind of a deal. Either way, the former US Navy officer would most likely prefer to put the great Iraqi terrorist in front of some very senior people rather than just lead him to the local sheriff.

The main problem was, surely, how to get into the United States without being apprehended by the immigration authorities and swiftly handed over to the merciless agents of the CIA. Adnam believed the straight London–New York and London–Washington routes were very tight at the immigration desks. He decided to find another, quieter path into the customs halls of the Great Satan.

As he drove back past the rolling hills of Lammermuir, he weighed up the factors which ranged against him: The fact that Lt-Commander Baldridge had spent time with the MacLeans meant they all knew who he, Adnam, was; he felt reasonably sure Douglas Anderson would have alerted the admiral that someone had been inquiring after Laura; and, knowing the mind of old MacLean, Ben was prepared for anything . . . *My Teacher remains consistent, missing nothing – not then, not now.*

In Ben's view, he now had to get out of Scotland and into another country without his British passport being freshly stamped. From there he could try to make his way unobtrusively into the United States. There was only one country from which he could be certain of being able to pull off such a move: Eire, because he wouldn't need a passport to get in – not from the UK. If MacLean had alerted his American friends, they would be keeping a rigid watch on passengers coming into the United States from London, Manchester, Edinburgh or Glasgow. But perhaps they would not be paying quite such stringent attention to passengers from Shannon.

Bill, Laura and the girls arrived back from Edinburgh shortly after seven in the evening. Laura had signed a stack of legal papers in her solicitor's office, and Bill had had to countersign several of these. It was beginning to look as if she would be granted full custody of the girls, with Douglas having them for vacations only. Admiral MacLean's powerful intervention with the judge had worked a miracle, and it seemed increasingly likely that they would ultimately attend their new step-grandmother's alma mater, Wellesley College, outside Boston, Massachusetts.

The admiral met the Range Rover as it drove in with Laura at the wheel. He told Mary and Flora to run along to the kitchen where their grandma and Angus had their supper ready. He then suggested that Laura and Bill might join him in the drawing room for a drink before dinner because there was something he needed to discuss.

They could both see the concern on his face. They noticed he was silent as he poured three glasses of Scotch and soda. He wasted no time beating about the bush, except to hope that Bill liked the Scotch, which was a single malt, distilled locally.

'Ben Adnam showed up this afternoon at Douglas Anderson's house,' he said. 'He was looking for Laura, who he apparently thought was still in residence. Douglas called to let me know – the description fitted and the visitor told Douglas that he and his wife met you in Cairo – at the Mena House Hotel, to be precise. A bit close to the bone, eh?'

'God, Daddy, I didn't know even *you* knew that.'

'Well, I didn't until about two years after the event. But I tend to come stumbling along a bit behind the rest of the world. Nonetheless, the Cairo clue is decisive. It must have been Ben.'

'Correct. Couldn't be anyone else. And you say he was asking for me?'

'According to Douglas, he was.'

'But why?'

'Oh, it's hard to know really. But chaps in his line of country lead very strange, lonely lives. And, when they finish their various projects, it's nearly impossible for them to return to anything normal.'

'Yes . . . I suppose so. Do you think we're in any danger?'

'Possibly. I mean, when a chap has already killed several thousand people, you don't quite know what his state of mind might be. All kinds of odd thoughts can pop into such a disturbed mind. It's not completely beyond the realm of possibility that he may have gone to the house intending to kill Douglas and kidnap you. Let's face it, he might be planning to kill *Bill* right now and kidnap you. Either way, we're going to have to be very careful indeed until he's caught. I've had a talk to Arnold Morgan, who is just as concerned as I am about your safety. He thinks you should leave Scotland and return to Kansas – that'd be the morning flight to Chicago tomorrow.'

'You think it's that serious, Iain?' asked Bill.

'Actually, no. Even so, you can't be too careful with this man. I'm taking it seriously enough that I've changed your reservations and organized a Navy car and escort to get you to the airport with the girls by 0900 tomorrow.'

'Does Adnam know where we live in the States?' asked Laura.

'I don't think so. He didn't, after all, even know you weren't married to Douglas any more. But I'd better bloody ask Douglas. I should have thought of that when he rang. Must be getting old.'

'What's Admiral Morgan doing?'

'Stepping up security at all airport points of entry to the USA, looking for Adnam, in case he should try to go there. If I know Arnold, it'll be quiet but thorough. I just called him back. He's organizing a Navy helicopter to run you from Chicago to Kansas, and for the time being there'll probably be some military security at the ranch – firstly to protect you, secondly to catch the bastard. We now think there's no doubt he was somehow responsible for all three of those aircraft disasters.'

'Do you think Ben might really be planning to kill my husband, Daddy?' said Laura.

'Well, we have to work on the theory that he may be thinking along those lines. Dementia can easily enter the mind of a mass murderer. But I don't think so. Because there's an edge of hysteria in that type of thinking – murdering husbands in order to run off with their wives. Doesn't sound like Ben to me. He's too cold-hearted for that – too reasoned, too clever. In my view he may have wanted some kind of favor from you this afternoon, but he might have turned very unpredictable if you'd refused to give him any help. None of us knows where his professionalism ends and his madness begins.

'And we can't take any chances. Adnam must for the moment be treated as a rabid dog – simply because he's been operating on an entirely different wavelength from most of the human race for a very long time. He may be erratic now in his actions – maybe even irrational. But we don't want to assume *anything*. And the quicker we get you both home, with the girls, and under the personal protection of the President's National Security Advisor, the better I'll like it.'

'Have you told Mummy anything?'

'No. And I see no reason to worry her unduly. You can leave that to me.'

They finished their drinks, and Bill and Laura went upstairs briefly to change before dinner. They went into the bedroom which overlooked the loch, and the ex-lieutenant-commander was quite surprised at his wife's reaction. She threw her arms around him, and he could feel deep within her an uncontrolled trembling. 'Ben really scares me, darling,' she whispered. 'There's something so absolutely terrible about him. And to think he's out there somewhere. He found Douglas, and he knows well enough where this place is. My God, he's been here before. For all we know he's out there watching.'

'Ben Adnam is not the kind of man to be scratching around in some field, watching a house like some pervert,' said Bill. 'That's not him at all. He operates to carefully drawn-up plans. I'd be surprised if he came anywhere near here. I mean, Jesus, your father knows him. So does your mother. This is the last place he'd show up.'

'I suppose so. But if Daddy and Admiral Morgan are worried, then I oughtn't to take this lightly. I'll get Angus to start packing up the girls' and my things while we're having dinner.'

'OK. And I'll make my own arrangements. But I'll tell you one thing — I wouldn't be searching for Ben here in Scotland because I'm guessing he's on his way out of here right now.'

'Why?'

'Well, he knows now that you don't live here. He's played that card and lost. But there's a Mr Anderson who's seen him, and Ben'll know that just a routine phonecall from Douglas to either your father or yourself will stir up a hornet's nest. In my view he'll have been on his way out of the country instantly.'

'But where to?'

'That's the big question, Laura. Maybe back to the Middle East. Maybe to Switzerland, to collect money — he's sure to have unnumbered accounts there. Maybe South Africa, which he mentioned. But not, I suspect, to the USA, where he's the most wanted man in history, having just murdered our saintly Vice-President and a half-dozen congressmen.'

The farewell dinner at the home of Admiral MacLean was deeply traditional. Annie served Scottish smoked salmon from the Tay with a bottle of Olivier Leflaive's superb 1995 Puligny–Montrachet. The thick Aberdeen Angus steak fillets were accompanied by a 1990 Châteaux Lafleur from Pomerol.

'It took a bit of courage to risk steak on a world expert beef-producing rancher from the Great Plains,' said the admiral. 'I hope we've measured up.'

'Fantastic,' said Bill, swallowing luxuriously. 'And this is probably the best glass of wine I've ever had.'

'Yes. They all got it right in Bordeaux in 1990,' agreed Sir Iain. 'Took five years for it to come right again. By the way, I'm really sorry you four have to go tomorrow, but I think it's for the best.'

'I agree. And now we got Morgan on the case, I wouldn't be surprised if they picked our man up very soon.'

'I hope it's before he does any more damage, Bill. I still have it in my mind he somehow took out those two soldiers on St Kilda – otherwise they'd still be there. Imagine that, two lives for a few gallons of fuel. I suppose that's how you become, in his business . . . in the end.'

'Guess so. And of course those terrorist guys always believe they're in the military, so to kill a couple of enemy soldiers hardly counts.'

'Well, he knows you were in uniform, doesn't he?' said Laura. 'I hope he doesn't think *you* hardly count. Because, if he does, I'll hunt him down and I'll kill him in cold blood.'

Laura Baldridge did not have even a semblance of a smile on her face when she spoke those words. Her parents both looked quite shocked.

CHAPTER ELEVEN

$\mathbf{B}$EN ADNAM DINED alone, occasionally listening to the rumble of the trains deep beneath the Balmoral Hotel. Was that his way out of Scotland? South and west on the railway to the coast of North Wales and the ferryport of Holyhead? Or should he play it safe and drive, anonymously, right through England and then pick up a ferry to Ireland at the port of Fishguard, 14 hours away on the remote southwestern coast of Wales?

He guessed that by now Admiral MacLean would know about the mysterious visitor to Galashiels Manor that day, and have deduced that visitor's identity. That meant there would be some kind of security in place – he should avoid airports in big cities like Edinburgh, Glasgow, London and Dublin. His every instinct told him to stay rural, in his unobtrusive car, to travel alone and be seen by as few people as possible.

He studied his little map throughout an excellent dinner of cold smoked trout and roast pheasant. By half past ten there was no doubt in his mind. The way to Ireland was through West Wales to Fishguard, and then into the Emerald Isle via the quiet southeastern Irish port of Rosslare. He wouldn't need a passport if he was British. He decided to spend some time with a travel agent before leaving Scotland. The one right around the corner from the hotel, in the High Street, would do fine.

He slept late the following morning, read the papers downstairs in the hotel lounge, and sipped three cups of coffee. Then he checked out, leaving his bag with the concierge and asking for his car to be brought up at midday.

Inside the travel agency he studied a pile of brochures dealing with travel to and from Ireland. He bought himself a single ferry ticket from Fishguard to Rosslare, sailing at three fifteen the following morning. He intended to stay in Ireland for a few days organizing a B–2 multiple-entry business visa into the United

States, and then to leave via Shannon for Boston, thus travelling between the two closest points on the North Atlantic route.

There was one excellent reason for this. The US immigration authorities have a fully-staffed operation in Shannon for checking passengers straight in to the States: you go through by the US desk in the sprawling Irish airport, and your passport is stamped right there and then, so that the Shannon–Boston flight becomes essentially an internal journey, as if it were Chicago–Boston.

Ben Adnam reasoned he had ten times the chance of slipping through the US desk in Shannon, with a return ticket and a new US business visa, than he ever would at a mainland-US port of entry, where the CIA might by now be watching every incoming passenger from the UK.

He arranged for and prepaid his Dublin hotel, which he understood was just a short walk from the US Embassy in Ballsbridge. He strolled back to the Balmoral to pick up the Audi and to phone his bank and to tell them to send his credit cards overnight to the Berkeley Court in Dublin. Then he tipped the doorman, slung his bag onto the Audi's rear seat, and set off south out of Edinburgh, heading for the long, lonely A7 road which runs down through Galashiels and Hawick for 100 miles to the English border city of Carlisle.

It took him a couple of hours to get to the grim Scottish wool town of Hawick, tracking a line of three trucks in pouring rain for most of the way. He thankfully watched them peel off in the middle of the town, and was pleased to hit the open road once again south of the great cashmere center.

It had stopped raining now, and he was able to drive quickly down the almost empty winding highway as it followed the tortuous course of the Teviot river for mile after mile, through spectacular border valleys and between magnificent hillsides. South of Langholm, the A7 picks up the Esk, and follows in turn this new river's twisting course through the stark border mountains, with deep-green fields for grazing cattle and sheep to either side of the road.

At Longtown the Esk swung away westward toward its long estuary at the head of the Solway Firth. Ben pressed on south for six more miles before joining the fast, wide M6 motorway which would take him almost 200 miles into the Midlands of England, the backbone of his journey.

He reached Penrith, the gateway to the Lake District, by half past three in the afternoon, the Audi now cruising at 80mph east of the long rolling hills which guard the high waters of Ullswater, Haweswater and Lake Windermere. He refueled at the Tebay service station, picked up a sandwich and a cup of coffee, and drove on south.

From here the M6 skirts the waters of Morecambe Bay opposite Barrow-in-Furness, recent home of HMS *Unseen*. But the relentless southward progress of the freeway offers no opportunity for sightseeing, and Commander Adnam just kept driving through northwestern England, past Lancaster, past Blackpool, Preston, Southport and Wigan, past Warrington, Manchester and Liverpool, past Newcastle-under-Lyme, Stoke-on-Trent and Stafford – all the way to Birmingham, where the M6 turns into the M5, the fast road to Bristol 90 miles further south. Ben made it to Bristol by nine o'clock in the evening, and crossed the great span of the Severn Road Bridge just twelve minutes later.

He paid the toll and pulled into the Magor service station, where he refueled once more, parked and found a quiet window table inside for supper. He glanced at the plates of the other diners, and was careful to select popular choices so that his presence would not be fixed into the memory of the waitress. Bewildered as always by the eating habits of the English public, he ordered sausages, chips, fried eggs and baked beans – like just about everyone else.

With Bill, Laura and the two girls now well on their way to Chicago, Admiral MacLean and his wife had a peaceful, elegant dinner of grilled river trout, new potatoes and spinach, accompanied by a bottle of Sancerre. They each had a glass of port at the table while they finished the final edges of a full Stilton cheese.

Lady MacLean retired early, but the admiral was very restless. Finally, having moved over to his study to read the newspaper in front of the dying log fire, he stood up and dialed the number for Galashiels Manor. The phone was answered by the butler.

'Oh, good evening, Beresford. This is Iain MacLean. I wonder, is either Mr or Mrs Anderson still about?'

'Oh, good evening, sir. I'm very sorry but they've gone to

France for a few days. But Mr Douglas will be in London next Tuesday, I believe.'

'That's a pity. Still, it wasn't important. Just a quick question I wanted to ask him. Will he be staying at his Club?'

'I believe so. But I couldn't be sure.'

'Very well, Beresford. Thank you, anyway. Goodnight to you.'

There was a very worried frown on the face of the admiral as he made his way to bed.

Ben Adnam checked his watch. It was almost half past ten at night as he drove along the slip road from the service station and back onto the M4, which runs almost the entire length of the South Wales coastline, way beyond Swansea and into West Wales. It was pitch dark now, and beginning to rain again. The motorway was busy and the Iraqi found the Welsh-language road signs highly confusing. He stuck to the middle traffic lane, not going too fast, watching the big white lettering which signified he was passing Newport, then Cardiff, then Pontypridd, then Bridgend, Maesteg, Port Talbot, Neath and Swansea. This was the old industrial heartland of Wales, the southern end of the steep valleys from which they once mined the finest shipping coal in the world, Welsh anthracite.

Ben Adnam had learned much about rugby football while studying in Scotland, and he recognized the names of those towns and mining villages, almost every one of them with a place in the folklore of world rugby. Beyond Swansea he watched for the signs for Llanelli, the West Wales mining town reputed to have produced more world-class stand-off-halves than all the rest of the British Isles put together.

Ben had watched the Royal Navy play rugby several times, and he remembered meeting three of the massive tight forwards, all of them submariners, all of them from Wales. Irrationally he wondered if they might now be living near here, and whether their lives were less lonely than his. He would have given anything for a conversation – with anyone, even with Able-Seaman Berwyn James, the big, cheerful 1988 Navy forward from Neath, whose neck measured 24 inches round, whose forehead was nonexistent, and whose IQ was only a shade higher than that of plantlife. Ben remembered Berwyn well.

The M4 ended to the northeast of Llanelli, and now he sped

on down toward Carmarthen, slashing through the rain at 75mph. He'd have liked to cruise at 90mph-plus, which the car could have managed with ease, but he didn't: leaving a trail which would inevitably be uncovered within at most a month was one thing; getting arrested by the police for speeding would have been crass.

The roads were deserted down here in West Wales, and now the signposts were beginning to pinpoint the port of Fishguard. Ben raced past St Clears at midnight, still heading due west. At half past midnight he turned north at Haverfordwest for the last 15 miles of his 560-mile journey. Cardigan Bay and the ferryport lay due north before him. The sausage and chips he had had earlier lay heavily upon the stomach of a weary Commander Adnam.

Even though it was the small hours of the morning, the traffic grew much heavier now, and Adnam found himself in a convoy of trucks all trundling up the narrow, winding road to the ferry. Those last 15 miles took him 45 minutes, and the rain and spray made it impossible even to contemplate overtaking the trucks. They meandered in line astern through ghostly quiet Welsh villages like Tangiers, Treffgarne, Wolf's Castle, Letterstone, Newbridge and Scleddau before the trucks turned left along the country road which bypasses Fishguard itself and leads down to the port.

Ben decided to go straight into the middle of Fishguard and look for a gas station. At a quarter past one he drove into the desolate town square and began to follow the signs to the ferry. He was surprised at the town's height above sea level, making it seem to perch on the giant headland over the cold waters of the Irish Sea. He could see the harbor lights, way below down a steep curving road, and out to the west of the harbor wall there was the huge lighted bulk of Stena Line's massive car ferry, the *Köningin Beatrix*.

There was a gas station open on the wharf and he filled up the Audi to ensure that he would have a full tank for his journey when he arrived in early-morning Ireland. Then he made his way to the ferry, showed his ticket at the kiosk, and collected his boarding pass. The route took him through the Customs shed, where a police officer stepped from the shadows and beckoned him to stop. Ben did so, and wound down the window.

'British passport, sir?'

'Yes.'

'Straight ahead.' The officer did not ask to see it.

Outside the ferryport shop a line of half a dozen early arrivals waited in their cars. Ben got out and went inside to buy a cup of coffee, but did not linger to drink it there. He tipped in a couple of small packets of sugar, stirred, and returned to the car, where he sat, sipped, and contemplated the world which lay ahead of him.

At ten past two the attendant seamen called the drivers forward, and, in a long snaking line, they made their way a half-mile along the dock, with the harbor waters to their right and the street-lights of Fishguard high above to the east. Seamen ordered each of the 27 cars into a designated place, deep in the hold, balancing the weight on the port and starboard sides of the nine-deck ferry.

By the time the trucks boarded, ten minutes later, Adnam had made his way, following the signs, to the executive lounge, right up on deck eight. It was warm, deserted, and comfortably furnished. He sank into an armchair and drifted off to sleep before he had even had time to remove his coat. He did not stir until the ship was underway, reversing out of its berth and then moving forward, to the north, around the long harbor wall into the easterly waters of the Irish Sea. Subconsciously Ben could tell they were just leaving – he could easily pick up the changing beats of the engines as the *Beatrix* settled on to her westerly course, running fair through the sheltered waters, with the rugged, towering cliffs of the wave-washed coast of Pembrokeshire a mile off their port beam.

Waking, he sensed the rain had stopped now. He walked out onto the windswept upper deck, staring over the rail at the strange moonlit coast of Wales, feeling again the old familiar rise of the ocean beneath the keel. He had already studied the route on a map he'd bought in Scotland. Adnam leaned forward on the rail, peering into the darkness for the lights of another ship.

But this part of the Irish Sea was deserted. He waited on, alone, watching for the flashing light of the lighthouse on Strumble Head which he knew marked the end of the British mainland, the point where the giant ferry would enter the rough open waters of St George's Channel, where the great Atlantic swells roll in from the southwest. He felt the waters before he saw the light;

felt the angle of the ship increase just slightly as she pitched slowly forward, then rose with the wave, hesitated, then angled down again, the foam-white spray slashing out wide from a great curl of water off her bow as she drove her way westward.

And now at last he could see the light on Strumble Head. Four short flashes, then a seven-second gap, and then four more.

The Commander walked back inside, feeling curiously less tense than he had all day. The sensation of the open sea, where he was used to being the acknowledged master, had a calming effect. It was, he understood, home. The only home he had ever had – and now, possibly, the only home he ever would have.

He sank back into the armchair and closed his eyes. Sleep again engulfed him immediately and when he next woke it was a little after five thirty in the morning.

Along the wide companionway at the end of his lounge was a big right-angled ship's bar which served alcohol, soft drinks, coffee and biscuits. A few passengers were scattered, mostly sleeping, at various tables. No one was speaking.

Ben strolled along to sit at one of the high bar stools and ordered black coffee and a small package of shortbread, which had a Scottish tartan emblem on the wrapper. He remembered shortbread from Faslane, and he munched the biscuits slowly, thinking again of the days he'd spent training with the young British submarine officers at Commanding Officers' Qualifying under the all-seeing but fair eye of the young Commander MacLean, their Teacher. Adnam smiled despite himself, despite everything.

Five more minutes went by before his daydreams were interrupted. An unshaven young man, no more than 19 years old and dressed in a cheap black leather jacket, jeans and trainers, came and sat one stool away and ordered a pint of Guinness. Except that he just said, 'Stout,' pronouncing it 'Stoht.' The barman knew what he meant, and, slowly allowing the creamy head to settle, placed the glass of jet-black Irish nectar before the young man.

'Good luck,' the youth said. Turning to Ben, he added, 'Will you have a jar?'

It was not until that moment that Ben realized the newcomer was extremely drunk, and would be a bit lucky to make it to the car deck, never mind to the road out of Rosslare. 'No, I won't, thank you,' he said. 'It's a bit early for me.'

'Early? Jaysus, I thought it was a bit late.'

Ben smiled. The Irishman was a handsome kid, with black hair and a narrow serious face. He smoked deeply, taking inward breaths which pulled the tobacco fumes deep into his lungs. Ben judged him to be a man with a lot on his mind, despite his youth.

'Now what might you be doing on this terrible bloody ship at this time of the night?' the young man asked with that disarming frankness so often displayed by the Irish.

'I missed the earlier ferry, and had to hang around in Fishguard,' replied Ben. 'How about yourself?'

'I've been attending to a bit of business. Late finish. Had to get down from London on the train. Takes for bloody ever. You change at Swansea.'

'Should have got a plane,' said Ben.

'Not worth it. Costs a fortune. And I live in the south. Waterford. When I'm there, like. Someone'll pick me up at Rosslare.'

Ben had not had a harmless chat like this for literally years. It went against everything he knew. Idle chatter. Loose thoughts. Leaving an impression upon another person. Practices which are forbidden to men who work undercover. He had to stop himself spilling out any salient facts, and he told himself to tell only lies. That way he would be more or less immune to indiscretion.

'What line of country are you in?' asked the Irishman, but before Ben could answer, he leaned over, quite suddenly, thrust out his hand and added, 'Paul, Paul O'Rourke. You don't live in Ireland, do you?'

Ben shook his hand and said, 'Ben Arnold. I'm from South Africa. Mining's my trade.'

'Oh, right. I'm in politics myself.' And Paul drew deeply on his Guinness.

There was silence between the two for almost a minute, and then Paul spoke again: 'Now, then. You, sir, I can see are a man of the world, so you'll not mind my mentioning this. But there's been a lot of trouble in your country over the years – you know, the poor native blacks striving to get some of their lands back from the whites who took it away. What do you think about that? About a people who were savagely dispossessed, and are trying to assert themselves, to get a decent life?'

'Well,' said Ben, 'We don't quite look at it like that You see there were almost no indigenous blacks in South Africa when the whites settled it. They have arrived from the north over the years, trying to get work in a country built from scratch by Europeans – Dutch and English.'

'Jaysus. I t'ought the buggers had always been there.'

'Paul, you thought wrong. South Africa was always white.'

'Is that why it's so bloody rich, unlike the rest of Africa?'

'I suppose so. All its industry was built by the whites. My own corporation employs thousands of black workers. But I'm not saying we didn't make mistakes. We did. We should have provided more opportunity, years ago, to bring the blacks on-side, into white society. Apartheid was never right. And it turned out to be very damaging.'

'I read a lot about it in college,' said Paul, 'before I dropped out. I was doing a degree in world politics at UCD. But I missed the part about the blacks being itinerant workers, visitors to the white state.'

'Well, that's what they were. And that's how most of 'em got there in the beginning. Streaming over the borders from places like Nyasaland. And, of course, many more immigrants came from India.'

Again there was silence. And then Ben asked quietly, 'And what was it, Paul, that was so pressing in your life that you decided to abandon your university degree?'

'Oh, not much really I just got caught up in politics.'

'What kind of politics? You thinking of running for office sometime?'

'Perhaps sometime I might. But I got into the more practical end of things.'

Ben sensed that Paul O'Rourke was about to say more than he should. He watched the boy, smoking nervously, gulping great swallows of Guinness, his hand trembling slightly.

'My people are Republicans,' Paul said eventually. 'We've always believed in a united Ireland. My dad was an activist. So was his dad, and his.'

'What kind of activists?'

'Well my great-grandda came to Dublin with Michael Collins from Cork in 1916. He died in the fighting at the post office – the English gunned him down. My great-uncle was wounded but

299

he got away. He was with the group that retreated to Boland's Bakery. I think about it every time I go to Dublin. They never had a chance against the English artillery, but Jaysus, the lads were brave on that day.'

Ben nodded, saying nothing.

'My whole family is Sinn Fein,' said Paul. 'It means in Gaelic, "Ourselves Alone." We want Ireland to be one country, with no English here at all. That's why there's the IRA – that's our military wing.'

'I know,' said Ben. 'Are you a member?'

Paul, silent, shook his head, then said, 'Let's just say I'm sympathetic.'

He gulped some more Guinness. 'I don't think you'd understand, Mr Arnold,' he said. 'We're from different sides of the tracks, you and I. You belong to the rich ruling class. I belong to an organization struggling to break free from a cruel and wicked oppressor.'

'You think the English are cruel and wicked?'

'We've nothing to thank them for. They raped and pillaged our country for centuries. And by whose right? The right of their bloody guns, that was their only right. But it may be *our* guns that finally put an end to it.'

'When did you first get interested?'

'I think I must have been about 13. There was a little party at my granddad's house down in Schull, on the Cork coast, and some English people were invited back from the pub. I remember they were all singing songs, each person taking turns, and when it came time for the Englishmen to sing, they did "It's a Long Way to Tipperary."

'At that moment my grandfather went berserk. I was standing right next to him, and he smashed the flat of his hand down on the table, and he shouted, "I'll not have that song sung in this house! I'll not have it! damn you – damn you to hell!"

'Well, the party broke up right then. Everybody left, but the next day I asked my dad what had upset Grandpa so much. And he told me that song was an English marching song, and the Black and Tans used to sing it.'

'Who were the Black and Tans?'

'Oh, that was the English occupying army in Ireland, before we drove them out. My dad told me they had shot Grandpa's mother and both of his sisters when he was about 14 years old, down in Cork. He said Grandpa stood on the doorstep of the house, covered in the blood of his own dead mother, and he could hear the English soldiers marching off, singing "It's a Long Way to Tipperary." '

'Does that mean you want to become a terrorist, a soldier of the IRA?'

'I'm not sure. And I can't explain it. You'd never understand what it feels like to be prepared to die for something you believe in, Mr Arnold. I hate the English, and so does everyone in my family. They'll never be forgiven for what they've done in Ireland. And it's up to just a few of us to get the last of them out of here. The best way to do that is to bomb their bloody country until they leave.'

'I should be careful, Paul. It's a lonely life you're considering. Hunted by the English, the feeling that every man's hand is turned against you. And the constant danger of high explosives and British Army marksmen. Worse yet – you end up not daring to trust anyone.'

'I've already studied the subject pretty carefully, Mr Arnold. I'm brave enough, and I think I might be smart enough. I've helped in a few missions, but never in a real way. My father commanded an IRA squad, but he never told us what he had done.'

'Well, I think you should think it over very carefully first, Paul. It's a big step. And you'll have a lot of time to regret it if it turns out to be wrong for you. Not to mention that you might get killed.'

'Ah, you say that because you can't quite understand what it's like to believe in something and be ready to die for it. It burns right into you, the hatred, and the feeling of being right, being justified. All terrorists are men apart.'

'So they are, Paul,' replied Benjamin Adnam. 'So they are.'

1600, Wednesday, April 5. Office of the National Security Advisor, the White House.

Admiral Arnold Morgan was on the secure line to CIA headquarters, Langley, Virginia. 'Yeah. Well, I don't know where the hell he is, or where the hell he's headed. But I know he was in

Scotland last night. And I have no real reason to suspect he may be trying to get into the United States, but he might be . . .

'Yup. I gotta picture the Mossad wired us – it's on the way over. Excellent quality. Well, I'd be inclined to get some guys into the main ports of entry from Britain – flights from the northern airports, Edinburgh, Glasgow, Manchester . . . Just because they're nearer to his last known position. Yeah, and we'd better watch flights in from London Heathrow and Gatwick as well, in case he heads south first. The Brits are watching all those too.

'Yeah, I've sent a physical description. Remember he's a naval officer – he usually looks smart. And he speaks with a very correct British accent. But remember, too, he's no fool and he's unlikely to oblige us by looking like a gentleman . . . Right . . . right. Well, I guess New York, Washington. Possibly Philly, possibly Boston – maybe Chicago.

'Yeah, alert immigration, the passport guys, for anyone fitting this description. OK. No, I'm *not* sure. For all I know he might be going back to the Middle East, but he *could* be coming here. Yeah, possibly Kansas. Right. No. I don't think he'll have a visa – he won't have had time to get one. No, he could forge a passport but the modern US visas are almost impossible to forge accurately. I'd guess he wouldn't dare try that – too big a risk. If he does try to enter the States, we're looking for a guy with no visa, traveling just as a visitor, for less than 90 days.

'OK, let's stay right on top of this. Remember, this bastard is the worst terrorist in history, and if he comes here I want the fucker caught. So does the President – so don't screw it up.'

Arnold Morgan banged the phone down, yelled for coffee, then yelled for Kathy O'Brien. Three seconds later, when the door didn't open, he strode towards it, snapping 'Dumbass broad!' just as the President of the United States entered, chuckling.

'Who, me?'

'Christ, no, sir. Sorry. It's just that bastard Adnam gets me on the raw. I've no proof, and it's a real longshot, but he just could be on his way here.'

'Hell, that we don't need.'

'Not if he plans to blow up another warship or a goddamned aircraft, or even an airport. He really spooks me. I just think the fucker might do anything.'

'I agree. If your theories are right, we might be in big trouble. Yet again. We gotta catch him, Arnold. What's the latest?'

'Well, I just heard from Iain Maclean in Scotland.'

'Oh yeah? What does he think?'

'Well, it was Iain who alerted us that Adnam was in Scotland. He thinks he's trying to locate Laura.'

'Jesus. You don't think he's going to try to kill Bill, do you?'

'Hell, I hadn't even thought about that. But when a guy's killed as many people as Adnam, you don't know what he might do.'

'We must find him, Arnold. Christ, he's just killed the Vice-President, among others. You got Langley on the case?'

'Absolutely.'

'Keep it tight, Arnie. We gotta get him. Use as many people as it takes. How 'bout Kansas? You think we need guys out there?'

'Not yet. He probably won't even come here. I don't want to alert the entire country. Right now I thought we'd just get a rigid handle on all the incoming flights from Britain. We got good photos, good description. We might just have a shot at picking him up.'

'OK, buddy. I'll leave it to you. Keep me informed.'

'Aye, sir.'

Ben Adnam had said goodbye to Paul O'Rourke and was making his way down to the car deck. The *Beatrix* had passed the flashing light to port which marks the channel into Rosslare, and now she was reversing beyond the harbor wall into their berth on the Irish quayside. It seemed to take forever, but at ten minutes after seven on the morning of Thursday, April 6, Commander Adnam drove the rented Audi out onto Irish soil, making his way through the dock to the kiosk in front of the Customs shed, which was completely empty.

All of the cars from Fishguard just drove straight through, following the 'Exit' signs, then up the steep hill and out onto the main road to Wexford and, after that, 100 miles north to Dublin. It was growing light, and Ben could see he was driving over a long flat coastal plain, with only sparse houses and little traffic. Thankfully the fleet of heavy trucks from Wales was far behind and he settled down to drive fast along the wide, lonely Irish roads up to Enniscorthy, then to Ferns, Gorey and Arklow through the Wicklow Mountains to the southern suburbs of Ireland's capital city. Given the speed of its first part, he anticipated the whole journey would take him only two hours but, as he proceeded north up the east coast, the rain began again and the traffic grew heavier.

By the time he reached the outskirts of Dublin he was in a rainswept morning rush-hour, bumper to bumper all along the N11. Up ahead he could see his landmark, the tall tower of Ireland's television station, RTE. He was looking for the next right after that, at the Catholic church, and he finally turned into exclusive Anglesea Road at 10am.

Five minutes later he crossed Ballsbridge, swung right again into Shelbourne Road and ran down to the Berkeley Court Hotel in Lansdowne Road. He drove straight into the carpark at the rear, checked in at reception, and crashed onto his bed on the fourth floor – exhausted, hungry, too tired to eat, but safe. And anonymous. In a new country, in which he had never even shown his passport.

Adnam slept until midday, and left the hotel in a light drizzle. He took a cab to Grafton Street and used his Royal Bank of Scotland credit card to purchase a raincoat and an umbrella in Brown Thomas, Dublin's excellent answer to London's Harrods and New York's Saks Fifth Avenue. Then he walked back up to St Stephen's Green and picked up a cab from the rank. He was driven to the great round building of the US Embassy, which sits in its own grounds behind a black wrought iron fence at the end of Shelbourne Road. He walked through the small gateway, crossed the cobbled courtyard and walked up the slope to the visa office. He explained to the duty guard that he wanted to pick up application forms for a B–2 multiple-entry business visa.

The guard waved him through the security X-ray. The Iraqi terrorist soon found himself to be the only person seeking help at the counter. The official, an Irishwoman, was polite and genial. She gave him the form and pointed out that he must fill it in carefully, explaining that he must pay the fee into the Irish Bank, along the road, and collect a receipt. He must also provide a passport-size photograph and then acquire a note from his bank or employer to confirm that he was a man of substance and would not be entering the United States in order to receive welfare payments.

Ben thanked her and took a cab back into the center of the

city to the office of the Royal Bank of Scotland. There he explained that he was an established client of the bank's, Helensburgh branch and would like a letter explaining that he had run an account from there for many years, and that it currently contained a sum well in excess of £50,000 Sterling. They said they would fax the request to Helensburgh immediately, and that he should call in the next morning to collect the letter of recommendation, which would be marked for the attention of the US Embassy.

He picked up another cab and returned to the Berkeley Court, retired to his room, and worked on the long detailed form, electing to use his UK passport as the one into which the coveted B–2 businessman's visa, valid for ten years, would be stamped. The notice in the Embassy had specified that the process would take two working days, but the woman behind the counter had explained that, if he could return the completed documents the following morning, Friday, they would almost certainly be ready after 2.30pm on Monday.

Faced with a lonely weekend in rainy Dublin, Adnam reflected that, when he entered the United States, officials wouldn't be looking for a man with a visa. He suspected that at Shannon Airport they might not be looking for anyone at all.

But first he must insure that visa was actually issued. He checked every question carefully, making certain all his answers were those of a stable, well-to-do Scottish businessman from Helensburgh – Ben Arnold, mining executive, with interests in the South African coal and copper fields, now residing in Dublin for six months. He had invented his address, invented his profession, invented his corporation, invented his name and forged his UK passport. The only truthful document he would present to the US consular officials would be the letter from the Royal Bank of Scotland.

The next morning, when he picked the letter up from their Dublin office, it was precisely as he had asked:

'To the US Embassy, Dublin. This letter is to confirm that Mr Benjamin Arnold has had an account with us for more than 15 years, and that his current balance shows in excess of £50,000 Sterling.'

He walked to a supermarket, where he had four passport pictures taken in a machine. Then he stopped at the Bank of Ireland, paid the fee of 16 Irish pounds, collected his receipt, and strolled the quarter-mile to the US Embassy. There he placed his UK passport, his signed application form, his photograph, his letter from the bank and his receipt in a brown envelope and deposited it in the polished wooden drop-box. As he left, the security guard smiled and said, 'After 2.30 Monday, sir. It should be ready.'

Adnam then walked over the wide bridge which spans the River Dodder toward the headquarters of the Dublin Horse Show. He crossed the road to a shopfront marked Ballsbridge Travel and went inside, requesting a business-class return ticket from Shannon Airport to Boston next Tuesday, April 11. He was looked after by a trim, pretty Irish girl named Loraine, who checked and accepted his credit card and booked him on the Aer Lingus Flight that leaves Dublin at midday and arrives in Shannon 25 minutes later. Ben in fact planned to drive from Dublin, leaving early in the morning and making Shannon by 11.00am to check in, and to arrange for the return of the car to Helensburgh, but he didn't tell Loraine that.

He took his ticket and walked back to the hotel. After a light lunch, he traveled by taxi out to Dublin's suburb of Clonskeagh to spend the afternoon at the Islamic Centre and Mosque, a truly stunning religious and educational establishment founded in 1996 by Sheikh Hamdan al Maktoum of Dubai, for the 7000 Muslims who live in Ireland, mostly in Dublin. The mosque, a magnificent stone building set beneath a vast copper dome, holds 1200 people. Ben Adnam answered the Friday evening call to prayer, kneeling with several hundred others of the faithful, begging his God for guidance and forgiveness.

All through the rest of that long weekend Adnam went back and forth from the Berkeley Hotel to Clonskeagh. He read the Koran in the library, he attended prayers throughout the day and early evening, and on the Sunday afternoon he succeeded in gaining a private audience with the Imam, a wise and considerate Egyptian sheikh whose teachings had brought comfort to many of his countrymen.

Ben Adnam was unable to reveal the truth about himself, but he tried to explain his predicament: that he had worked for governments, carrying out their bidding, because he believed in their motives. He spoke of his betrayal by those governments, and tried to define his current dilemma and his desperate need to attain the understanding of Allah.

The Imam was thoughtful and encouraging. But, as with all Sunni Muslims, he stressed that Benjamin must continue to nurture his own faith, that no one could help him with that. But he assured the now-weeping ex-naval commander who knelt before him that Allah was merciful – that in his opinion Allah would not damn him, and that in the fullness of time, subject to prayer and devotion to the teachings of the Prophet, Benjamin would one day be welcomed into the arms of his God.

By night he slept only fitfully in his luxurious bedroom in the Berkeley, fighting off the persistent nightmares, awakening in the dark and spending hours trying to reconcile the brute instincts of the international terrorist with his devout and pious yearnings to be closer to the Kingdom of Allah. The result was always confusion, as the images of death and destruction in his mind's eye raced on with the glancing speed of all disconnected dreams.

At 2.30pm on Monday afternoon he walked into the consular section of the US Embassy. The guard waved him through the security X-ray and told him to go straight to Window Three. The woman behind the glass recognized him, and smiled. 'Mr Arnold?' Ben nodded. She handed him an envelope in which had been placed his passport and the letter from the bank.

Outside in the courtyard, beneath the great fluttering Stars and Stripes at the top of the flagstaff, he stood for a moment and opened the envelope. Taking up one full page in his passport was the official entry visa to the United States of America, printed along the ornate lines of a bank note in green and pink with a wide yellow band across the great Seal of the United States. Ben's photograph, name and passport number faced the predatory head of the American bald eagle. The visa, the B1/B2, was good for ten years, until the year 2016.

The next morning, Tuesday, April 11, six days after Arnold Morgan had alerted all inlets to the USA, Ben checked out of the Berkeley at first light and headed southeast out of Dublin bound for Shannon Airport and then Boston. He took the city route, running along Dublin's Grand Canal to the Crumlin Road, and heading southwest through County Kildare, past Naas, and on to Roscrea and Limerick. The road was lonely throughout the second half of the 130-mile journey, and Ben pulled easily into the precincts of Shannon Airport at ten minutes before eleven.

He parked the car in the longterm parking lot, took the key, and paid a £28 fee which would cover the parking until late Saturday. He taped the key to a piece of card he had brought with him and placed it, together with the parking-lot ticket and a check for £1000, drawn on his Helensburgh account, in an envelope addressed to the garage in Helensburgh. The accompanying note read: 'Sorry about the distance, but I had to go to Ireland. The Audi is in the long-term car park at Shannon Airport, bay M39. I expect you'll have to send someone over, so I enclose enough money to cover expenses and inconvenience. Thanks for cooperating – Ben Arnold.' He was sure the Scots mechanic would be irked at the prospect of the journey, but equally sure the cash bonus would undoubtedly make it worthwhile.

He purchased two Irish airmail stamps inside the airport and mailed the envelope from the box next to the Hertz carhire desk. It was, he thought, an easy way to avoid raising any questions about a mysterious missing Audi in Helensburgh which ultimately turned up in Shannon Airport, the same Audi which perhaps Douglas and Natalie Anderson had seen parked in their drive. His £1000 payment to the garage might pay for itself a hundred-fold in covering his trail for the next couple of weeks.

He checked in his bag at the Aer Lingus desk and was directed to the business-class lounge. At 1pm he was escorted by a stewardess down to the line of US immigration desks, through which the passengers from Dublin had already passed. There were only 23 passengers beginning their journey in Shannon, and only two of those were business-class – Adnam and an off-duty travel agent.

Ben moved through first. The uniformed officer, an American, leafed through the passport without looking up. 'Purpose of trip?'

'Business. Meetings in Boston first, then New York'

'Ah-hah. How long do you intend to stay in the United States, sir?'

'Maybe three weeks. No longer.'

The immigration official looked through a large black book containing clipped-in pages of computer printout. Finding nothing to concern him, he took his stamp and confirmed in Ben Arnold's passport that he had entered the US on April 11,

2006 at the port of Shannon. In the space marked 'Admitted until . . .' the officer just wrote 'B–2.'

Essentially, the world's most wanted man was in the USA already. 'Enjoy your flight, sir,' said the immigration man, handing him a Customs form to be completed for Logan Airport, Boston.

1300, Tuesday, April 11. Loch Fyne, Scotland.
Admiral MacLean was still trying to track down Douglas Anderson. He called Boodle's in St James's and was irritated to find the Scottish banker was not in residence at his club, and furthermore was not expected. He called the Connaught Hotel and then Brown's with the same lack of success. Finally, supposing that Douglas and Natalie had stayed another couple of nights in France, he called Galashiels Manor again and asked Beresford to please insure that Mr Anderson called him on a matter of some urgency – whatever time of the day or night he received the message.

1400, Tuesday, April 11. International Arrivals Building, Logan Airport, Boston.
Dick Saunders, the CIA chief at the Boston Station, had been on duty since 0700. In company with two field officers, Joe Pecce and Fred Corcoran, he had been combing passenger lists for incoming flights from Great Britain, especially from Scotland.

Right now was the busy time, with big jets trundling in off the Atlantic every five minutes until 1500: the morning flights from Europe. There were British Airways 747s from Glasgow, Edinburgh and Heathrow. There were American Airlines planes from Heathrow and a North Western out of Gatwick. Virgin had one from Manchester. All these were interspersed with flights from Paris, Frankfurt, Madrid and Rome, plus one from Dublin–Shannon.

The three CIA observers would have their work cut out, as had been the case every day for the past week since the command had come down from on high to try to find a traveling Arab named Ben Adnam, probably from Scotland, maybe from England, no visa, probably under an assumed name. But each agent had a good photograph, and they placed themselves strategically in the glassed kiosks with the immigration staff, making it well-nigh impossible for *anyone* to walk through without being stopped who looked *anything* like the dark-skinned foreigner in naval uniform shown in the photographs held by the CIA men.

Their problem was that Ben Adnam did not have to pass through the glass kiosks into the United States. He had already completed that formality back in Ireland. Aer Lingus Flight 005 came in on time at 1410 and, along with the rest of the passengers, Adnam walked straight through the immigration area and down the steps to the Customs hall, where he collected his bag.

Admiral Morgan's last line of defense was Field Officer Pecce, who was down in the hall, standing at one of the main desk search centers watching the incoming passengers from Edinburgh. Ben Adnam walked right by him, 25 feet to his left, with his head high, bag in hand. He handed his Customs form to the waiting official, who initialed it and told him to present it at the door. Half a minute later he was out in the arrivals hall, taking his time, walking with his bag toward the exit.

Ben turned left outside the international building and headed for Terminal D, where he hoped to locate either American or United Airlines. He proposed to take a direct route to Kansas, openly buying a ticket; he was no longer terribly concerned about leaving a consistent trail.

Thus, with just one change at Kansas City, Missouri, he flew straight to Wichita, and from there on a small local flight down to Dodge City, the old Wild West town in the southwest of Kansas, a 45-mile car ride from the big ranch run by Bill and Laura Baldridge. Arnold Morgan had not yet ordered a team in to protect Bill's household.

Ben arrived at Dodge City Airport on the evening of Thursday, April 13. He rented a dark-red Ford Taurus station wagon for a week using his Scottish credit card and his British license. He was checked into a new hotel out near the airport before 9pm.

At this precise time Bill and Laura were sitting alone beside the big fire in their living room, half-watching the television news, half-reading magazines. They had dined early with Laura's daughters and Bill's mother that evening, and now they were each sipping a glass of port, a habit they'd brought with them from the home of Iain MacLean in faraway Scotland.

Bill's days were always busy during the early spring. He had to keep track of the herds — which his brother Ray tended on a day-to-day basis — and watch the beef-stock markets, deciding when to buy and what to sell. The warmer weather sometimes comes late to the High Plains, and it was often frosty and still freezing cold when the master of the great Baldridge spread marched out onto the frozen ground before first light. Sometimes he was so tired in the evenings he could have crashed into bed at seven o'clock, but he treasured the peaceful later hours with his beautiful Scottish wife, and so he always stayed up until about half past eleven.

They had both talked to her father this evening. Sir Iain had been unusually tense, explaining to them that he still thought it was possible that Ben might try to get into the United States, despite Admiral Morgan's dragnet around the points of entry. The veteran Royal Navy submariner begged Laura to be careful, and when he spoke to Bill he practically forbade him to allow her to be alone at any time of the day or night. 'I don't need to tell you how dangerous or how mad he may be,' said MacLean, 'but I intend to ask Admiral Morgan to get some heavy security into the ranch within the next 24 hours. I simply do not consider it's worth taking any chance.'

By half past nine that evening Ben Adnam had completed his study of a detailed map of the counties which surround Dodge City. There, just west of Burdett, he noted in red letters the sign 'B/B,' then, in parentheses 'Baldridge.' It looked as if the main ranch buildings were right off Route 156, where the Pawnee river and Buckner Creek converge before winding on down to the Arkansas river. The Scottish newspaper which had described Lt-Commander Baldridge as a farmer was right. Ben assessed thousands and thousands of acres out there in the flat grazing land which straddles Pawnee County and Hodgeman County. 'About twice the size of Baghdad,' Ben murmured. 'It could be hard to find the house, but you couldn't miss the land.'

Dressed in his dark tracksuit and soft black trainers, Ben left the hotel with his bag at about a quarter to ten and drove fast out along Route 50 from Dodge City. He turned north up 283 to Jetmore, and then went east 23 miles to Burdett, the little town which sits almost on the border of Pawnee County. He checked the road signs every few minutes. They stayed consistent. There were no turns. He was running dead straight along 156.

He drove through the little township of Hanston, which he guessed was his halfway point from Jetmore. He checked the reading on the speedometer and resolved to start slowing down and searching after ten more miles.

Instinct more than navigational skill guided him, and approximately one and a half miles before he reached Burdett he made a sharp right turn into the pitch darkness of a south-running country road. Way out to the left he could see lights. As he came to a bridge he slowed and stopped, winding down the window and hearing the unmissable sound of a flowing river not far below. 'Too far. That's the Pawnee,' he muttered. 'In full flow at this time of the year after the winter snow, melting down from the Rockies. Like the Tigris around now, back home. Different mountains, same sound.'

He reversed the car, swinging in reverse into a gateway, and heading back to Route 156, where he took the next right turn into an equally dark country road. But there were lights dead ahead now, floodlighting the great iron gates and archway of the B/B Ranch. He could see the entrance was closed, and that the post-and-rail fence ran right up to stone pillars which guarded it. He caught sight of two carved wooden longhorn steers on each post. He kept going, driving at 50mph past the B–Bar–B where Laura now lived.

He continued for a mile further on dipped headlights. The fence had run out now, and he could see a clump of trees on the edge of the frosty road. He pulled off onto the grass verge and parked behind the trees. Then he pulled on an extra sweater, leather gloves and a dark woolen hat. He checked his big desert knife was firm in the back of his leather belt, and, after locking the car, began to jog back toward the main gates of the Baldridge ranch.

Before he reached there, he cleared the fence and made his way crosscountry toward the distant lights. The moon was up and very bright, and he wanted to come into the ranch compound behind the buildings with the shadows in front of him rather than behind. This was difficult – he realized he would have to circle the ranch buildings in order to achieve it – but he didn't want the clear, pale light of the moon in his face.

He reached the buildings and flattened himself behind them. Inside he heard a sharp thud on the wall, followed by another. *Stables*, he thought. *And the horses have heard me.*

He began his circle around to the main house, creeping silently through the shadows with the soft, light steps of the Bedouin. He hoped to God no one would see or hear him, because he had no intention to kill anyone – except perhaps Baldridge, if he had to. If it became obvious that Laura would leave with him. There was a corner of Ben's brain which was not functioning in any way rationally, and the master of all these Kansas acres was right in that corner.

The Iraqi made his way softly into a place where he could observe the house with his back to the moon. His plan was to take Bill and Laura by surprise. There was no point walking up to the door and trying to be reasonable. For all he knew this damned cowboy would gun him down in cold blood. No, he had to engineer the situation so that he was the one in control, and to do that, he must put them both on the defensive. That way he would be able to see how the land lay.

He planned to enter the house, through an upstairs window whose drapes were not drawn, the sure sign of an empty guest room. The trouble was that *none* of those upstairs drapes were drawn right now, unlike those of the downstairs windows. And he could see light crossing the hallways between the upstair rooms. He had seen one room on the far side of the house with drawn drapes but no light, and he guessed that Laura's daughters must be asleep in there.

He waited for a half-hour, until 11.45pm. The drapes were being pulled over now by a figure he could not identify. Ben made his move. He slipped quietly across the yard and climbed easily onto the roof of an outhouse. From there he swung up onto a second-floor balcony, and then went higher, to a gently sloping roof, leading up to the one window which still didn't have its drapes drawn.

Crouching on the ledge, he inserted his knife between the sliding panes and flicked the catch back.

At exactly that moment Laura Baldridge walked in, switched on the light and saw the big blade of the desert knife jutting upwards in the gap. She also saw a dark figure beyond. She yelled at the top of her lungs, '*Bill! Bill! Come quick! There's someone breaking in!*'

Outside on the roof, Ben Adnam nearly died of shock. Two dogs were barking furiously below. He ducked low and moved higher, the only way he could go, up toward the chimneys.

Bill Baldridge unlocked the gun cupboard in the back hall and grabbed a D.M. Lefever 9FE shotgun. He snapped two 16-gauge shells into it, cramming four more into his jacket pocket. He took the stairs two at a time and found Laura pressed against the passage wall outside the spare room.

'Right in there,' she whispered. 'I saw Adnam close against the window with a big knife. It *was* Ben – I *know* it was him! If we don't kill him, he'll kill us. Jesus, wait here, I'm going for a shotgun myself. This is bloody ridiculous.'

'I guess there are advantages in marrying a girl whose family trade is war.' He smiled. 'They don't lose their nerve that easy.'

At that moment, on the other side of the Atlantic, Douglas Anderson was waking up in a sleeping car in Edinburgh's Waverley Station on the overnight express from London. It was six o'clock in the morning. The red light on his cellular phone was flashing. He pressed the button as he realised he'd been lax in checking his messages. There was just one. The familiar voice of Beresford informing him that Admiral MacLean wished to speak to him on a matter of the utmost urgency; Mr Douglas could call him at whatever time of the day or night.

Douglas was usually somewhat unnerved by the Admiral, and he did precisely as he was asked, wakening Sir Iain on a misty Scottish morning just before dawn.

The great submariner awakened fast. He asked his former son-in-law to hold for one moment, pulled on his dressing gown and hurried downstairs to his study.

'I say, Iain, I'm awfully sorry about the time, but the message did say . . .'

'Don't worry about that, Douglas. I'm delighted you made it. I want to ask you something very important, and I wish I'd been able to reach you before. You remember that South African chap who called to see Laura the other day? Did he, by any chance, ask where Laura now lived? I don't mean just America – he didn't ask for her address, did he?'

'Yes, he did. He said his own wife would very much like to send her a Christmas card, just to show they had tried to make contact in Scotland. Natalie wrote the address down in full on a piece of paper for him. It seemed a reasonable request.'

Admiral MacLean's heart missed a beat. But he steadied himself while Douglas went on, calmly, 'The ranch in Pawnee County, Kansas, correct? I remember it – sounds like something out of the Wild West.'

'Yes . . . it does. Thank you, Douglas. I'm sorry to have been a bother.'

His heart pounding, Admiral MacLean replaced the receiver. 'Fuck,' he said, uncharacteristically. Then he picked up the phone again and placed a call to Admiral Arnold Morgan's office in the White House, where it was currently one o'clock in the morning.

The main switchboard patched him through to Kathy O'Brien's house immediately and the National Security Advisor came promptly on the line. 'Iain – hi. This has got to be important.'

'It is. In the last few minutes I found out that Adnam is almost certainly on his way to the Baldridge Ranch. He's walking around with their complete address, right down to the zip code, in his pocket. That's what he went to Anderson's house for. Arnold, trust me. He's on his way. My God, he's capable of blowing the ranch up!'

'Holy Topeka!' grated the Admiral, slipping into Kansas mode. 'Leave it with me, pal. I'll have a team of heavies in there inside two hours.'

He rang off and called the CIA duty officer, telling him to get him through to Frank Reidel, the agency's chief military liaison man. They connected in less than 60 seconds, and the admiral wasted no time with explanations – just told Frank to get a half-dozen heavily armed hardmen by helicopter to the Baldridge ranch in Pawnee County, Kansas, *right now.* He told Frank the guys in the control room at MacConnell Air Station, Wichita, knew the way. No, he didn't care if they used civilians, agents, US Marines, Navy SEALs or King Kong. Just so long as they moved fast. Who were they looking for? An escaped Arab terrorist, Benjamin Adnam, Commander Benjamin Adnam. 'Certainly armed. Extremely dangerous. Pre-emptive action if necessary. But try to keep him alive.'

Then Arnold Morgan called Bill Baldridge, and waited with mounting concern while the phone rang and rang before an answering machine picked up and requested that he leave a message.

It was just a few minutes after midnight back in Kansas, and Laura was heading downstairs at high speed to the gun cupboard in search of the shotgun left to her by her grandmother, the Countess of Jedburgh. Bill Baldridge went into the small office next to his bedroom and spent five minutes adjusting the zones on the burglar alarms, activating the entire downstairs area but only one part of the upstairs system.

He positioned himself on the main landing, in the shadows near the big fireplace along the corridor from his old bedroom. If anyone entered the house they'd have to come through one of two rooms on the second floor or else the alarms would go off, floodlighting the house, alerting every ranch worker and the local police.

Bill believed Laura – it had to be Ben. His own plan of action was clear. If the Iraqi came through either of those bedroom doors onto the landing Bill would gun him down like a prairie dog, no questions asked. If he tried to make entry through the downstairs doors or windows, the alarm system would surely frighten him off.

However, the five minutes he had taken resetting the zones was critical. Out on the roof, Ben Adnam had been startled, by being spotted, but had not panicked. Like any good submarine commander he elected to press home his attack while the enemy was in disarray. He moved from the chimneys back down the roof and opened the window where he had pried open the catch.

Laura, in her haste, had not relocked it. Ben Adnam climbed in through the window, crossed the room and turned out the light, positioning himself behind the door of the empty third-floor spare room. It was Bill he wanted, because that way everything else would fall into place, when Laura could see clearly who the master was.

Ben stood breathing hard after his exertions, gathering his thoughts, trying to work out which he wanted most – Laura, or access to the US National Security Chief. The problem was confusing him now. He knew he wanted Laura more than anything he had ever wanted. But he sensed that was just his heart speaking. His brain was a still small voice in the background, telling him, whispering: 'If you kill Bill Baldridge, you'll probably have to kill Laura as well. You'll never get out of this state, never mind this country, alive. They'll hunt you down and send you to the Chair. Don't be a fool. Negotiate with Baldridge, because that way may lie sanctuary, and a life . . .'

And yet . . . and yet he longed for Laura. The memory of her touch and her laughter, and their love for each other, was as vivid tonight as it had ever been. Ben Adnam would have cut off his own right arm just to have her once more.

At four minutes after midnight he stepped through the doorway into the upstairs corridor, his desert knife clutched now in his right hand.

One story below him, Bill leaned against the wall, his rifle cocked, watching the two doors along the southern corridor. Ben saw him first, saw the glint of the barrels of the Lefever, which was not so much an advantage as a clarification. The Iraqi's task was plain: he had to descend thirteen steps without being heard, and then Bill Baldridge would be his.

Downstairs he heard Laura yell, 'Where do you keep the shells for this damned thing?' Bill, standing not 15 feet below Commander Adnam, shouted back, 'Cupboard by the back stairs — top shelf — right-hand side — leather box . . .'

Ben took three steps downward while Mr and Mrs Baldridge communicated. He pressed himself against the wall, deep in the shadows of the upper staircase of the big, heavily timbered house. He pressed on down three more steps. Bill took a pace forward, then another, peering down over the balustrade to the first floor. Then he stepped backward into his original position.

Ben Adnam was just seven feet away now, and suddenly, as if emerging from the dark tunnel of his own self-pity, all of his old sense of cold-blooded reason came flooding back. He wasn't going to kill Bill. But he pounced noiselessly, with a menace that was guided by cool intent.

Lt-Commander Bill Baldridge felt the cold steel of the Iraqi's wide desert knife pressed hard against the left-hand side of his throat.

'Good evening, Lieutenant-Commander,' said a British voice. 'I don't need to tell you it would take me less than five thousandths of a second to sever your jugular, do I?'

Bill Baldridge said nothing.

'But, actually, I do not intend to do that. Now, walk carefully and place your gun on that chair.'

They both moved four paces across the hall, close to the

corridor which Bill had been guarding. He put the loaded shotgun down.

'Excellent,' replied Adnam. And, with a move that absolutely astonished Bill, he removed the big desert knife from his captive's throat and placed it on the chair also, right next to the Lefever.

'There,' said Adnam. 'I have not, of course, come to kill you. I have come to claim your attention. Because I want to bargain for my life. I believe you know who I am, and I should like to think we can now talk on equal terms.'

That might have been possible 20 seconds previously. But it was not possible now. Because jammed hard against the base of Commander Adnam's skull were two cold rings of steel – the barrels of a loaded 12-bore Purdey sporting gun which had once belonged to the Ninth Earl of Jedburgh.

'Hello, Ben,' said the soft voice he had traveled across the world to hear. 'If you keep very still I may not blow your head off. But if my husband tells me to do so I shall not hesitate. I expect I'll be given the Congressional Medal for my marksmanship.'

Ben Adnam froze. But he kept his composure. 'Hello, Laura,' he said. 'What a nice surprise. Are you sure you know how to use that thing?'

Bill Baldridge, whose childhood heroes had been local men like Wyatt Earp, Bat Masterson, the Dalton Brothers and Wild Bill Hickok, was amazed by the coolness of their conversation – the Scottish heiress and the Arab assassin. For a few seconds he was dumbfounded, and then he heard Laura say, 'Ben, both my grandfather and I could hit a high pheasant flying downwind at 50 miles an hour with this particular gun. I assure you, I am even better with a closer target.' She shoved both barrels a little harder into the dark curly hair at the base of the skull of her former lover.

Bill, like the Commander, by now believed she might actually do it. And he stepped forward to confiscate the knife and reclaim his own gun from the chair. He took the greatest care to stay well clear of the front of Adnam's face, just in case his wife got carried away.

Then he spoke for the first time. 'Commander Adnam,' he said, 'step through that door over there, turn left, and face the wall with your hands on your head. If he makes one move, Laura, kill him. Or I will.'

Ben walked slowly forward, Laura's magnificent shotgun –
bearing Purdey's classic rose-and-scroll pattern engraving – still
rammed against his head. Inside the office, Bill searched him
carefully, warning Laura, 'This man is lethal. He could kill the
pair of us with his bare hands in under 20 seconds. Keep that ole
Purdey rock-solid against his brain and keep your finger on the
trigger – twitching.'

'Don't even think about the mess you'll make,' said Laura to
Ben. 'I was going to have this carpet changed anyway, and the
room's being redecorated next month.'

Bill couldn't help smiling, but the deadly nature of the game
kept him focused. He moved behind his desk, keeping his own
gun trained on Adnam, who was still standing pressed against the
wall. Bill held the weapon straight with one hand and pressed a
button on the telephone with the other.

He picked up the receiver. 'Ray – hi . . . yeah, sorry it's so late,
but we gotta big problem here. I want you to come over right
now, dressed and armed. Bring your shotgun and some rope.
Round up McGaughey and Razor. And make it fast.'

He put down the phone, turned off the burglar alarms and
then walked round to stand next to Laura. No one spoke, no one
moved for eight minutes until, with a crash of the front door, the
big prairie-hard Ray Baldridge came clumping in accompanied
by the veteran herd manager Skip McGaughey and the ranch
hand and groom Razor Macey.

'Up here, guys!' yelled Bill. The three people in the frozen
tableau heard the men climb the stairs and walk along to the light
in the office. Ray came in first, holding a shotgun and a lariat.
McGaughey had a six-shooter in his belt, as did Macey.

'Hey, little brother, you got a visitor?'

'He's a bit more than that. This is the bastard who killed Jack,
sunk the *Jefferson* and did God knows what else. Make him secure,
willya? Treat him like a steer . . .'

The very mention of Bill and Ray's brother, Captain Jack
Baldridge, who had been Group Operations Officer in the lost
US aircraft carrier four years previously, galvanized the Kansan
cowboys.

Ray eased Laura away, took Ben by the back of the neck,
kicked his feet from under him, and dropped expertly down on
one knee, his other shin rammed into the Iraqi's throat as he lay

prostrate. He wrapped the rope tight around his captive's wrists, behind the man's back, looped it round and through, and did the same to Ben's ankles. Houdini himself would have been there for life. 'He ain't goin' nowheres,' said Ray. 'You want me to put a hot branding iron to him?'

'Not yet,' said Bill. 'Depends a lot on how he behaves. Can you put him in that chair? I wanna talk to him.'

They manhandled Ben upward and sat him down, facing Bill. Laura stayed behind the chair, as if trying to avoid gazing upon the man she had once loved.

'What do you want, Ben Adnam?' said Bill. 'What the hell do you want?'

Ben smiled. 'I want you to get me in front of the President's highest national-security officer. I have much to say, and much to sell.'

'Are you kidding?' replied Bill. 'They'll put you in front of a firing squad in about 20 minutes. After the crimes you've committed – not just against America, but against humanity.'

'Maybe they will. But perhaps not. Do you know of anyone else who knows as much as I do – and who has also deliberately placed himself in your power?'

Bill Baldridge looked pensive. 'No, offhand I guess I don't.' After a moment's thought he picked up the telephone again and dialed the number of the main switchboard in the White House. It was a little after 1am on the morning of Friday, April 14.

Everyone in the room heard Bill's terse request. 'Hello, this is Lieutenant-Commander Bill Baldridge in Kansas. Please connect me right now to the President's National Security Advisor, wherever he is. Yes, correct. Admiral Morgan. Admiral Arnold Morgan.'

None of them noted the narrow smile on the face of Commander Adnam as the White House operator prepared to awaken the admiral for the second time this night.

CHAPTER TWELVE

E VERY SEAT WAS occupied in the sleek US Air Force C20
Gulfstream 4 as it raced at 450 knots above southern Illinois
toward the Missouri border. Admiral Arnold Morgan was next
to the Deputy Director of Central Intelligence, Stephen Hart.
Opposite them sat Frank Reidel, the Associate Director of Central
Intelligence in charge of military support, the linkman between
Langley and the US Joint Command.

Next to Reidel was the Secret Service agent who bore the
communications system tuned directly to the Oval Office. Behind
them were two other armed Secret Service agents, plus an armed
US Marines staff sergeant with his corporal. The Gulfstream
seated eight only.

They flew to the north of St Louis and picked up the
meandering Missouri river as it swerved through Jefferson City.
At 1003, two hours out of Andrews Air Base, Maryland, they
cleared the eastern border of the State of Kansas, flying 30,000
feet above the old cavalry outpost of Fort Scott.

Twenty minutes later they began their descent, sliding swiftly
down out of gray clouds which scattered cold, spring showers
over the eerie rolling contours of the Flint Hills, the last remaining
expanse of tall-grass prairie in the United States. Arnold Morgan
was tired. He'd been awake half the night, ordering hit squads,
canceling hit squads, talking to Iain and to Bill, even to Laura,
insuring that the Iraqi prisoner was tightly bound and under the
heavy guard of three armed Kansan cowboys, supervised by a
former lieutenant commander in his own Intelligence staff.

Now he stared out of the window on the starboard side of the
aircraft, gazing at the geographic phenomenon below, six million
acres of bluestem grass, rising and falling in jagged, uneven granite
hills, none of them more than 300 feet high, right across the
otherwise clean flat billiard table of central Kansas – north–south,

from the Nebraska border 200 miles to the State of Oklahoma. A good steer gains two pounds a day grazing down there. That bluestem is the finest nutritional pasture for raising beef cattle on earth.

The Gulfstream continued to lose height until it shrieked down across Butler County and headed into McConnell Air Force Base on the outskirts of Wichita. It touched down on the runway at 1038. The door was opened immediately and all eight of the men from Washington were escorted directly to an awaiting Army helicopter, a howling Sikorsky Black Hawk, its rotors already running.

The transfer took less than four minutes. Seatbelts were tightened, the door was slammed shut and the helo clattered into the sky, flying to the south of the city before altering course to the northwest, low over the Great Plains for more than 100 miles, straight toward the southern border of Pawnee County. The pilot knew the way – he'd made the journey several times before; done it twice on Bill and Laura's wedding day.

Bill Baldridge spotted the Black Hawk when it was still more than ten miles out. He could see it as a faint dot low on the horizon, drawing ever nearer, moving over the prairie at 250mph – a mile every 15 seconds. Soon he could hear the steady thump-thump-thump of the rotors, and he could see the downward blast of air flatten the pasture as Arnold Morgan came barreling out of the sky to meet the terrorist he had loathed for so long.

Bill signaled the Black Hawk in to land on the lawn to the west of the main house, 50 yards from the barn in which Ben Adnam was still securely tied like a steer in the Flint Hills Rodeo. He had been there for nine hours now, guarded by two of Bill's ranch hands at all times. He'd slept on a pile of straw with a couple of horse blankets to keep out the cold. And during the night Ray Baldridge had stopped by specifically to let him know that for what he'd done to his brother Jack Ben'd be 'goddamned lucky to survive the night. Someone's gonna kill you, that's for sure. Might be my mommy, might be Bill. Might be any of the guys around here. Just don't count any on waking up, hear me?'

With that Ray had gone off to bed. He felt better for having got it off his chest, and felt he had achieved his objective – frightening Ben Adnam half to death. But that he had not in fact done. The Iraqi commander knew he was safe until this Morgan character arrived, but after that – well, it would be a journey into the unknown. Adnam knew that if the top National Security man in the United States wanted him dead, then dead he would quickly be. But at least he knew he was safe, relatively, until midmorning.

He too heard the US Army Black Hawk come shuddering into the B/B ranch. After it had landed there came the shouts of the Americans out beyond the heavy wooden walls of the horse barn. Then he heard the sound of the rotors die away, and almost instantly there was a shaft of light through the small barn door set into the huge dark-red double doors which were opened only for tractors.

By now both of Ben's 'jailers' were on their feet – the big rangy Skip McGaughey, his gun leveled at the Iraqi's head, and young Razor Macey, toying with his six-shooter. First man through the door was Bill Baldridge, wearing a sheepskin ranch coat, stetson and high boots with spurs. Right behind him came a smaller, thickset man wearing an expensive dark-blue overcoat and a wide-brimmed dark-brown trilby hat. Ben noticed his piercing blue eyes immediately – the craggy face, the scowling expression. *That's Morgan*, he thought. *That's the National Security Chief. That's the man I'm looking for.*

Almost before the CIA chiefs and the secret-servicemen were in the door, Adnam's assessment was confirmed.

'Is that the sonofabitch over there, Bill?'

'Yup, the one trussed up like a steer. The other two are my trusted herd manager, Skip McGaughey, and my groom, Razor Macey.'

Admiral Morgan walked over to them immediately. 'Good to see you, men. Been keeping an eye on this bastard, have you?'

'Yes, sir. Most of the night.'

'Did he behave himself?'

'Yes, sir. Never gave no trouble.'

'Guess that makes a fucking change,' growled Morgan. 'If he steps outta line, shoot the sonofabitch right between the eyes, right?'

'Yes, sir.'

By now the marine staff sergeant was inside the door, blocking it completely. His corporal was patrolling outside. The secret-servicemen formed a posse at the end of the line of open horse stalls. Adnam was in the third one along, next to Bill's beloved Irish-bred bay hunter Freddie. The two CIA men flanked Admiral Morgan as he made his way across the wide stone walkway towards the man who had sunk the *Thomas Jefferson*, blown both Concorde and Starstriker out of the sky and obliterated *Air Force Three*, along with the Vice-President of the United States and his staff.

Arnold Morgan gazed down at the arch-terrorist, still tied by the ankles and with his wrists tethered behind his back.

'You've caused us a lot of trouble,' Morgan said carefully. 'Too much for any one man to have caused. And I've waited a long time to meet you. Now gimme your correct name, rank and country.'

'I'm Commander Benjamin Adnam, sir. Islamic Republic of Iraq.'

'Is that an Iraqi Navy rank?'

'No, sir.'

'What is it, then?'

'Israeli, sir.'

'Did you serve in the Israeli Navy?'

'Yes, sir.'

'Were you an Iraqi spy working undercover?'

'Yes, sir.'

'And now?'

'Iraq, sir. I returned to work in Iraq.'

'Iraqi Navy?'

'No, sir. Intelligence.'

'Commander Adnam, did you sink the *Thomas Jefferson?*'

'Yes, sir.'

'Did you also command a stolen Royal Navy submarine in the North Atlantic earlier this year?'

'Yes, sir.'

'And did you cause that submarine to fire surface-to-air missiles which brought down three civilian aircraft?'

'Yes, sir.'

'And was that submarine operating under the command of the Islamic Republic of Iraq?'

'Yes, sir.'

'Then might I ask what the hell you are doing in the one country which wants you dead more than all the other countries in the world put together? And why have you made it so easy for us to nail you, right here?'

'I've come here to bargain for my life. I possess unique information which I believe has a value to you. You are correct to notice that I made my trail here relatively easy for you – but not so easy that you got here first. And I expect Mr Baldridge will confirm I have shown no sign of a serious threat to anyone. I am here to meet *you*, sir. Because you, of all people, will realize I am of more value to the United States of America if I'm breathing than if I'm not.'

'And what gives you the idea I couldn't get any information I might need out of you for nothing?'

'You probably could get much of it from me – but not all of it. Not without my conscious, willing cooperation. And perhaps we should talk about that. I would, however, ask you to remember that I have always been prepared to die for my country and my beliefs, sir. That is the one thing that has never changed. You'll either employ me or I'll quite happily die with my secrets.'

'I guess we'll see about that . . . Bill, can you take me to the house for a cup of coffee before I get angry with this fucking towelhead?'

'Sure can, Admiral. How'd you like it?'

'Black, asshole . . . I mean, former asshole. With buckshot.' Both men laughed, and Bill put an arm around the wide shoulders of the great man as they headed for the house, accompanied by two secret-servicemen.

Bill called back, 'I'll send coffee out for everyone in a minute. Guard that bastard – he's dangerous.'

Admiral Morgan walked with Bill, silent for a moment. Here, trussed up in the barn, was the man he had hunted for years. The fact was that Morgan could have him taken out right now – and that was what his instinct told him to do. At least most of it did. But Arnold Morgan was a longtime Intelligence officer, and Intelligence officers do not take out foreign terrorists without getting something in return. Ben Adnam was not only a foreign terrorist but an Iraqi Intelligence officer. His knowledge ought not to be wasted. Which meant that, for now, Ben himself could not be wasted either.

Inside the house, Bill led the way to the big log fire in the hall and suggested the two agents might like to go into the kitchen, where his wife Laura was with the housekeeper, Betty-Ann Jones. But at that moment Laura came into the hall, dressed in snappy Western garb – light-brown suede tailored trousers, white shirt and a dark-green Indian patterned waistcoat. She walked straight over to the admiral and kissed him on the cheek. 'Arnold,' she said. 'How lovely to see you. Will you stay for a couple of days?'

The admiral slipped his arm around her waist. 'Wouldn't you rather I got rid of the world's most dangerous man for you?' he said. 'Can't stay this trip. We're outta here by five at the latest. Will you invite me again?'

'Of course. Did Bill tell you how we caught the Iraqi?'

'Not yet. I'm ready, though.'

The former submarine commander then recounted the adventure that had taken place the previous evening, culminating with the pivotal moment when Laura had rammed her grandfather's Purdey into the back of Adnam's head, with a view to blowing it off. 'She told him she expected to get the Congressional Medal of Honor for marksmanship,' said Bill with a chuckle.

'Damn' right, she would,' said the admiral. 'And any other award she wanted. What happened then – your boys just moved in and made him secure?'

'That's it. Tied him up good and tight. And kept him under guard till you guys showed up. What now? You taking him back?'

'Yup. I wanna have another little talk to him in a minute. He seems ready to tell us anything we want to know right now.'

'That's how I'm reading it, Arnold. He told me last night he wanted a deal, and for his part he would disclose anything we wanted.'

'And in return for that he wants his life?'

'Guess so. But I'm getting the feeling he's been betrayed by Iraq. Otherwise he woulda gone straight home to Baghdad and kept his head down. Also, I have to say that, before Laura made her dramatic entry with the Purdey, Adnam had essentially turned over his weapon. He had placed his knife on the chair. He was unarmed. He was actually volunteering.'

'Hmm. Bill, let's go through this thing the way we used to, back in Fort Meade. Let's think it through, item by item. I'm going to write down a list of the certain facts.' The admiral pulled out his little notebook and pen, and wrote down his prime thoughts thus:

1. Adnam, despite knowing that almost any American would kill him as soon as look at him, has given himself up, laying an obvious trail to the B–Bar–B in the process.

2. He does not appear particularly repentant.

3. He perhaps does not greatly value his life.

4. He must know a great deal about the Middle East – not all of which can be obtained without his conscious cooperation.

5. The history, and the fine details, will be of questionable value. Agents tend to be told only what they need to know. But this one is special: he will know more than most, and his real value is likely to lie in the future.

6. He has outwitted me, Arnold Morgan, every inch of the way. Christ! I've just fucking well reported to him! Can I now use him? Is that what he is really offering?

7. Or is this some other tortuous plan, intended somehow to fuck up my life.

8. Might this sonofabitch be on a suicide mission to kill the President's National Security Advisor? (NB: Keep said sonofabitch manacled and disarmed for now.)

'That, Bill, is how I see this equation at the moment. But one thing is immediately interesting: do you think he might tell us where to find that goddamned submarine?'

'Dunno. But I think he might. *If*, as I suspect, the Iraqis have dumped him.'

Betty-Ann brought in the coffee and the two former US Navy colleagues sat companionably in big leather armchairs that had Kanza Indian blankets thrown over them.

'Seems real strange, after all these years, to think Ben Adnam's out there in that barn, eh?' Admiral Morgan was thoughtful. He sipped the hot coffee and then he asked Bill: 'Do you think we could, under any circumstances, use this bastard for our own purposes?'

'I think it'd be a political impossibility. Christ, if the public ever found out precisely who he was, and even a half of what he'd done, we could end up with the biggest lynch mob of modern times.'

'Hmm. I wonder what he knows? I wonder if he could put a finger on any of that germ-warfare activity that's been going on in Iraq? What about their agents in this country and in the UK?'

'I'd guess he knows more than they think. Whether he tells us may depend on how badly they've pissed him off. My own view, Arnold, is that his great value to us will be to give us a first-class psychological profile of the Iraqi mindset.'

'I agree. I'm certain they've pissed him off real badly, otherwise he couldn't possibly have contemplated coming here. Not even to see your beautiful wife – which possibility has been scaring the life out of me these past two or three days.'

Bill grinned. 'Bet he never thought she'd nail him with the Earl of Jedburgh's pheasant gun.' He smiled.

'No. I wouldn't think that was any part of his plan. But the question is, do we think Adnam is just too risky, too treacherous, too big a liar even to consider doing business with? I must say, Bill, my immediate instinct is to kill him now. Although I could be persuaded to wring him out first before eliminating him. But, but, but, *but* I wonder whether the bastard isn't too valuable for that.'

'Admiral, comfortable and pleasant though this is, let's get back out there and you have another go at him. Let's ask him about the submarine – the part that was worrying my father-in-law. That and the fishing boat.'

'OK, old pal. Let's go and see how forthcoming he is.'

It was raining lightly now and both men put on their hats for the short walk to the horse barn. Inside, they found the two CIA chiefs working on a detailed report of the journey and the preliminary interrogation which had already taken place. Everyone had coffee, and Adnam was still sitting on a bale of straw, tightly bound. There had been no further conversation since the admiral had left, and no one was untying the Iraqi until Morgan gave the word – which, understandably he was not inclined to do.

But now he moved in very quickly. 'Commander Adnam, there is no submarine in the world equipped to fire short-range surface-to-air missiles fast and accurately enough to bring down a supersonic aircraft. How and where did you convert HMS *Unseen* to possess this capability?'

'We did it at sea, out in the Atlantic near the equator in the Doldrums.'

'What kind of missile system?'

'Russian in origin. But we didn't get it directly from them.'

'Exactly what missile system, and who did you get it from?'

'That information is for sale only, sir. Not for money, you understand. For my life.'

'How did you know it would work? Did you test it?'

'Yes, sir.'

'Where?'

'Down in the Marshes in the south of my country, east of Qal'at Sālih.'

'How?'

'We test fired four down there. Then one more in the Gulf on a live aircraft. Pilotless, of course.'

'Of course. Perish the thought you should kill someone.' Admiral Morgan was trying unsuccessfully to avoid the sardonic. 'Did you hit it?'

'The test was successful, sir.'

'How did you make such a huge alteration to a submarine out in the ocean?'

'It was not huge, sir. We simply modified the regular radar in the boat to locate the target at long range. We then had ample information for us to fire the missiles into a steady oncoming target at a known cruising height. The actual launcher was bolted onto the deck, behind the fin.' Adnam spoke his apparent secrets with the finesse of a man who knew his captors were going to find out anyway. And he added, as an apparent statement of good faith, 'I could show you how to achieve something similar any time, should you decide to work with me.'

'Thank you, Commander.' But the admiral turned to Bill and, speaking as if there were no one else in the barn, exclaimed, 'Can you believe this crap? I'm just getting a high-tech lesson in submarine weapons conversions from a fucking Marsh Arab – Jesus Christ.'

Everyone laughed, even Adnam. 'Sir, I'm not from the Marshes. My home is further up the Tigris on the edge of the desert.'

'Oh, Jesus, yes. So it is. The situation just fucking worsened . . . I'm being told how to put an advanced weapon onto an American nuclear boat by a fucking Bedouin.'

Then he turned back to the Iraqi. 'Right,' he muttered. 'Now listen, I know you're probably some fucking von Braun of the desert, but I wanna dead straight answer, right here. Did you really lower that huge missile launcher over the side of a supply ship on a crane and manhandle it into position, seal it and sail for the North Atlantic?'

'Yes, sir. Yes, we did. In less than two days.'

'Jesus Christ. Whose idea was it?'

'Mine, sir.'

'How did you come up with such an invention?'

'It was not an invention, sir. The Israelis came up with it several years ago. And they had such a system made and tested. I merely stole a copy of the plans back in 1999, and adapted their ideas on a much grander scale.'

'Was that HMS *Aeneas*?' asked the Admiral, displaying as usual his encyclopedic memory for ships and previous conversations.

'Yes, sir. Yes, it was.'

'Hmm. And then what? You just set off for the Atlantic and sat there on 30 West awaiting your prey? And how did you get away to Scotland?'

'Again, sir, that information is only for sale. Also, I have no intention of informing you of anything which might incriminate me with another country.'

'In your shoes, pal, I'd dispense with the formalities and start trying to make a few allies. Before I agree to anything I'm gonna need a lot of information. Give this bastard some coffee, someone, while I confer with my former employee.'

The admiral and Bill walked out of the barn together, leaving everyone else inside except the marine corporal on guard outside the door.

'OK,' said Morgan to his former lieutenant-commander, 'he's telling the truth so far, right? But I really want to know more about how Iraq got that Kilo in 2002, and how they got that Upholder out of Plymouth. Christ, to the best of my knowledge no one has ever stolen a submarine before. At least not from a major naval power. And this man has stolen *two*!'

'Well,' Baldridge responded, 'he said he wouldn't tell us anything that would incriminate him outside the States. I suppose we can't blame him for that. I think we should try him on the technical problems of driving the submarine, training the men and, above all, what the Iraqis now plan – and where the hell they're taking *Unseen* right now.'

'I'll go for him on the theft, but he'll duck that, I'd guess. The real issue for me is, who's driving it now and where the hell is it?'

They walked back inside the barn. Arnold Morgan returned immediately to the fray. 'You wanna tell me how you got the submarine out of Plymouth?'

'I drove it, sir.'

'How many crew did you have?'

'Forty, sir.'

'All Iraqi?'

'Yes, sir.'

'Who trained them to drive a British Upholder-Class diesel–electric?'

'I did, sir.'

'Where?'

'Iraq, sir.'

'How?'

'I used a full-scale model.'

'Who built it?'

'We did, sir?'

'Based on what?'

'Plans, sir. Plans of the Upholder-Class.'

'Where did they come from?'

'I presume England, sir. I was never told.'

'What do you mean, you were never told? How did you know they were genuine?'

'Because I've driven an Upholder-Class boat, in Scotland, and so I knew the plans were what I'd been told they were.'

'What about all the Brazilians on board? How did you get rid of them?'

'I won't incriminate myself to another nation, sir.'

'How about the Royal Navy officers? What happened to them? Are they still alive?'

'I won't incriminate myself . . .'

'Yeah, I know,' interrupted the admiral. 'How did you get into the exercise area, and out again, without being discovered for 36 hours?'

'I found *Unseen*'s orders in her CO's office, and I just kept sending in the right signals at the right time.'

'*Jesus H. Christ!* This is unbelievable. How far from the area were you when you decided to miss the diving signal?'

'About three hundred miles.'

'And from there you just headed south, around South Africa and back to the Arabian Gulf?'

'No, sir.'

'Whadya mean, "no, sir"? Did you take *Unseen* into the Gulf of Iran?'

'No, sir. The supply ship serviced us at sea in the Atlantic. I stayed with the submarine while the missile system was fitted.'

'Very well . . .'

The admiral then conferred for the first time with Stephen Hart and Frank Reidel, discussing briefly the formalities of the arrest. Morgan suggested that, since Adnam was plainly a sea-going military enemy of the United States, he should be taken into custody under the direct auspices of the US Navy. The CIA would then be entrusted to undertake the debriefing, working in conjunction with the US Joint Command.

Reidel thus became a key man in the operation, working as he did as the senior liaison man between the CIA and the Pentagon. All three men agreed that the matter ought properly to be kept under the tightest imaginable secrecy rules throughout. The admiral thought the interrogation should take place at CIA Headquarters in Langley, Virginia, and that Adnam should thus be held during this time under the normal procedures governing the arrest of a designated 'Enemy of the United States.' As such, he would be held more securely than anyone had ever been held before. Guards from the US Marines would supervise his captivity, night and day, but would never be told who they were guarding. Accommodation would be organized by the CIA.

The admiral then returned to Commander Adnam and addressed him formally. 'Commander, you are under the arrest of the Government of the United States of America. Your crimes against this nation and against humanity are of such a dimension as to deny you any rights whatsoever, under any treaty ever enacted by the member nations of the United Nations. You will be held on an indefinite basis until it is decided whether you should stand trial or simply be made to disappear.

'At this stage we shall not be working with any other nation, but you may assume that Her Majesty's Government in London will be informed in due course that we are presently holding the Iraqi terrorist who destroyed Concorde Flight 001 in February. Do you understand me?'

'Yes, sir.'

'OK. Untie his hands and someone feed the fucker. Bread and coffee – don't want him to get too comfortable. Bill, I'm gonna beg Laura for a roast-beef sandwich and then I'm gonna sit in the kitchen and annoy her for a half-hour. Maybe we can send down to the local town for lunch for these guys.'

Bill Baldridge and Arnold Morgan returned to the house, both men heading for the kitchen where the dark-haired daughter of Admiral Sir Iain MacLean was supervising the production of sandwiches. 'Just us, Laura,' said the admiral. 'The rest of the crew are eating out – eating out in the barn, that is. I don't expect you to feed half of Washington. In my view you've already done quite enough.'

'Well, Admiral, that's very kind of you. Now why don't you and Bill go and sit by the fire in the hall? I'll bring lunch in, and perhaps I might join you for a while.'

'That's the only reason I came out here,' said the admiral. 'I just wanted to have lunch with you. These other ruffians can take care of the business.'

Laura laughed. 'Will I assume Benjamin will not be joining us?'

'That'd be safe.' Arnold Morgan chuckled. 'By the way, have you called your father?'

'Yes. I did that – right after Ray and Skip tied Ben up and carried him over to the barn for the night. It was past seven in the morning in Scotland, so it wasn't too bad.'

'What did Iain say?'

'Well, he was just so relieved we were both safe – but he laughed like hell when I told him I'd captured Ben with Grandpa's shotgun, and he did ask me to pass on his best regards to you and Kathy.'

'But not to Ben?'

'Certainly not to Ben,' she said, laughing.

'Do you realize, Laura, your father and I were calling the shots on this one almost a year ago? We both somehow sensed that, if *Unseen* had been stolen, there was only one person who could have done it – just one person in all of this world who would be that audacious, that damned clever. And right now he's out in your barn.'

'What will happen to him?'

'Now that's a question. Men like him, and there aren't many – I really mean spies like him, even without his operational brilliance – they rarely get executed. They just know too much, they're too useful alive.'

'But surely a man who has committed such shocking crimes, brought that much grief to so many families – surely he must be executed?'

'Not necessarily. What would execution achieve? Although Bill does not quite agree with me . . . yet.' And he smiled at the proprietor of the B/B.

'He's just too darned notorious, Arnold. There'd be a public outcry if it were found you'd kept him alive.'

The admiral nodded, and was silent for a moment. He took a sportsman-sized bite out of his beef sandwich. Then he stirred his coffee and had a couple of swigs. When he spoke it was to Laura. 'What would *you* say to Ben if he told you he would finger Saddam Hussein's old germ-warfare plants – the ones which could wipe out half the Middle East, or Europe, or the US? If you would spare his life? What *would* you say? I'm not saying he could – I'm just making the point. If we execute him we get nothing. If we wring him out, we might get a whole bunch of Christmas presents. What would you decide?'

'I'd spare him. And take his damned knowledge and use him as long as he was useful. Not a day longer.'

'And that, my dear, is why agents like him rarely get executed.'

'There *are* no other agents like him,' said Bill. 'He's completely different. He's a one-man demolition squad. And he's brought endless desolation to endless families.'

'But there's one important thing.'

'What?'

'Hardly anyone knows who he is, or what he has done. The public don't even know the *Jefferson* was hit by a foreign terrorist. We've never admitted it. Neither do they know there was a lunatic sitting in the middle of the Atlantic knocking down passenger aircraft. Certainly not that it was the same lunatic. In the collective minds of 250 million Americans, including the press and all but a few of the military, no one knows the bastard even exists.'

'True,' said Bill Baldridge. 'It just seems such a gigantic secret to keep under wraps. And if he somehow escaped and got out from under our control and did something dreadful – like blow up the Pentagon or something – then it would all come out: that this Administration had been working under cover with the most evil terrorist in the history of the world, and now look what'd happened. You'd end up more reviled than Ben.'

'That is indeed a risk. But I'd cope with my disgrace in the private knowledge that I had probably saved thousands of lives, and that I had acted in accordance with my beliefs and my conscience.'

'You're a big man, Arnold Morgan,' said Laura. 'Just don't let him get out of your control.'

'Not I,' said the admiral. 'And when I'm done with him, I'll probably still have him eliminated.'

'That's my man,' said Bill. 'And that's the way to look at it. Ben Adnam deserves nothing. Certainly not fairness. Ask the friends of Martin Beckman.'

'The biggest problem with Ben,' said the admiral, 'is his unbelievable cleverness. When you think about it, he's been a couple of jumps ahead of everyone in all his projects – ahead of Israel, ahead of me, I suspect ahead of the Iraqis and certainly ahead of the US Navy and the Royal Navy. And, even now, of the entire US Government. Remember, he came here determined to get in front of people in high office to plead for his life, and he's done it. First time. He was a couple of jumps in front of the immigration authorities, a couple of jumps ahead of the CIA guys, and certainly a couple of jumps ahead of me, again.'

'He wasn't always far in front of me,' said Bill quietly, thinking of his days in active service.

'No, he wasn't. But he was far enough. You did identify him, and basically caught him – or, at least, you caught his ship, and then only with his help. You and Laura's dad, between you . . . The problem is, is he just too clever and too devious for any of us to work with?'

'Probably,' said Bill. 'But you'll have to try to wring him out. And then decide, I guess, what further use he could be.'

'That's about it,' said the admiral. 'And now I think we have to get him out of here.' He rose from the armchair and put on his coat. He and Bill headed for the door, and 20 minutes later the Black Hawk was revving up and ready to go. All eight men were strapped in, Ben Adnam securely bound on the floor between the marine staff sergeant and his corporal.

Bill and Laura watched them rise up above the ranch and then hover over the prairie, and the sun came out briefly as the Army helicopter set a course southeast, clattering away toward Wichita, where the Gulfstream 4 waited. About a dozen people in all of the world knew that the United States was in control of the arch terrorist who had caused havoc above the North Atlantic.

0930 Monday, April 17. The Memorial Garden, CIA Headquarters, Langley, Virginia.
Admiral Morgan, Stephen Hart and Frank Reidel were seated together on the wrought iron garden bench in front of the pond. It was one of the first warm spring mornings, the third day of the relentless grilling of Ben Adnam by the CIA's professional interrogators, some of whom had been flown in specially from the Middle East to test and retest the validity of the Iraqi Intelligence officer. Thus far he had neither cracked nor, so far as they could tell, lied to them in any way. But on the previous evening, tired and battered by the endless questioning, the Commander had said something to Morgan which he plainly believed was a critical card.

'Tomorrow, Admiral, I will give you something which will show you once and for all that I am sincere in my desire to switch my allegiance to your country. I have told you my price is my life, but tomorrow I will write something out for you. Then you can decide for yourself my usefulness to you.'

The second night of interrogation had ended at 0230, long after Admiral Morgan had left. Commander Adnam was due to reappear at 1015. Morgan and the two CIA Chiefs had agreed to meet here beforehand, in this outdoor cradle of US patriotism and loyalty, to discuss tactics.

It was peaceful in the garden. The constant cascade of the falling water broke the silence and muffled their words. Admiral

Morgan was reflective as he stared at the fieldstone wall around the pond. It was inlaid with an almost obscured bronze plaque on which were inscribed the words: 'In remembrance of those whose unheralded efforts served a grateful nation.' Whenever he read them, a chill went through Arnold Morgan and he thought again of the terrible dangers unknown US agents had risked over the years. And he wished, irrationally, that he could somehow meet them again right here and rise to his feet and shake the hand of every last one of them. They were his kind of people. Hard, unsung heroes, concerned with the well-being of their country, never for personal glory.

The three men chatted for 20 minutes, trying to decide what course of action to take – whether to eliminate the mass murderer in their midst and say nothing (thus avoiding the awkward problems of having to alert the general public to the known danger they had been dealing with since 2002 and risking exposure as complete incompetents) or to come clean and admit everything and put the terrorist on trial for crimes which carried a compulsory death penalty. Finally, there was the enticing third option: to say nothing, but to utilize Adnam and carry out a few harrowing strikes against the fundamentalist Islamic regimes of the Middle East.

All three options had support. But it was the third which intrigued them most.

At 1005 they returned to the main building and made their way up to the interrogation room. They all picked up coffee on the way, and were sitting down when Commander Adnam was escorted in by four marine guards. He was handcuffed but free to walk in the direction the guards indicated.

Once seated, the bracelets were removed while he placed his hands on the table in front of him, where there were pens and writing pads. Immediately he began to write neatly at the top of one of the yellow pages. His message was short. He requested it be torn out and handed to Admiral Morgan.

'201200APR061855S5220E. Refueling.'

Morgan looked up sharply and snapped, '*Unseen*?'

'Yes, sir.'

'Indian Ocean, right? Whereabouts?'

'Two hundred miles due east of Madagascar.'

'No bullshit?'

'No, sir. This is another way to help convince you of my worth.'

Admiral Morgan left the room and charged straight into the office of the Deputy Director. He grabbed the secure line and told the switchboard, 'Get me Admiral Mulligan right now, either in the Pentagon or wherever he may be.'

It took just five minutes to locate the Chief of Naval Operations, who at the time was on board the cruiser *Arkansas* in the Navy Yards at Norfolk, Virginia.

The conversation was brief.

'You secure, Joe?'

'No.'

'Go to SUBLANT right now and call me secure at Stephen Hart's office, Langley.'

There were very few people these days who handed out instructions to Admiral Mulligan. None who spoke to him quite like that. But he and Morgan were old friends, and Joe Mulligan knew that was just Arnold's way. He also knew, when he heard it, the edge of gravity in the voice of the National Security Advisor.

Mulligan left *Arkansas* immediately and a waiting Navy staff car took him on the short drive to the headquarters of SUBLANT. Reconnected with Arnold Morgan, he had to stay right on top of his game to keep up with the President's right-hand man, who, he knew, was now deep into the interrogation of Commander Adnam.

'Joe. I'm not saying we've cracked him. But he's just come up with something – the position of HMS *Unseen* at midday this Thursday. She's gonna be in the Indian Ocean, which seems about right given she probably left the North Atlantic at the end of February. He has her position as 18.55 South, 52.20 East. He says it's 200 miles due east of Madagascar. I'm just looking at a map now. It's 1500 miles from Diego Garcia. Can we make it? 1200, Thursday, April 20. Yeah . . . yeah. OK, Joe, I'll leave it with you. Let's go. I'd prefer them alive, but I'll take 'em dead if necessary.'

Crash! The phone went down like a sledgehammer as Morgan marched resolutely back to the room where Ben Adnam was being systematically wrung out. Or, at least, a substantial group of people were trying to wring him out, the trouble being that

Ben Adnam gave the impression of telling nothing which he did not want to tell.

Mulligan conferred quickly with COMSUBPAC, Vice-Admiral Alan Cattee in Pearl Harbor, formally requesting that USS *Columbia* be released to Black Ops Control. They opened up a conference line to the battle group which operated around the 100,000-ton Nimitz-Class carrier *Ronald Reagan*, which was stationed off Diego Garcia for a few more hours. Cattee did the talking on the secure line, and was patched through to Admiral Art Barry, who commanded the group.

The former Captain of the *Arkansas* checked his watch, which said almost eight o'clock in the evening, nine hours in front of Washington. He confirmed *Columbia*'s position and said, 'She's ready to go anywhere. To make that location by midday on Thursday she'll need to clear DG by midnight. Leave it with me.'

Commander Mike Krause and his crew had already had a long day testing a new sonar fitting out in the deep water south of the US Naval Base. He and his XO, Lt-Commander Jerry Curran, had dined together on board, but some of the crew were ashore – on-base but ashore.

The US Navy is trained to move quickly. The entire crew was located and back on board the submarine inside two hours. At 2345 Commander Krause signaled the engineers to answer bells. Up on the casing, still warm in the hot tropical night, the deck crew prepared to cast her off. The Officer of the Deck ordered, 'Let go all lines. Pull off . . .'

The tugs began to haul the jet-black 7000-ton Los Angeles-Class nuclear boat away from her jetty.

'Engines backing two-thirds . . . The ship is underway. Ahead one-third . . .' The commands were succinct as always, spoken calmly from the bridge by Krause, the tall New Englander from Vermont, who had previously served as the Executive Officer in *Columbia*.

And now the great bulk of the nuclear boat moved forward down the channel, running fair at 12 knots, out toward the open water of the Indian Ocean surrounding the island of Diego Garcia. America's sole operational naval base in this part of the world is situated bang in the middle of absolutely nowhere, 1000 miles south-southwest of the tip of the Indian subcontinent, seven degrees south of the equator, 1600 miles east of the Horn of

Africa. It feels like the hot end of the earth, and the nights are dark and silent. It is not a favorite place of United States Navy personnel.

Commander Krause ordered a course of two-two-five, heading southwest, away from the Chagos Archipelago, a group of towering underwater peaks which rise up from an ocean depth of 16,000 feet between DG and the southern end of the Carlsberg Ridge.

The Navigation Officer, Lt Richard Farrington, who stood on the bridge with the captain, put the total distance to the search area at 1587 miles. *Columbia's* two nuclear-powered turbines, which generated 35,000 horsepower, would have to drive her at a high-speed 27-knot average, 24 hours a day, to give them a chance. That meant well over 600 miles a day, which the commander thought was touch-and-go, even with no stops. Six miles off the island he ordered her deep: 'Make your depth 400 feet. All ahead flank. Steer two-two-five.'

Columbia raced toward the southwest. On the first day her objectives were simple; she wanted to be over the line of 70 degrees longitude by midday and out over the north end of the Mid-Indian Ridge by midnight. On Wednesday it was even simpler: she needed to be across the Nazareth Bank, south of Mauritius, and the 60-degree line of longitude before midnight. That would give her a reasonable ten-hour run to the search area. All of that assumed there would not be the slightest problem in running. The only slow-down factor would be periodic moves to the surface for GPS checks and satellite comms.

And they very nearly made it. A CO_2 scrubber went on the blink after 12 hours, which cost them 90 minutes fixing it and ventilating the boat afterwards. But they were only two hours late at the Nazareth Bank, and they made good speed into the area west of the 53-degree line of longitude, where *Columbia* came to periscope depth. Lt Farrington had them bang on 18.55°S, and at 1139 on Thursday morning, as they slowed down to come to periscope depth, they picked up some odd noises directly ahead. Through the periscope they thought they saw something about ten miles off their port bow – but it was difficult to identify.

The captain himself finally expressed the view that it could have been the fast-disappearing fin of a submarine, beam on. They had caught just a glimpse, and it was gone. POSIDENT

340

was very difficult. It could have been an Upholder-Class submarine, but it had disappeared before he'd properly seen it, just
as *Columbia* had come to periscope depth. The fact was they were
too far away to do much about it except watch, and proceed
cautiously in the same direction using passive sonar for the
moment – active sonar was not an option, for fear of alerting
their target.

But they never saw it again. *Columbia* continued her careful
approach, the sonar revealing nothing. And it was with great
reluctance that the US team had to admit to themselves they had
missed their quarry. The carbon-dioxide scrubber, which allowed
them to breathe, had cost them the mission.

For a further half-hour they moved forward, now steering
course three-one-five, still on passive, still watching the screen for
the slightest indication. But it was to no avail. HMS *Unseen*
possessed all of the most diabolical attributes of stealth and silence
that were common to the Russian Kilo. If she stayed slow, at
around five knots, she was literally impossible to hear. And *Columbia* was hearing nothing. The only information Mike Krause
and his sonar team had was that the submarine was probably an
Upholder, clearly the tiresomely named *Unseen*. She had showed
up right on time at 18.55°S, 52.20°E, and had last been seen
heading north 200 miles off the east coast of Madagascar, destination unknown.

The CO knew if he opened up an active sonar he could
probably pick up his fleeing opponent, but that course of action
had its dangers. HMS *Unseen* was a very quiet, possibly hostile
submarine, and she could be within ten miles of him. He had
been told not to sink anyone without POSIDENT and he
couldn't swear that he had it. And there was the possibility of a
pre-emptive shot against him, at short range and short notice.
Krause was not too happy about any of that.

So it was with some irritation that the CO came back to PD
at 1300 and accessed the satellite to inform SUBLANT he had
traveled flat-out, but had been too late – by about 15 minutes.
Mike Krause felt he needed new rules of engagement before he
could start giving chase on active sonar. Caution was his watch-
word. He was no Boomer Dunning.

By now Admiral Morgan had joined Joe Mulligan on the line to

Alan Cattee in Hawaii, and news of the near-miss spread an aura of gloom, lightened only by the fact that Ben Adnam had certainly provided valid data. Nonetheless Morgan decided to test him again. He went back into the interrogation room and barked at the captured terrorist: 'Sonofabitch wasn't there! The goddamned ocean was deserted! You told me there would be a fueling tanker in the area and my team found nothing. If you're bullshitting me, Adnam, you might be spending your last day on this earth.'

If Adnam's nerve was going, he betrayed nothing. 'Admiral Morgan, I gave you the best information I have. But you know and I know that a refueling point can be changed without much notice. The time and position can be pushed forward or back. My reading of this situation is that the submarine had already fueled and gone by, and is still proceeding north for possibly another 3000 miles, into the deep waters of the Arabian Gulf toward the Strait of Hormuz.'

He was uncertain of the precise destination but he knew the projected route. When he had left *Unseen* the plan was to run north in shallower coastal water toward Oman. He thought it unlikely, he told Morgan, that Iraq would be able to keep the submarine, and that the Iraqis might scuttle it in the Arabian Sea. Alternatively, he believed it possible they might sell it to another Middle Eastern country, possibly Iran, which had superior submarine facilities and which might pay very highly for such a boat.

'It's a pretty goddamned hot property for that, isn't it,' grunted Morgan.

'True, but ships can be altered. And Iran has excellent facilities for working on submarines. I do not, however, have firm information about the Iraqis' intentions. The plan was always that I should leave the ship in the Atlantic. When my mission was complete.'

Either way, Commander Adnam had assessed the newly refueled *Unseen* would make for a point 400 miles east of Mombasa. From there, he said, it would run up the long coast of Somalia, past the Horn of Africa, and across the Gulf of Aden into the national waters of Oman, west of the ops area for the American CVBGs.

Right now Admiral Art Barry's battle group was steaming north under the clear skies of the southern Arabian Basin, way south of the Gulf of Arabia, in depths of more than 17,000 feet.

The giant carrier *Ronald Reagan*, pitching heavily forward through great ocean swells at over 20 knots, was surrounded by a formidable arsenal of naval firepower – two cruisers, three destroyers, four guided-missile frigates, a nuclear submarine, and a big fleet oiler.

SUBPAC sent in a signal to Admiral Barry which arrived at midnight. In broad terms it detailed the possible route of HMS *Unseen* as supplied by her former CO to Admiral Morgan. Admiral Cattee had been advised that *Columbia* was planning to follow that route in the hope of catching the fleeing Iraqi captain. The stolen Royal Navy submarine was expected to make the final 300 miles into the Strait of Hormuz on her battery, and thus could be expected to come shallow to snorkel-charge, maybe twice, when she was between 500 and 350 miles south of the strait, close to the Omani coastline.

Admiral Mulligan suggested that Admiral Barry conduct a search in that area beginning two weeks from today – starting May 10. The ideal solution, so far as he was concerned, was to hunt the submarine to exhaustion, force her to the surface and then board and search, identifying precisely who the crew were and who had controlled her operations. Then sink her. No word was mentioned about her precise activities over the past three months, but Art Barry was quite sure about the tone of the signal. Urgent.

He sent immediately for his destroyer escort squadron commander, COMDESRON, Captain Chuck Freeburg, and his group operations officer, Captain Amos Clark from North Dakota. The three men ordered coffee and pondered the charts. It was no problem to arrive off the Omani coast in plenty of time. The question was whether to take the entire force, or just peel off three destroyers or frigates and send them on alone.

Admiral Barry thought they might need fixed-wing aircraft as well as helos for such a search. This would mean the whole force would move over to the western reaches of the Arabian Gulf. That decision was up to him, and he made it quickly. Everyone would go to help find the Royal Navy submarine which was causing so much angst at headquarters. 'Jesus,' said Captain Freeburg. 'Right here we got the CNO and COMSUBLANT acting on information from Arnold Morgan. That's not big. That's monstrous. Guys, we better find this sucker.'

The trouble was the sheer size of the new search area. Basically the Americans would have to take a northwest–southwest line 500 miles from the strait and conduct their search in a seascape of almost 200,000 square miles. The fixed–wing aircraft would be crucial to the operation, and the carrier itself would need to operate from the center of the area.

Barry made his course adjustments and reduced the speed of his flotilla. Meanwhile, nearly 3000 miles to the southwest, Commander Krause searched in vain for a sign of the vanished *Unseen*. But still there was nothing.

On the morning of May 4 the first two Lockheed ES–3A Viking ASW aircraft roared off the deck of the *Ronald Reagan* and headed in toward the Omani coast, cruising at 300 knots. Both of these Navy ASW aircraft could carry four Mk 5 depth charges and four Mk 46 torpedoes. But today their mission was not to destroy, just to locate.

Like *Columbia* they found nothing, even though they searched for three days in relays. On May 7, however, one of them picked up a radar contact 400 miles to the south of the strait. The Viking came in low and dropped sonobuoys, but by then the contact had long disappeared. To the trained Navy pilot, that meant just one thing – the submarine had been snorkeling and had picked up the radar of the aircraft, as a result of which it had instantly slipped away beneath the surface. But the Viking pilot was definite. He had had it. The clue was strong: the contact was snorkeling 180 miles east of the Omani port of Al–Jawarah.

The Americans knew two things. They had interrupted and hopefully curtailed *Unseen*'s full battery-charge, and from now on it must be continuously harassed. The sub *must* come to periscope depth again soon, probably within 100 miles. Art Barry's pilots were ready. And in due course they got it again – surprisingly, 110 miles to the north – and this time they had a guided–missile frigate within strike range: Captain Bill Simmonds's 4000-ton Oliver Hazard Perry-Class USS *Ingraham*, patrolling 15 miles to the east.

Right now *Unseen* was 90 miles east of the southern tip of the island of Masirah. Again she picked up the Viking's radar and instantly vanished below the surface. It was early in the afternoon. The Americans knew the submarine would be forced back to the surface within hours to charge that battery. And, on his way in,

344

at high speed, was Captain Simmonds, the former CO of the destroyer *O'Bannon,* his face still terribly scarred from flying glass from the same nuclear blast which had destroyed the *Thomas Jefferson.*

He ordered *Ingraham* to her maximum 29 knots, and the sleek, heavily armed frigate, with her crew of 206 at battle stations, came swiftly into the main search area, just to the north of *Unseen's* last known position.

The Americans now had a hot datum. They had two radar fixes from the Vikings. They knew the submarine's speed of advance, 5 knots, and they knew her course, zero-four-zero, which would probably go to zero-zero-zero as she struggled north, now in desperation, toward the Strait of Oman, gateway to the Gulf of Iran. Essentially they had 270 miles to catch her before she turned into more populated narrow waters, patrolled by the Navies of Oman and Iran.

Captain Simmonds had an excellent intelligence assessment from Langley. '*Your target has acoustic characteristics of Brit U-class. Mission: hunt to exhaustion, board, POSIDENT submarine, arrest crew. Shoot only in self-defense.*'

Tactics for the frigate commander were clear. He must use every available asset to flood the now quite limited area with fixed-wing, helicopter and surface-ship radar. That way *Unseen* could not come up without being detected. That way Captain Simmonds could home in for the final moves in this elaborate and lethal game.

At 2205 the rogue submarine was forced to periscope depth by her dying battery. Again she put up her snorkel mast, because by now she was gasping for air – air to flow through the diesel generators while she tried to restore her electric power. *Unseen* was like a drowning whale, and the harpoonists picked her up instantly on the radar screen of their patrolling helicopter. The US pilot began tracking the submarine, reporting her every move back to *Ingraham.*

Simmonds reacted swiftly, ordering his sonar active and sending his own helicopter in to assist. *Unseen* picked up *Ingraham's* electronic beam immediately, but her latest 15-minute battery charge was insufficient. The battery had been just about dead flat a half-hour previously. Time was running out for the stolen submarine.

Commander Alaam ordered *Unseen* deep. But he knew it must

345

be for the last time. They were simply running out of power, and the US frigate was very close. *Unseen* was caught in the classic chess position – Morton's Fork – when the rook checks the king but threatens the queen at the same time. If *Unseen* stayed deep she would run out of power completely. If she came to periscope depth the Americans would force her deep again or blow her mast away. If she came to the surface the Americans would capture them all and execute them. There was no escape, Commander Alaam knew. This was checkmate. And Simmonds knew his opponent was trapped.

Five minutes later, at 2255, *Unseen*'s onboard lights and other systems suddenly wavered. Lt-Commander Rajavi reported the battery was at zero-percent charge – flat, that is. So flat you could barely see it sideways. Shortly before 2300 Commander Alaam ordered *Unseen* to periscope depth to try to snorkel for the last time.

Simmonds, 4200 yards off *Unseen*'s starboard beam, picked her up before her diesels had even started. He ordered his Italian-built OTO Melara 3in gun into action. Sixty seconds later the top of *Unseen*'s ESM mast had been blown off, ending all communications. The American gunners had blasted the periscope, rendering the submarine 'blind,' and they had obliterated the snorkel mast, making further recharging at PD impossible.

Unseen was now, finally, forced to the surface. She came rising out of the dark Indian Ocean, the water cascading down her hull.

But there was no sign of her crew. The US helicopter circled the submarine and, with the aid of flares, photographed her unique missile system from several angles. But the pilot reported no onboard activity.

The frigate commander ordered Mk 46 torpedoes to be loaded into tubes one and two. Then he sent an immediate communication to the Flag, explaining that HMS *Unseen* was stopped on the surface with a flat battery, no communications and no periscope. Engines not running, so probably all hatches shut. He believed boarding might be difficult. The crew had not surrendered, nor even come to the bridge – indeed they appeared to be battened down inside the hull and Simmonds was afraid they might just scuttle her. However, he confirmed he was quite prepared to press on and break into her, using whatever explosive was necessary, then neutralize the crew. He would await further instructions.

Admiral Barry considered this was one for the hierarchy and sent an immediate signal to SUBPAC, who appeared to be running the operation. The three US admirals – Morgan, Mulligan and Cattee – separated by thousands of miles, spoke tersely together on the conference line.

'Look, I'm not sure we need this bullshit,' said Morgan. 'We know exactly who these guys are. We know where they got their ship, and we know what they've been doing. We also know they're Iraqi. We've got their goddamned former CO just up the road calling the shots for us.'

'Right,' Mulligan concurred. 'And boarding is dangerous. These maniacs might just blow the ship apart with a lot of our guys on the casing. I really don't want to run this sort of a risk, because it's not necessary. My opinion is therefore that we should bang it out right now, before the fucking thing breaks loose again.'

'Agreed,' snapped Morgan. 'Go to it, Alan.'

The message which was relayed via the satellite to the *Ronald Reagan* was, as ever, crisp: '*Cancel existing ROE. Sink your contact.*'

The order reached *Ingraham* before 2330. There was still no sign of life from the crew trapped in HMS *Unseen*. Captain Simmonds again sent the helo up for one final look, and then something amazing happened. A figure appeared on the submarine's bridge and began rattling away at the US Navy helicopter with some kind of a machine-gun. It was like writing a suicide note. The pilot wheeled away, heading for the deck of the missile frigate.

Captain Simmonds gave the final orders. 'Ready numbers one and two tubes.'

Seconds later a Mk 46 MOD 5 blasted out of the frigate and set off in a dead straight line towards *Unseen*, which was now wallowing 4050 yards off the frigate's bow. There was a dull explosive thump as the torpedo punched a killer hole into the pressure hull. *Unseen* and her Iranian crew were gone inside a minute, sunk in water almost three miles deep. No one lived for more than 30 seconds. And no one in the Middle East would ever know what had happened to the terrorist missile boat.

On board *Ingraham*, of course, everyone knew what had happened – that in the course of their mission they had sent probably

50 men to their graves. No one dwelt upon the humanity of their actions, only on their sense of duty, that high and mysterious anthem of fighting men. And their world quickly fell into tune with it.

Meanwhile, back on board the *Ronald Reagan*, Captain Barry took some delight in the fact that not all US carriers are prey to marauding diesel–electric submarines. 'We had a bead on her from the moment we stepped up to the plate. That sucker never moved without us knowing,' he told Amos Clark. 'In the end we only needed a couple of good ASW search aircraft and a good frigate and they were dead at first base.'

'Yes, sir. The only time the rules change a bit is when you don't know the fuckers are out there. Sneaky little bastards.'

Art Barry reflected on the incontrovertible fact that all surface group commanders *hate* submarines. Especially non–nuclear boats.

His signal back to SUBPAC confirmed the destruction of HMS *Unseen*, sunk 145 miles off the coast of Oman shortly before midnight on May 9. No wreckage. No survivors. No US casualties.

The photographs wired back to HQ via the carrier arrived in the late afternoon. After a brief study of them, the two Washington–based admirals headed home with copies, a Navy helicopter delivering Admiral Mulligan to the Pentagon and Arnold Morgan to Langley, Virginia, where Ben Adnam was going into his fourth week of debriefing.

He had held up night and day, through question after question, checks and re-checks, until his words were proven either true or false. Thus far he had not faltered, and the CIA were becoming more and more impressed by him – especially Frank Reidel, who had deep experience of field officers, having been head of the Far Eastern Desk for several years.

The photographs of HMS *Unseen*, brought to the interrogation room by Morgan himself, showed of course the incredible sight of the missile-launcher behind the fin. And upon this the admiral felt Adnam's story lived or died. Everything else fell into place, he knew that. But the question remained: That System.

He sat down to grill personally the former pirate CO of *Unseen*. He kept going for four hours.

'How heavy was it? . . . What kind of crane did you use? . . . What was the name of the supply ship? . . . How many people did it take? . . . Who were they? . . . Where does Iraq get ahold of such engineers? . . . Who trained them? . . . Where are the holding bolts situated? . . . What kind of seals did you use? . . . Was it pressurized inside? . . . Where did you test it? . . . How many missiles did you take on the journey? . . . Did you intend to commit more crimes against civil aircraft? . . . Who liaised with you in London on the departure times of Concorde and *Air Force Three*? . . .'

The admiral tried every trick known to the master interrogator – and, as he had once been Director of the National Security Agency, that was a substantial number of tricks. But Adnam held firm. He answered every question. He knew every answer. By 2200 there was no doubt in Admiral Morgan's mind. Iraq had perpetrated the atrocities, under the guidance of their hero, and Iraq must be taught a lesson. The issue would be to find one sufficiently severe.

The admiral called it a day – or a night – just before 2300. He had left his own car at Langley, parked in the Director's private space, like always, and he drove himself to Kathy's house, which was less than four miles away across the American Legion Memorial Bridge into Maryland.

She was waiting up for him, as promised, and poured him a large rum on the rocks as he marched wearily through the door and crashed into a large armchair without even taking his coat off. 'I am beat. Nearly,' he said. 'And I still love you. Even after dealing with more bullshit than a field of longhorns.'

Kathy O'Brien looked wonderful. Her long red hair, just washed, fell about her shoulders. Her slim figure was encased in a dark-blue silk housecoat. She wore no makeup except lipstick, and Arnold Morgan was once more amazed that she should care about him. She handed him his drink and kissed him, and told him to get up and take off his coat, and anything else which might make him happy. She put on some music and told him, in answer to his request, that, no, he could not have a beef sandwich.

'First of all, they're not good for you to eat all the time. And, secondly, in anticipation of your late arrival I have prepared a nice late dinner for us.'

'Dinner! Jesus, it's the middle of the night.'

'Pretend you're Spanish, El Morgano.'

The great man laughed. 'Do you know I've never been there,

but I've always heard those crazy pricks have their dinner at midnight and then stay out drinking wine till about four.'

'That's right. But they don't start work until ten, and they have a two-hour siesta after lunch. They go back to the office from about four in the afternoon to eight.'

'Guess it works for them. You don't hear of many Spanish secret-servicemen though. They're probably eating or sleeping or drinking. Anyway, what do we have?'

'Dining room, Barbarian. I don't serve picnics, as you well know.'

The admiral dragged himself up, reluctant to move, but Kathy had candles lit in the elegant room beyond, which was furnished entirely with antiques. On its walls were four small oil paintings.

'Sit, and pour us some wine,' said Kathy. 'I'll be right there.' Three minutes later she came in with some perfectly cooked veal piccata, thinly sliced in a lemon-based sauce, accompanied by spinach and new potatoes. In the middle of the table was a wooden board containing a small baguette, real French brie (no butter) and big white seedless grapes. The wine was a five-year-old white burgundy from Sancerre.

'Jesus, this was well worth waiting for. Will you marry me?'

'No,' she said cheerfully. 'Not while you're still employed. But I do love you.'

The admiral took a large bite of veal, and a swallow of wine. 'That does it,' he said. 'I'm resigning, soon as I finish this.'

'Yeah, right,' she said. 'Now tell me about your day, and the inquisition of Commander Adnam.'

Despite the clear overtones of massive secrecy involving the entire scenario, it was plainly impossible for it to be kept from the lovely Mrs O'Brien, who had anyway been present when Ben's name had first come up, a year ago, and who, as Arnold's secretary, had taken so many calls regarding the capture of the terrorist that she'd lost count of them. She was as bound by the official secrets code as her future husband, and was equally as trusted.

'Well, he seems to want to stay here.'

'In a casket?'

'No, as an employee. He makes the point, like most major spies who are captured, that he has information which is priceless.'

'And has he?'

'He sure does. But he'd need such a thorough change of identity I'm not sure it'd be possible.'

'Arnold, that could never work. Think of all the families he's destroyed, just in the Navy. Think of all those people in Concorde. How about all the families of Martin's staff? How about the memory of Martin? And Zack Carson, and Jack Baldridge. It would be like hiring the Boston Strangler.'

'I know it would. But this guy has knowledge – *real* knowledge. In my view he may be the most valuable agent anyone has ever caught, including all those faggot Brits who worked for Moscow.'

'You're not supposed to use that word any more. It's politically incorrect,' she remarked with studied seriousness.

'Not when *they* were lifting each other's shirts,' he replied, chewing the veal and drinking the white Burgundy with relish. 'I'm in the past tense. An old, dead faggot is an old, dead faggot.'

Kathy giggled at the admiral's unfailing, irrepressible aim at any subject. Then she said, more seriously, 'I suppose you don't need reminding that you didn't really catch Ben Adnam. He came here unaccompanied, of his own accord, and effectively gave himself up. Plainly he could have killed Bill, and he might have got Laura as well. But she says he never intended to kill anyone. He just wanted to get in front of you. He's probably regretting it right now.'

'The problem for all men like him, Kathy, is they end up having nowhere to turn. No one needs 'em. No one wants 'em. In the end, the only country which does want them is the one they have always worked against. Just because of what they know.' He paused for a moment, then said, 'Men too deep in national intelligence can often become outcasts because, finally, they just have no one to talk to.'

Kathy gazed at him quizzically. 'Are you really planning to use Adnam on a long-term basis?'

'I do not have that authority. The question is, will I recommend something of the sort to the President of the United States?'

'Well. Will you?'

'Kathy, that's the second item to which I don't have an answer.'

'What's the first?'

'Whatever would happen to me without you?'

CHAPTER THIRTEEN

THE FINAL BARRAGE of questions fired at Ben Adnam by the President's National Security Advisor concluded the principal interrogation of the Iraqi terrorist. He was still under the control of the CIA, and under 24-hour guard by the US Marines, but he was now moved to a CIA safe house 15 miles south of Washington, west of the Potomac river.

He posed, obviously, the most enormous problem. The *simple* solution was to get rid of him – quickly, professionally, and illegally. The *best* solution, however, was to use him in every possible way to guide US military dealings in the Middle East. But the *moral* solution was to put him on trial, to answer publicly for his horrendous crimes against the United States and other nations.

Arnold Morgan hated Solution Three.

He hated it because it opened a zillion cans of worms. It would bring in the UK judicial system to deal with the downing of Concorde; it would let the media run riot all over the world; it would cause desperate problems for the airline industry because the media would go on and on about 'Could This Happen Again?' And, worse yet, it would force US Government and military authorities to admit what had happened to the *Thomas Jefferson*. And that would cause the media to go collectively berserk for about six months, possibly threatening even the President's tenure in office.

In the interests of a quiet life, Admiral Morgan knew that Solution One was the simplest answer. Just get rid of the sonofabitch. Very few people in the States even knew he existed, never mind what he'd done. If he should suddenly disappear, the difficulties vanished with him. There was no other Ben Adnam. The problem would be completely solved. Why not just proceed as if nothing had happened? Ben *who*?

The trouble was that Arnold Morgan did not operate like some other military and political careerists. He operated only in the specific interests of the United States of America. And he knew, as surely as he knew the sun rises in the east, that Ben Adnam had real possibilities. Morgan knew of no one else in the world – indeed, he had never met anyone in his long career – who could in such a short space of time have completely outwitted the entire politico-military establishment of the United States. And not just once, but twice. Not to mention the Brits, the Russians, and the Israelis. Arnold Morgan reckoned Adnam was as close to priceless as made no difference.

The National Security Advisor knew as well as anyone about the restrictions all governments place on classified information. But Ben Adnam was not just any old Intelligence officer: he was some kind of a military genius, and in Arnold Morgan's opinion he was likely to have found out *anything* he really wanted to know. In his present plight, Adnam had two commodities to sell. Knowledge, and lateral-minded cunning. And Morgan's instinct told him the Iraqi was unlikely to come up light. Certainly Adnam would probably know more than Langley about all kinds of matters in the Middle East.

Before Ben Adnam had left Baghdad he had deposited the full story of his operations in three different safe-deposit vaults in Europe. The written account was split into several parts, no one of them complete. He had allowed the CIA to check out one part of one deposit in Paris. Neither the CIA nor Arnold Morgan, who had spent a lifetime in the dogged pursuit of such data, was disappointed. The admiral could not bring himself to have Adnam eliminated, nor could he risk him going into a public trial before a jury. Morgan already knew that what he really wanted to do was 'run' him.

Which was why, broadly speaking, he and two Secret Service agents were driving fast down Route 1 to the Woodley Hills district, the admiral himself at the wheel. Arnold Morgan sensed there was something in the nature of a showdown in the air between him and Adnam, because sooner or later someone was going to have to decide something. Right now the admiral did not know what course of action to advise the President, but he would by the end of the day.

They pulled into the tree-softened driveway which led through languorous lawns that were turning green with the advance of spring. At the end was the big, white, gabled house which represented the most unlikely-looking prison in the United States. Only the presence of two uniformed Marine guards inside the glass of the front porch betrayed the secret nature of the proceedings.

Admiral Morgan parked and walked into the house, nodding at the two guards. Inside, two CIA field officers met him and took him into a living room which enjoyed rural views out to the trees; here there were three more guards.

Sitting in an armchair, reading the *Washington Post* despite his manacled wrists, was Commander Benjamin Adnam. He wore a blue shirt, dark-gray trousers and brown loafers, all of which he had bought in Helensburgh two and a half months ago. He stood up immediately upon the arrival of the National Security Advisor and nodded a greeting. 'Admiral,' he said calmly.

'Commander,' replied Arnold Morgan, unable to bring himself to reduce to the ranks the submarine genius he wanted to hire. He turned to his secret-servicemen and the CIA field officers who had accompanied him into the room, and said curtly, 'I'll let you know if I need you.'

One of the CIA men nodded to the Marine guard, who was plainly ready for this instruction, and, before leaving, he hand-cuffed the prisoner both to the chair, by the wrist, and to the table, by the ankle. Ben Adnam was not going anywhere, even if he had had anywhere to go.

'I want to talk to you about your future, if any,' said the American gruffly.

'I'd be glad to join you,' said Adnam, smiling.

'We won't waste each other's time on trivialities, because we both know I could have you eliminated any time I think suitable. And, like Laura Baldridge, I'd probably get a medal from a grateful nation.'

'If you say so, Admiral.'

'However, I would like to touch base with you on the question of a trial, should my government decide to charge you either with crimes of mass murder against the state or, alternatively, with war crimes against humanity. What would your reaction be?'

'I should plead Not Guilty to everything. I should deny ever having been in anyone's navy. I should say I was just trying to get a job here. Then I would leave you to persuade the Iraqis to give evidence against me. You could ask them to swear I was the world's greatest terrorist and acting on their behalf. Or you could try Israel, get their government to admit in front of that beleaguered nation that their military had been made to look absolutely ridiculous, by me, for the biggest part of 20 years.'

Arnold Morgan shook his head, frowning.

Then Adnam added, 'You could of course try to nail me with the Royal Navy submarine, the one you have undoubtedly hit by now, illegally, in international waters, drowning the innocent crew, as if you were a group of gangsters. That would probably go down very well in the United Nations. And in your own press, which has been told nothing of all this. Personally I wouldn't really know. You see, I've never been in a submarine. I'm in the mining business myself.'

'We could bring in evidence from Scotland,' growled Morgan. But he was only testing the waters.

'Where's that, Admiral? I've never even been there, as my passport will show. You have only one witness that fool Anderson, whom any good lawyer would rip to bits.'

'You have told me plenty, Commander. And the CIA.'

'Yes. Your methods of torture, like some Third World despot, have been very effective. You and your henchmen could make a man admit anything. On the other hand, real evidence, as you know, is very hard to find. I can't help thinking a public trial is not in anyone's best interests. And you will never get anyone to admit I had anything to do with downing those aircraft.'

Admiral Morgan had always known that the cooperation of Benjamin Adnam was good only so long as the man made his plea for life. Once that was achieved, and he was put on trial, things would be very different. And in his soul Arnold Morgan knew this man never would, never could, come to public trial. The ramifications, on all sides, were just too difficult. No good could possibly come of it. Not for anyone. Especially not for the United States of America.

'Should we decide to take a more agreeable route, and make you a clandestine employee of our government, what would your expectations be?'

Benjamin Adnam refrained from even a cautious smile. He had, after all, planned this moment for weeks and weeks. This moment represented his entire reason for being in the United States. But when he spoke it was slowly.

'Admiral Morgan, I would plainly need a new identity. Which I imagine you would have little trouble in providing. I would also need somewhere to live, and some money. My own country treated me less than generously. I imagine you would wish me close to Washington, where my knowledge could best be put to use.'

'Would you wish to become a citizen?'

'I think I would leave that to you.'

'Do you put a high price on your worth to us?'

'I always put a high price on my worth to anyone.'

'Have you considered that you might owe us something?'

'No, sir. I work for money. Or else I leave – if I can.'

'Try not to forget Solution One.'

'I have not forgotten it. But, if you are planning to exercise that, then we ought not to be talking at all.'

'No, we ought not. But lemme ask you this, how much money do you think we should pay you?'

'Sir, that depends how long I stay, and how long you would wish to employ me.'

'How long would you like to stay here in the United States?'

'Until I die.'

'Which could be tomorrow.'

'But I hope, and think, not.'

'Why? Are you not our most intractable enemy?'

'*Was*. Not any more. And I doubt it has escaped you that there are very few places I can go. In my trade you tend to have a downward spiral in your number of friends, and the supply in the end runs out.'

'Commander, I understand that very well. But I would like to pursue finances for a moment. If, for instance, we wanted to employ you over a ten-year period, there's no way we'd give you a major lump sum of cash before that time was up. Just in case you decided to vanish. However, we might think about a monthly arrangement, with perhaps a capital sum accruing to you each year, which you could not of course touch until the end of the ten-year period.'

'What if I wished to buy a house here?'

'No problem. We'd own it until your service time was up.'

'Then, under such circumstances, I would expect to accrue money at the rate of $1.5 million a year, on top of my normal living salary. The interest to come to me.'

'Uh-huh.'

'After all, I can probably show you how to get Iraq out of your hair permanently. What would that be worth alone?'

'Commander, you do not need to waste your time convincing me of your worth. I know it. That's why we're sitting here.'

'Excellent. We could probably make a very good team. You remind me in many ways of my Teacher. Different style, but same analytical mind.'

Despite an uneasy feeling that he was being patronized, the admiral smiled. He stood up and walked to the window. Then he turned around quite suddenly and said, 'I wonder how wise it would ever be for me to turn my back on you.'

'Admiral, I have nowhere else to go. That's why I'm here.'

'Again, that's why we're talking. I guessed your situation. The only catch may be that you are already working for someone else.'

'If you can trust me long enough to make a deal, I give you one promise. I can prove my former employer became my enemy, and I will do so to your satisfaction as soon as we seal our arrangement. If I fail, either you may execute me or I will take cyanide.'

'Accepted. The burden of proof is on you. That's between us. And now I'm outta here. Hope you get a decent dinner. We'll talk tomorrow.'

'Oh, Admiral, just one thing you should know before you go. I forgot to tell you before, but I've written out my *whole* story – you know, the aircraft carrier, and the passenger airliners, with suitable backup material – and it is to be released to the media by my Swiss bank should I disappear or die. You know, if I fail to report to them every six weeks.

'I've arranged for the material to go mainly to foreign newspapers – the UK, France, Germany, and of course the *Washington Post*. I thought that might deter you from deploying Solution One – the fact that I might come back to annoy you from beyond the grave, as it were. How will the President laugh off the decision to take out three Iranian submarines when Iran had done nothing? How will you excuse your lies about the loss of the *Jefferson*? Your more recent cover-up over the airliner "accidents" will seem like kids' stuff in comparison.

'Matter of fact, I think you should be extremely relieved you did not go to Solution One in the first hour before we had time to talk. Anyway, see you tomorrow.'

The admiral scowled and without another word headed back out to his car, walking resolutely, his chin stuck out in front of him, looking as if he were about to declare war. He was in the driver's seat and had the engine running before the secret-servicemen had time to scramble out of the house and join him. Admiral Morgan did not like being outwitted, as he suspected he was being right now by the Iraqi.

Morgan drove on to his lunch appointment, first heading north to the Richmond Highway. From there went further south, away from the city, for another nine miles before turning first onto a secondary road and then onto a shaded woodland drive, at the end of which was a majestic white Colonial house.

He told his secret-service detail he would be two hours; one of them should go find lunch for the two of them and the other should bring the communications system inside. Both agents knew they were at the private residence of the Chairman of the Joint Chiefs, Admiral Scott F. Dunsmore. They also knew Dunsmore himself could not possibly have purchased this spec-tacular property, overlooking the Potomac river to the Maryland Heights, with his Navy salary. The scholarly Scott Dunsmore, it was well known, was from a Boston banking family. He had also been the cleverest admiral in the Navy. That too was well known.

Dunsmore stepped out to greet his old friend Arnold Morgan, and they stood chatting for a few minutes below the tall, greening trees, some still in blossom. A couple of bobwhite quails called from quite close in the woodland, and above them the sky was clear blue. The idyllic rural scene contrasted darkly with the grim, subversive, and murderous subject they were about to discuss. Standing here in the lovely grounds of the house was to postpone the enormity of their decision – what to advise the President when they met him in the White House at 1600 this afternoon. The subject, as it had been so many times before, was Benjamin Adnam. Scott Dunsmore had suffered the shuddering distinction of being Chief of Naval Operations when the *Jefferson* was sunk.

Inside the mansion the two admirals retired to a high summery room which faced out directly to the river and the distant Maryland shore. It was a room familiar to Arnold Morgan, and he settled himself into a wide, comfortable armchair, expensively upholstered in a rose-patterned chintz – the unmistakable touch of the urbane Grace Dunsmore.

Admiral Dunsmore spoke first. 'Well, Arnold. As the brains behind this operation, what do you think? Do we shoot him, jail him, or hire him?'

'Hire him . . .'

'Right. Now we've got that over with, let's go get some lunch.'

They both laughed, still avoiding the magnitude of the subject. 'Well, what did he say?' Admiral Dunsmore finally asked.

'As you and I both feared, the question of a trial is a total disaster area. He told me he would plead Not Guilty, drag the trial out and reveal everything he knows to our disadvantage. He would deny ever having been in anyone's navy and leave it to us to get the Iraqis to give evidence against him.'

'Fat chance.'

'Which he knows as well as we do. He also added that he is now certain, thanks to his own information, we have demolished a submarine illegally in international waters, drowning 50 people, and generally behaved like wild men before the world community.'

'In a sense, the bastard's right about that as well.'

'Only in a sense . . . And he also says we won't get a scrap of help from the Israelis, who will be unwilling to look ridiculous by having to admit he made a fool of them for almost 20 years.'

'He's got that bit right, too. Christ, you sure it *is* him?'

'Of course. Laura MacLean, remember?'

'Yes. Just kidding. Of course we have his passport. British, right? With a couple of South African stamps from Johannesburg Airport?'

'Yup. That's it. He'd just leave it to us to prove who he really is and what he's done. He added that he'd say we tortured him to get an admission.'

'Which confirms what we both think. He's a clever little bastard and a trial is out of the question. Correct?'

'Correct. It would be a huge embarrassment to the Government, and cause an uproar in the airline industry. The liberal media would have the best time since Watergate, bringing down this excellent administration.'

'Arnold, we could just find him guilty ourselves and, er, dispense with him. It seems absurd staging some kind of a trial in order to seek revenge by taking his life when he's cost so many thousands of other lives. It's not even a hundredth of the way toward a reasonable exchange.'

'Absolutely. Which brings us to the real issue. Do we unload him, right now, and act as if nothing's happened? Before you answer, I must tell you he has written out his whole story – the *Jefferson*, the aircraft, the submarine and all – and has instructed his Swiss bank to release it to the media should he not report in every few weeks. God knows what else he has up his sleeve, but my instinct tells me to kill him would be damned nearly as bad as putting him on trial.'

'Sounds like it, Arnie. Except it might be worse.'

'Which brings us to the much more difficult but much more fruitful course of "running" him, using him for our own purposes.'

'Well, "running" him is certainly the most appealing option if you don't care about your career. Which I don't, since I'm retiring at the end of this president's tenure. You don't, because you're probably unsackable and anyway you and Kathy have a lot to look forward to in retirement – with *your* pensions. I don't think the President cares either. He's halfway through his second term. So I suppose we should all act in the strict interest of this nation and, if it goes wrong . . . we just take it on the chin, and retire gracefully from the fray.'

'That means we "run" him,' said Arnold Morgan. 'And that's one hell of a challenge. He actually said this morning he could show us how to get Iraq out of our hair for good. Christ, he'd be useful in all of our dealings in the Middle East. And he's not expensive, relatively. *And* he says he wants to stay here – nowhere else to go.'

'The danger is, of course, he might still be working for Iraq.'

'I know. I did bring that subject up. And his reply was quite strange. He said he would prove to us conclusively that Iraq plainly tried to kill him. He also said that if he failed to prove it, he was quite prepared to take cyanide.'

'Hmm. If we were dealing with a normal person that'd be impressive, but with Ben Adnam involved, there's almost always going to be more to it than meets the eye.'

'I know. I'm just trying to think what that might be. All the evidence I have tells me I'm wasting my time – which, paradoxically, is why I want him on our team.'

Lunch passed swiftly as the two US admirals wrestled with the problem of the captive terrorist a dozen miles away. By the time they had worked through ham and cheese omelettes and salad they had agreed that Ben Adnam must live, at least for the moment. But a new problem emerged. Who, eventually, would 'run' the ex-Israeli submarine commander on a day-to-day basis? 'Aside from the fact that he needs a rock-solid Navy background, whoever it is has to be as clever as Adnam,' said Morgan.

'Any suggestions?'

'Not really. I shouldn't think his old Teacher, Sir Iain MacLean, would make himself available. But he'd do fine.'

'How about the Teacher's son-in-law?'

'Bill? Can't see that happening. He's got that cattle operation to run, and he's quite recently married. I shouldn't think he'd want to up sticks and move to Washington. And Laura seems very happy out there in the wide open spaces.'

'I know, Arnold. But do you think he might do it for, say, six months while we got ourselves organized with a permanent guy?'

'Well . . . the first six months are probably going to be the most difficult. I don't think Bill would consider it. But you never know – I guess he might.'

'OK. Let's get back to the factory and see if the President has any strong views. If he does, this could all become strictly academic. After we finish there, we'll make a new plan.'

'Hey, Scott, thank Grace for a delicious lunch, will you? I caught a glimpse of her, but she looked like she was leaving.'

'She was. So are we. I'll ride with you. My car's meeting me at the White House.'

At 1600 precisely, Morgan and Dunsmore presented themselves to the President of the United States. He was waiting for them in the Oval Office, and rose to greet them with his usual affability.

'Good to see you both. Thanks for coming. How's our terrorist?'

'He's not bad, sir,' said Arnold Morgan. 'A bit awkward, like you'd expect, but nothing we can't deal with.'

'Good. Now, I believe we are going to touch base on what to do with him?'

361

'Yes, sir. And it's a very trappy subject – I'm not sure how deeply you want to be involved. If you wish, you can of course lay down the law right away. But I wouldn't really advise that. And I wonder whether you might not consider whether the President actually *needs* to be involved in the nitty-gritty of our decisions concerning some foreign terrorist . . . All I'm saying, sir, is that you don't have to if you don't want to.'

'I hear you, Arnold. And I thank you for your consideration. Could you give me a very private rundown on the situation right now?'

'Scott's damned good at that, sir. When I arrived at his house this morning, he just said, "Right. Are you gonna shoot him, jail him, or hire him?" '

The President chuckled. 'That's why he's Chairman of the Joint Chiefs. He never gets involved in trivia.'

'Exactly, sir. Anyway, the most complicated area is the prospect of a trial for either crimes against the US or war crimes against humanity. In our opinion, it is a political nightmare, a no-win situation, and anyway Adnam told me he'd deny everything. He didn't think Iraq would be anxious to give evidence on our behalf.'

'I've already thought of that,' said the Chief Executive. 'Forget a trial. It'd take a year and it'd drive everyone mad. It'd also probably drive me out of office. The left-wing media would kill us, especially if the beans somehow got spilled about the *Jefferson*.'

'Exactly, sir. It's a total nonstarter. Especially since no one really knows what happened to either the carrier or the civilian airliners. And no one in this country knows Adnam even exists – just us and our most trusted people.'

'Which means his removal would be extremely simple, hmm? No one would ever know anything.'

'It's not quite that simple, sir. He seems to have made quite elaborate arrangements for substantive disclosures as to our activities in the event of his sudden disappearance and failure to communicate. The hard way is the only way we'd ever find out for real. So, making him disappear might ultimately prove as embarrassing for us as putting him on public trial.

'We already believe he's a mine of information. We also know, to our considerable cost, that he has a brilliant mind. And I would dearly like to use him. He could change our lives in the Middle East.'

'I see,' said the President. 'He seems to have thought it through, doesn't he? The question is, do I need to know, or care, if you decide to remove him, or if you decide to use him?'

'I think not, sir,' said Admiral Dunsmore. 'Let's just suppose for the moment we have the man who hit the *Jefferson*. My own view is that it is unnecessary for you to be involved – *unless* we decide to go to trial, *or* if we decide to make any military retaliation against another nation, based on information provided by Adnam. I don't think we could avoid your involvement then.'

'I understand, Scott. And I realize you two do not want to have him executed privately. Rightly. Quite apart from the political consequences of postmortem exposure, it might be a waste of a major asset – not to mention a purely futile act of revenge on our part. The crimes committed were so monstrous there could be no revenge anyway. Not with just one man's life. Therefore my conclusion must be that I need not be involved at this stage. I will leave the fate of the mysterious Commander Adnam to the offices of my military commanders. But you will inform me, Arnold, should we consider a strike against anyone?'

'Absolutely, sir.'

'One further point, before you go. Are we now certain that the airliners were knocked down by Iraq?'

'Yes, sir. Yes, we are.'

'I would personally consider it very remiss of us, if we failed to make known our extreme displeasure to that pariah of a government.'

'Understood, sir. I will keep you informed.'

The two admirals rose and said goodbye to the President, returning down the long corridors to Arnold Morgan's office. Kathy O'Brien was at her post but on the telephone; she offered just a small wave of greeting as they arrived. 'Coffee,' murmured her boss. 'And hold all phonecalls for a half-hour.'

Inside his office Morgan took off his coat and exclaimed, 'Jesus Christ! Did you hear that last remark?'

'I sure did, Arnold. He wants us to hit Iraq. Obviously not publicly, but it sounded like he expected something impressive.'

'Fortuitous, huh? We just happen to have the very man we need to guide us through those tricky waters.'

'Isn't it, though? Benjamin, old buddy, I think you just got yourself a job.'

'He might have, Scott. But I'm not sure what exactly he meant us to do. Bomb Baghdad? Take out a few streets? Knock down some missile sites in the desert? Hit their main seaport? Maybe a military airfield? A few oil wells? What do you think?'

'I'm not sure, but I presume he's looking for something like their strikes against us. Too awful to be admitted, too much of a loss of face. And too secret for anyone to know *quite* who was responsible.'

'Guess so. But it's a tall order.'

'No doubt, Arnold. But it was a very presidential order. He's a man who just hates to see his country humiliated in any way whatsoever. And no one gets away with it. Not indefinitely.'

'Iraq got away with the *Jefferson*.'

'Not any more. Not by the sound of things.'

'We better start thinking about plans. It just seems overwhelming at the minute. I'm not sure where to start. But this is military, Scott, and you're the Chairman of the Joint Chiefs. I think this ball's in your court, and I'm waiting for your creative input.'

'You think I'm a film director? Well, I'm not. Basically I'm an organizer. And this is what I propose. I think we have to get someone in here who's going to work with Adnam on an initial plan – subject to your striking a deal and reminding him of his words about Iraq.'

'Right. Who?'

'Bill Baldridge, despite what you said earlier. For the following reasons. He's in deep already. He's damned smart. He knows Adnam, and you and he work very well together. Now that the kids have gone back to Scotland, he and Laura will certainly come to Washington for a few days if we make it quick and urgent – she could come to my place and stay with Grace, if necessary. Or else we'll put 'em in a hotel. That way the three of you can try and thrash something out. We'll pay Bill a fee; and, if the mission is successful, it might just give us the opening to persuade him to "run" Adnam for another six months.'

'Can't fault any of that. Who's gonna call Bill – you?'

'No, you. Tell him Adnam's balls are on the line. The bastard said he knew how to deal with Iraq, and now we're giving him the chance to prove it. That might just titillate the master of the B/B sufficiently.'

'Yeah, I guess it might at that. Leave it with me, Scott. I'll call him later. I'll check how the herds are. See if they can manage without him for a few months.'

Two hours later, at 1900, speaking from Kathy's house in Chevy Chase, Arnold Morgan made contact with the former submariner in Kansas. Baldridge listened laconically to the proposition and contributed a lot of 'Uh-huhs,' 'Is that rights?' and general 'Get outta heres.' But in the end he did not turn it down. He just said, 'When?'

Arnold Morgan replied, 'Now.' It was his most favorite word.

Baldridge said, 'How long?'

Morgan replied, 'A week, max.'

'Okay. You sending transport?'

'Yup. Tomorrow morning, 1000. In front of your house.'

'We'll be there.'

'See ya.' The admiral clenched his fist and gritted his teeth. 'Now something *will* happen,' he muttered. 'With Commander Adnam and Bill working as a team. Just so long as we watch, monitor, and check every step Adnam makes. Maybe, one of these days, we'll even come to trust him.'

But he was pleased with the Kansan's response, and he visibly brightened. '*Kathy!* Drinks! Then we're going out for a little celebration.'

1600, May 12. The White House lawn.
The helicopter from Andrews Air Base touched down lightly, leaving its engines running for immediate takeoff down the Potomac. Laura remained on board while Bill disembarked and was given a pass by the Secret Service agents and escorted into the West Wing. Arnold Morgan came to meet him in person. 'Hey, good to see you. Grace is waiting at the house for Laura. You and I will be there by seven. We're all having dinner there and we're all staying overnight.'

Bill followed Arnold down to his office, where his briefing began. Morgan explained everything – the potential deal with Adnam, the hopelessness of a public trial, the consequences and wastefulness of executing him . . . and the President's expressed wish that a strike be organized against Iraq.

Bill was particularly interested in the avowed statement from the ex-Israeli submariner to Admiral Morgan the previous day, that he could rid the United States of the menace of Iraq. 'Christ. What do you think he has in mind?'

'Who knows? But when he does have something in his mind, we know, to our cost, that he is not usually joking.'

'Ain't that right.'

By 1800 the helicopter was back, miraculously bearing Admiral Dunsmore. The three old friends, in company with two Secret Service agents, took off from the White House in good time for the 1900 rendezvous with the ladies. Only Kathy O'Brien was absent, but she would have to hold the fort, first thing in the morning, in Admiral Morgan's office.

The flight was swift, and the pilot brought them in over the Potomac before dark, touching down on the wide back lawn above the river.

There was a chill in the air, as there often is in the late spring on the East Coast, but Scott Dunsmore said that the cool would not deflect him from his plans: he was cooking outside tonight, come hell or high water. It would be the first barbecue of the season and he intended it to be memorable. Therefore he expected a full attendance around the gas-grill while he perfected a perfect butterflied leg of lamb, just the way his cook had taught him during his days in the Navy as a Fleet Commander.

The fact that the huge leg of lamb had already been carefully cut by Grace's butcher and carefully marinated and half-cooked in the oven by Grace herself did not discourage Admiral Dunsmore from claiming full credit, in advance. Grace mentioned that it would be a real shame if he burned it, like he did the last one, on her birthday two years ago.

'I was under a bit of pressure then,' said the Chief of the entire Pentagon. 'There'll be no mistakes tonight. Let's get in there for some drinks – and then you'll see me in action, putting a 40-minute charcoal finish to this banquet.'

Laura, who had not met the Dunsmores before, was captivated by them both. Grace had been charm itself during the late afternoon, but the arrival of the admiral, the most powerful man in the United States Armed Forces, was something she had viewed with some trepidation – even though both her father and her husband had always told her that Scott was a prince of a man, and she would like him, as she had liked all of the high-ranking military Americans she had met. Even Arnold Morgan, who was not precisely everyone's cup of tea.

Now, just as Admiral Morgan always assumed that everyone had coffee black 'with buckshot,' Admiral Dunsmore assumed that anyone who had endured a long day would be revived by the dark smooth taste of Johnny Walker Black Label Scotch with club soda. With this drink he was something of an artist: in the high summer he allowed two cubes of ice in a tall glass, with a lot of soda. On Labor Day he eliminated the ice for the season, and then, as the days drew in and the temperature dropped, he reduced the soda water, until by Christmas it became quite a short drink.

Tonight, only six weeks off Memorial Day, when the ice went back in, the drinks were medium-long but warm. He brought five Scotches and soda on a silver tray into the big room at the front of the house. They each took one, and Arnold Morgan stepped forward to propose a toast.

'We are here tonight for several reasons, some of which can be talked about and some of which cannot. So I'll confine myself to proposing the health of Laura's father and our friend, Admiral Sir Iain MacLean, who has, as before, been some way ahead of us.'

They all raised their glasses, smiling at the thought of the urbane Scottish officer, who would have been mortified with embarrassment had he been in attendance. But Arnold Morgan was not prone to mawkish sentimentality. If he said that Iain MacLean was out in front in his thinking, then that was so. And, if it hadn't been after midnight on Loch Fyne, they would have all called him right there and then to congratulate him.

By now the gas-grill was at full power and Scott Dunsmore had the leg of lamb in prime position. Wearing sweaters, they all stood around outside, admiring the dusk over the dark Potomac, sipping their drinks and watching the Chairman of the Joint Chiefs strategically adjusting the angle of the gently sizzling lamb.

By common consent he got it right this time. And dinner was outstanding, not least because Dunsmore decided to open his last two bottles of 1961 Haut Brion. 'Bill and I drank a bottle to the memory of his brother right after we lost the *Jefferson*,' he said. 'This seems the right time to finish the vintage . . . on a high note, at the conclusion of an unhappy episode.' The fact that the rare bottles were worth about $500 each was not lost on anyone. And the 45-year-old Bordeaux from the Graves district lived up to its towering reputation, casting a deep warm glow over the gathering. No one discussed the project which lay uppermost in their minds. Indeed, during the entire evening it was touched upon only once, lightly, when Admiral Dunsmore raised his glass and said quietly, 'Welcome back on board, Bill.'

The following morning Admiral Morgan's chauffeur arrived at 0830 to drive his boss and Bill the short distance back to the CIA safe house where Benjamin Adnam awaited them. They both walked straight into the room where the terrorist was reading the newspaper, and the admiral wished him a 'Good morning, Commander.'

But Morgan did not waste one further second on formalities. 'Right now,' he said, 'I'm here to hack out a deal. And this is what I propose. I have a project and I would like your guidance and general input. If this is deemed to be a success, we will then settle down and make some kind of a long-term agreement for you to work with us on the lines we discussed yesterday. Naturally, we can have nothing in writing, but in your business I expect you are accustomed to that.

'The project we are working on is against Iraq, and will be a one-off. It will either succeed or fail. If I judge your role to have been critical, which it will be, and we are successful, we will make a single payment to you of $250,000 to start off your life here in America. You will not be required in an operational capacity – only in strategic planning.'

'Since I am sitting here thinking and reading the paper,' replied Adnam, 'I suppose I may as well earn some money for it.' But then he smiled and said, 'Admiral, I think that would be an excellent way to start off our relationship. Might save me the trouble of taking cyanide.'

'Then we are agreed? You trust me sufficiently?'

Commander Adnam held up his handcuffed wrists. 'I don't really have very much choice, do I? If I do not agree, you could always go immediately to Solution One, despite the uncomfortable consequences for you.'

Admiral Morgan nodded. 'Yes. And now I would like to talk to you, and so would Bill, who I believe you know well enough?'

'Yes, I think so. We have a few things in common.'

'Right. If I yell "Coffee!" loud enough around here, will something happen?'

'I think so. There is a housekeeper for the agents and the Marine guards.'

'I'll go and find someone, Arnold,' said Bill. 'But I bet they don't have buckshot.'

The admiral grinned, but he was very preoccupied as he turned to Ben Adnam and said, deliberately, 'My President does not believe that Iraq should get away with shooting down three airliners, in the process murdering our oil-negotiating team, six congressmen, and the Vice-President of the United States. Neither has it escaped him that we, as yet, have taken no retribution against them for the loss of our aircraft carrier.

'We now propose to attend to these matters, with or without your help. But I hope with.'

Adnam nodded.

'Now, you mentioned yesterday that you could offer a way for us to deal with Iraq on a long-term basis. Could you elaborate on that?'

As the Iraqi again nodded his assent, Bill came in with the coffee. Three mugs. All black. A blue tube of sweeteners on the side.

'That's one fucking miracle,' said the admiral, firing the little white pellets into the coffee, somehow making the clicker sound like a six-shooter. 'Now let's see if young Ben here can come up with a second.'

Despite himself, Commander Adnam laughed. He thought he might enjoy working with this American cowboy. 'Admiral,' he said, 'one of the biggest problems in Iraq is water. We have two great rivers, the Euphrates and the Tigris. Both of them flow out of Turkey, and the Euphrates crosses Syria. Those two rivers are the lifeblood of Iraq. They are the reasons civilization flourished in ancient Mesopotamia, the old name for modern Iraq.

'The rivers still control the country's agriculture, wheat and barley, in terms of both irrigation and direct pumping. They control fertilizer plants, cement-making plants, light industry, the production of steel, the growing of dates. They control Iraq's drinking water and hydro-electric power. For centuries, when the water level dropped and in some areas occasionally dried up, there was something close to national panic. But it was even

369

worse when they flooded, as they often do at the end of the winter. Right back to biblical times – I expect you both know that Noah and his Ark were in Mesopotamia when that great flood happened.

'In order to control these waters, various governments have built a succession of dams and barrages and canals. These in turn have helped to form lakes and reservoirs, which first of all absorb the floodwater and secondly provide enormous backup when the rivers are very low.

'There is one at Dukan on the Tigris; others are at Mosul and Al Hadithah. There is a huge one at Darband–I–Khan, right up in the Kurdish Mountains on a tributary called the River Diyala. There is another at Basdush and another at Fathah, both on the Tigris. There's a further one on a tributary, the Great Zab; a critical one at Sāmarrā, the Sāmarrā Barrage. There are several also on the Euphrates, at Habbaniyah, Hindiyah and Ash Shinafiyah.

'But the most important ones are those at Darband–I–Khan and Sāmarrā. The Darband Reservoir stands at the southern end of a massive lake. It is surrounded by mountains, 130 miles northeast of Baghdad. It contains three cubic kilometers of water. Imagine that? A reservoir four miles long, three miles wide and a quarter-mile deep. The Sāmarrā Barrage, about 76 miles north of the city, right on the Tigris, holds 85 billion cubic meters of water.

'If I were you I'd blow out both those dams and Iraq's economy would collapse – and stay collapsed for several years.

'Once you get out of the northeastern mountains, Iraq is a flat country, and the flooding would be ruinous. But the distances are so great there would be no serious loss of life. The water would rise relatively slowly over the key areas along the river. People would have time to get away. I know that because the Government has made careful studies of the consequences of a dam failure and I've seen them. We'd just have a lot of factories that no longer worked, a lot of crops which would not grow, a lot of flooded oilfields. And a lot of flooded towns and villages. The country would be forced to throw itself on the mercy of the West.'

'Jesus,' said Arnold and Bill, almost simultaneously.

'The trouble is, Admiral, that you don't have long. I read that winter stayed late in the mountains this year, which buys you some time. But, if you want to strike hard, you need to do it while the snows are still melting, when the water in the reservoirs is at maximum height. I'd say you have about another four weeks, maximum. By mid-June the levels start to evaporate in the heat. All the Iraqi Government's studies show that the flooding would be 50 percent worse if it happened at the end of the snow-melt.'

'Jesus Christ,' said Morgan. Baldridge looked amazed.

'I know it sounds perfect for our purposes,' said Arnold Morgan after a while, 'but it'd be absolutely impossible. We'd have to use Special Forces, train 'em, get 'em into the mountains somehow through Turkey, and then have 'em operate deep underwater, against the inner walls of the dams. Christ, we'd need about 50 guys. It would be like declaring war. And they might get caught.'

'How marvellously old-fashioned,' said Commander Adnam. 'That's out of the question. Admiral, you don't use people, you use missiles. Cruise missiles.'

'Missiles? Jesus, that's like a *world* war. We can't just stand a ship off in the Gulf or the Med or somewhere and start throwing big missiles at a couple of major Iraqi dams. The world community would go crazy with indignation. And we could never admit why we were doing it. I'm sorry, Commander, but that would be out of the question. Everyone would see a big missile launch from a US warship. The whole world would know what we'd done, and we couldn't afford that.'

'They wouldn't know if you did it from a submarine.'

'A submarine . . . Of course.' The admiral never minded being outthought. 'We could do that, maybe from the middle of the Gulf. But a missile big enough to come straight in and blow the wall of the dam right out? I don't think there's a missile big enough to do that. At least not one which would fit into a submarine.'

'Not just one. How about six of them, Admiral? One after the other, all hitting the wall of the dam in precisely the same spot until it gives way?'

'Commander, can you just imagine the scene? The Iraqi defensive force at the dam – and I'm sure they have one – standing there watching these big missiles coming in, belching fire, slamming into the wall, one after the other. It would be like Hiroshima. And within hours it would be world news, because there's only one nation which could send in cruise missiles like that. The United Nations would hang us out to dry – leave us swinging in the wind.'

'Not if the missiles came in from the other side, and made their final approach in the dark, right above the water,' replied Commander Adnam. 'Then dropped into the water a couple of hundred yards short.'

For the first time Arnold Morgan was totally silent.

'By which time, sir, the submarine which fired them would have slipped under the water and headed out of the Strait, deep and quiet – long gone, and no one would ever know.'

'Holy Shit,' said the President's National Security Advisor. 'This is fucking unbelievable.'

'No it's not, Arnold,' interjected Ben. 'You have a missile which would do it. But you'd have to modify it because it would have to make its final approach *under* the water.'

Arnold Morgan took a deep swig of his coffee and rubbed his chin in a gesture of rumination. 'Commander Adnam, I want to say just one thing. I knew you were extremely clever, but your grasp of this kind of warfare has surprised me. Welcome to the US of A.'

It was Bill Baldridge who was now completely preoccupied. He ignored the admiral's compliment to the prisoner. 'Ben's thinking about the Hughes Tomahawk land-attack missile,' he said. 'One of those big submerged-launch cruises. It has a special navigation system – they call it TERCOM-aided. You know, pre-programmed into its computer – you just bang in the waypoints. This is the sucker that can be launched from a Los Angeles-Class boat, and it has a hell of range – 2500 kilometers, about 1400 miles, which I think would get us up the Gulf from Hormuz.'

'Yes. Yes, it would,' said the admiral thoughtfully. Then, turning to Ben Adnam, he said, 'Lt-Commander Baldridge was a weapons officer in the US Navy. Submarines. Nuclear specialist.'

The Iraqi nodded respectfully.

The admiral continued, 'Didn't we fire some of those missiles at Iraq from submarines in the Med during the Gulf War?'

'We did,' said Baldridge. 'Those Tomahawks can hit just about anything within range. No mistakes. They're accurate now to within about six feet.'

'Remind me, how many can the submarine carry?'

'Eight, minimum. Maybe more.'

'How about this underwater bullshit?'

'That's the special part,' said Ben. 'I don't think it should be too difficult. The Brits solved it 60 years ago. What was he called? Burns Morris? You know, the dambuster fellow.'

'I guess you're referring to Professor Barnes Wallis,' said Bill, pompously for a cowboy.

'Burns Wallis, Barnes Morris, what the hell? I refer to the World War II inventor who came up with the bouncing bomb. Our problem is, cruise missiles don't bounce. So the trick is going to be slowing the missile up for entry into the water. We'll have to use parachutes, because the speed's gotta come down from Mach 0.7 – from about 450 knots to 30. Then it has to hit the water for the last 200 yards, making a slow shallow trajectory along the preprogrammed course, down to the target, somewhere near the base of the dam wall, which is probably 100 feet thick and 100 feet below the surface.'

'Just one of those missiles wouldn't breach it?'

'No. But the first payload should smash the outside concrete layer, driving cracks maybe 40 feet into the wall. Then the second one bangs into the precise same spot, and makes those cracks wider and deeper, maybe 80 feet into the wall. Then the third one smashes in, and probably drives the cracks right through. The wall might go right then, but it'll certainly go with the impact of the fourth one. The last two are just for good measure, in case one of the earlier missiles failed. As you well know, a cruise missile of this size could knock down the White House or blow up a destroyer, so that dam wall wouldn't have a prayer against four of them, never mind six.'

'How about the propulsion of the missile under water?'

'That's not a problem. We can do it using the weapon's residual speed. Fast through the air, then into the water for the last couple of hundred yards, where it'll turn into a kind of torpedo.'

'Commander Adnam, are you sure of the extent of the damage if we hit the Darband and Sāmarrā dams?'

'Very sure. If you remember, there was a fierce battle during the Iraq–Iran war at a place called Halabajah – a Kurdish town in the southeast of their area, right up there in the mountains, a couple of miles east of Darband. The Iraqis fought like tigers for that town after the Iranians captured it in the winter of 1988. And they succeeded – they drove the Iranian tanks back. There

373

were even allegations – perfectly justified, in case you didn't know – that Iraq had used chemical weapons in retaking Halabajah – which must have seemed strangely extreme, just for the sake of this little place up in the mountains. But there was more to it than that. Iraqi Intelligence had heard the Iranians were planning to blow the big dam at Darband, and Iraq could not allow that. No price was too high to pay in order to stop them – even the fury of the whole world over the use of chemical weapons. That dam and its massive hydro-electric plant, and the one at Sāmarrā, very nearly represent life and death to the very fragile economy of Iraq. If they were both blown at the same time it would cause havoc. Imagine the situation after the Sāmarrā Barrage had gone: massive flooding right down to Baghdad, and then another vast volume of water cascading out of the Darband Mountains to meet the mainstream of the Tigris just below the center of the city.'

'Doesn't sound great,' agreed Morgan. 'How long do you estimate such a body-blow would keep Iraq out of action?'

'I'd say ten years. At least, that's what they thought when the Iranians threatened the Darband Dam back in 1988.'

'How far would the missiles have to travel to the dams, Bill?'

'Well, that's the problem – the eternal problem for weapons officers. Bigger the target, bigger the warhead you need. Otherwise you end up kicking away at an iceberg with a toothpick. Unless you want to end up with a missile the size of the Washington Monument, you always have to sacrifice range. What I'm really saying is you can send a minor warhead 1500 miles, but the same missile will carry a big warhead only, say, 500 miles. The maximum mass the missile can have is finite, so you end up with a choice between fuel and explosive. Every time you increase one, you have to cut back on the other. We'll have to make significant adjustments in design.'

'Bill, you're not saying we can't do it, are you?'

'No, Arnie, 'course not. I'm just cautioning everyone we do have to trade a lot of range for a lot of extra bang. When I last looked at this sort of tradeoff, range was *the* limiting factor for the payload. Not the other way round.

'Back in '91, we were taking a very serious look at those Iraqi dams, and for a while we thought we could knock 'em down with modified Tomahawk missiles. We were looking at two launch-area options – one at the eastern end of the Med, one at the northern end of the Gulf.

'We knew we would need a ton of missiles per dam, which meant we had to fire half of 'em from the Med. But that option required the missiles to fly at least 600 miles. And that gave us a *real* problem. We just couldn't get a big enough warhead to travel that far. Couldn't hold enough fuel if we were carrying that much explosive. Not without a complete redesign of the entire airframe and power-plant – really, what we were talking about was a brand-new missile, because the 600-mile range was a fixed nut. The best we ever did was get it down to 30 missiles per dam. Right about then we stopped thinking about it.'

Bill Baldridge stood up, paced the room and drank some coffee. 'I do seem to remember that Hughes went right ahead with the project. They completed operational trials, but no one ever told me how they came out. By the time they were ready, the god-damned war was over. But I did once hear they made a few. Shouldn't be difficult to find out what happened to 'em.'

Ben Adnam nodded, already a comfortable member of the team. 'It is indeed about 600 miles from the Mediterranean to the more easterly dam, Admiral,' he said. 'But I have a problem with that routing, simply because it cuts down so drastically on our ability to optimize the actual route. We just don't have enough gas for a lot of ducking and diving. The bird will have to fly on a steady course almost all the way, quite possibly through heavy Iraqi radar and anti-aircraft defense. That has major implications for the survivability of the weapon in transit. And it has impli-cations all of its own – if we want to get six home, and we're calulating a possible loss of two, we need to fire nine. Basically that's why I hate to launch from the Med.'

The admiral looked up and nodded, a kind of rueful half-smile on his face. He just said, 'Uh-huh.' But to himself he was thinking, *Jesus Christ, is this guy something, or what? He's only just fucking got here, and he's talking like a lifelong US weapons officer.*

'How many of these missiles do you think we got, Bill?'

'Dunno. Hughes may have bagged 'em, for all I know. I'll check it out right away. Even if we were lucky there, we'd still need two launch vehicles.'

'That better not be a problem either,' growled Morgan. 'Because, if it is, someone's in deep shit.'

Bill Baldridge continued: 'Look, we might get this thing done at short notice. But I have to check out, for a start, the status of those missiles. Then how many ships we have modified to launch these birds, and where they are, who's nearest our launch-areas. I ought to get through with that today. The main routing stuff gets done by the target computer team, and before their machine can start spitting out all our options we need to feed in every scrap of information – the topography, every hill and valley, every intelligence report detailing Iraqi defensive positions along the way. All right up to date – which it always is, of course. But I shall want to talk further to Ben here. He might have some input.

'The computer guys will understand right away that our 600-mile maximum flight path is the critical factor. They'll come up with options for us. Then we can start to make a few hard decisions about the launch-area and the vehicles which could fire the missiles.'

'OK, Bill. Sounds like you two are getting on top of this. But remember: this thing isn't simply a high-tech problem. We have to give real consideration to the political side as well. We have to find a way to make some serious evasions in-flight, otherwise those bastards may leave a trail which goes straight back to the Pentagon. We gotta try the best we can to keep 'em right off the Iraqi radar – we gotta try every twist and turn to stop anyone ever finding out where they came from.'

'And we don't want to make it too obvious where they're headed *to*, either,' said Adnam. 'I suppose if you *do* happen to see a line of these things whipping through the skies at 600 knots you don't have a lot of time to do much about it. Better not to take any chances, though.'

'Right,' said Morgan. 'That's the thinking. Anyway, I'm outta here, so I'm leaving it to you two. Get the computer whizzes to do their thing, and let's take a look at the routing options ASAP. Also, let's get ahold of a real good hard-copy map, so we can take a careful look and choose the right options. Second-guessing a computer is a dangerous business, but we have to get this dead right. You have any trouble with the goddamned eggheads and their fucking software – you know the kind of thing, resentment at a couple of outsiders like you and Ben – just use my name. And use it hard.'

'You sure it might not be better for you to pave the way yourself, Admiral? One quick phonecall before you go?'

'You're right,' Morgan snapped. He picked up a phone, and a few moments later they heard him in action. Adnam smiled a smile of pure admiration. Baldrige grinned wistfully, memories drifting back of stressful nights in Fort Meade with the Big Man.

'Right. Admiral Morgan, that's me. Yup, that's it. Iraq. All the way north from Basra to the Turkish border. Right. Take in Syria out to the west. Right, that's it. Same thing for the Gulf. And lemme have a chart of the Gulf itself. Right. From the Strait of Oman alla way up to the northern end. Right. When do I want 'em? *Now!* Car? Forget all about that. Get 'em down here in a chopper. What? *Five minutes ago.* And tell the pilot to keep it running when he gets here, and to pick up Lt-Commander Baldrige and his colleague and run 'em down to SUBLANT in Norfolk.'

Morgan banged down the phone, as usual, without missing a beat. 'OK, I guess you got about an hour before he arrives. Meanwhile, work on the details – and then make SUBLANT's Black Ops cell your headquarters. We'll probably want one of their boats anyway. The thing is, we want this done with a high degree of secrecy but at the same time we need to be fast and efficient. The cell has all the facilities. Get to it. I'll be at SUBLANT at 1600.'

And with that Arnold Morgan was gone, like a Texas tornado, sweeping all before him, frightening the life out of everyone who stood in his way.

The day passed in a frenzy of helicopter flights, harassed computer technicians, phonecalls, checks and re-checks, satellite communications to the CVBG in the Arabian Gulf, clearances . . . and the development of a cold-blooded plan to attack the two great dams which kept Iraq alive as a world economic power.

At 1600 both Bill Baldridge and the Iraqi Naval officer were unsurprised when the door to the Black Ops cell burst open and Admiral Arnold Morgan marched in. 'Just tell me we're on,' he barked. 'No bullshit. No major snags.'

'We're on,' said Bill. 'No bullshit.'

'Beautiful.'

'The best news first,' said Bill. 'We got a good choice of launch platforms. We can fire from surface ships or submarines, and we can position adequate assets into the northern Gulf or the Med, or both, without any trouble. We got two cruisers in the Med, both available at short notice. And we got two SSNs plus another cruiser out in the Indian Ocean with the Battle Group. The whole lot of 'em can fire these weapons.

'The main drawback in firing from the Med is we have to fly the weapons out there. We'd probably have to use a Fleet Auxiliary stores ship but that would mean a long surface transit as well, and it might be pretty difficult to hide the sonsabitches.

'If you ask me, it would be a whole lot better to use the platforms in the Indian Ocean. That way we can fly the weapons direct into Diego Garcia and load 'em right there in private. Then it's 2700 miles up to the northern end of the Iranian Gulf, leaving us a missile flight of only 400 miles to the most easterly of the dams, flying direct.

'That option would allow us plenty of indirect routing, but we'd have to conceal the launch-platforms. That means sub-marines. And, because of the number of weapons, we need both of them.'

'Just as well they can both fire the birds, right?' grunted Morgan. 'And what about the goddamned birds? Have we got any? Hughes got 'em stowed away somewhere?'

'They sure have. I could hardly believe our luck. They'd gone right through to 24 production models, on the shelf, ready to go. They're not gonna be cheap – probably double normal cost, because Hughes wanna get their money back. And you can bet your goddamned life they'll charge us plenty to make a rush modification. But they can do it and have them ready to ship out in ten days flat.'

'Well, get on the horn and do it – *now*!'

'I already have, Admiral. In your name. You got plenty of cash?'

Ben Adnam shook his head ruefully at the apparent ease with which the Americans could deploy really major weapons of war, like big guided-missile nuclear submarines, and he pondered briefly all the troubles he had encountered just trying to acquire a diesel–electric submarine for his missions. Aloud he said, 'I can't see much of a problem getting the submarines into the Gulf and up to the launch-area around latitude 29 North. But it's not as deep as we would like up there, especially if we have to evade any opposition. And the high seawater temperature does place limits on maximum reactor power and speeds.

'On the other hand, the Iraqi Navy does not possess any real threat to an American SSN – except in the unlikely event they had a patrol craft lurking right in the launch-area. I suppose our COs could either blow it away or wait a few hours till it left.

'Even after we'd fired off the missiles, even if the Iraqis were somehow able to trace the flight paths back to our launch-area, they still couldn't do a damn thing about it. They simply don't own a weapons system capable of catching an American SSN. Fortunately they don't have any allies in the area either. I imagine the Iranians could make things quite awkward for us down in the Strait of Hormuz with their new Kilo. But I can't see them helping the Iraqis, of all people, can you?'

Bill Baldridge shook his head. 'Not a chance,' he said. 'But, of the launch-areas on offer, the Iranian Gulf wins it hands down – just on the basis of the spare 200-miles range it gives us for a deceptive approach and defense avoidance. Arnold, I could recommend the Med only if you have overriding political reasons.'

'Well, I can think of one overriding political reason why we should consider only the Gulf!' replied the admiral, grinning. 'If we let 'em go from the Med, just a little further to the north, it would look as if they were coming in from Syria. Or taking a slightly more roundabout route from Israel, which would have the effect of causing a full-scale war in the Middle East, and no one needs *that*. Let's just bag the Med and everything to do with it.'

'The same thing would apply to routing the missiles in anywhere from the West,' said Commander Adnam. 'But I do have one thought. Surely even the Iraqis know that no one except the USA can fire this kind of a missile accurately?'

'We're not sure of that any more,' said the ex-weapons officer from Kansas. 'The Brits have something similar. And the French, and the Russians. Probably the Indians and possibly the Iranians. But the Iraqis are gonna look no further than the Americans unless we give them good reason to do otherwise, so we wanna leave them with a few nice little choices. Then we can sit back and try to let them prove it was us. Which will be just about impossible.'

'If we're very careful,' said Adnam, smiling. 'Oh, by the way,

Admiral, we did find out the water levels in the dams were unusually high all over Iraq. It's been a hard and wet winter. A lot of flooding.'

Admiral Morgan stood up. 'Right,' he said, with an air of finality, 'that's it. I want you to set up to use the south and southeastern approach routes. Send the missiles in along the western foothills from the Iraq–Iran border. East around the Baghdad city defenses is also sense. If anyone should say anything to us, we'll just ask politely if they are *absolutely sure* the Iranians weren't somehow involved. I don't think there's any doubt in any of our minds: the southeast route, the one the computers put up, gives us all the advantages. You'd better get back to the program-mers and have 'em produce a few more alternatives, to give us a bit more variation. Otherwise we'll have a dozen missiles all flying down a straight line like a fucking clay-pigeon shoot.

'And make sure the goddamned eggheads understand we're using *two* launch-platforms, firing at the same time, each SSN taking a separate dam, in case one of 'em doesn't get to the launch-area right on time. We don't want one platform *almost* taking out two dams; much better to hit one, and hit it good, and then let the later SSN bang away at a new target hundreds of miles away an hour later. The computer guys will have to work at it, because we want the individual routings deconflicted. The missiles have to arrive at the respective dams at 30-second intervals. Both lead missiles hitting at roughly the same time. We're looking for precision.'

'Aye, sir. You want me to work on these clearances right away?'

'No, Bill. We have to go right to the top on this one. Just get it set up to move into gear, real quick, as soon as I've seen the President. Keep it moving, guys. This one's gonna fly.'

The admiral picked up his briefcase and decided to take just the big chart with him, the one on which Bill Baldridge had sketched out the projected route of the Tomahawk cruise missiles. Then he got on the secure line to Admiral Mulligan, warned him of the broad requirements he was about to make of the US Navy, and told him to meet him in the outer office of the Chairman of the Joint Chiefs in 45 minutes. The Navy helicopter was already running as the President's National Security Advisor marched resolutely forward, preparing to teach the government of Iraq a very severe lesson.   ★

Inside the Pentagon, Admirals Morgan, Mulligan and Dunsmore studied the general plan. The launch-platforms would be two SSNs, both 7000-ton boats of the Los Angeles-Class: *Cheyenne* and *Columbia*. By 1800 they were ordered into the US Naval Base at Diego Garcia. The loading of 14 modified Tomahawks, prepared and flown direct from San Diego, would take place on Thursday, May 25.

Both submarines would clear DG at first light the following morning and make their way north to the Gulf, submerged and fast, stopping off 600 miles out for a test-firing of one missile each. They would clear the Strait of Hormuz and enter the Gulf of Iran on June 1. Moving more slowly up the Gulf, they were scheduled to arrive in the small hours of June 2. Launch time was dusk – 021910JUN06.

Both *Cheyenne* and *Columbia* would turn south immediately the missiles were away and head back to the open waters of the Gulf of Arabia, which they should reach by midday on Saturday June 3. By this time the Iraqis should have a great deal more on their minds than the whereabouts of a couple of SSNs, should they indeed make such a connection.

It took only a few minutes to brief Scott Dunsmore. Arnold Morgan was happy. First thing in the morning he and the CJC would go straight to the White House to obtain formal clearance of the plan from the President. Both men assumed this would be instantly forthcoming, since the entire operation was being mounted on behalf of the Chief Executive.

They arrived at the White House at 0900 the next day. Both men had permanent passes, and so they were able to walk immediately into the West Wing, where a Secret Service agent escorted them to the Oval Office. The President was waiting. Coffee was served as soon as they arrived. 'Morning, gentlemen,' he said. 'Are you going to frighten me to death?'

'Absolutely not, sir,' replied Admiral Morgan. 'But we're about to frighten the President of Iraq to death.'

'Could I ask you to inform me *only what I need to know?*'

'Certainly.' The Chairman of the Joint Chiefs took over, formally. 'In retribution for Iraq's attack on the *Thomas Jefferson*, and subsequently for their unwarranted attacks on three civilian airliners, which ended the lives of several US citizens, including six congressmen and the Vice-President, we intend to strike against that country early next month. The operation is Black. It will be conducted by the US Navy and will involve a missile strike against two Iraqi structures. We envision minimal loss of life, but massive economic damage to that country. We estimate it will take up to ten years for them to make a full recovery.'

'Christ, Scott. Are you guys taking out the two big dams?'

'Yes, sir. How did you guess?'

'Well, a couple of years ago it was the suggestion of our friend Admiral MacLean.'

'It was a good suggestion, too. Like most of his.'

'Yes. In light of the short time-frame you must be using missiles?'

'Yes, sir. Two sets of cruises. Fired top-secret by submarines. Preprogrammed underwater missile approach from the reservoir side of both dams.'

'One of them's the Sāmarrā Barrage on the Tigris, isn't it?'

'That's right, sir. The other's about five times bigger – the Darband–I–Khan.'

'Ah, yes, I remember now. Well, I don't know if we'll be accused of international banditry, but I assume our policy is to say absolutely nothing.'

'Correct, sir,' replied Admiral Morgan. 'We'll just let those bastards understand who they can fuck with and who they can't. But we cannot allow the flag of this nation to be fired upon by anyone. Not without massive retribution from us.'

'My sentiments entirely. These rogue regimes are gonna learn it the hard way. They either play by the very fair rules laid down by us, or we'll make them wish they had. By the way, might I judge from the expeditious manner this has been set up that we received help from an, er, unusual source?'

'You may, sir.'

'Thank you gentlemen. I'll look forward to the evening news next Friday night.'

021840JUN06. USS Columbia. *28.55N 49.48E. Periscope depth. Speed 5. Course three-one-five.*

Commander Mike Krause, conscious of the critical nature of his mission and of the proximity of the sea-bottom to his keel, had checked on the underwater telephone: Commander Tom Jackson's *Cheyenne* was running quietly 500 yards on his starboard beam – same course, speed and depth. Both SSNs were on top line to fire. Tubes ready. A hundred checks had been made, the missile men had completed all the prefiring routines and settings. There could be no mistakes, barring missile malfunction or enemy action. The preprogramming was immaculate. The big self-guided Tomahawks were ready to do their catastrophic job.

At 1845 precisely Commander Krause ordered, 'Stand by tubes one to six.'

Then, 'Tube one, *launch*.'

The first of the specially modified SLCM Tomahawks blew out of the submarine, slid up to the surface and roared into the black night sky, adjusting course at its cruise altitude of 50 feet above the water, heading north, a fiery trail crackling out behind it for the first few seconds of its flight. Then it hit flying speed, and the gas-turbines cut in, leaving no tell-tale trail in the sky. Nothing could stop it now – at least, nothing in the maritime armories of the Gulf nations.

Within four minutes, the remaining five missiles had screamed onward and upward, all under the control of the launch sequencer. All were fired at exact, but different, intervals, each one designed for the specific route of the respective Tomahawk. No matter what the route-variations, the big cruises would arrive on their target, from their separate flight paths, precisely 30 seconds apart.

Now the Tomahawks, in a murderous salvo of destruction, fanned out and hurtled above the dark waters of the Gulf. Though Mike Krause could not tell this, they were surprisingly quiet as well as fast. Once they were over land they could scarcely be heard at all before they were already past. Too late. Much too late for the dam on the Darband–I–Khan.

At 1850 Commander Krause heard that *Cheyenne*, too, had completed her firing sequence. Commander Jackson had drawn a long-range bead on the Sāmarrā Barrage.

Now the Americans must get out of the Iranian Gulf. Mike Krause ordered *Columbia* sharply around to the southeast, co-ordinating his turn with the other SSN. The two Black Ops submarines headed off together 500 yards apart.

By dawn both boats would be creeping softly through the Strait of Hormuz – deep, fast and in the center of the channel at the safety separation of 100 feet in depth. Soon the Gulf of Oman begins to shelf away to the unfathomable sandy depths of the

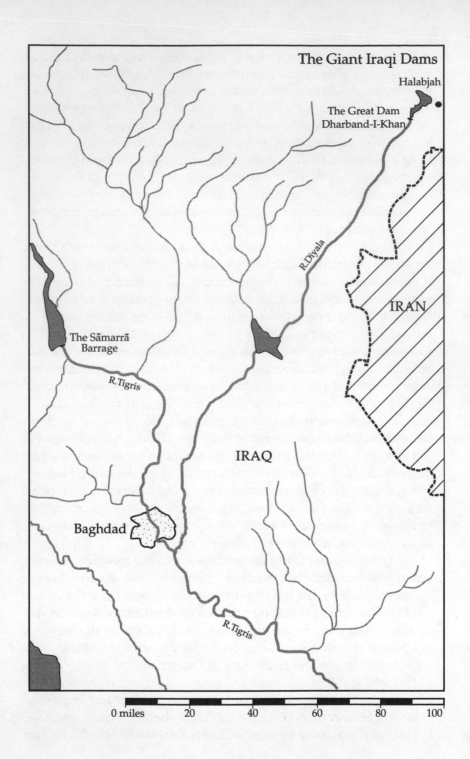

The Giant Iraqi Dams

Halabjah

The Great Dam
Dharband-I-Khan

R.Diyala

IRAN

The Sāmarrā
Barrage

R.Tigris

IRAQ

Baghdad

R.Tigris

0 miles   20   40   60   80   100

Arabian Gulf, and it was here that the Americans would angle to the right, running south down the coast of Oman, passing almost directly over the shattered tomb that had once been HMS *Unseen*.

022015JUNE06. 35.07N 45.42E. The guard room, western end of the great wall of the Darband–I–Khan dam.

Corporal Tariq Nayif, at the age of 21, was the duty soldier charged on this night with walking out along the wall to the midway point and back every half-hour during his four-hour watch. The eastern half of the wall was patrolled from the guard room on the other side.

Tariq's immediate superior, Staff Sergeant Ali Hasan, a veteran Iraqi combat soldier in charge of the western guardhouse, was resting until midnight. The officer on duty, Second Lieutenant Rashid Ghazi, was reading, which left Tariq out on the wall on his own – armed with his standard-issue Russian Kalashnikov, but nonetheless alone. To his right there was a low wall, then a yawning 500-foot drop to the River Diyala; to his left were the still dark waters of the reservoir. The wall was well lit all the way across, and swept by a personnel surveillance radar and infrared detector at all times. Their end of the wall could be viewed on a television monitor in Tariq's guardhouse.

Tonight, like every night, it was cool, silent and peaceful up here in the mountains. Tariq wore a greatcoat, hat and gloves as he walked slowly toward the east, his steel-tipped boots making an unusually loud noise above the gusting wind which blew directly into his face. He was not a Kurd, and it was beyond his reasoning why anyone should want to live up here in the cold, barren peaks of northeastern Iraq.

There were other things beyond his reasoning tonight, principally the knowledge that less than 150 yards away, already 70 feet below the surface, a big US-built cruise missile with a thumping 1100-pound warhead was quietly making its final approach to the front of the wall, to a detonation point down at the base of the dam. It was still making 10 knots through the water, and would explode with shuddering impact 100 feet below where Tariq now stood.

It hit at 2018, detonating with a massive underwater explosion – which, strangely, made little sound in the air. Hardly a ripple disturbed the calm water immediately beside the dam. But the force of the underwater blast shook the giant structure to its foundations as cracks like lightning bolts ripped 40 feet into the concrete. But the dam held firm. As the waters subsided there was complete silence again save for the pounding feet of Tariq Nayif, running back to the safety of the western guardhouse to report what little he had seen or heard.

By now Staff Sergeant Ali Hasan was on his feet outside the building, yelling, demanding to know what the hell was going on. Tariq could not help much there, and, as he struggled to explain the dull, muted thunder, his words were cut short by a second stunning impact on the wall, again well below the surface. Both men felt the reverberations of the thud on the soles of their boots.

And then again there was silence. No attacking fighter-bombers screamed through the sky. There had been no sense of a rocket attack − or, indeed, *any* attack. The area was undisturbed, and the lapping of the wavelets on the shore was lost against the low gusting of the wind.

Then the third SLCM missile nosed into the dam wall, going right into the gaping hole on the north side before it blew. Once more the force of the exploding warhead lasered those lightning-bolt cracks deep into the structure, this time going right through. The two Iraqi soldiers, backing away from the now-obvious tremor along the great wall, could not see, but one giant jagged crack ran one hundred feet diagonally down the southern face of the wall − the face that now held back three cubic miles of water.

Staff Sergeant Hasan − joined now by Second Lieutenant Rashid Ghazi − was just saying that there seemed to be no military explanation, that this must be some kind of an earthquake, when Mike Krause's fourth cruise missile blasted into the underwater cavern on the north side of the dam. It blew with spectacular impact a gigantic breach into the dam, 150 yards across. Millions of tons of concrete finally gave way to billions of tons of water. The 100-foot-high wave surged through the gap with unimaginable force, and then began to crash down in slow motion 500 feet to the quietly flowing river below.

And, of course, it kept coming − the outpouring of one of the biggest reservoirs in the world, followed by an entire lake, the waters rushing in behind from a deep mountain lakebed more than six miles long.

On both sides, the great wall held firm for a span of about 50 yards. It was the middle that was missing. The three Iraqi soldiers stared towards the east in terror at the wrath of Allah. And, turning in the direction of Mecca, they knelt before God and prayed for guidance.

Below them the friendly River Diyala was now a raging, cascading torrent, 40 feet higher than normal, roaring down its course southeast toward the Tigris, 100 miles away. Toward the fertile southern farmlands south of the city of Baghdad. Toward the factories in the industrial delta of Iraq.

1857 (EDT) June 2. The CIA safe house in the Woodley district of Virginia, south of Washington.
Lt-Commander Baldridge, Admiral Arnold Morgan and Commander Benjamin Adnam were sharing a pot of coffee and preparing to watch the seven o'clock evening news. The only information they had was that the missiles had been launched and the submarines were on their way home.

An aura of gloom began to descend upon the trio as the summary of the program's content was given and no mention was made of the havoc they expected to have broken out in the Middle East.

'I know these media bastards are parochial in outlook,' growled the Admiral, 'but this is ridiculous.'

1915 came and went. Still no mention. At 1920 Arnold Morgan was about to call the station, but restrained himself.

At 1922, there was an interruption. 'We're just breaking away from that story for a moment because of a breaking news story,' said the commentator with heavy emphasis. 'There are reports of some kind of a natural disaster in Iraq. Baghdad is reported to be under four feet of water at the northern end of the city. We have conflicting reports right now, but one of them suggests that the great dam on the Tigris, the Sāmarrā Barrage, has breached. Another report suggests it is the northern dam in the Kurdish mountains, the Darband–I–Khan, which has burst. Right now we have no further information – communications seem to be heavily disrupted. But we'll keep you informed of what appears to be a huge disaster in Iraq. Now, back to the Gay Rights March in LA.'

Arnold Morgan walked across and shook the hand of Bill Baldridge, and then that of Ben Adnam.

But the Iraqi seemed very preoccupied. In fact, he was wondering how the flood water was rising in a little stone house off Al–Jamouri Street, the one in the dark, narrow alleyway next to the hotel.

He hadn't seen it for two years, since May 26, 2004, the night the Iraqi President's men had come to murder him. Since then the full moon had risen above the desert 26 times. It had been two years, plus one week. He had just missed the anniversary – which was a pity, because he liked anniversaries.

But nevertheless Eilat smiled. *Perfect*, he thought. *Almost*.

EPILOGUE

COMMANDER BENJAMIN ADNAM was given a US passport on September 18, 2006. It bore the name Benjamin Arnold and gave his birthplace as Helensburgh, Scotland.

For the mission against the Iraqi dams he was paid the agreed $250,000. With this he made the down payment on a medium-sized white Colonial-style house quite near the Dunsmores' mansion in Virginia, on the west side of the Potomac. He purchased an unobtrusive dark-green Ford Taurus and began work in the head office of the Central Intelligence Agency in Langley, Virginia.

A new position was created for him – Special Advisor to the Associate Director of Central Intelligence. This was Frank Reidel, Langley's linkman between the Agency and the military Joint Command. Commander Adnam moved into an office adjacent to that of Reidel, a short walk from the CIA's Middle Eastern Desk, to which the former terrorist was seconded on a permanent basis. The normal strict vetting procedures for employees of the CIA were dispensed with, on special orders from the White House.

Adnam had requested that he be permitted to use the rank which he had earned in the Israeli Navy. Admiral Morgan insured this was granted, and so Adnam was henceforth referred to in the Agency as 'Commander Arnold.'

On the first Thursday of each month Adnam attended a private briefing on Middle Eastern Developments inside the White House with the President's National Security Advisor.

His salary was $150,000 a year, but Morgan negotiated him out of the annual lump sum in excess of a million dollars which the Iraqi had demanded. It was agreed that at the conclusion of ten years' service he would receive a bonus of $2 million. In return for this, Morgan insisted that all incriminating documents be returned from Adnam's Swiss bank, and sent special agents to Geneva to pick them up.

As Arnold Morgan had guessed, Benjamin Adnam's insights into the mindsets of the Middle East were extremely valuable. Within a matter of weeks, it was plain that he would make a major contribution in helping the Americans ease the political cross-currents, to calm the warring factions among the sheikhs and dictators in the turbulent, oil-rich crucible of the Middle East.

For himself, Ben found a peace he had never known. Away from the frontiers of hands-on terrorism, separated from the high-risk areas of Intelligence field agent, he settled into his smooth, suburban American life with considerable ease. For the first several months he made few attempts at befriending colleagues, instead concentrating on living quietly at home, reading and watching the news and international current affairs programs on television. For the first time for as long as he could remember he was out of the front line, and no one was hunting for him. At least, not in the United States they weren't.

For the moment Ben Adnam was content to keep the lowest possible profile, and to thank his God he was out of the lethal world of international terrorism.

On one autumn morning he was jolted into the reality of that judgment. Reading the *New York Times*, he caught sight of a story which detailed a long police chase and a minor gun battle in the Kilburn area of northwest London. It involved the IRA and the capture of a suspected cache of explosives and guns. The shootout lasted only ten minutes, and only one man was hit, although quite badly. His name was Paul O'Rourke, aged 20, from County Waterford. They charged him under the Terrorism Act, while he lay in hospital with a collapsed right lung.

Ben shook his head. *To be prepared to die for a cause.* He pondered his own years ahead, and how he would deal with civilian life should the Americans permit him that permanent luxury. He had, of course, one further score to settle: Iran, and its brutal if ill-planned attempt on his life. Not to mention the $1.5 million the Iranians still owed him. One day they would pay for that.

Confident now in the goodwill of his new masters, Ben picked up the telephone and requested a private talk first thing in the morning with Admiral Morgan. Perhaps this was the time, he thought. The time to come clean with the National Security Advisor, perhaps to consolidate his position even further.

At 0900 the following day he was sitting in the West Wing recounting in graphic detail to Arnold Morgan how the big US cruise missiles had slammed the wrong country in revenge for the dead Americans in the destroyed airliners.

He could not know for sure how the ferocious White House admiral would react to the revelation that he had been used as a pawn in the Iraqi's grand scheme of vengeance, but he felt that Morgan would look beyond the obvious deception and perhaps begin to consider a big strike against Iran. The destruction of the Iraqi dams had of course merely avenged the deaths of 6000 US Navy personnel in the *Thomas Jefferson*. The demise of the regime in Iraq was justifiable simply on those grounds, not to mention that country's proven aim of producing weapons of mass destruction.

He edged Morgan along the thought process that Iran's day would surely come. Of that he was certain. In the end the Iranians would step out of line on the international stage of the Gulf. And then he, Arnold Morgan, could move in for the strike against the Ayatollahs which had for so long been coming.

It was clear to both men that Commander Adnam's days of illusion were over. Where once there had been hope and idealism, there was now an empty place. What remained was the skilled, unique military mind of the world's most successful terrorist. And Morgan had bought that mind at a bargain price.

They were together for less than one hour, and as he left Commander Adnam was certain he had been correct in clarifying the situation – correct in his assessment that the US admiral would appreciate knowing, now, the full truth. They shook hands formally at the conclusion of the meeting.

This time, however, Commander Adnam had misjudged his man.

Admiral Arnold Morgan was furious. Furious at having been outwitted by the scheming terrorist every step of the way. Furious that he had been hoodwinked once more during the interrogation. And really furious that he had moved major US muscle against a country which had known nothing of the acts of terrorism against the passenger aircraft. Right now Morgan was about ready to murder Ben Adnam, and not just figuratively. This was not on the basis of some terrible attack of conscience toward any of the troublesome nations of the Middle East but because he, Morgan, was sick and tired of being made to feel a damned fool in front of 'this crooked fucking towelhead.'

The Iraqi was not four yards down the drive before the NSA was storming through the White House on his way to talk to the President.

Their conversation lasted five minutes. Admiral Morgan briefed the Chief carefully, and then said with icy indifference, 'Sir, I've had enough of him. He's gotta go.'

'I could not,' replied the President, 'agree more. Please don't mention his name to me, ever again.'

'No, sir,' Morgan replied. He returned to his office.

It was at 2200 that evening that two CIA cars and a private government ambulance pulled into the driveway of Commander Adnam's house. Three armed Marine Guard marksmen took up sniper positions while Arnold Morgan walked into the front door alone. Ben Adnam was reading in the living room.

'Commander,' said the admiral, 'it is my duty to inform you that we have no further use for you.'

'Sir?' replied the Iraqi, betraying nothing.

'We have decided to dispense with your services on the grounds that we do not trust you, and that you may become an embarrassment to the USA.'

'Does this mean you intend to execute me, after all, for my crimes against humanity?'

'It would, with any other prisoner of your category, Commander. But you are somewhat different.'

'I see. But I imagine that nevertheless you have men with rifles trained upon me as we speak?'

'Yes, Ben. I do. Your time is, shall we say, limited.'

'I think I misjudged you today. Perhaps I should never have told you the truth.'

'Perhaps not. But this day would have come anyway.'

'Are you going to tell them to kill me now?'

'No, Commander. Strange as it may seem, I have a respect for you. Not for your callous murder of so many people, but for the professional military way in which you did it. Therefore I am going to offer you an old-fashioned form of chivalry in your departure.'

Arnold Morgan reached into his coat pocket and drew out a big, wooden-handled military service revolver. Loaded. And he placed it on the table between them.

'You understand, Commander, that your death in the next ten minutes is inevitable?'

'Yes, sir, I do. And I am not regretful. I have no further heart for a fight. I have nowhere to go. No one to speak to. My options have run out.'

'So, Ben, if I may call you that again, I am offering you an honorable way out, in the tradition of a serving officer. And now I am going to leave you. I wish you goodbye. In a way I'm sorry – but not in other ways. I will turn my back on you briefly as I depart, but if you should even look at that revolver before I am gone the honorable option will be obviated. My men will shoot you down like a cheapskate little terrorist – which would not do you justice, certainly not in your mind and nor in fact in mine. I hope you follow me? Because I regard this as personal, between us.'

Ben Adnam nodded. But he never moved.

The admiral left.

The Iraqi heard the CIA cars reach the end of the drive. He did not, however, hear the admiral disembark and stand with two agents beneath the tall trees on the edge of the road.

They all heard the veranda door slam. They heard slow, dignified footsteps walk down the wide wooden stairs, and then the soft tread of the Bedouin across the gravel.

Then there was silence for three minutes before there came the unmistakable crash of a single echoing gunshot in the silence of the night.

When Arnold Morgan's men went in with their flashlights and the big zip-up plastic bag and the stretcher, they found the body in a damp leafy corner of the garden.

Commander Benjamin Adnam, the side of his head blown away, was still in kneeling position, facing 90 degrees on the compass, due east . . . toward a distant God in a distant heaven, somewhere out by the shifting desert sands of Arabia.